SECRETS AND LIES

Stephanie Harte

Book

This paperback edition first published in the UK in 2021
by Head of Zeus Ltd
An Aria book

9 7 5 3 1 2 4 6 8

A CIP catalogue record for this book is available
from the British Library.

ISBN (E): 9781800245761
ISBN (PB): 9781800246270

Cover design © Cherie Chapman

Typeset by Siliconchips Services Ltd UK

Printed and bound by CPI Group (UK) Ltd, Croydon, CR0 4YY

Aria
c/o Head of Zeus
5–8 Hardwick Street
London EC1R 4RG

www.headofzeus.com

ALSO BY STEPHANIE HARTE

Risking it All
Tangled Lives
Forgive and Forget

SECRETS AND LIES

For my son, James, thank you for the endless cups of coffee and delicious meals you made while I wrote this book. You are a fantastic cook and a force to be reckoned with in the kitchen. Long may that continue!

I

Ella

November

To set the scene for a relaxing evening, I'd lit the candles at the end of the enormous high-tech tub and poured myself a large glass of wine. After letting my pale pink dressing gown drop to the floor, I hit the button to switch on the whirlpool and climbed into the bathful of scented bubbles. *This is the life*, I thought, as I wallowed in the warm water with my eyes closed, listening to the soothing music I'd added to a playlist on my phone, imagining I was in a luxury spa. After a couple of minutes, I opened my eyes and reached for my drink. The ice-cold liquid ran down my throat, and I looked around the room, which was bathed in a soft glow. Taking in a deep breath, I allowed my mind to drift while watching the flickering flames dance and cast shadows on the marble tiles.

Eventually, I glanced down at the skin on my shrivelled fingers; I'd been soaking for almost an hour, so I reluctantly pulled out the plug before I turned into a prune. I wrapped a fluffy bath sheet around myself, picked up my half-drunk glass of wine and headed into the living area. I was standing in front of the full-length sliding doors sipping my Pinot Grigio rosé when something caught my eye. My heart pounded, and my relaxed state of mind disappeared in an instant. I willed myself not to panic, but I was alone in the house, and I'd always been scared of the dark. With shaking fingers, I reached behind me and put my glass down on the coffee table. Wrapping my arms around myself, I peered into the darkness. Maybe I'd just imagined things – the security lights hadn't come on, and they would have illuminated the garden if a prowler or burglar had triggered them, wouldn't they?

For a split second, I thought about phoning my dad but then decided against it. I didn't want to worry him, and it was one o'clock in the morning; far too late to call somebody. I wasn't sure he'd appreciate being woken up in the early hours of the morning, as we were barely on speaking terms. But running to him for help was a hard habit to break. Before Conor had come into my life, my dad had been my protector and my go-to person if something scared me.

I let out a deep breath and forced myself to find a plausible explanation. Given that the lights weren't on, the most likely thing that could have happened was that a neighbour's cat or possibly a nocturnal creature of some sort was out on a hunting expedition. London was overrun with foxes, badgers and hedgehogs.

I went to bed but woke up at four o'clock when I heard noises outside, and this time I could see the light was on. My pulse pounded against my neck as I pulled the quilt around my chest then backed myself into the headboard. I was considering calling the police when the light went out. Relief washed over me, but it was short-lived.

I knew I wasn't going to be able to go back to sleep, so I walked down the stairs and into the kitchen. While I was making a cup of tea, I craned my neck so that I could see out into the garden. Daylight wasn't starting to creep through yet. At first, I saw nothing; then my blood ran cold. I saw the silhouette of a hooded man outside the window before he disappeared into the shadows. I ran from room to room, switching on all the lights until the house was lit up so brightly it could have been visible from outer space.

I stayed at the front of the house to keep myself out of sight, but I was surrounded by glass, and that made me feel incredibly vulnerable, like I was on display in a shop window. Everything had gone quiet apart from the sound of my ragged breath. I stood where I was, frozen to the spot, trying not to make a sound so that I didn't have to confront the situation on the other side of the door. It seemed like an eternity, but in reality, it was probably no longer than a matter of minutes. As the seconds ticked by, I wondered if I'd imagined the whole thing. Then I heard the man climb over the gate, and his heavy footsteps echoed into the distance.

That was when I allowed myself to crumple. I slid down the wall until I was sitting on the tiled floor. I pulled my knees into my chest and sobbed my heart out. Conor couldn't get back soon enough for my liking.

2

Ella

I remember the first time we met like it was yesterday. Conor Baxter walked into the Thames-side pub, where I worked part-time as a barmaid while I studied at uni, on a scorching day in mid-June, and my day instantly seemed a little bit brighter.

I was stuck behind the bar, daydreaming of winning the lottery so that I could give up my course and move to Spain. Being a student wasn't shaping up to be the carefree experience I'd been expecting; it wasn't one long round of parties and socialising into the early hours – it was hard work trying to juggle coursework and shifts in the Riverside Tavern.

The two men Conor had arrived with headed to a table at the back of the room, which I'd found surprising; most of our customers opted to sit at the tables on the decked jetty and admire the view of the river, especially during the summer months.

'Three pints of Estrella, please,' Conor said in a smooth London accent as he stood in front of me.

Conor had the most mesmerising deep blue eyes I'd ever seen. They were the colour of blue diamonds, and when he fixed them on me and hit me with his dazzling smile full beam, my heart skipped a beat.

'No problem,' I replied.

I'd served the round he'd ordered loads of times before, but for some reason, my hands trembled as I lifted the first embossed glass down from the shelf and angled it under the stainless steel tap. As the amber liquid started to fill the glass, I glanced up and noticed the tall, dark-haired man's eyes scan over the surface. I switched off the tap and examined the pint.

'I'm sorry, this glass is a bit smeary. I'll get you another one,' I said.

'There's no need. I'll give that one to Bobby.' He laughed.

It was all I could do not to spill the lager all over the bar as I lined the drinks up in front of him. 'Fifteen pounds seventy-five, please,' I said, having run the order through the till.

Conor pulled a black leather wallet out of his back pocket and handed me a crisp fifty-pound note. 'Keep the change,' he said before bunching the three pint glasses together and carrying them over to the table in the far corner of the room.

I must have looked ridiculous, standing there gawping at him with my mouth ajar. But in my defence, I'd worked at the Riverside Tavern for over a year, and nobody had ever tipped me before, so it was hardly surprising that a mixture of shock and delight washed over me. The amount Conor gave me was incredibly generous; I wouldn't earn as much as that on my four-hour shift. He'd basically doubled my wages, and I was seriously impressed.

'Thank you,' I called after him, suddenly remembering my manners, as his broad-shouldered form retreated into the distance. I wasn't sure whether he heard me or not because he didn't acknowledge what I'd said.

It was unusually busy for a Friday afternoon – considering the lunchtime rush had finished, and the vast majority of London's workforce hadn't yet clocked off for the weekend. In between serving customers, I'd busied myself arranging the freshly washed glasses back on the shelves. It was a tactical move. I was attempting to spy on the handsome stranger I'd just encountered while being as discreet as possible.

I was intrigued by him, but I didn't think he'd noticed me. He was engrossed in conversation with one of the well-dressed men he was sitting with, whose raucous laughter had made me jump on more than one occasion as it blasted out across the room. His strawberry-blond eyebrows took on a life of their own as he chatted to his younger, better-looking companion. The other man at the table had a shaved head and a bushy ginger beard, and didn't appear to be involved in the conversation. He sat in silence, eyes darting around, taking in the scene while sipping on his pint. That seemed odd to me. When I go out for a drink with my friends, we all participate equally. But they might not be friends; they could be business associates. They were all smartly dressed in suits, and given the temperature outside today, that was probably more likely. I stopped deliberating about their relationship when I saw the group stand up and shake hands.

'Leave it with me, Bobby,' the dark-haired man said.

They were about to leave, so I considered, if only

briefly, rushing over to clear their glasses. I wanted another opportunity to get close to the man with the most gorgeous eyes I'd ever seen but then decided against it. I'd embarrassed myself enough for one day. No good would come of it anyway, so what was the point? I stole one last glance as he headed out of the door.

Fast-forward forty-eight hours. The handsome stranger was back at the Riverside Tavern, and this time he was on his own. My heart pounded in my chest as he approached the counter. As he sauntered over to the bar, the smell of his aftershave wafted towards me on the warm summer breeze.

'Hello again, beautiful,' Conor flirted. I couldn't believe my luck and had to stop myself from squealing with delight.

'What can I get you?' I asked in a semi-squeaky voice; then I felt my cheeks begin to burn.

'I didn't come here for a drink.' Conor smiled, and I felt my stomach somersault as my pulse rate soared.

This man seemed to have it all. He was drop-dead gorgeous, as well as being incredibly generous. That wasn't a bad combination by any means. I figured he could have his pick of any girl he wanted.

'What time does your shift finish?'

I was flattered that he was showing an interest in me, but I had a feeling there was a considerable age difference between us. If he asked me out and we went on to have a relationship, I was pretty inexperienced in matters of the heart and scared of making a fool of myself. But I pushed the thought from my mind and decided to live for the moment. Why wouldn't I? Age was just a number, wasn't it?

His question had left me speechless, and I suddenly realised I hadn't replied, so after what seemed like an endless pause, I turned around and looked at the clock.

'I get off in twenty minutes,' I replied as I turned back to face him.

'That's great! In that case, I'd like to take you out for dinner. Indian or Chinese?' he said, flashing me a winning smile as my legs turned to jelly.

3

Conor

Isabella Dawson was the most beautiful woman I'd ever seen. She had huge dark eyes and a thick mane of dark brown hair that fell in loose curls down her back. Ella's heart-shaped face had an innocence about it that was in complete contrast to her body; she oozed sex appeal and had curves in all the right places.

When I'd noticed she was filling a grimy glass, I would normally have stopped her in her tracks, but I hadn't wanted to offend her by asking for a clean one; I could see she was nervous and I didn't want to come across as a bellend. I'd watched Ella in the mirror's reflection to pass the time while Bobby Parker held court in the Riverside Tavern that day. Every time she'd glanced over in my direction, she had me going weak at the knees.

It had been a chance meeting; I'd never drunk in that pub before. But I was determined that our first encounter wouldn't be our last. I'd never been interested in having a serious relationship – my mum's disastrous love life had well and truly put me off; it looked like that was about to change. There was something different about Ella; she seemed so pure, so innocent, and my heart pounded when she got near me. I couldn't ignore the effect she was having on me.

With the top down on my convertible Z4, I pulled onto the Arnold Estate five minutes early, accompanied by the nerves of a man on death row, and had to fight the urge to chew my nails down to the quick. As Ella stepped out of the door and walked towards me, my heart started pounding in my chest. She looked incredible in the strappy pale pink dress and heels she was wearing.

'You look amazing,' I said when Ella got into my car, and an intoxicating smell of perfume drifted in with her.

'Thank you. You don't look too bad yourself,' Ella replied, smiling at me.

Her compliment went straight to my head like a shot of alcohol and made my brain feel fuzzy. When she finished talking, I struggled to reply with anything intelligible and appeared to have lost the ability to function properly.

'Shall we make tracks?' I said after grinning at her for several seconds.

Ella's dark brown hair whipped around her as we drove along, and she laughed as she tried to keep it under control. 'I'm going to look like I've been dragged through a hedge backwards by the time we arrive,' she joked.

'Do you want me to put the roof up?'

'No, as long as you don't mind me looking like Hagrid's sister.' Ella turned towards me; the way her dark eyes gazed into mine made my pulse rate soar.

'As if.'

Although there was a space outside the restaurant, I

parked up a short distance away. I'd intended to hold Ella's hand on the walk back, but I wasn't sure if that was too forward, so I abandoned that idea.

When we stopped outside the door, I opened it. 'After you,' I said, placing my hand on the small of her back to guide her inside. The tips of my fingers tingled when they made contact with the soft fabric of her dress, like an electric current was running through my veins.

The Mandarin Palace was a place normally only frequented by couples. The interior was romantic, with soft lighting provided by the Chinese lanterns, and pink cherry blossom branches suspended from the ceiling giving the space a rosy glow.

'It's so beautiful in here,' Ella said, tilting her chin towards the canopy of flowers suspended overhead.

I'd chosen this restaurant because I was confident Ella would love it. The décor alone was so incredible that it made the place worth a visit; it was an added bonus that the food was also first class.

The waiter handed us both menus. 'What are you going to have?' I asked when Ella looked up from the pages.

Ella leaned across the table. 'It's so expensive in here,' she said in a hushed tone.

'Don't worry about that; order whatever you fancy.'

I didn't care how much the meal cost; I wanted to impress her, so I was happy to push the boat out. Ella ordered vegetable spring rolls while I had zesty chilli tiger prawns.

'So tell me about yourself. Do you work at the pub full-time?' I asked.

'No, part-time. I'm a student. I've just finished my first year at King's College London.'

'So you're clever as well as beautiful. What are you studying?'

'Modern languages – Spanish and French,' Ella replied.

We were just finishing our starters when Bobby Parker and his bodyguard, Stumpy, walked into the Mandarin Palace. If it hadn't been for Stumpy's sizeable frame, I might not have noticed them as my date had my undivided attention. The only time I'd taken my eyes off her was when I'd noticed an almost invisible stain on the tablecloth. Its presence had threatened to derail the whole evening, but then I clapped eyes on Bobby's bald head, making its way across the room, and I lost interest in it.

'Fancy seeing you here!' Bobby said.

Who was he trying to kid? It was obvious he'd come here deliberately to bump into me. We'd ended up sitting almost shoulder to shoulder. That wasn't quite what I'd had in mind when I'd booked a table for a candlelit dinner.

'I wouldn't have thought you'd like this kind of establishment,' Bobby continued before his laugh echoed through the small space.

'Likewise,' I replied. 'Romantic meal for two, is it?'

I could see Ella stifle a laugh out of the corner of my eye. She was trying to clamp her lips shut to stop them from breaking into a huge grin but was losing the battle. Meanwhile, Bobby bristled then started twisting the large sovereign ring he wore on his little finger around while he considered his response.

'Unfortunately, Stumpy's not my type,' Bobby replied with a smile on his face, but the tone of his voice was telling a different story.

I very much doubted Stumpy was anyone's type. He was

a six-foot brick shithouse from Glasgow with a shaved head and a ginger beard so bushy something could be living in it. He was a mad bastard with an evil temper. For everyone's sake, I thought I'd better change the subject in case he took offence at being the butt of the joke. Trust me – nobody wanted to see him lose his shit. I'd seen it before, and it wasn't a pretty sight. The occasion that sprung to mind was when a cocky lad made a smart remark to his friends when Stumpy went to walk out of a pub after a business meeting with myself and Bobby. Blinded by fury and fuelled by alcohol, Stumpy decided to leave the teenager with something to remember him by: a Glaswegian kiss. He smashed his sizeable forehead into the startled boy's face, crushing the bone in his nose. People looked on in horror as blood spurted everywhere, but nobody was brave enough to say a word. I didn't want Ella to witness anything that might put her off me before I had a chance to win her over.

'On a serious note, you're making me feel paranoid, Bobby. Are you following me?' There was no point in skirting around things, so I decided to be blunt.

The waiter came over to take Bobby and Stumpy's order, but instead of placing it, Bobby pushed his chair back and got to his feet. He gripped onto the edge of the table with both hands as his gold sovereign ring collection glinted under the restaurant's lights.

'My friend and I have lost our appetites. We won't be eating here after all,' he said. The waiter nodded, then turned on his heel. When he was out of earshot, Bobby crouched down and whispered in my ear. 'Stop fucking about, Conor. You haven't got time to wine and dine your latest conquest.

You've got a job to do. You need to find me a new supplier. Capeesh?'

Ella looked decidedly uncomfortable when Bobby straightened his posture and stood glaring at me with his strawberry-blond eyebrows knitted together.

'Enjoy the rest of your evening,' I said, giving Bobby his cue to leave.

'Goodnight, God bless,' he replied, throwing me one last filthy look before he walked out of the Mandarin Palace with Stumpy trailing behind him like a well-trained Labrador. I thought about ignoring their intrusion but decided it would be a better move to apologise for it instead.

'Sorry about the two ugly sisters turning up unannounced.'

'That's OK.' Ella smiled.

'So you're a student. Do you still live at home?' I asked, going off on a tangent.

'Yes,' Ella replied just as the crispy aromatic duck and pancakes arrived at our table, putting an end to the conversation.

The phrase 'shut up and eat' sprung to mind. Ella's beautiful brown eyes were like saucers when the waiter placed a platter of shredded meat and thinly sliced vegetables in front of her. I'd like to say that Bobby's visit hadn't put a dampener on our evening, but I'd be lying. I tried to make a habit of not allowing my work life to spill over into my personal life and keep both areas separate. If Ella was going to be on the scene, I had even more reason to strike the perfect work-life balance. I hadn't appreciated the bald-headed bully showing up out of the blue. Thankfully, Ella hadn't started asking me awkward questions, but she was probably wondering what the hell was so important to warrant this man gate-crashing our date.

There was an insatiable demand for cocaine in London, and everyone involved in it was raking in cash. I'd been desperate to get involved and knew enough dodgy people with contacts, but a while ago I'd decided I was done working for somebody else. I'd wanted a fresh start. My days of following orders were over.

I'd wanted to get in on the action on my own terms – and that was when an idea had come to me: if I became a middle man, I could bridge the gap between the suppliers and the dealers. Not everyone wanted to purchase drugs at source, because they feared being arrested. Once I'd done my research and realised it was a viable option, I'd decided a change of career was in order. I'd put forward a proposal to Bobby. As expected, he'd jumped at the opportunity I'd offered him.

Bobby had fallen out with his regular cocaine supplier a while ago and was keen to find a new one, which had left the door open for me. I wasn't surprised he'd wanted out of the deal; the guys had turned out to be con artists. There was no denying Bobby was a difficult man to please, but on this occasion, he had every reason to be pissed off. The last two shipments he'd received had increased in price but not in quality.

The feedback Bobby had received from the street backed up his concerns. According to some of his customers, the coke had been cut with some dodgy substances. It was an inferior product to what they were used to, which meant the distributors couldn't dilute it any further, and that affected the resale price. If things didn't change, they'd told Bobby they were going to take their business elsewhere. Bobby stood to lose a small fortune if they'd carried out their threat. He wasn't about to let the scammers get away with trying to double-cross him.

The moral issue of working for the people who ran the cartels hadn't weighed heavily on my mind. I was acting as a go-between, merely representing someone higher up the ladder – and at the end of the day, I had bills to pay. People do what they have to do to keep a roof over their heads. Thanks to my previous profession, I'd had the right credentials for the role. I'd worked as an enforcer for a local gangster, so I was streetwise and used to the type of violence that went hand in hand with this line of work. I wouldn't hesitate to demonstrate my proficiency with a firearm if the occasion arose.

That was then; this was now. I'd been so desperate to branch out on my own I hadn't considered the bigger picture. I was beginning to wish I hadn't got involved with Bobby Parker now. He was a demanding bastard; there were no two ways about that. Whenever he clicked his fingers, he expected me to come running, no matter what time of day or night it was, even though I wasn't part of his firm. We were business associates. Nothing more. Nothing less. I ran my operation single-handedly. That was the way I liked to do things. I hated working for other people. I preferred being my own boss. That way, I never had to do something I wasn't comfortable with. If the going got too hot for me to handle, I could bail at a moment's notice without answering to anyone.

I knew Bobby was keen for me to find him a new

supplier, but these things took time, so he'd have to be patient. Breathing down my neck every minute wasn't going to speed up the process. The huge list of requirements the dealer needed to meet meant it wasn't going to be an easy task, but I was determined to find a source that fitted the bill.

Spurred on by the way our date had gone, I took hold of Ella's hand as we walked back to the car. I felt a jolt of electricity flow through my body again when our skin met. When she tilted her face towards mine and smiled up at me, I knew I couldn't wait a second longer; I had to kiss her even though this wasn't the most romantic setting. I stopped walking, turned Ella around to face me and took hold of her other hand. She gazed up at me with a smile on her face. If I was reading the signs right, she liked me too, but I wasn't sure whether she'd be up for snogging on a first date. There was only one way to find out.

'Can I kiss you?' I asked.

'Yes,' Ella replied.

She'd given me the green light, so I leaned straight in. A surge of adrenaline flooded my body. My heart rate sped up, and I felt my blood flow increase to a particular organ.

'I've been wanting to do that all evening,' I said after we pulled apart.

'That makes two of us,' Ella said.

4

Ella

After my date with Conor, I floated in the front door, tiptoeing across the landing to my bedroom so that I didn't disturb Mum and Dad as they'd already gone to bed. I was ready to burst with excitement, and even though it was late, I decided to call my besties and give them the low-down. I couldn't wait until the morning.

'I've put you on speakerphone so you can tell us all the gory details,' Lucy said when she answered the phone.

'How did it go?' Amy added.

'Like a dream; my feet still haven't touched the ground. It was seriously the best date I've ever been on. My cheeks are aching from smiling.'

'That's fantastic, but we need to hear hard facts,' Lucy said. 'Where did Conor take you?'

'To a really expensive restaurant. The food was to die for, and on the way back to the car, he kissed me.'

'Blimey, he didn't waste any time; he made sure he got his money's worth.' Lucy laughed.

'It wasn't like that. You know I wouldn't normally kiss on a first date, but I couldn't help myself.' Conor's aftershave must have had spellbinding powers.

'Did you only kiss once?' Amy asked.

'Let's just say there was more than one smooch.' I laughed.

'I take it he's a good kisser then?' Lucy said.

'The best. There were fireworks and violins.' I swooned.

'It sounds like you had a brilliant time. You can tell us all about it tomorrow,' Lucy said.

I could have talked for hours, but we had an early lecture, so I understood why she'd ended our call. I lay back on my pillows and closed my eyes, but I was too filled with adrenaline to sleep. My body was still tingling from our first touch, our first kiss. It had been an amazing night, and I couldn't wait to see Conor again.

Even though I hadn't been looking for a relationship, things moved very quickly. After that first date, we started seeing each other every day. Conor soon became the centre of my world; he made everything look and feel a bit brighter. Unlike some of my friends, I wasn't attracted to bad boys. I always found myself migrating to nerdier males. Suffice to say, Conor wasn't my usual type, but there was something about him that drew me towards him. It was more than just his good looks; an air of excitement surrounded him like a magnetic force. The saying 'opposites attract' never seemed more fitting. The chemistry between us was instant. Even if I'd wanted to, I wouldn't have been able to resist the pull.

It was another blisteringly hot day when Conor and I went on our second date. I wasn't as nervous this time around, although I did still have butterflies in my stomach when I walked towards Conor's car.

'You look stunning,' Conor said as I took a seat next to him.

Because it was so hot, I'd chosen to wear a white floral playsuit. I felt a smile spread over my face when I saw Conor's eyes skim over my bare thighs before he reached across and planted a kiss on my lips.

'Thank you,' I replied.

'Where would you like to go?' Conor asked.

'What about one of the London parks?' It was such a beautiful day; it would be a shame to be cooped up inside.

'Really?' Conor seemed surprised by my suggestion.

'I like the simple things in life,' I replied.

'That's good to know. So what else do you like? I want to know every single thing about you.' Conor turned his mesmerising gaze on me and smiled.

My cheeks flushed as a heady feeling and flood of emotions overpowered my senses, but rather than making me open up, I became lost for words as my first-date jitters returned with a vengeance.

'So tell me about your course; you're studying languages, right?'

'Yes, Spanish and French.'

Something inexplicable was happening. I would normally talk the hind legs off a donkey, but I suddenly felt tongue-tied. I needed to make an effort; I didn't want Conor to think I wasn't interested in him.

'What do you do for a living?' I asked, turning the focus onto my date.

'I distribute IT equipment,' Conor replied as he parked his car.

'That sounds interesting,' I replied, finally finding my flow.

'It's not.' Conor laughed.

We strolled hand in hand through Hyde Park, chatting and getting to know each other. The more we talked, the more my nerves melted away.

'Do you want to go in here and get something to eat?' Conor asked, stopping outside the Serpentine Lido Café. 'Or we can go somewhere else if you prefer.'

'This looks perfect.' The large alfresco dining area had stunning views along the Serpentine and was more low-key than the last restaurant we'd been to.

'I know I probably shouldn't ask, and I'll apologise now if it's a rude question, but how old are you? I'm twenty-nine, by the way,' Conor casually dropped in. He tilted his head to the side and fixed me with his blue diamonds while he waited for me to reply.

I wasn't sure why I was a bit taken aback; he'd confirmed what I'd suspected, and I didn't have an issue with Conor being older. He was a sizeable step up from the cider-guzzling lads I was used to; better in every way, in my opinion. But I wondered how my mum and dad were going to react. They were usually really chilled about everything. We were more like siblings than parents and child. Even so, I was scared they might have some concerns. I knew I was falling hard for Conor; he was intoxicating, and my family's approval meant everything to me.

I'd felt my heartbeat speed up, and I briefly considered lying; I was scared he might be put off if I admitted the truth. But then I reasoned, it would be worse if it came out at a later stage, so I decided to lay my cards on the table and hope he didn't have an issue with the age gap either.

'I'm nineteen.'

Conor nodded, unfazed by my answer.

Being romantically inexperienced, I threw myself headfirst into the relationship, allowing myself to enjoy the rush of excitement the new experience was giving me. I was totally infatuated; from the moment our eyes met, I was intrigued by him. Conor exuded sex appeal, so he was easy to fall for, but it wasn't just a physical attraction; we shared an instant emotional connection to each other as well. It was hard to keep a level head; I felt giddy and euphoric. Our relationship felt magical, fated. Without warning, my heart told me to jump into the waters of the abyss.

We all succumb to a vice that causes us more harm than good, and mine was getting involved with Conor. Looking back, I know we rushed into things. Within a few weeks of meeting, I moved into his house. If I'd known what a disastrous decision that was going to turn out to be, I would never have made it. I would have turned on my heel and put as much space between us as humanly possible.

I had to pinch myself every time I went out with Conor. I still couldn't believe he'd chosen me to be his girlfriend. It felt amazing when I walked into an expensive restaurant on his arm, and everyone turned to look at us. I can still picture my friends' faces when he picked me up from uni before one of our dates in his flash car. When the gunmetal grey convertible BMW Z4 glided to a halt at the kerb, Lucy and Amy practically had to lift their jaws up from the pavement. Just thinking about it still brought a smile to my face.

At first, we didn't discuss what Conor did for a living in much detail. Now I realised why he'd been so guarded. All he'd told me was that he was involved in the distribution of IT equipment, and at that stage, I had no reason not to believe him. I was besotted with him, and that had clouded my judgement, unsaddling any rational thoughts I might have had. Conor was in a different league to anyone I'd been out with before. When you were an impressionable teenager like me, it didn't take much to make you feel sophisticated, so I allowed myself to be swept off my feet. I was blissfully happy, enthralled with the connection I'd found – the kind of connection that, up until now, I had only imagined existed for a few lucky people. My brain was pumping me full of hormones, and I was unable to resist.

My new boyfriend was worldly, whereas when we started dating, I was living at home with my parents. The council estate I grew up on was nestled between Shoreditch High Street and Bethnal Green Road. It was the kind of place where everyone knew each other and news travelled fast. I'd knew I'd have to tell Mum and Dad about Conor before one of my nosy neighbours did it for me. They'd always been hugely supportive of everything I'd done in the past, so I wasn't sure why I felt apprehensive about it.

'I've got some great news,' I said when I walked into the room and saw Mum and Dad cuddled up together on the sofa.

It gave me a warm, fuzzy feeling to think my parents were still completely in love with each other after all the years they'd been together. They were a great advert for the elusive happy-ever-after some people never managed to find.

'Ooh, that sounds intriguing,' Mum replied. She extracted herself from my dad's arms and positioned herself on the edge of her seat.

'I've met somebody.' I felt my face break into a huge grin, and my parents smiled back at me in response.

'That's fantastic, Ella. Did you meet him at uni?' Mum asked, keen to find out the details.

'No. I met him at the Riverside Tavern. He came in for a drink, and we just hit it off.'

'How exciting. We're delighted for you.' Mum was brimming over with happiness. 'What's his name?'

'Conor.'

'So tell us all about him.' Mum wriggled in her seat, then turned to Dad and smiled. 'We're dying to hear all about him, aren't we, Scott?'

Dad nodded, but his head movement lacked enthusiasm, and the fact that he was biting down on his lip showed me that he wasn't as excited about my announcement as my mum was. I knew dads sometimes struggled to let go of their daughters and worried about how a prospective love interest would treat their precious child. But he had nothing to worry about; I was sure of that.

'Dad doesn't seem convinced.' I laughed. I wondered if he could sense that I felt differently about Conor than anyone I'd been out with before.

'Don't I?'

My dad's reply was non-committal. I wasn't trying to put his nose out of joint; I wanted him to be happy for me. He was the man who'd set the standard for future men in my life to follow, and he'd placed the bar high, so I didn't give up my heart easily.

'I really like Conor, and I'm sure you're going to love him too.'

'I'm sure we will,' Mum agreed. 'You'll have to bring him over soon.'

'I will,' I replied before heading off to my bedroom and closing the door behind me.

My excitement was reaching fever pitch, but that was all I was prepared to say for the moment. I could see Mum was eager to hear more details, but Dad was sitting on the fence. I'd decided to keep the conversation brief in case Mum asked how old he was. I didn't want to make an issue out of the fact that Conor was ten years older than me – because it wasn't a big deal to me, and I was the one who was going out with him, so it wasn't anybody else's business.

5

Conor

Bobby's supplier was chancing his arm; he'd recently hiked up the cost of the merchandise to make extra profit, and Bobby wasn't best pleased. He was on the warpath, so he'd passed on a message to the Colombian cartel that their game was up. They either stuck to the original agreement, or the deal was off. The Colombian cartel called Bobby's bluff; if that was his attitude, he could get his cocaine elsewhere. They didn't think he would be able to find a product superior to theirs, so it was an idle threat.

I was beginning to think they were right. Locating an alternative source was proving to be difficult as the Colombians controlled the majority of the market, which was why they were able to get away with changing the terms of the agreement without Bobby's consent. They'd swallowed up all of their rivals and done away with the competition, inflating prices, reducing choice, and eroding trust as they expanded. Bobby was a small fish in a big pond, and even though he was keen to throw his weight around, he was powerless to stop them.

Finding a replacement supplier was a risky business, so I'd have to tread carefully. The goal was to build a rapport and strike a good deal with a manufacturer. That sounded simple enough, but when you bought illegal drugs, getting ripped off was sometimes part of the territory, especially before you established a proper connection with the other party. Bobby wanted to buy at source to ensure he was getting the best price, but he had to remember we'd be dealing with professional criminals. As we knew only too well, they had varying degrees of trustworthiness. I'd heard the horror stories; all too often, scammers took the money for the drugs and never delivered, or the long-awaited shipment of cocaine arrived, and when it was unpacked, it turned out to be a worthless substance. I'd never hear the end of it if that happened.

I was just a link in the chain, but at this stage, I had more at stake than Bobby Parker. I had no intention of languishing behind bars because he was hounding me to finalise a deal without checking it out properly. I had to make sure I covered my tracks and be certain that I wasn't walking into a trap. This was a corrupt business. Everyone was on somebody's payroll. Bobby needed to stop breathing down my neck and let me do my job.

After digging around on the darknet, I came across a group whose operation appeared to fit our needs. From what I could establish, they were a small family-run firm. I didn't see that as a disadvantage. Bobby had a lot of money to spend, so he could end up being one of their biggest customers, perhaps *the* biggest. I knew without a doubt that he'd love the idea of that. The only downside I could see was that they only operated out of Spain, so if I wanted to meet them, I'd have to be prepared to travel.

The Gómez cousins came from humble beginnings. They started out in a modest way, smuggling hashish from Morocco before they began working for a Colombian firm as low-level employees so that they could learn about the business from the inside. They weren't significant players in the distribution chain so were able to walk away from the operation unnoticed. Once they felt confident that they knew enough, they set up their own business. The key to their success was that they learned from the mistakes of their former employer. They deliberately kept their operation and labour force small, to escape the attention of the larger cartels and reduce their overheads. Attempting to expand too much would be a bad move. The cousins were shrewd enough to realise that if they posed a threat to the big players, they'd bring trouble to their door.

'Bobby, it's me. Can you meet me at the Riverside Tavern in an hour?' I said. I wanted to pass on some info, but I didn't like having sensitive conversations over the phone. You never knew who might be earwigging.

I was propping up the bar chatting to Ella when Bobby and Stumpy arrived.

'Let me guess, three pints of the usual,' Ella said as she filled the first glass with Estrella.

I carried the drinks over to the table, then took a seat opposite Bobby.

'So what's so important that you had to drag me here at a moment's notice?' Bobby asked in his usual charming manner.

'I've got some good news. I've managed to set up a meeting with Diego and Pedro Gómez.'

'About bloody time too. I thought I was going to die of old age before you got around to that.'

'I'm flying out in the morning,' I replied, ignoring the barbed comment.

'Good, make sure you keep me posted, capeesh?' Bobby fixed me with his piercing blue eyes.

A stretch limousine picked me up from the hotel on Spain's north-west coast where I was staying and took me to a modern office block in the heart of Vigo that overlooked the bay and large marina packed with expensive-looking yachts. On arrival, I was met by a man dressed in a navy polo shirt and beige chinos who introduced himself as Juan. He led the way into the foyer of the air-conditioned building and, as we waited for the lift to arrive, made polite conversation in broken English.

Behind a wood-panelled door, a huge cherrywood table dominated the conference room. It would easily seat twenty people, but only three were sat around it. As I hadn't been introduced, I presumed they were the leaders of the cartel.

The person at the head was flanked by a man on one side and a woman on the other. He stood up when I entered the room and walked across the cream marble floor to meet me with his hand outstretched.

'I'm Diego Gómez, pleased to meet you.'

'Conor Baxter,' I replied, shaking his hand firmly.

Diego was older than I'd expected. He had long grey hair that fell past his shoulders, and the lines that etched his skin bore all the hallmarks of a troubled life lived under the hot Spanish sun. Dark liver spots covered his weather-beaten complexion, and the puffy bags under his eyes indicated that he wasn't a man who slept well at night. But he was friendly and welcoming. That was the best I could hope for at this stage.

'I would like to start by apologising to you. I'm afraid the rest of the Gómez family has a poor grasp of the English language, but we will do our best to communicate with you. Please come and meet the others,' Diego said, gesturing with his gnarly hand for me to follow him.

As we approached the table, Juan took over the introductions. 'This is Diego's cousin, Pedro,' he said, pointing out the man with jet-black curly hair, an ultra-bushy moustache and mutton-chop sideburns.

'Pleased to meet you,' I said as I shook his extended hand.

'Welcome to Spain.' Pedro smiled.

'And this is Valentina, Pedro's wife,' Juan said, pointing to the lady cradling a toy-sized dog under one arm.

'Hello, Conor,' Valentina said, rolling the r at the end of my name.

If the soft purr of her voice and the intense gaze of her dark eyes was meant to cry sex kitten, it wasn't having the desired effect. I wasn't sure whether she was trying to intimidate me or seduce me. Either way, she made me feel uncomfortable. I felt like I was being sized up by a hungry tiger.

'Hello, Valentina, it's a pleasure to meet you,' I replied with a wide smile pasted on my face before I averted my eyes from the heavily made-up woman wearing bright red lipstick and a top so low-cut it showed off her crepey cleavage.

First impressions told me that Pedro's wife wore the trousers in their relationship. Although I'd only just met her, I couldn't help thinking she was mildly terrifying. I wouldn't want to be left alone in a room with her. Valentina had man-eater written all over her.

'We use Spanish companies as fronts for our drug money to throw the authorities off the trail. Please assure your client that the Spanish courts are notoriously inefficient at prosecuting businesses suspected of money laundering.' Diego smiled. 'Despite their best efforts, in most cases, they can't trace money they suspect is generated by a criminal activity back to the bosses.'

That was something I knew Bobby would be pleased to hear.

'A lot of our merchandise passes through the Port of Vigo. It's a good cover as global fishing companies are based there,' Diego said, explaining how the cartel's operation worked. 'We can arrange a tour if you'd like to see it for yourself.'

'That won't be necessary.'

I was keen to get back to the UK as soon as possible. I knew Bobby would be champing at the bit for news, and I didn't want to be away from Ella any longer than I had to be. I couldn't get enough of her and wanted to spend all my time with her. From the moment we met, we formed an instant attachment; we just clicked right away, and when I wasn't with her, I felt like part of me was missing.

6

Ella

Money was tight. It didn't seem to matter how many shifts I did, I was always struggling to make ends meet. I wouldn't go so far as to say I was living a mundane life, but I felt like I was stuck in a rut. Working to pay my way through uni wasn't exactly a bundle of laughs, and it was playing havoc with my social life. I hadn't seen Conor for a couple of days, but tonight he was taking me out on a date. I couldn't hide my excitement at work and tackled the most tedious tasks with boundless energy. Keeping busy was the best way to pass the time and stop me from watching the clock.

When Mum knocked on my bedroom door while I was getting ready, I'd fully expected her to tell me to keep the racket down. I was singing along to Lewis Capaldi's 'Someone You Loved' at the top of my voice like a true hairbrush diva.

'Can I come in?' Mum asked, poking her head around the door.

'Of course,' I replied. Without looking away from the mirror, I carried on coating my lashes with black mascara.

'Are you going out with Conor again?' Mum asked.

'Yes. How did you guess?' My face broke into a cheek-aching grin.

I watched Mum in the reflection. Instead of smiling back at me, she cast her eyes to the floor, then her brow furrowed. I stopped what I was doing and turned around so that I was facing her.

'Is everything OK?'

'Not really.'

'What's the matter?'

Mum looked like she had the weight of the world on her slender shoulders.

'Dad and I are worried about you?' Mum said, looking into my eyes.

'Why?' I shrugged.

Even though I'd asked the question, I had a horrible feeling I knew what the answer would be before she opened her mouth. She took a deep breath before she spoke, and the words spilled out of Mum's mouth in a steady stream.

'We don't think it's a good idea for you to go out with Conor.'

She'd obviously been nominated to be the bearer of bad news and was keen to get the unpleasant job over and done with as quickly as possible.

'Why not?' My tone was sharp.

'Dad and I think he's too old for you, and we're worried you're going to get hurt.'

I rolled my eyes. At least Mum had the good grace to look embarrassed before she broke eye contact with me.

My parents hadn't been introduced to my new boyfriend yet, but they must have sneaked a peek at him when he'd picked me up from the flat the last time we went out. I was shocked that they seemed to have taken an instant dislike to him. They're generally not judgemental people.

'Things seem to be moving so fast between you and Conor.'

'For God's sake, Mum, I think you're overreacting. It's not as though we're getting married. We're only going out for dinner...'

'Even so, you've only just turned nineteen, Ella.'

'And you had a toddler by the time you were my age.' I knew that was a low blow, but I couldn't help myself. I didn't appreciate Mum poking her nose into my business.

Mum looked startled by my outburst, but she didn't let it throw her off her stride. 'Listen, Ella, I don't want this to sound harsh, but Conor's a fully grown man; you need to ask yourself, why would he want to go out with a teenager?'

Mum's words were like a slap around the face. Anyone would think Conor was about to start drawing his pension or was some kind of sex offender trying to groom a child the way she was reacting. This wasn't the first time in history that a younger woman had fallen for an older man, and it wouldn't be the last.

I considered explaining why I'd been drawn to Conor in the first place. If my parents knew that unlike men my own age, he didn't behave as though he had endless options on Tinder, maybe they'd see things differently. Conor had got his life sorted, so he didn't feel the need to play games or mess with my emotions. But I was silently seething that they were trying to interfere, so I kept my thoughts to myself.

Mum reached towards me and tried to take hold of my hand, but I pulled it away. 'I'm sorry if I've hurt your feelings, but I'm just trying to protect you. Seriously, Ella, don't get too attached to Conor, or he'll end up breaking your heart. I know you don't want to hear this, but Dad and I think you really need to cool things off with him.'

As if I was going to do that. I was falling in love for the first time, and nobody was going to stop me. Investing myself fully into our relationship felt natural. Conor had opened my eyes and taken the blinkers off. He'd awakened my desire for wanting to experience everything life had to give and provided the medium for me to explore new things. Why couldn't my mum and dad just be happy for me? No matter what they thought about my relationship, they needed to accept that I wasn't a child anymore. I was a woman, and an independent one at that, so I'd make my own choices whether they liked it or not.

Mum waited for me to respond, but a long pause stretched out between us. When she opened her mouth to speak, I cut her off before she had a chance to continue the lecture.

'Can you close the door on your way out, please?' I said before turning my back on her.

After she'd left my room, I stood in silence for a moment so that I could absorb what had just happened. The way Mum had spoken to me was really out of character for her. She was usually laid-back about everything. She'd never been the type of overprotective mother who suffocated her child and destroyed their confidence. She usually stood ten paces back and let me make my own mistakes. That was the way people learned how to stand on their own two feet, wasn't it?

STEPHANIE HARTE

Although I was sure her intentions were good, there was no way I was going to listen to Mum's advice. Things were just getting exciting between Conor and myself, so her warning fell on deaf ears. I'd never felt like this before; it was a unique experience, completely overwhelming, partly wonderful, partly terrifying. It was difficult to explain, but it was like wading into the deep end of the pool when you couldn't swim. I was trying to be cautious so that I didn't lose my footing, fully aware that I'd be in way over my head if I did. But the thought of plunging into the unknown, knowing I wouldn't be able to swim in the deep end, was so exciting, it outweighed any reservations I might have had.

36

7

Conor

'Fuck me, for a minute there, I thought my eyes were deceiving me, but they weren't, the prodigal son's finally decided to return to the flock. You took your time,' Bobby said, adjusting one of his sovereign rings before he cackled at his own joke.

'We all know the Colombian deal's dead in the water; we can't continue to do business with people who keep changing the terms of the agreement, but trying to get someone I've just met to trust me enough to get on board with us is a slow process,' I replied, brushing off Bobby's remarks, not that I owed him an explanation.

Bobby seemed to have forgotten that he wasn't in a position to piss me off; he was totally reliant on my services. He didn't know the first thing about setting up a deal with a new supplier, and paired with the fact that he had about as much charm as a polished turd Bobby wouldn't get far without me, so he'd do well to remember that.

'When's the shipment arriving then?'

I had to stop myself from shaking my head. Talk about jumping the gun. We were only in the early stages of the negotiations. The terms of the deal hadn't been agreed yet, let alone finalised. It could be months before we received a delivery, but Bobby wouldn't be happy about that. He wanted everything done yesterday and was used to getting his own way. He hailed from humble beginnings and was now one of the most powerful men in the East End of London.

'It's too early to say.'

Bobby twisted the large sovereign ring on his little finger around before he crossed his arms over his chest. 'I'm sure I don't need to tell you that's not what I wanted to hear.'

Bobby lowered his strawberry-blond eyebrows a couple of inches and glared at me, then he turned on his heel and walked out of the office. I stood and watched his suited frame disappear out of sight as he went off for a sulk. He could be a difficult man to deal with at times. Bobby upset everyone he came into contact with; he had a habit of rubbing people up the wrong way.

I was on my way to pick Ella up and already running late when Leo Carr called again. He'd left me numerous voicemails while I was out in Spain, but I hadn't had a chance to get back to him yet. I'd been putting off making the call, secretly hoping he'd get bored of chasing me and find somebody else to do his dirty work.

'Long time no speak. You're a difficult man to track down. Where have you been hiding?' Leo said.

'I haven't been hiding anywhere, but I'm up to my neck in work at the moment,' I replied, hoping he'd take the hint.

I'd been trying to cut ties with Leo for as long as I could

remember, but he was still clinging on, like a persistent skid in a toilet pan.

'I've got a job that needs sorting, and I can't think of a better man than you to do it.'

I let out a loud sigh. I should have realised he'd ignore my attempt to let him down gently. As far as I was concerned, our working relationship had come to an end, but he was impossible to walk away from. It used to be part of my job description to threaten a person who'd failed to repay a debt and extract extortion money from some unfortunate members of the population, but I'd left those days behind me now, and I had no intention of returning to them.

'On this occasion, I'll have to say no. But thanks for thinking of me.' Leo wasn't the sort of man you turned down, so I knew he wouldn't be happy.

'For a minute there, I thought you were blowing me out.' Leo laughed, but I could tell he wasn't impressed.

I wasn't in the mood for a discussion. Having my ear bent by a man who wouldn't take no for an answer was beyond frustrating, and I'd had as much as I was prepared to take for one day.

'Are you still there, Leo? I can't hear you. The reception's bad,' I lied before hanging up.

Leo liked to think he was a big player, but he was small fry compared to a lot of the other local villains. He ran a protection racket with a bit of money lending thrown in on the side to boost his earnings, and he made a modest living compared to some of his rivals, but he was probably still raking in more cash than the average man on the street.

Leo was another one of those characters who liked to go around upsetting everyone. Leo and Bobby both hailed from Mile End. It made me think there must be something in the water.

Until I'd branched out on my own, I'd held down a succession of jobs. All of the roles had varying degrees of legitimacy. I was only twelve when my mum's boyfriend at the time asked me if I wanted to earn a bit of pocket money. I had Roy to thank for setting me on the wrong path. He was a small-time crook and got me involved in all sorts of illegal activities. Roy used to pay me a pittance to work on his market stall selling counterfeit designer goods, anything from sunglasses and handbags to tracksuits and trainers. His stock varied depending on the hooky gear he could get his grubby little hands on. As a sideline, we also used to peddle marijuana. The rate Roy paid for the risk involved amounted to child labour. I was glad when my mum split up with him. It was a good excuse to stop working for him and go it alone.

It was also down to Roy that I'd become saddled with Leo. I hadn't seen the rotten-toothed wonder for years until that fateful day I'd been picking my way through the crowd to get to the bar in my local. Roy had caught my eye and had gestured for me to come over. So much for popping in for a quick pint on my way home. No doubt he'd be trying to ponce a drink off of me, I'd thought as I'd made my way to where he was standing. But I was wrong; he'd wanted to introduce me to a man whose eyes were out on stalks. Roy had described Leo Carr as a good acquaintance. I'd heard the name before but couldn't say I'd ever had the pleasure.

'See you around, Conor,' Roy had said before he'd scuttled off into the shadows like the cockroach he was, leaving me behind with his bug-eyed associate.

'Take a seat, son,' Leo had said.

Although this was ancient history, I could still picture the way his dyed dark brown hair had drained his already sallow complexion. For his own good, somebody should have pointed that out to him, but nobody, myself included, would have been brave or foolish enough to do it.

He seemed to have taken a particular interest in recruiting me. Before I'd left the pub that evening, Leo had hired me as an underworld enforcer, a line of employment I'd never enjoyed and was keen to leave behind. I'd wanted to focus on my latest venture. But when you worked alongside the dregs of society, you couldn't afford to upset anyone, or you'd be constantly watching your back.

8

Ella

I paced backwards and forwards on the pavement outside my block, wiping the palms of my hands on my stonewashed skinny jeans while I waited for Conor to arrive. There was an awkward atmosphere in the flat after Mum and I had words earlier, so I couldn't wait to put some distance between us. Even though I couldn't see them, I could feel my parents' eyes boring into the back of my head. I knew they'd be watching me from the window, and if I turned around suddenly, the net curtains would twitch.

I checked the time on my watch; Conor should have been here fifteen minutes ago. It wouldn't have been a big deal if I didn't have a ringside audience watching the drama unfold. He'd never been late before, so I was sure he had a genuine reason, but after the conversation I'd had with my mum, I suddenly felt concerned. Doubt flooded my mind. What if Conor had had a change of heart and decided he didn't want to go out with me anymore? Would he let me down gently, or would he just not bother to turn up? The longer

I waited, the more certain I was that he wasn't going to show. Nobody would want to get stood up in public; the humiliation would be unbearable. I felt tears stab at my eyes and had to blink them away. I didn't want my mum and dad to realise I was upset.

It had been one of the hottest June days on record, and although the sun was now low in the sky, the temperature remained high. As the fabric of my fitted top started to stick to my skin, I wished I'd worn something looser. Even my feet were beginning to swell; the paving stones were red hot, and the heat was seeping into the soles of my Adidas trainers. I would have loved to have taken refuge inside, but I decided to grin and bear it to avoid an interrogation from my parents.

Why hadn't Conor text me to say he was running late? Surely that wasn't too much to ask, was it? As I considered what might have happened, I became aware that my body language, foot-tapping and arms folded, was sending silent signals to my parents. The last thing I wanted to do was give them any ammunition if the worst happened, and Conor turned out to be a no-show. I knew being left in the lurch wasn't that big a deal. It happened to people all the time. But who was I trying to kid? I'd be absolutely devastated if he failed to arrive. To stop myself from getting too flustered and going into a complete meltdown, I scrolled through the photos stored on my phone. I couldn't think of anything worse than having to do the walk of shame back to the flat and face my mum and dad.

I willed myself not to assume the worst, but I was just beginning to think that I was going to have to admit defeat when Conor's BMW turned onto the estate. My heart pounded as it drew closer. My stomach felt all fluttery as my excitement grew. Conor jumped out of the driver's side as soon as the car came to a stop.

'I'm so sorry I'm late,' Conor said, holding his palms out as he rushed towards me with a look of concern on his face.

'Don't worry,' I replied. The butterflies inside my stomach were doing cartwheels of joy. I'd never been more relieved to see anyone in my life.

'I feel terrible. I got caught up on a work call and couldn't let you know I was running late. I didn't realise you'd be waiting outside in this heat. I hope you haven't got sunstroke.'

Conor had presented me with the golden opportunity to explain what had happened with my parents, but I didn't want their negativity to overshadow our evening, so I decided not to mention it.

'You weren't to know. It's such a beautiful evening, I thought I'd make the most of the sunshine. Being stuck behind the bar when you can see the sunlight glinting on the River Thames is torture.'

'I really do feel awful about it; I'm normally good on time. I promise I'll make it up to you.' Conor smiled with a glint in his eye.

Conor slid his arms around my waist, and when he kissed me, my body tingled, and all the uncertainty I'd felt earlier melted away in an instant.

'I thought we might do something different tonight,' Conor suggested once we were both sitting the car.

'That sounds intriguing.'

'If you don't mind, instead of going out for dinner, I'd like to rustle something up for you at home.'

'That sounds great!' I was seriously impressed that he could cook. I'd never been very domesticated, so the fact that Conor knew his way around the kitchen was definitely a big plus point.

'You seem quiet. Is everything OK?' Conor asked, glancing across at me as he pulled out of the estate.

'Yes, everything's fine.' I smiled. Now that we were together, my worries had vanished into thin air.

Conor's house was situated in a quiet tree-lined cul-de-sac of just six individually designed properties. It was a million miles away from the two-bedroomed flat where I lived with my parents on the council estate. The leafy suburb of Highgate was like a village, yet it was only fifteen minutes from the heart of London.

'I thought it was about time I gave you a guided tour,' Conor said as he parked his BMW Z4 on the driveway.

I got out of the car and stood looking up at the charcoal-coloured exterior of the detached house, barely able to believe what I was seeing. Conor smiled and took hold of my hand, then led me toward the contemporary door with central glass panels and a long chrome handle down one side.

'What do you think?' Conor asked when he opened the front door of the cube-shaped house. A massive skylight above the hallway flooded the minimalist interior with light.

'Wow,' I replied. I was at a loss to know what to say and couldn't find the right words to do the place justice.

With a smile on his face, Conor guided me into a large double-height reception room with floor-to-ceiling black-metal-framed windows that overlooked the landscaped garden.

'Do you like it?'

'I love it. It's incredible!'

If I hadn't known somebody lived in this house, I would have thought it was a show home. Everything was spotlessly clean, but there was no sign of life. It didn't look like the contents had ever been used. As my boyfriend guided me through every room in the house, I quickly concluded that electrical devices were as essential to Conor as the air he breathed. His house was fitted out with every smart home gadget under the sun. I hadn't had him down as a techno-geek up until now.

This house was the epitome of a swanky bachelor pad. There wasn't a feather cushion or a scented candle to be seen. Although stylish, in my opinion, the absence of soft furnishings and any unnecessary clutter made the beautiful house seem almost clinical. It seriously lacked a woman's touch.

Conor pulled me into his arms and gazed at me with his hypnotic eyes that were the colour of blue diamonds. 'I'm glad you like the house... I want you to move in with me.'

My mouth fell open. Not for the first time since arriving, I didn't know what to say. We'd only been going out for a few weeks.

'Don't you think it's a bit soon?'

'It's not too soon for me, but if you need more time...'

My head was telling me not to be ridiculous, but my heart wasn't listening. I wanted to spend all my time with Conor. What better way was there to get to know a person properly than living with them? It would give us the opportunity to strengthen our physical and emotional bonds with nobody interfering.

Alarm bells should have been ringing, but at the time, I was too busy swimming in the currents of passion to notice the red flags. My brain had turned to mush, which stopped me being able to focus on anything other than Conor. Every time I clapped eyes on him, my heart skipped a beat, and I felt a rush of excitement through my body.

I was seriously tempted to take him up on his offer, but I was worried about what my parents would say. Mum had already voiced her opinion about our relationship, so I knew if I announced that I was leaving home, it would go down like a tonne of bricks. I'd have to play this carefully; I didn't want to fall out with my parents over this.

I bit down on my lip and considered my response. 'Living together is a big commitment; we haven't been going out with each other very long.'

'I understand. I wasn't trying to pressure you. Someday maybe?' Conor smiled, then leaned down and pressed his lips onto mine.

I allowed myself to become lost in his kiss. Conor took my hand and led me to the bedroom; he pushed my hair over my shoulders and began to kiss my neck, sending shock waves through my body. Conor lifted my top over my shoulders, unclasped my bra then stripped off the rest of my clothes. I reached forward and undid the button of his jeans. He pulled off his black Hugo Boss T-shirt, and as he did, he exposed a well-maintained six-pack.

Conor lowered me back onto the bed, and I closed my eyes as his hands explored my body. Cupping my buttock with one hand, he ran the fingertips of his other hand gently up the inside of my thighs. A moan escaped from my lips. I wanted him inside me. As he slowly entered me, I dug my fingers into his back. Conor was making love to me. He wasn't trying to perform sexual gymnastics like my previous boyfriend, who had felt the need to experience as many positions as he could think of in the short space of time before he climaxed. This was no teenage fumble. Conor took charge and brought me to the edge of earth-shattering moments over and over before we collapsed in a heap of tangled limbs.

As we lay breathless in each other's arms, I wished we could stay like this forever. He didn't need to do anything else to talk me into moving in with him. My mind was made up.

9

My parents didn't need to say a word; disappointment was written all over their faces. I'm not blaming them for pushing me into Conor's arms, but if everything had been all right at home, I might not have made the same hasty decision. The more they wagged the disapproving finger in my direction, the more I seemed determined to rebel against it.

There was no denying I was besotted with my new boyfriend. I knew I was falling in love with him, but taking the step to move in together after you'd only been an item for a couple of weeks was a reckless thing to do, and I wasn't a natural risk-taker by any means. Although we'd been pretty inseparable since we'd met and had spent every available moment in each other's company, the fact remained, we barely knew each other. There was a nagging doubt at the back of my mind that this was all too much, too soon. Part of me was terrified; it wasn't the right thing to do, but I was caught up in the moment, so I pushed the thought to the back of my head and forged ahead with my plans.

I was about to find out that once I scratched beneath the surface, there was a very different man waiting to meet me than the one who had breezed into my life and swept me off my feet. I'd hoped my parents would be happy for me, but I was an only child, and they were struggling to let me go. This day was going to come around sooner or later. Some of my friends had gone away to study and were now scattered all over the country. I could have easily been one of them. I was beginning to wish I hadn't chosen to do my degree at a London university. They wouldn't have known what I was up to if I wasn't still living under their roof, but money had forced me to make that decision.

'What do you mean, you're moving out?' Dad put his hands on his hips and glared at me.

I'd had a horrible feeling the news wasn't going to go down well, but the last thing I wanted was to get into a huge argument over it. I normally had such a good relationship with my parents, but since Conor had been on the scene, we weren't seeing eye to eye on anything.

'I'm nineteen, Dad, so you can't stop me.'

'Can't I? We'll see about that.'

Dad clenched his teeth, and his face flushed. I could see he was fuming, but I wasn't going to change my mind. I loved him dearly, but sometimes he treated me like I was still a five-year-old.

'Why can't you just be happy for me?'

Earlier, when I'd run this scenario through my mind, I'd had visions of them helping me pack up my stuff and then driving me around to Conor's to settle me into my new home, excited about what the future would bring. But I should have known that wasn't the way things were going to play out. My parents didn't even want me going out with Conor, so it was obvious they were going to be less than impressed when I told them I was moving in with him.

The longer this hostile scene played out, the more my happiness began to unravel. I needed to get out of the flat before all hell broke loose, and we ended up saying something we'd later regret.

'Where do you think you're going, Isabella?' Dad shouted in his best stern voice when I walked away, putting an end to the Mexican stand-off.

He never called me by my full name unless he was angry with me. 'I'm going to pack my stuff,' I replied without looking back.

When I reappeared fifteen minutes later, having thrown some essentials into my pink hard-shell case, Mum and Dad were sitting on the sofa talking to each other in a low whisper so that I couldn't overhear their conversation. Dad stood up and blocked my path as I went to leave.

'Your mum and I are really worried about you, Ella,' Dad said, trying the softly, softly approach. He'd realised laying down the law wasn't going to work, so he'd adopted a change of tactics. 'It's not easy to let go of your child, especially your only little girl. As your dad, it's my responsibility to protect you, and if you get hurt, I'll feel like I failed you.' Dad's mouth was downcast.

'There's no need for you to worry.' I glanced over at my mum and gave her a half-smile. 'I'll be fine.'

'But how are you going to manage?'

I rolled my eyes and let out a loud sigh.

'You barely earn enough to stay afloat while you're living at home with us.' Dad's voice was rising. He was starting to lose it again. 'Your wages aren't going to stretch to rent, bills and food, young lady.'

If he was going to speak to me like I was still a child, there was no point having this conversation. It was obvious Mum and Dad didn't approve, but that made it all the more exciting – like we were engaged in an illicit romance. The more they insisted I stay, the more I couldn't wait to walk out the door and seek solace in the arms of my forbidden boyfriend.

'I'm going to start working full-time to bring in extra money. I'm dropping out of uni,' I announced as I pulled my suitcase across the beige-coloured carpet.

My parents were staring at each other, open-mouthed and speechless. I didn't know why I'd said that. I had no intention of giving up my course, not for one minute, but it was a knee-jerk reaction. I'd done it to hurt them. I knew how important my education was to my mum and dad. They'd wanted me to be the first person in the family to have a degree.

'Wait, Ella, are you sure you know what you're doing?' Dad asked.

A pang of guilt stabbed at my heart as I slammed the front door behind me. I didn't want to fall out with my parents, but they needed to back off and let me make my own decisions, my own mistakes, or I would end up resenting them. At the moment, I felt like I was trapped in two half-lives, one with my parents and one with Conor. I didn't want to be stuck in the middle, torn between both sides.

When I pushed open the exterior door, Conor's car was parked outside the building. He was leaning against the passenger door, with his tanned arms crossed over his chest, waiting patiently for me. A smile lit up my face as I wheeled my case over to him.

'Are you OK?' Conor asked, with a look of genuine concern on his face.

I nodded. I didn't trust myself to speak. There was a lump at the back of my throat that was so big it was threatening to cut off my windpipe.

'Are you sure? You look upset.' Conor tilted my chin upwards, and he stared at me with his beautiful blue eyes. 'You haven't changed your mind, have you?' Conor searched my face for the answer to his question. When I didn't reply, he continued to speak. 'It's OK if you have; I don't want to make you rush into anything if you need more time.'

'Don't be silly; of course I haven't changed my mind,' I managed to blurt out. I had enough to worry about without him questioning my feelings for him.

Relief washed over his handsome face. I didn't want Conor to read anything into my silence, but I was scared that when I opened my mouth, there was a real chance I might burst into tears. Thankfully, I didn't, so I forced out a smile and tried to forget about the argument I'd had with my parents.

I knew deep down they were just looking out for me. In hindsight, I should have done things differently. Mum and Dad hadn't even been introduced to Conor yet, so no wonder they were being wary. But it had all happened so quickly there hadn't been time. I was certain that once they got to know my boyfriend, they'd like him as much as I did.

I didn't want to be forced to choose between them. Surely we could come to a compromise. My parents had always been there for me through thick and thin, and I couldn't imagine them not being a part of my life.

'How did your parents take the news?' Conor smiled as he asked the question I'd been dreading.

'They were a bit shocked, but I'm sure they'll get used to it,' I replied, not wanting to go into details. I tried to make my words sound breezy to cover up how worried I was about the situation. But the bottom line was, whether my mum and dad liked it or not, the decision wasn't theirs to make.

Conor threw his arms around me and pulled me towards him. He prised open my lips with his tongue and kissed me in the middle of the estate. Now that would give the neighbours something to talk about, I thought.

10

Conor

Ella was a nineteen-year-old girl living at home with her parents when we'd started going out. She was so trusting and had an unquenchable enthusiasm for anything and everything, the way people did before they'd been exposed to the cruel reality of life, so part of me felt guilty for tainting her world with my murky lifestyle. But her doe eyes and bright smile were impossible to resist. Common sense told me we were a mismatched pair, but any logic I might have possessed seemed to have gone out of the window. I was smitten by her. Ella had captivated my attention from the first moment I'd laid eyes on her. I couldn't ignore the effect she was having on me.

It was true I had a dark side, but it was too early in our relationship to come clean about what I did for a living. I wasn't prepared to risk Ella walking away from me if she knew that I took part in illegal activities to fund my lifestyle. I felt guilty about being this devious, but in the short time we'd been together, Ella had got under my skin, and that was where I wanted her to stay. I didn't want to put her in danger, but my desire to be with her outweighed everything else.

I felt incredibly lucky to have found Ella and was flattered that such a beautiful girl would be interested in me. She had an energy about her that was infectious; I couldn't get enough of her. Her age never came into it for me; if anything, being young was a bonus. Ella's history was blissfully uncomplicated; she had a clean slate, which was a rare thing to find.

I'd concluded from my limited experience that, more often than not, women my age were either looking for the kind of commitment I wasn't ready to make, or they brought so much baggage to the table, it put me off before we even got started. They were either divorced, had kids, or psycho exes that they couldn't get rid of; I didn't have the time or the patience to deal with all the drama that accompanied them. Maybe it was the women I attracted, but they seemed to want to make me pay the price for every bad relationship they'd ever had. Which was why I'd thought I was destined to stay single.

Despite being older, I'd never bothered having serious relationships; short-term flings were more my style. But since I'd met Ella, I'd done a complete U-turn and felt like I was finally ready to settle down. In a short space of time, she'd changed my mindset and perception. I was a natural sceptic when it came to love, but Ella had stirred something within me I didn't know existed. I was addicted to her; when I wasn't with her, I craved her company like a junkie craved their next fix.

There was no doubt, Ella brought out the best in me. She

appreciated everything I did for her, which made me feel good about myself. Being with Ella boosted my confidence and self-esteem, but there was a flip side to my happiness; I was scared of letting my guard down and allowing her to get close to me in case she didn't like what she saw.

I hadn't had the best start. My dad had been unaccounted for my entire life, and although my mum was around, she'd done a lousy job and failed the most basic parental test by not providing a solid foundation for her five children's upbringing. For want of a better description, we were dragged up. Being the oldest, a lot of the responsibility fell at my feet. She took complete advantage of me. I'd work in the market for a pittance, and then she'd take the small amount of money I'd earned off me to buy fags and booze, knowing there was nothing in the fridge for our dinner. Mum was very hard on me if I didn't pick up the slack that she created in our home life. To ensure that no one would ever exploit me again, I forced myself to become a badass and gained people's respect.

As a young man, I was desperate to get away from home and make some serious cash, so I got in with the wrong crowd. But once you stepped over that line, it was almost impossible to go back. I'd chosen to break the law; now I had to live with the consequences of that decision for the rest of my life. I hoped in time, I'd be able to come clean with Ella about how I made a living without her bailing on me. But it was too soon to take the risk. If she knew what a shady business I was involved in, she might be tempted to cut her losses and walk away.

When I came out of the en-suite bathroom with a towel wrapped around my waist, Ella was sitting with her back against the leather headboard. I walked over to her and planted a kiss on her soft lips. She looked beautiful without a scrap of makeup on her face. She was wearing one of my T-shirts, which was oversized on her, and her mane of dark brown curls was pulled into a messy bun.

'How did you get that scar?' Ella asked, running her slender fingers over the skin on my stomach.

I glanced at the faint line to buy myself some time before I replied. 'I had my appendix removed when I was a teenager; it hurt like a bitch.' I laughed to cover up the little white lie. I couldn't tell Ella what really happened, or she'd run a mile.

'It's in a funny place, isn't it?' Ella inspected the scar that ran from just below my ribcage to the top of my belly button.

I shrugged my shoulders. 'You'll have to take that up with the surgeon.'

Glossing over the truth was a bad habit of mine. But if I wasn't careful, I could end up tying myself in knots, and the lies would destroy the trust that we were building in our relationship. I was a lot of things, but I'd never claimed to be an honest person. In my line of work, weaving deception went with the territory.

11

Ella

Conor was making our breakfast in the state-of-the-art fully fitted kitchen when his mobile rang. I glanced up at him, and he threw one hand out apologetically before he disappeared out of the room, the way he always did when he was taking a call. We hadn't been living together long, about a month, and I was still getting used to how different my life had become. I kept pinching myself to check I wasn't dreaming, but this was really happening to me.

I was slowly spinning around on the hydraulic bar stool when Conor came back into the kitchen; his bare feet padded across the shiny black tiles. Stopping in front of me, he swept my long hair over my shoulders and looked at me with those eyes. My heart fluttered in response.

'Is everything OK?' I asked.

'Yes,' Conor replied, but his face told a different story.

Moments earlier, my boyfriend had seemed on top of the world. With a tea towel thrown over his shoulder, he'd poured freshly squeezed orange juice into tall glasses, having just popped two almond croissants into the oven to warm. Now he appeared deflated.

'I've got to go away for a while,' Conor tried to casually drop in as he took the croissants out of the oven and put them on two plates.

The second those words left his mouth, they hit me with such force they almost winded me and pinpointed the moment I realised I'd fallen in love with Conor. I couldn't bear the thought of being separated from him for one minute, let alone a period of time. It felt like the end of the world, and if I wasn't careful, I'd begin to crumble. It was all I could do not to burst into tears.

'Where are you going?' I managed to utter.

'There's a business deal going on that I need to oversee.'

We'd still not discussed in detail what Conor actually did for a living. All I knew was that he was involved in the distribution of IT equipment.

'I'm sure I could get time off work. Can I go with you?' I smiled. Travelling was my passion, so I was always up for going away.

'I wish you could, but I'm afraid not.'

I was in danger of throwing a hissy fit; I didn't want to be parted from my gorgeous boyfriend, not even for a short while, but he didn't seem the slightest bit bothered about leaving me behind, which made me doubt whether he had feelings for me.

'Don't be sad.' Conor walked over to me and went to pull me into his arms, but I wriggled out of his grip. 'What's up?'

'Really?' I said, placing my hands on my hips and glaring at Conor. 'Do you really need to ask?' Conor looked at me blankly, so I felt the need to clarify what was bothering me. 'You've just told me you're going away, and you seem surprised I'm upset about it. I thought we had something special, but you obviously don't feel as strongly about me as I do you.' The idea of that paralysed me with fear, and my mum's warning echoed in my head; she'd been worried I was going to get hurt. I hated feeling this vulnerable.

'What the hell are you talking about?' Conor looked genuinely shocked. 'I wasn't trying to make you feel insecure. I love you, Ella.' My boyfriend pulled me into his arms and, this time, I didn't resist.

'I love you too,' I replied. Relief washed over me when I realised we were on the same page. Conor hadn't tried to play it cool; he wanted to reassure me.

Spending time with Conor made me feel content; we were totally comfortable in each other's company. We'd already formed a deep connection, and the chemistry between us was incredible. I didn't want to be that needy person who didn't feel complete without their partner by their side, but I couldn't seem to help myself. Since we'd moved in together, I'd become even more enraptured by my boyfriend and had spent hours studying every little detail about him. It occurred to me that probably nobody else had noticed he had a freckle on his right earlobe, and he always arranged things in straight lines, be it the cans in the kitchen cupboards or the toiletries in the bathroom.

'I wish you didn't have to go,' I said, burying my face into the soft fabric of Conor's T-shirt as he rested his chin on the top of my head.

'I'll only be gone for a couple of days, a week at the most.'

'A week?' I questioned. My heart sank. Pulling back from his embrace, I looked up into his handsome face.

'I'll be back before you know it.' Conor kissed the tip of my nose.

'Is that a promise?'

'Yes. Now let's eat before our breakfast gets cold.'

'OK,' I replied, then let out a sigh.

Carrying a tray, Conor walked across to the doors on the far side of the kitchen. He slid back the black-framed glass panel then stepped out onto the outside deck. Pulling my dressing gown around me, I followed him outside. It was August, but there was a coolness in the air, one of those misty mornings towards the end of summer where the sun was struggling to break through the dense white cloud that covered the sky like a blanket.

The gloomy landscape matched my current mood. I tried to shake it off, but I couldn't seem to make myself snap out of it. We were still very much in the honeymoon phase of our relationship, so being parted from Conor was going to be a nightmare for me. But I couldn't allow my eternal optimism to take a beating. What was one week out of a lifetime?

I took a bite out of the almond croissant, and as crumbs rained down onto the plate and table, Conor started wiping them away while I was still eating. What was the point? I was about to make more crumbs! I could see him becoming anxious that I was making a mess, and it put me off my food, so I put the half-eaten croissant down on the plate. He instantly pounced on my discarded breakfast, whisked it away and began a tidying frenzy while I stood by and watched.

Later I sat on the edge of the bed, gazing at Conor as he packed for his trip. He zipped up the black hard-shell suitcase and lowered it onto its four wheels. Pulling the case behind him, he walked over to me and caught hold of my hand.

'I'm going to miss you so much.'

'I'm going to miss you too,' Conor said, pulling me onto my feet. He slid his tongue into my mouth before I had a chance to answer.

My body was still tingling from Conor's touch, and I could taste my boyfriend on my lips as I watched him walk out of the door moments later. They say absence makes the heart grow fonder, but it wasn't possible for me to feel more for Conor than I already did. Corny as it sounded, I would be counting the minutes until he came back to me.

It wasn't in my nature to mope about. I'd been told on many occasions that I had a sunny personality, so I'd just have to keep myself busy and hope the time passed quickly. I wasn't interested in the London scene; I'd rather go for coffee with friends or stay in and watch a movie than go clubbing. No doubt that was pretty unusual behaviour for a teenage girl, but I'd never been one to follow the crowd.

'Hi, Ella, it's Lucy. I just wanted to let you know there's a party tonight. Amy and I are going. Do you fancy joining us?'

I was buoyed up at the sound of my friend's voice, and if I was still single, I'd have been up for it. We used to have a great laugh plying ourselves with pre-drinks so we could nail a cheap night out on a student budget. I smiled at the thought of the drinking game forfeits that usually revolved around some form of hideous punch mixed up in a baby bath. And having warded off the wandering hands of horny fellow students, we'd try to stagger home afterwards with blisters on our feet from dancing all night in uncomfortable shoes.

Although I had happy memories, being in a room full of tanked-up people now that I had a lovely boyfriend didn't hold the same appeal, and I couldn't face the thought of going. At the risk of sounding prematurely middle-aged, my days of attending student piss-ups were going to stay in the past where they belonged. Instead, I resigned myself to an evening of Netflix.

'Thanks for the offer, but I'm going to get an early night,' I replied. I could sense Lucy wasn't impressed that I wasn't going to join them.

Having realised that there was only so much popcorn a person could handle, I decided to sign myself up for all the overtime that was on offer, much to my manager's delight. At least the extra money would come in handy and buffer my overdraft if nothing else. And keeping busy would help to get me through the next few days. Boredom was well and truly starting to set in.

12

Conor

I was dreading the latest business meeting with the Gómez family. We were meant to be ironing out the final details of the deal. Even though Bobby was tightening the thumbscrews, I didn't feel comfortable negotiating the terms of a large contract at this stage. I wasn't sure if I could trust the cartel's interpreter, Juan, to translate the agreement word for word. Maybe I should opt for a small drop in the first instance. That way, we could test out the merchandise without investing too much money. I figured once we established mutual trust, the size of our orders would automatically grow.

Diego greeted me like an old friend when I walked into the conference room, clasping my hand in his; he gave me a firm handshake and invited me to join his partners seated around the cherrywood table. Pedro was too preoccupied with smoothing down his wiry moustache to reach out, but he smiled and nodded to acknowledge me when I took a seat.

'It's good to see you again,' I said.

Clasping her tiny dog under one arm, Valentina held out her other hand in front of me.

Did she think she was European royalty? Valentina's action threw me for a moment as I wasn't up to speed on the etiquette of hand-kissing, but I thought I'd better not snub her request as I was trying to cultivate a good relationship with the Spaniards. So I gave her a quick peck just to be polite and tried not to snort with laughter as I did. If that's what it took to keep her sweet, I was more than happy to oblige.

'Conor, you are so charming, darling,' Valentina said with an r roll and a bat of her false eyelashes.

'How nice of you to say,' I replied, flashing her my brightest smile, then I turned my attention back to Diego. 'My client would like to place a small order initially to make sure he's happy with the product.'

Diego's weather-beaten face broke into a grin. 'Our cocaine is top quality. I can assure you, your contact won't be disappointed, but we'll agree to the terms so that he can sample it for himself.'

'But only on this occasion,' Valentina added, flashing me a warning look. She wagged a manicured finger at me like she was scolding a small child before she went back to stroking her pooch.

'Are you deliberately trying to put me out of business?' Bobby asked, puffing out his chest. He put his hands on his hips, then fixed me with his piercing blue eyes.

'Far from it,' I replied. 'But with all due respect, we don't know if we can trust these guys yet, so I thought it was safer to err on the side of caution.'

It was common knowledge that drug dealers weren't pillars of the community. The Gómez cartel could take our money and disappear into thin air without delivering the goods, and if they did, it wasn't as though we could go running to the police about it.

'Don't fuck this up for me, Conor, or I'll make sure you're finished in this business.' Bobby jabbed his chubby finger in my face.

Maybe that wouldn't be such a bad thing. I'd thought about turning my back on the underworld before now; sometimes, the aggro didn't appear to outweigh the benefits. The way Bobby kept kicking off, trying to control me and call the shots, made me feel like I still wasn't my own boss or in charge of my destiny.

And besides that, I had Ella to consider now. She'd totally overreacted when I'd told her I had to go away on business. I dreaded to think what she'd say if I came clean about the nature of my work. I didn't know for sure, but I was fairly certain it wouldn't go down well. I knew it wasn't a good basis to build a relationship on secrets and lies. They would jeopardize the trust between us; it was fragile, and once damaged, it wasn't easy to rebuild. But it was a chance I was going to have to take; my hands were tied at this stage. I wasn't prepared to tell her the truth. I was scared I might lose her. She was so important to me; I had to hold on to her at all costs. I did feel guilty about what I was doing, but I justified keeping Ella in the dark because I was lying about my profession; it wasn't as though I was cheating on her.

I hadn't intended to upset Ella by leaving her behind. But

what else could I have done? Bringing her to Spain with me might have put her in danger, and I wasn't prepared to take that risk. My trips away were going to become a regular occurrence; I didn't want that to become a source of conflict for us. Ella was my world, and the last thing I wanted to do was make her feel insecure.

For Ella's sake, as much as my own, I'd love to have been able to earn an honest crust, but it wasn't as simple as that. My desire to escape my upbringing had made me obsessed with being successful. My ambition had been a powerful driving force, but in my desperation to succeed, I'd allowed myself to be controlled by people around me, which had led me down a dark path. I'd been involved in this game my whole adult life, and I didn't know any other way to make the kind of money I was used to; the simple truth was I needed a lot of it to fund my lifestyle.

13

Ella

There was no denying I was missing Conor, but I was really out of sorts, a feeling that didn't just come from pining for my boyfriend. I'd been off-kilter for a good couple of days before I considered the possibility that I might be homesick. Living away from my parents for the first time was exciting but also a bit daunting and nerve-racking. The familiarity I was used to had disappeared overnight, and everything was new and different, and I had to admit I was finding the experience a little overwhelming.

I'd tried to keep myself busy while Conor was away by working and listening to French and Spanish audiobooks so that I didn't forget everything I'd learned by the time I went back to uni, but nothing seemed to be helping. So I thought, why fight it when a trip to see my parents could rectify the problem. What I hadn't anticipated was that I'd feel even worse after the visit.

Dad was at work, and Mum was making dinner when I'd breezed into the flat as though nothing had happened. I wasn't sure what I'd been expecting, but I didn't receive a hero's welcome, which made my mood plummet. It suddenly occurred to me that our relationship was damaged beyond repair, and the thought of that terrified me, triggering a feeling of separation anxiety. I wanted to reach out to my mum, so she could wave her magic wand and make everything instantly better like she used to when I was little, but the atmosphere was so tense between us; I didn't stay long enough to finish my mug of tea.

Seeing how hostile my mum was with me made me question the way I'd gone about things. She was obviously hurting too. Maybe if I'd explained that while I didn't know what was going to happen in the future, right now, I was blissfully happy and didn't regret moving in with Conor and that I wanted nothing more than her and Dad to get to know my boyfriend. Then she might have understood how I was feeling and been able to accept the choices I'd made. I wasn't trying to cut her and Dad out of my life; that was the last thing I wanted.

I managed to hold it together on the journey back to Conor's house, but I let it all out once I was behind closed doors. Crying was good for the soul, wasn't it? So why didn't I feel any better? I knew the reason; Mum had always been my go-to person when I was upset. My relationship with Conor was jeopardising our once unbreakable bond. The thought of that was agonising. I couldn't remember the last time I'd been so distressed.

Beautiful as it was, I didn't like being in this big house on my own. I was used to being surrounded by others. Mum often said I was a social butterfly, and she was right. I couldn't take any more of the isolation; I was a people person, so I decided to invite my two besties over. Some female company was just what I needed to take my mind off things.

'So this is it, girls. What do you think?' I asked.

Lucy and Amy stood looking up at the grey cube house with their mouths wide open.

'Bloody hell,' Lucy said. 'No wonder you were in a hurry to move in! By the way, I've been meaning to ask you, has Conor got any brothers?'

'Yes, he's got two,' I replied.

'Oh, fantastic! We can have one each, Amy.' Lucy laughed. Then she ran her fingers through her platinum blonde bob.

Even though the house belonged to Conor, I felt a huge sense of pride when I showed my friends around the four-double-bedroomed property.

'How the other half lives,' Amy said. Her greeny-blue eyes shone brightly when I opened the door to the master suite.

I walked across the ivory-coloured carpet past the super-king-sized bed and slid open the glass door, which led out onto a decked balcony.

'Oh my God, it's incredible!' Lucy's eyes widened as they scanned over the manicured surroundings and the treetop view.

'That's an understatement,' Amy added. Flecks of gold and copper in her beautiful red hair shimmered in the bright sunshine.

'I love the way the steps go down into the garden,' Lucy remarked.

'I've left the best until last,' I said when I led my friends out onto the rooftop deck where a large hot tub took centre stage.

'If I lived somewhere like this, I'd never leave the house!' Lucy said.

My friends had been a welcome distraction. I was so glad they'd come over. Spending the day binge-watching episodes of *The Last Kingdom* on Netflix while eating take-away pizza in the home cinema had worked wonders. Lucy and Amy's company and a large helping of junk food had been just what I'd needed to banish the case of loneliness I was feeling.

'We'd better head off now,' Lucy said just before midnight.

'Thanks for everything,' Amy added.

'My pleasure. Text me when you get home.'

As I closed the front door and put the alarm on, I felt my mood take a tumble. It was time to put a stop to my wallowing. Conor would be back tomorrow, so I had nothing to feel down about.

'I missed you so much!' I ran across the tiles towards Conor and threw my arms around his neck.

'Now that's what I call a welcome.' Conor laughed before he dropped his case in the hallway and lifted me off my feet. 'I missed you too.'

Moments later, we were tearing each other's clothes off. I couldn't get enough of the feeling of Conor's lips on mine. His strong hands roamed over my bare skin as our limbs entwined, locked together in a lovers' embrace.

'I'm starving after that workout.' He smiled.

'Me too.'

Conor rifled through the fridge, then began rustling up some dinner. A short while later, he was stirring a steaming pot of chilli con carne. If it tasted half as good as it smelled, I was in for a real treat. I couldn't help thinking, as I sipped on my glass of Merlot, there was something undeniably attractive about a domesticated man.

I leaned forward and inhaled deeply as Conor scooped a large helping of the sauce onto the fluffy white rice. The smell of the aromatic spices mingling together was divine, and my stomach rumbled in response.

'Can you take the plates out, and I'll bring the nachos?'

The full-length doors were already pulled back when I stepped onto the paving; potted blue hydrangeas stood like sentries on either side, guarding the open space. The garden looked a vision bathed in the soft glow of spotlights and large outdoor candles, so I paused for a moment to admire the view. Conor caught up with me. He was skilfully balancing a pitcher of frozen margarita mix in the centre of a tray with bowls of guacamole, sour cream dip and cheesy nachos surrounding it.

'I could get used to this.' I smiled. My boyfriend kissed the side of my head before he walked forward and put the tray down on the solid wood table.

Conor poured us both a glass of the tequila-based cocktail then handed one to me. 'Cheers,' he said, clinking my glass.

'Cheers,' I replied. 'So, how was your trip?' I asked before spooning some of the spicy beef into my mouth.

'It was OK, I suppose,' Conor replied, not going into any details.

'All work and no play then,' I joked.

'Yeah, something like that.'

There was no point questioning him. My boyfriend was a man of mystery. From what I'd witnessed so far, Conor wasn't the type to bring his work home with him. Maybe he'd tell me more about his business at a later stage.

'You've gone to a lot of trouble,' I said as my eyes scanned the contents of the table.

'It's nothing more than you deserve,' Conor replied.

I felt my cheeks flush. Despite what my parents thought, I'd really landed on my feet. Conor was a gentleman. He hadn't laid a finger on me until I'd practically begged him to, and that impressed me more than I could say. Boys my age only ever had one thing on their minds. Their bodies were flooded with hormones, and they were far too immature to hold my interest. Conor was on a different level in every way.

14

Conor

Diego Gómez was keen to finalise the deal, so any thoughts of a lie-in with my beautiful girlfriend were shattered when he treated me to an early morning call. I was tempted to put the pillow over my head and ignore the ringtone, but a vision of Bobby's ugly mug popped into my head. I knew I wouldn't be able to go back to sleep now anyway, so I might as well answer it.

'Diego, it's great to hear from you,' I said, doing my best to sound delighted as I walked out of the bedroom, down the stairs and into my office so that we wouldn't be overheard. I was probably being over-cautious as Ella was sound asleep, but I didn't want to take any chances all the same.

'You sound half asleep. I hope I didn't wake you,' Diego replied in a strong Spanish accent. 'I just wanted to run over some details with you. Is now a good time to talk?'

'Yes, of course.'

*

'What's the matter? Don't you like the food?' I asked, looking across the table. My girlfriend's eyes were fixed on her scrambled eggs as though they held the key to a great mystery.

Ella stopped pushing her breakfast around her plate, and her beautiful face broke into a smile, but I could tell it wasn't genuine. 'It's lovely, but I'm not hungry.'

'You're not having second thoughts about us, are you?'

In my eyes, we'd spent an idyllic evening together, but maybe I was reading it wrong. I'd never been in love before; this was a totally new experience for me. Being a naturally suspicious person, I found it difficult to trust and made a habit of jumping to conclusions and second-guessing situations.

'Of course not.' Ella reached over and covered my hand with hers to reassure me.

I wanted to believe her, but I could tell something was off; my girlfriend didn't seem herself today. Over the years, I'd learned to trust my gut, and if something didn't feel right, it usually meant I should tune in to my internal voice and listen to what my body was telling me. The unconscious mind was more powerful than we realised, and mine had become an expert at alerting me to dangerous situations or times when I thought somebody had a hidden agenda or was keeping something from me.

'So what's up? If you tell me what's bothering you, I might be able to help.' I turned my palm over and squeezed her hand.

'I went back to my parents' flat while you were away.

I was hoping the dust would have settled by now, but Mum was still being frosty with me,' Ella said, then let out a long sigh.

I felt bad for her; I could see Ella was stressed about the situation, but I was relieved that it wasn't me causing the problem.

'I'm sorry to hear that; I don't want to come between you and your parents. Maybe they'd feel better about everything if you introduced me.'

Ella bit down on the side of her lip. 'I'm not sure it will help.'

'It can't do any harm.'

It didn't seem right that Ella and I had moved in together before I'd met her family, especially as she'd always been so close to her parents. Looking at it from their point of view, I could see why they'd have the hump about it. Things would only get worse if we didn't try to rectify the situation.

The last thing I wanted was for our relationship to cause Ella problems. I didn't want her to fall out with her mum and dad, so I was determined to do my best to build bridges between them and act as a mediator if need be.

Ella and I had grown up on the same estate, living only streets apart. Despite the close proximity of our family homes, we'd never crossed paths before I met her in the Riverside Tavern, which wasn't that surprising as I'd left home when I was seventeen, while Ella was still at junior school. I couldn't wait to get away from the place; it was a shithole, and I was fed up of being my mum's live-in babysitter. My childhood was pretty tough.

The fact that we'd both been brought up on the Arnold Estate was where the similarities in our backgrounds ended.

Ella was an only child, whereas I was the oldest of five. Mum was a single parent of three boys and two girls. None of us shared the same father or had benefitted from having a male role model in our lives. Suffice to say, the kind of men my mum hooked up with were the love-them-and-leave-them type.

Ella had a good home life. Her mum and dad were childhood sweethearts and were very young when she was born, so they were more like friends than parents and child. They might not have been able to afford to give her material things, but they loved and cherished her, and that counted for a lot. They'd done a better job at raising their daughter than people twice their age, and I admired them for that. It can't have been easy; they must have faced countless challenges and had to grow up overnight.

'I've got an idea, why don't you text your mum and dad and invite them out to dinner? My treat.' I smiled.

'I don't think they'll feel comfortable with that,' Ella replied. 'Can't we cook a meal here instead?'

I lived a very private life, so having people I'd never met over to my house was out of the question. But I was sure I could come up with a solution.

'How about you suggest we go for a drink. Somewhere on neutral ground, just in case things turn ugly.' I laughed and immediately regretted being insensitive when I saw the look on Ella's face.

'It's not funny. I've never known them to be like this. My parents are usually supportive of everything I do.'

I wished I could say the same, but my mum didn't give a shit about me, and as for my dad, he hadn't even bothered to make himself known to me and had happily remained anonymous for my entire life.

'I'm confident we'll soon have this sorted. Invite them out tonight, and I'll unleash the Baxter charm on them.' I winked.

'I'm not sure my mum will know what's hit her if you do that.' Ella roared with laughter.

'Don' worry; I'll be gentle with her. Breaking the ice in awkward situations is one of my specialities.'

15

Ella

'Hi, I'm Scott, pleased to meet you,' Dad said, holding out his hand to Conor when we walked into the pub. 'And this is my wife, Joanne,' he continued, pointing towards Mum standing next to him at the bar.

'Pleased to meet you both,' Conor replied. 'These are for you. Ella looks so much like you. The two of you could be sisters,' he said with a twinkle in his blue eyes as he handed my mum an enormous bunch of flowers.

Mum's face flushed slightly, flattered by his compliment, then her eyes lit up at the sight of the brightly coloured blooms. They'd only just met, and she was already putty in my boyfriend's hands. I was looking forward to sitting back and watching him woo her. Winning people over was an art form, but Conor made it look effortless.

I'd been worried that we were going to sit around the table with an uncomfortable silence looming over us. There was nothing worse than being stuck in a situation where you had to frantically scan through all forms of small talk in your head before deciding which form of idle chit-chat would be the least painful. But Conor had opened up the conversation in such a way that Mum seemed completely at ease with him. Within minutes of being introduced, she was telling him stories about my childhood like they were best friends. His easy manner appeared to have thawed the frostiness between us, lifting the tense atmosphere that had been hovering over us the last time we'd met.

Even though autumn was fast approaching, it had been a beautiful day, so in an attempt to hold on to summer, Mum and I decided to order a pitcher of Pimm's. By the time we were at the bottom of our second jug, the alcohol had loosened our tongues, and we were back to our old selves, gossiping away. It was good to catch up on all the things we'd missed out on while we'd been estranged. As I fished out a chunk of strawberry from my glass, I glanced over at Dad and Conor. They were downing pints of lager, engaged in conversation like they'd known each other for years, and that brought a smile to my face.

'I know we got off to a bad start, but once you get to know him better, I'm sure you'll love Conor as much as I do.'

'I don't doubt that. Dad and I shouldn't have interfered; we should have known better. When I found out I was pregnant with you, I don't mind telling you the news was met with pity and disapproval. Everyone had an opinion on what your dad and I should do for the best. The whole world and his dog got involved.' Mum shook her head. 'Busybodies the lot of them!'

My mum was only seventeen when I was born, and my dad had just turned eighteen. 'It must have been hard for you.' I couldn't begin to imagine what it was like for my parents; by the time Mum was my age, I was two years old.

'As far as your dad and I were concerned, there was only ever going to be one option. People I barely knew said I was too young to be a mum, and I wouldn't be able to cope. But you know me, I was determined to prove the doubters wrong.' Mum laughed.

'And you did!' Despite her age, she was a fantastic mum. I had a happy childhood, and a person couldn't ask for a better start in life than that.

'When I fell pregnant, your grandparents were shocked, but all of them were supportive and didn't try to interfere. My mum and dad were a bit worried that my relationship with Scott might not last and that I'd have to raise you alone. At the back of my mind, I thought that might happen too, but I couldn't let that influence my decision.'

'That's understandable; a lot of men shoot through when the going gets tough, but look at the two of you. You're still going strong after all these years.' Anyone could see my parents still loved each other more than ever.

'It just goes to show, if something's meant to be, it will be. Granny and Grandad were worried about nothing, just like Dad and I. You're old enough to make your own decisions. Ever since you were a little girl, you've always been comfortable in adult company, so it's not really surprising that there's a bit of an age gap between you and Conor.'

'I couldn't think of anything worse than going out with a spotty teenager who only had one thing on his mind. I'd rather be single any day.' I laughed.

Everyone was getting on brilliantly; my parents and boyfriend's first encounter had been a great success; I was so glad I'd let Conor talk me into it now. There was something very therapeutic about sitting in a pub beer garden on a beautiful evening; you couldn't fail to relax and unwind.

Conor and I were sitting in the back of a minicab on our way home when a text came through from Mum. I let go of Conor's hand and took my phone out of my bag. Mum's message brought tears of joy to my eyes when I read it.

> Dad and I just wanted to say we're sorry that we fell out with you and that it's taken us a while to come around to the idea, but we both think Conor is amazing! We can see how happy he makes you and understand why you've fallen head over heels for him 😄 Enjoy the rest of your evening. Love you x

'Is everything OK, Ella?' Conor asked with a look of concern pasted on his handsome face.

'Yes, they're happy tears,' I said, patting my cheeks dry with my fingertips. 'You were a big hit.' I smiled.

'I told you I would be. When I unleash my charm offensive on a person, they're powerless to resist.' Conor laughed before leaning towards me and bumping his broad shoulder into mine.

'So modest of you to say.'

I knew Conor wasn't being cocky; he was joking. But it was true; he had a magnetic personality, and once people were drawn to him, his friendly manner put them at ease. I should have realised Conor would put Mum and Dad's concerns about our relationship to bed once they met him.

To end off our perfect evening, Conor opened a bottle of champagne and – after pouring a glass for me and grabbing a beer for himself – led me out onto the roof terrace. He threw one arm around my shoulder, and I cuddled into him as we sat in the hot tub, feeling flushed with love. Conor was so romantic; he showered me with love and attention. I'd fallen under his spell and was completely infatuated by him. As I sipped from the long-stemmed glass, I didn't think anything could burst our blissful bubble, but that was before I mentioned that I'd invited Lucy and Amy over while Conor was away.

'I missed you so much; I was counting the hours until you'd come back. I've never been so bored, so to help me pass the time, I asked a couple of my uni friends over. We had a great time binge-watching *The Last Kingdom* on Netflix.' I smiled.

Conor's body stiffened, and when I gazed into my boyfriend's incredible blue eyes, I saw the expression on his face change.

'You don't mind, do you?'

Conor didn't need to reply; it was obvious he wasn't impressed. What was the big deal? It wasn't as though I'd thrown a massive rave and ended up trashing the place. I suddenly felt like a naughty schoolgirl caught doing something without the teacher's permission.

'I only invited Lucy and Amy, not hundreds of people.' I laughed.

I was trying to lighten the mood, but I could tell Conor was pissed off with me when he stared stony-faced at me, silently fuming. What the hell was his problem? A long pause dragged on between us. The water bubbling and bursting on the hot tub's surface was the only sound filling the tense atmosphere between us.

'You should have asked me first before you invited your friends over. I don't like people I don't know coming to my house.'

'For God's sake, Conor, the way you're carrying on, anyone would think I opened the front door and dragged in some total strangers.'

I'd never seen Conor react like this before. He was being a total dick. Emotions were running high, and we were about to come to blows over something petty and ridiculous.

Conor knocked back his drink then reached for a towel. As I watched him drying himself off, I couldn't help feeling he was overreacting. I was a sociable person by nature and wasn't sure I would feel comfortable living somewhere, no matter how nice it was, if I couldn't have Lucy and Amy over occasionally. I suddenly felt uncomfortable. Admittedly it was Conor's house, but I was living with him now, so surely I was entitled to treat the place as my home.

'Where are you going?' I said as Conor started to walk away.

He didn't reply, so I climbed out of the hot tub, wrapped a large, fluffy towel around myself and walked over to where he was standing, resting his elbows on the cool chrome railings as he took in the view of the garden.

'What's got into you?'

'I'm a private person, and I'm not comfortable having people I don't know in my personal space. You should have checked with me before you invited Lucy and Amy over.' I could see Conor clench his jaw when he spoke as he tried to hold in his anger.

I shook my head and blew out a loud breath. 'Oh, I'm sorry; I didn't realise I needed to ask your permission.' My words were laced with sarcasm.

I considered telling Conor that I'd been lonely and homesick while he'd been away. Being alone in the house had made me miss my parents, so I'd toyed with the idea of staying with them until he came home. But once I'd been to visit, I realised going back to my old room wasn't an option. After the frosty reception I'd received, I'd felt like I was grieving the loss of my relationship with my mum and dad as well as everything else that was familiar to me. If I was completely honest, I was struggling to adjust to my new life and was in dire need of some company to cheer me up. But I shouldn't have to justify my reasons for inviting my two closest friends over, should I?

'I'm sorry. I'm being a prick.' Conor locked eyes with me before he leaned down and kissed me on the cheek.

'Yes, you are, but for what it's worth, I'm sorry too.'

Conor pulled me towards him and wrapped his arms around me. 'I love you, Ella; I don't want to fight. Let's forget about it. You weren't to know.'

We'd need to discuss this further, but now wasn't the right time. We'd both been drinking, and things had got heated, but it would be easy to get into a full-blown argument over it. It was a well-known fact that alcohol often ended up fuelling a fight. The best option I could see was to sleep on it and talk things over in the morning. My boyfriend had only just got back from a week away, and the last thing I wanted to do was fall out with him.

16

Conor

I knew Ella was upset with me, but I had my reasons for not wanting strangers in my house. I should have probably gone about things in a more tactful way than I did, but it was a knee-jerk reaction. I was shocked when she'd told me what she'd been up to while I was in Spain. I understood for most people, having your two best friends over wasn't a big deal, but I wasn't most people.

Ella climbed into the front seat of my BMW when I picked her up at the end of her shift. The start of term was approaching, so she'd been putting in extra hours, and I couldn't help noticing that she looked tired. Scott and Joanne didn't have the money to fund Ella's higher education, so she'd been working at the Riverside Tavern to supplement her maintenance loan. It was fine at first, but doing long shifts for minimum wage was hard; it was taking its toll on her and wearing her down. I was worried about her. While I admired her principles, it was clear she'd taken on too much.

'I've got a surprise for you.' I covered Ella's eyes and led her into the open-plan dining room.

'Wow, this looks amazing,' Ella said as her big brown eyes scanned over the rose-petal-strewn tabletop. 'It's the most romantic thing anyone's ever done for me.'

'Take a seat,' I said before I lit the candles, got myself a beer and retrieved the pink champagne from the fridge. I popped the cork and then handed Ella a glass. 'There's something I've meant to ask you.'

Ella turned her heart-shaped face towards me. 'Ooh, that sounds intriguing! Fire away,' she replied.

'I want us to spend as much time together as possible. Why don't you give up your job?' I'd decided to take the softly, softly approach. I knew how much Ella valued her independence.

Ella laughed, then turned the corners of her lips down and covered her heart with her hand. 'Aww, how disappointing.'

I tilted my head to one side and studied my girlfriend. That wasn't the response I was expecting.

'When I'd walked in and saw the champagne and rose petals, I thought you were going to drop down on one knee and propose to me, not suggest I quit my job.'

'Oh shit! I'm such an idiot sometimes. I was trying so hard to be romantic. I should have realised what this would look like,' I replied, scooping up a handful of red petals and letting them fall through my fingers. 'Just out of curiosity, what would you have said if I'd asked you to marry me?' I could think of worse things than being engaged to the beautiful woman sitting opposite me.

'I would have said "no".'

Ella's reply shocked me. 'Thanks a lot. That's done my

ego a world of good, and all the while, I thought I was a great catch.' I turned out my bottom lip and pretended to wipe away tears with the back of my hand.

'Don't get me wrong, at some stage, I'd love to get engaged, but I'm only nineteen, and we haven't been going out very long, have we?'

'It's OK; don't try to spare my feelings,' I said, putting my palm out in front of me. 'I'm a big boy; I can handle your rejection.'

Ella shook her head and smiled. 'To answer your question, I'd love nothing more than to give up pulling pints, but I need the money.' Ella swept her mane of dark brown curls over her shoulders and settled back in her chair.

'I earn enough to support both of us. Let me do this for you. Then you can concentrate on your degree, not trying to make ends meet.'

'It's a lovely offer, but I can't accept it,' Ella replied.

'Why not?'

'You know I value my financial independence. I'm worried that if I don't make my own money, I'll lose it.' Ella's smile brimmed with confidence.

My girlfriend was determined to be self-sufficient, even though I was offering her a simple way out. Sometimes it was easy to forget she was so young. Most girls her age wouldn't have to be asked twice if you presented them with the same opportunity.

'Of course you won't.' I tried to reassure her. 'But you've taken on too much. You look exhausted all the time.'

'I am pretty tired. It can be hard work being a cash-strapped student.' Ella laughed.

I reached across the table and took hold of her hand.

'Then, don't be. Phone the pub and give in your notice. Honestly, it's not a big deal; let me take care of you.'

'I can't give up my job just like that.'

Ella wasn't about to budge, so I tried a different tactic.

'Oh, that's a shame. I'd planned a surprise to celebrate your newfound freedom, but if you're determined to carry on working...' I trailed off to keep my girlfriend in suspense.

'Don't be such a tease, Conor.' Ella laughed. 'Tell me what's going on.'

'I booked us a last-minute holiday, but it's short notice, so you might not be able to get the time off.' I smiled.

Ella's eyes were like saucers when my words registered. 'It wouldn't hurt to ask,' she replied, and the corners of her mouth lifted.

I was hoping that if I applied enough pressure, eventually Ella would give up the struggle and jack in her job, but she wasn't backing down easily and was testing my powers of persuasion.

'If you can't get the time off, I suppose I'll just have to go on my own.' I knew Ella wouldn't be happy about that and hoped it might give her a nudge in the right direction. But I had no intention of leaving her behind.

The smile slid from Ella's face, and I suddenly felt a bit worried that I'd taken things too far. So I reached under the table and handed her a Victoria's Secret bag before I leaned forward and planted a kiss on her soft lips. Ella looked at me under her long dark lashes before she delved her hand into the bag and pulled out a black bikini. She held it up in front of herself as her eyes scanned over it.

'Oh my God, I love it, thank you. Where are we going?' Ella asked, clapping her hands.

That was music to my ears. It looked like her mind was made up. I resisted the urge to gloat at this stage because I didn't want to tempt fate, but I appeared to have won the battle. With any luck, the pub would refuse her request for annual leave, and then she'd be forced to resign from her position or miss out on the holiday of a lifetime. Ella loved to travel, so I was confident I knew which option she'd choose.

'If I told you where we were off to, it wouldn't be a surprise, would it?' I winked.

17

Ella

'I love you, Ella,' Conor said, fixing me with his amazing blue eyes.

'I love you too.'

I felt like a celebrity, sipping champagne in the VIP lounge while we waited for the plane to board. When Conor told me that he was taking me away on holiday, I hadn't known what to expect. It was a lovely surprise, and I would have been happy with a long weekend at Butlins, but Conor had spared no expense.

My generous boyfriend tried to keep the location a secret, but through sheer persistence and determination, I eventually managed to wear him down. When he'd told me we were going to Mexico, I'd thought he was winding me up. I didn't believe him until he showed me the booking confirmation.

Brimming over with excitement, I'd phoned my mum and dad to tell them the good news, but I should have known better. They were seriously unimpressed that I was going away for two weeks during term time, especially as I'd only just started back at uni. They felt my education should come first and were bitterly disappointed that I wasn't taking it seriously. I tried to explain that the opportunity was too good to pass up, and I'd have a chance to try out my Spanish for real instead of in a classroom environment. But they were having none of it. I felt like we were taking one step forward and two steps back. Maybe some time apart would be good for all of us.

'I've never travelled long-haul before; this is going to be a new experience for me,' I said as we stood in the queue waiting to board.

'You're going to love it,' Conor replied, squeezing my hand.

Conor had upgraded our tickets, so I almost felt embarrassed when I took my seat and saw the look of envy on the faces of the other passengers as they filed past us towards the back of the plane. Although my parents took me away every year during the school summer holidays, I'd only ever been on a budget airline before. I'd never been a high-maintenance sort of girl and appreciated the value of money more than most, so the five-star luxury wasn't lost on me.

'Wakey-wakey, sleeping beauty,' Conor said as he lifted the side of my eye mask away from my face. 'We're nearly there now.'

I pulled off my mask and stretched before I opened the blind and glanced out of the window at the vibrant colour of the sea, striped in shades of turquoise blue. 'Oh my God, the water looks incredible.'

'How did you sleep?'

'Surprisingly well,' I replied, stifling a yawn.

Some people could sleep standing up, but for the rest of us, there was an art to dropping off. Conor and I had flown through the night. After polishing off a few glasses of champagne, I'd settled down in my makeshift bed. I'd expected to toss and turn, but I'd gone out like a light.

'How about you?'

'So-so,' Conor replied. 'I dozed off for a bit, but I've never been able to sleep well on planes.'

After we disembarked Conor swung our cases off the carousel and placed them on a luggage trolley. As he wheeled it into the arrivals area, a dark-skinned man was holding up a plaque with 'Baxter' written on it.

'Let me take that for you, sir,' he said as we approached.

As we entered the luxury beach resort's lobby, which overlooked the lagoon and a large banyan tree, we were greeted with flower bracelets and scented washcloths. While I took in the lovely surroundings, a waiter brought over a tray containing freshly prepared chaya, orange and pineapple juice and offered it to us. Having turned down the option of a ride in a golf buggy, we walked hand in hand through the extensive grounds on the way to our ocean-side villa. The landscaped gardens were like a tropical paradise, with brightly coloured exotic flowers and lush green plants around every turn.

'I hope you have a pleasant stay,' the hotel employee said as he unlocked the door to our private oasis.

'What do you think?' Conor asked after we'd explored the king-sized suite with private plunge pool.

'It's incredible. I've never been anywhere like this before,' I replied, stepping out onto our terrace.

I felt like I was in a dream. This was our first trip away together, and so far, everything was perfect. We'd arrived without the stress of lost luggage or flight cancellations. It was too early to tell if we'd have to deal with sunburn, food poisoning or days of unbroken rain. But my enthusiasm for experiencing new things pushed that thought from my mind. I wasn't about to dwell on that.

Even though Conor and I lived together, being on holiday would allow us to really get to know each other. We had all the time in the world. The beautiful surroundings couldn't fail to make us relax and unwind. No doubt, the super-strength local cocktails, which I'm sure we'd be sampling very shortly, would loosen our tongues and act as a truth serum. Bring it on. I wanted to know every detail about my boyfriend and delve into his former life.

Once we allowed ourselves to open up to each other, I was sure our relationship would really start to thrive. Being with one person all day, every day, would take some getting used to, but I couldn't imagine it would be an issue for us. I was confident we wouldn't start getting on each other's nerves and bickering about stupid things, highlighting incompatibilities that were easy to gloss over at home. In my head, I imagined we were going to while away the hours, walking hand in hand by the edge of the crystal-blue water, sharing our hopes and dreams for the future.

Since we'd arrived, Conor had an unmistakable glint in his eye, so I'd be very surprised if I wasn't about to be treated to a hot bedroom marathon session very soon. One of the many benefits of dating an older man was that he knew his way around the female anatomy and never failed to leave me satisfied. Every time he made love to me, he blew my mind and left me with a euphoric feeling. Conor had introduced me to a whole new world of intimacy and sexually awakened me. Having gone my entire life without ever knowing passion like this, once I had tasted it, I wanted more, and from that moment on, I was addicted to Conor; my love for him was obsessive. All-consuming.

'According to the label on the jug in the fridge, this is a Paloma. It's tequila, grapefruit soda and lime,' Conor said, having poured us both a drink.

He brought them out to where I was sitting on the outdoor sofa admiring the view, and we sat side by side sipping the thirst-quenching cocktails when his mobile rang.

'I'll be back in a minute,' he said before disappearing back into the villa to take the call.

While I waited for Conor to return, I dug my toes into the powdery white sand and soaked up my surroundings. As I breathed in a lungful of orchid-scented air, I marvelled at the fact that I could walk into the Caribbean Sea from our suite any time I wanted. I'd always wanted to go skinny-dipping in the sea at midnight. Now that I had the chance, I wasn't going to waste it. No matter what my parents thought, being whisked away to an exotic location beat traipsing to lectures any day of the week.

18

Conor

'How are you enjoying Cancún?' Diego asked.

I must admit I was taken aback by his question. We'd been in the country less than two hours, and he already knew I was here. I wondered how he'd got wind of my trip. Not that the purpose of my trip had anything to do with him.

'It's great from what I've seen so far.'

'What made you visit Mexico? Did you think I wouldn't find out that you were checking out my competitors?' Diego laughed, but I could tell it was forced.

'Hardly, I'm on holiday with my girlfriend.' I didn't want to start discussing anything business-related.

'Of course you are. Mexico is a beautiful country, but it can be a dangerous place too. Be warned; things work differently over there. Towns can turn into a war zone in the blink of an eye. Rival gangs think nothing of fighting each other with AK-47s in the middle of a street full of unsuspecting people, to send a message to the authorities that they are untouchable.'

'I understand what you're saying, but don't all criminal organisations think they're above the law?'

'I'm just offering you some friendly advice.'

It didn't sound like advice to me; Diego was definitely trying to warn me off. But he'd got the wrong end of the stick. I wasn't checking out the competition; I hadn't been aware that the Gómez cartel had rivals in the area when I'd chosen the location. We were here purely for a holiday. I wanted Ella to have some well-deserved rest and relaxation and a chance to use her Spanish, but from the tone of my conversation with Diego, he was worried I was about to bail on our deal.

Diego's words hadn't fallen on deaf ears. I'd heard the rumours that a narco army ran Mexico's lawless Golden Triangle, and their organised crime groups were more barbaric than most. Allegedly, it was common practice for them to hang their victims from bridges or abandon them in public places. It was in complete contrast to the way things worked where I came from; gangs went to great lengths to hide or dispose of any incriminating evidence.

'I do appreciate you looking out for me, but I can assure you, I'm not planning to do any business while I'm here.'

Our call had gone on for far too long for my liking, and I wanted to get back to Ella. I'd spoken as sincerely as I could, so hopefully my words would put the drug baron's mind at rest.

'Enjoy your trip. But if you go sightseeing, be careful you don't get caught in the crossfire; bodies are left where they fall in the street – discarded like rubbish...' Diego said before putting down the phone.

Diego hadn't taken the blindest bit of notice of what I'd said; I hadn't managed to convince him I was telling the truth. But I wasn't about to dwell on it. In my absence, Ella had stripped down to the black bikini I'd bought her, and her hourglass curves looked sensational in it, so I had other things on my mind.

'Sorry about that,' I said when I walked onto the terrace. 'I hope you're not bored.'

'How could I be?' Ella replied, looking up at me from the tourist information leaflets she was scanning over. 'There's so much to do; I think we might need to extend our stay,' she said, then let out her adorable laugh.

'That's fine by me. I could think of worse places to be holed up.'

The resort was everything I'd hoped for and more, set among mangroves and lagoons and surrounded by the Caribbean Sea. It was paradise on earth. The company wasn't bad, either. Ella was the type of girl who never made enemies; everybody loved her. From what I could see, she was perfect in every way. Her heart-shaped face and huge dark eyes gave her an innocent look while her killer curves screamed seduction, an incredible combination if you asked me.

'Did you find anything interesting you want to do?' I asked.

After my conversation with Diego, I was hoping she'd say no. I didn't want to venture out of the resort and find we'd stumbled into the middle of a violent turf war or become the latest western tourists held to ransom. Diego had intentionally painted a grim picture, so it was no wonder I suddenly felt cautious. But it was a fact of life; bad things sometimes did happen to travellers.

'I've seen one or two things that caught my eye. I'd like to visit the Mayan ruins, the turtle conservation centre, go snorkelling, take a catamaran cruise, swim in a cenote, learn to surf and go tequila tasting,' Ella replied.

My heart sank, but I pasted on a smile. If Ella wanted to get out and see some of the sights while we were here, that was exactly what we were going to do.

'I can see my credit card's about to take a pounding, but it's my own fault for leaving you unattended.'

'I was only joking! Seriously though, this place is so beautiful; there's plenty to do without leaving the resort. I'd be more than happy to spend our time here, swimming in the sea and exploring the mangroves and lagoons.'

That was one of the things I loved about Ella. She wasn't a gold digger by any means and found joy in the smallest of things. She was grounded and not overly impressed by material possessions, which made a refreshing change. I couldn't abide women who demanded equality then expected a man to open the door for her and pay the bill. I was confident that Ella wasn't after my money; her interest in me was one hundred per cent genuine, which made me feel on top of the world.

Our time together in Mexico had turned out to be everything I'd hoped for and more. Once I'd got over my initial reluctance to leave the complex, we'd had a fantastic time visiting all the sights Ella had wanted to see without encountering any problems. Thankfully, we hadn't become the victims of a carjacking, a shoot-out or any other violent crime, and we'd been getting on brilliantly, so all in all, we'd had a great trip.

I'd noticed that Ella was using every opportunity to get inside my head, trying to peel away the layers of my character to understand how my brain ticked. I knew her intentions were genuine, though; she wanted to know everything about me so that we could grow as a couple. Still, the thought of letting my guard down so that she could get close to me made me nervous; I was terrified Ella wouldn't like what she found if she looked too deeply.

'So tell me more about your business; I think it's incredibly inspiring that you're a self-made man,' Ella had said while we were sitting on the terrace listening to the sound of the waves lapping against the sand on the last night of our holiday.

I always felt paranoid when people started asking me lots of questions in relation to my work and personal life. Ella's words sent shock waves through my body and put me immediately on edge, reminding me that the longer the truth was hidden, the bigger the hurdle it would be to come clean. I felt guilty being the secret holder, but certain topics were strictly off-limits. I tried to steer the conversation in a different direction, but when Ella continued to dig, I decided to excuse myself, pretending to need a pee so that I could seek solace in the bathroom for a while in the hope that when I returned, I could move our conversation on to a different subject.

I walked into what should have been a marble oasis and felt myself bristle. Ella's stuff was strewn everywhere; hair products, bottles of after-sun, perfume and makeup littered every surface, and I had to stop myself from swiping the lot

STEPHANIE HARTE

of it into the bin. As my eyes inched their way over the mess, I felt stress and anxiety building inside me. I struggled to stay in control when my environment was disordered. My mind flashed back to the flat I grew up in and my chaotic childhood. Having things neat and tidy made me feel in control. I couldn't help it; I couldn't bear it when stuff was out of place. I could feel the tension growing inside me; I knew I was in danger of losing my shit. Keeping my mental state on an even keel in a situation like this was a balancing act; I found it incredibly difficult to act rationally once my emotions were triggered. That was why I tried to avoid moments like this. I wouldn't be able to leave the room until I'd cleaned up the mess. My heart was racing as I got to work organising Ella's things.

'You've been a long time. Are you OK, Conor?'

The sound of Ella's voice brought me back to reality. She was knocking on the bathroom door, and I felt my pulse speed up at the thought of facing her. I needed to get a grip; we'd had the most fantastic time – I didn't want to ruin it by picking a fight over the state of the bathroom.

'Yes, I'm fine; I was just tidying up,' I replied, pasting a smile on my face before I threw open the door.

'Tidying up?' Ella seemed shocked.

'Well, somebody had to; you'd trashed the place. It only takes one second to put things back where they belong when you're finished with them.'

I tried to make my comments sound light, but by the look on Ella's face, she'd taken offence. Time to let the matter drop.

'Why don't we go for one last skinny-dip?' I suggested, catching hold of my girlfriend's hand.

'Good idea,' Ella replied.

I knew Ella wouldn't be able to resist a final swim in the Caribbean Sea, and when I pictured her naked body wrapped around mine, it banished all thoughts of her disorganised toiletries. Crisis averted; we'd be coming home on the same flight after all.

From the moment Ella and I stepped off the plane, it was clear trouble was brewing. Bobby Parker and Leo Carr were arch enemies. The feud between the two men could be traced back to the school playground, and their desire to get one over on each other hadn't waned over the years.

'Where the fuck have you been?' Bobby bellowed down the phone at me. 'You haven't answered my calls for the last two weeks.'

'I've been on holiday with my girlfriend, and the mobile reception wasn't great,' I lied.

Even though that wasn't true, it was too good an excuse not to use it. Not having to listen to Bobby's dulcet tones every waking minute of every day for the last fortnight had been an absolute pleasure and one of the highlights of my holiday. But I wasn't sure it would make his day if I shared that with him.

Bobby was on the warpath. While I'd been away, his old rival Leo had taken advantage of the situation. He'd used his contacts to establish a connection with a small-time dealer and was muscling in on the action. While I established a new supply chain, there'd been a delay in obtaining the product. Although Bobby had enough stock to see him through the dry spell, he couldn't compete with the knocked-down price Leo was shifting his gear for.

'Since you've been out of the frame, that jumped-up

tosser has moved away from harassing members of the population out of their hard-earned cash and bleeding the local businesses dry. Carr is trying to take over my turf.'

None of this was my fault, but Bobby was looking for a scapegoat. The timing was coincidental. There was no reason for Leo to wait for me to leave the country to start his new enterprise. Word on the street should have told Bobby loud and clear that his prices were inflated, so Leo had seized the opportunity and run with it. If I had to make an educated guess, I'd say that Leo was working on a very small profit margin so that he could build up a client base. That was good business sense, and he was still probably raking in more money than he did by coercing members of the public to part with their wages.

'What have you got to say for yourself?' Bobby demanded.

'I'm not sure why you think this is my fault.'

'You're dragging your heels with my new stock, and that's left the door open for that cheeky fucker.'

'Well, you know what to do, don't you?' My tone was abrupt, but I didn't give a shit at this stage.

'What?'

'Sell off the gear you're sitting on by undercutting Leo.' Anyone would think what I'd just suggested was rocket science. The same rule applied to any product a business was trying to shift.

'If I do that, I'll be making a loss.'

I very much doubted that. But Bobby wasn't interested in loose change; he wanted big bucks. His greed started this situation in the first place, so it was his fault that rival dealers were poaching his clients.

'If you don't undercut Leo, even by a small amount,

you won't have any customers left when the cheaper gear arrives.'

In this game, you had to be a straight-talker. There was no point in mincing my words. Beating around the bush wasn't going to get Bobby anywhere. We lived in a cut-throat world where competitors constantly nipped at your heels. Money was tight for the people who needed Bobby's product to get them through the day, and if they could save a few quid here and there, it made a lot of difference to their disposable income. If he wasn't very careful, his empire – which had taken years to build up – would come crashing down around his bald head.

'Get Diego on the blower and find out what's happening with my gear. I want it here pronto! Capeesh?' Bobby spat the words down the phone at me before he hung up.

Who the fuck did that meathead think he was talking to?

'Diego, how are you?' I asked, expecting to exchange pleasantries. When my question was left unanswered, I continued to speak. 'I'm sorry to bother you, but my client is keen to know when his shipment will be arriving.'

'I have no idea.' Diego's reply was so cold it was as though a bitter easterly wind had swept away his friendly manner and replaced it with frostiness.

'Is there a problem?'

'I don't know, Mr Baxter, you tell me.'

What the hell was that supposed to mean? I could hear Diego having a conversation with someone else in Spanish, but I had no idea what he was talking about. I was tempted to ask Ella to translate, but I didn't want to involve her. Something was going on. I'd have to find out what it was before Bobby got wind of it.

19

Ella

'How was the holiday?' Lucy asked when we met up for a coffee the day after I got back.

'It was incredible: endless sunshine, a tropical breeze, white sand and the bluest sea ever.' I sighed.

'Talk about rubbing our noses in it.' Amy laughed. 'It's done nothing but rain since you went away.'

'So did I miss much at uni?'

I knew it wasn't ideal to disappear for a couple of weeks at the start of term, but I'd probably learned more Spanish while I was in Mexico than I would have done attending classes.

'Not really,' Lucy said.

When I saw how many online recordings I was going to have to plough through to catch up with the lectures I'd missed, I nearly lost the will to live. I loved being able to speak several languages; that had been an ambition of mine since I'd been a small child. I also loved the socialising, the parties, and meeting new people. But I hated the course. I'd been finding the workload hard even before I'd met Conor, but now the pressure was really on; there weren't enough hours in the day, and everything was starting to overwhelm me. My heart sank even further when I opened the email regarding my attendance. Although we'd had a fantastic time, part of me thought it hadn't been worth it.

'Something's got to give. I've said it before, but I really think you should chuck in your job. I earn enough to support both of us,' Conor suggested when I'd complained about how much work I needed to catch up on.

'That's beside the point.' I exhaled louder than I'd intended to; I realised that made me come across like a petulant child, and I instantly regretted it.

'Why are you being so stubborn about this? If you let me help, you can concentrate on your degree and not trying to make ends meet.'

I couldn't deny Conor's offer was tempting, and I was seriously considering taking him up on it, but I'd promised myself I would never allow myself to be financially dependent on anyone.

'Ella, listen to me, you're going to make yourself ill if you carry on like this. What are you trying to prove?'

'That I'm independent,' I snapped. Then I immediately felt guilty when I saw the hurt expression on Conor's face. I shouldn't be taking my stress out on him; he was only trying to help.

'Nobody doubts that, but you've taken on too much.' Conor threw his arms around me and held me against his chest. 'At least think about it before you turn me down again. It's a genuine offer; I'd like to support you so that you can continue to study without the added pressure. I'm not trying to take your independence away. It really bothers me to think you'd rather struggle than let me make things easier for you.'

I hadn't intended to offend Conor by refusing to resign, but I could see he wasn't going to take no for an answer, so I allowed myself to cave in to his persuasion. 'OK, you win. I'll hand in my notice.'

I felt slightly deflated and a bit of a failure, knowing the independence I'd worked so hard to achieve had started to slip through my fingers. But the pressure was growing at an alarming rate and seemed to be closing in on all sides. I was finding it nigh on impossible to juggle everything. Now that Conor and I were living together, I had less free time, so I was battling to keep on top of my uni work. But I'd have to stop getting distracted and knuckle down to it. It was the only way I'd be able to catch up with the lectures I'd missed.

'That's fantastic, and brilliant timing. I'm going to Costa Rica in a couple of weeks, and I want you to come with me.'

'I can't go away again. We've only just come back from Mexico. I haven't even finished unpacking my suitcase yet.' I laughed.

'Yeah, I know, but I had a really shitty day today, so I thought I'd cheer myself up by booking a break.'

How the other half lived. It was hard not to be seduced by Conor's fancy lifestyle, and I found myself questioning why I was resisting fully embracing being part of it. Would I be better off just letting my old life float away?

'I thought you wanted to do some more long-haul travelling,' Conor replied, flashing me a beaming smile.

'I do, but I can't go in term time again.'

Giving me, a person who loved to travel, the opportunity

to fly to places I'd only dreamed of before was an offer I found difficult to refuse. Talk about dangling a carrot in front of my nose. I'd always wanted to go to Costa Rica and explore the waterfalls, volcanic peaks, lush rainforests and untouched beaches, but I'd already received a warning about my attendance. If I went on holiday again so soon, I knew I'd have to withdraw from my course.

I couldn't deny I was seriously tempted. It was all very well my parents pushing me down this route, but they didn't have any idea how stressful it was. Mum and Dad desperately wanted me to be the first person in the family to have a degree. Both of them had left school as soon as they were able to. My mum had done a variety of retail jobs over the years and was currently working as a sales assistant in Superdrug, and Dad had been a postman for over twenty years. Neither of them had reached lofty heights in their chosen careers, which is probably why they'd drummed into me that getting a good education was essential in life. It gave you options that would otherwise be closed off. I understood that, but it made me question whether I'd gone to uni for myself or to fulfil their dream.

Uni life wasn't all about getting wasted and partying all night; it was hard graft. Nobody in my family had followed this path, so they weren't qualified to comment. Having said that, I knew my mum and dad would go mental if I dropped out.

'I'm sorry, Ella, I didn't think; I'm still getting used to taking somebody else's schedule into account instead of just my own. The last thing I want to do is distract you from studying. How about we postpone the trip until you break up for Christmas?' Conor suggested.

'That sounds great.' I felt like a weight had been lifted from my shoulders now that temptation wasn't within my grasp.

I was so lucky to have Conor in my life. He was mature enough to understand that a couple had to compromise if they were going to make their relationship work. He was definitely a keeper; Conor was the most incredible man I had ever dated by far.

'I think it's amazing that you can switch between languages without giving it a second thought; I've never met anyone like you. I can barely get my head around English – all the different spellings for the same word, and don't get me started on grammar. It makes my brain ache just thinking about it.' Conor laughed.

'You're not the only one; English is littered with irregularities, which is why it's one of the most difficult languages to learn. In lots of ways, Spanish and French are easier.'

'I'll take your word for that. But don't sell yourself short; to become fluent in another language is a huge task. I'm proud of you.' Conor beamed.

20

Conor

Bobby Parker rubbed people up the wrong way; there were no two ways about that. He had a boxer's nose, and he hadn't got that from being in the ring. The man was a natural-born scrapper, and he'd had more fights than Frank Bruno. Bobby would argue with his shadow if he thought he could get a rise out of it.

I'd been racking my brains, trying to work out what had got into Diego, and I kept coming back to the same conclusion. My recent trip to Mexico must have something to do with his change of heart. He'd been so keen to supply us with cocaine when I'd gone out to Spain to visit him. We were on the cusp of finalising the deal, but he'd suddenly gone cold. Bobby's patience had worn thin, so I needed to sort the problem out.

Mastering the art of persuasion wasn't an easy thing to do. The ability to make a person change their mind once it was made up was a skill that needed to be honed. I'd been perfecting my technique over the years and found that persistence paid off nine times out of ten.

'Have I done something to offend you, Diego?'

At first, my question was met with silence. When Diego finally answered, I felt like my head was about to explode.

'My cartel has decided we don't want to do business with you. It's better for all of us to part ways at this stage.'

That wasn't what I wanted to hear. 'For fuck's sake,' I said under my breath. Balling my fingers into a fist, I wondered why he'd suddenly done a U-turn. 'That's terrible news. Is there any way I can convince you to change your mind?'

'I'm afraid not. We don't trade with people who also buy from our competitors.' Diego's reply was intentionally curt.

'I'm sorry, Diego, you'll need to rewind a little. I don't know what you're talking about.'

Diego let out a forced laugh. 'I was expecting you to say that, but there's no point trying to hide it anymore. You thought you could deceive us, but we know what you've been up to; we trust your recent business trip to Cancún was successful.'

'I've already explained to you that I didn't go to Mexico on business. I took my girlfriend on holiday so she could practise her Spanish. She's a language student.' I tried to keep the frustration out of my voice, but it wasn't easy; I felt like we were going over old ground.

'I remember you telling me that, but I'm afraid I don't believe you weren't conspiring with a rival drug cartel while you were in Mexico,' Diego replied.

'I can assure you I wasn't.' I'd have had more luck raising the wreck of the *Titanic* than getting Diego to believe my version of events, but I'd have to keep chipping away at him until I wore him down. There was too much riding on this to give up. 'What do I need to do to convince you?'

If I couldn't regain Diego's trust, I'd never be able to talk him around. I'd have to build a rapport with him to make him feel comfortable. Hopefully, then, he'd be more open to my suggestions, and I'd be able to get the deal finalised.

'I'll give you the details of the hotel where we stayed. They will vouch for the fact that every time Ella and I left the complex, we were accompanied by a guide, and nobody came to visit our suite,' I suggested when he didn't answer my question.

'If you're saying this is a big misunderstanding, why did you go all the way to Cancún for a holiday when Spain is much closer? You do know we speak the same language, don't you?'

Diego was like a cat playing with a mouse. I could tell by the sarcastic tone of his voice that I had a long way to go to convince him.

I could see why he might think that was strange, but there was a simple explanation.

'Ella's been to Spain loads of times, but she's never travelled long-haul before. That's why I decided to go further afield. I honestly didn't know you had a competitor in Mexico. I realise I've damaged our relationship and wish I knew how I could rectify the problem.'

'I need to speak to Pedro and Valentina. Then I will let you know if we still have a deal,' Diego said, and that gave me a glimmer of hope that all was not lost.

'Thank you; I appreciate you speaking to the other members on my behalf. I want you to know, the Gómez cartel is the only supplier I am interested in doing business with; my visit to Mexico was purely a personal one.'

Fingers crossed I'd done enough to convince Diego that he'd jumped to the wrong conclusion. The misunderstanding had damaged the trust in our relationship; only time would tell if it was repairable. Now that I knew he had eyes on me, I'd have to tread carefully in future and be completely transparent with any future travel plans. Maybe I should rethink whether visiting Costa Rica for Christmas was the best idea. If Diego had another rival hiding in the rainforest that I didn't know about, it would be the final nail in the coffin.

In the meantime, while I waited to see if we could salvage the deal, I'd have to give Bobby the run-around to buy myself some time. But that would be easier said than done. The man was like a starving hyena after an injured gazelle. He wouldn't rest until he got what he wanted. *Speak of the devil*, I thought when I saw his name flash up on my mobile.

'Any news on my shipment?' Bobby Parker's voice boomed into the earpiece when I answered the call.

'I'm still waiting on an update from the cartel.'

The words tripped off my tongue; what I'd said was true, but I didn't elaborate on the news I was waiting to hear. If Bobby realised the deal was teetering on the edge of falling through, he would blow a gasket.

'What's taking so fucking long?'

'There's been an unavoidable delay in the supply chain.' That seemed like a reasonable explanation, and it was the only thing I could think of off the cuff as Bobby had put me on the spot.

'Well, I'm not in the mood to hang about. Chase them up, Conor.'

'Will do,' I replied, trying to hide the frustration in my voice. Dealing with awkward customers was a major ball-ache.

I had no intention of harassing the cartel. But I would have agreed to anything so that I could get Bobby off the phone. Diego was playing mind games with me, dragging his heels and making me wait for his reply. I couldn't afford to let him know the delay was causing me a problem, or he'd use it to his advantage.

'If the cartel doesn't want my business, tell them I'll be happy to take it elsewhere. Capeesh?'

I could picture the veins throbbing at Bobby's temples; he sounded like he was foaming at the mouth. Bobby was talking as though he was a man with endless options. We both knew that wasn't the case, but instead of calling him out on it, I decided to humour him and let his comment go.

'I'll pass your message on to Diego,' I replied before ending the call.

21

Ella

'Why don't you invite your parents out for dinner tonight?' Conor asked, then he tilted his head to the side and studied my response.

'I'm not sure that would be a good idea.' I pasted on a false smile but shook my head as I spoke. 'We're not exactly seeing eye to eye at the moment, are we? They've still got the hump with me.'

'I know, but that's all the more reason to try and smooth things over with them. I'd like to treat them to a nice meal.'

I felt bad that Conor seemed to be putting so much effort into trying to appease my parents.

'They don't go out very often, do they? We could try that new Indian restaurant that's opened in Brick Lane.' Conor smiled and fixed me with his mesmerising blue eyes.

'That's very generous of you, but I don't think Mum and Dad would feel comfortable about that. You know money's tight with them. They wouldn't want to accept an invitation if they couldn't offer it back.'

'I'm not expecting them to repay the favour. I'm more than happy to pay. You don't give to receive.'

That was true, but I knew what my parents were like; they wouldn't want to be a charity case, and rather than help the situation, Conor's generosity would make things ten times worse.

'If you're hell-bent on seeing my mum and dad, why don't we rustle up something here? You're an excellent cook. I probably won't be much use, but I'd be happy to be your kitchen assistant.' I smiled.

'Nah, I'd preferred to take them out to a restaurant than entertain at home.'

I knew Conor liked to keep his private life private, but I was surprised that he was even reluctant to invite my parents over. It wasn't as though they were strangers.

'Don't you think it would be better to meet on neutral territory in case things turn ugly?' Conor added.

I hated it when my boyfriend used that turn of phrase, but he was probably right. The atmosphere between the three of us at the moment was hostile, and there was a good chance communications could break down even further.

'Let's leave it to another time; I can't face seeing them tonight.' I didn't want to risk making things worse than they already were.

It was a shame because we'd always been so close, but being in my parents' company had recently become hard work. My parents being so young when I was born meant it was as though we all grew up together. We used to be more like friends than parents and child. I know that was probably down to the fact that we had a smaller-than-average age gap between us than most.

I wondered what my school friends would think if they could see us now. They used to be jealous of the relationship Mum, Dad and I shared. Because of their age, my parents had a very young outlook on life and had boundless energy and enthusiasm for the things we did together. They clearly remembered what it was like to be teenagers and could relate to the things I was going through, which made the current situation harder to deal with; I felt alienated from them.

'Whatever you want to do is fine by me. But sometimes, the longer you leave these things, the worse they get.'

Conor had a point, but I wanted to let some time pass so that the dust could settle. On this occasion, I felt giving each other some space was the right thing to do. My parents needed time to calm down, and then they might be more open to seeing things from my point of view.

There seemed to be a recurring theme going on at the moment. Whenever I did something my parents didn't approve of, they became very vocal about it and tried to pull rank. But they needed to realise I wasn't a child anymore, and now that I didn't live under their roof, I could make my own decisions without consulting them. I wasn't trying to go out of my way to piss them off, but they needed to back off so that I could spread my wings.

We were stuck in a conflict between what I wanted and what my parents thought I should do. Firstly they hadn't wanted me to go out with Conor, but I'd come to realise taking a dislike to my boyfriend wasn't the real issue – because then they'd substituted him with my living arrangements, and now we'd moved on to my education. The bottom line was my parents thought they had the right to make decisions about my life even though I was an adult and more than capable of doing that myself. When I went against their wishes, they took it so badly it was driving a wedge between us. My connection to my family meant everything to me, but at the moment, I felt torn between their happiness and mine.

Getting a place at uni was my parents' dream, and I'd felt pressured to apply. I'd had to work incredibly hard to get myself into university; I wasn't what you'd call an all-rounder at school, but I had a gift for languages. My interest started from an early age after I became friends with two Spanish sisters while we were on holiday. In the beginning, we couldn't communicate because we couldn't speak each other's language, but by the end of the holiday, we'd learned enough to get by. I spent the whole flight home begging my parents for Spanish lessons and the rest was history.

I'd been dreading the start of term, but I'd made friends easily enough and loved the social side of uni. I had fond memories of the parties I'd attended in student accommodation where the rooms were filled with cigarette and marijuana smoke, and homemade bongs made out of two-litre Coke bottles littered the windowsills. One of the guys on my course lived in a particularly grotty place; sheets were nailed onto the walls to act as curtains, and mattresses were scattered across the floor. I remember being shocked when he'd told me he didn't have a fridge, but he didn't seem bothered because during the week he'd use the canteen and at the weekend he'd have drugs and beer for breakfast!

I knew my parents felt my education should come first, but the truth was I hated my course. It was nothing like I'd expected it to be, and I was struggling to stay engaged with it. I was tempted to tell them how I was feeling, but if I did, I'd be leaving myself open for another ear-bashing. The timing wasn't right. They were still furious that I'd gone off on holiday at the start of my second year. I could tell they thought Conor was a bad influence and distracting me. But he was doing everything he could to support me while I studied for my degree, encouraging me every step of the way. He knew that I was struggling with the course, and I hadn't even reached the halfway point yet. I should have been organising a placement in Spain for next September so that I could get some work experience in the language I was specialising in.

I'd always wanted to work abroad as an interpreter or maybe teach languages, but that was before I'd met Conor. I saw my future with him now, so I didn't even want to think about doing that as it would mean leaving my gorgeous boyfriend behind.

22

Conor

Until recently, the importing and distribution of cocaine in Spain was run exclusively by Colombian cartels. Sidestepping the usual routes, the Gómez family set up their own operation, bringing their cocaine directly into Spain from their base in West Africa. Since it had begun, it had ruffled a few feathers. Being the new kids on the block didn't seem to bother Diego, Pedro and Valentina. But I was pretty sure they needed our business as much as we needed their product, so it was time to call Diego's bluff. I'd given him plenty of opportunities to get back to me, but he was determined to make me sweat. I'd wasted enough time on this.

'My client is getting impatient, and I won't be able to put him off much longer. I need to know, do we still have a deal or not?' I asked.

I tried to keep the frustration out of my voice and my tone light so that I didn't do more damage to our fragile relationship, but it wasn't easy. I hadn't done anything wrong – there had been a stupid misunderstanding, so I wasn't prepared to eat a huge slice of humble pie; it would get stuck in my throat.

'We are prepared to go ahead with the deal,' Diego replied.

'That's good news. When can we expect to receive the shipment?' I felt like a weight had been lifted from my shoulders.

Diego laughed. 'You have only ordered a small sample, so it's not worth the risk involved for us to deliver it. You will have to come to Spain to collect it.'

I shook my head and let out a sigh; I was beginning to wish I'd chosen a different supplier. This transaction was proving to be one long headache, but I'd have to suck it up and get on with it. 'OK, fair enough. I'll be in touch when I've made my travel arrangements.'

Diego's headquarters were in Vigo on the north-west coast of Spain, which wasn't easily accessible from London. There were no direct flights from the UK, and even if I flew via Madrid or into Porto, I wouldn't be able to return by plane with the gear in my luggage because of all the security checks in place. As far as I could see, I had two options. I'd either have to charter a private plane, and that hardly warranted the expense for such a small drop, or I'd have to drive. Both were equally unappealing, but if I wanted to get Bobby Parker off my back, I'd have to choose one of them.

'Would you be able to increase my order to ten kilos?' I asked. If I was going to have to go to all this trouble, I might as well make it worth my while.

'It would be my pleasure,' Diego replied.

When I broke the news to Ella, she wasn't impressed

that I was going away again, but as I'd decided to charter a private four-seater plane from Biggin Hill airport in southeast London, I'd be able to complete my trip to Spain within the same day. If I'd driven, it would have taken me the best part of a week.

Although my airport source assured me I had nothing to worry about, the closer it got to boarding the plane, the more anxious I became. I needed a stiff drink to calm myself down. I'd started to overheat. I didn't often wear a shirt and tie. Every time I moved my head, the collar dug into my skin, and it was making me feel claustrophobic. The sooner I could get on board and unbutton it, the better.

I was approaching the final stage, but I still had to go through security. To ensure the process was hassle-free, my source had arranged for a corrupt official to x-ray my carry-on bag containing a vast amount of money. I had to stop myself from smiling when he handed it back to me and wished me a pleasant flight. Once on board, I loosened my tie and let out a long breath as I sat down on the leather chair. After switching my mobile off, I fastened my seat belt as the plane got ready to take off.

Sunglass-wearing, chino-clad Juan picked me up from the airport a couple of hours later and drove me to Diego's modern office block in the heart of Vigo. I sat in the back of the four-wheel drive, admiring the view of the bay and large marina packed with luxury yachts on the short drive. Carrying the bundle of cash in a black leather briefcase, I walked into the building along with Juan, who escorted me to a small office that overlooked the harbour. Although Diego greeted me with a handshake, it lacked the warmth of our previous encounter. It was clear our relationship had been damaged; it would take time to re-establish the trust between us.

One of Diego's men took the case from me and counted out the money while I inspected the product. The whole exchange took less than half an hour. Diego poured two large glasses of local Rioja to seal the deal. My heart sank when he handed one to me, but I drank it, trying not to pull a face as the liquid passed down my throat. I couldn't stand the taste of wine, but I didn't want to snub Diego's hospitality by refusing it in case I offended him. Then I placed ten one-kilo blocks of cocaine into my briefcase's concealed compartments before I left for the airport. I'd need to kill a little time to make my cover convincing.

'I want to buy my girlfriend a present. Can you stop somewhere that sells Jimmy Choo?'

'Of course,' Juan replied as he pulled up alongside Max-B, a ladies' designer shop. 'This place should have what you're looking for.'

A short while later, I reappeared, armed with a black-and-gold calf-leather bag and a pair of square-toed, block-heeled boots. Hopefully I'd be able to redeem myself with the gifts, I thought.

Posing as a businessman on a work trip, I'd dressed in an expensive suit and was carrying minimal luggage. I didn't think I fitted the profile for a drug smuggler, but I was about to find out. I'd gone through customs in the UK without a hitch; it was time to see if the same thing would happen on the Spanish side. My source had put English-speaking airport staff in place. Before we took off, I placed my case on the conveyor belt, and while it was scanned, I was ushered through security. To my relief, the process was quick and easy. I hadn't been subjected to the same checks I would have been on a scheduled flight.

As soon as I'd left the airport, I dropped the gear over to Bobby Parker. Although I wanted to get home to Ella, it was a detour I had to make.

'About fucking time too,' Bobby said when I took ten blocks of cocaine out of my briefcase and put them on the table in front of him. 'Get your lazy arse in here, Roy; I've got a job for you.'

My mum's ex sauntered in, with a fag hanging out the corner of his mouth, and I felt myself bristle at the sight of him. I ran my eyes over the front of his sweatshirt; it was peppered with unidentifiable stains as usual. If I had to guess their origin, I'd say they were from last night's Special Brew. The man was a disgrace; imagine turning up to work like that. His clothes looked like they needed a good wash or, better still, burning.

'Long time no see, Conor,' Roy said, holding his nicotine-stained fingers towards me.

'I didn't know you worked for Bobby?' I replied, reluctantly shaking his grubby mitt. I felt myself inwardly groan when his dirty skin came into contact with mine and I had to resist the urge to wipe the palms of my hands down the front of my Armani suit.

The last time I'd seen this lowlife had been when he'd introduced me to Leo Carr. Roy had described the man whose hair was far too dark to be natural at his age as a good acquaintance. I wondered if Bobby knew his employee fraternised with the enemy.

'Desperate times call for desperate measures,' Bobby replied.

'How's Trisha?' Roy asked.

'She's fine,' I replied.

But I had no idea how my mum was. I hadn't seen her for ages. Every time I went near her, she tried to make me feel guilty for not picking up the slack in my siblings' home lives. But as far as I was concerned, I'd done more than my fair share over the years. She'd created the chaos that surrounded them, so she should deal with it. My relationship with my mum was strained, to say the least. As the oldest child, a lot of responsibility had fallen onto my shoulders. I practically raised my younger brothers and sisters. Mum had a unique style of parenting; we were left to our own devices so that she could focus all her attention on her latest boyfriend.

'Give her my regards when you next see her,' Roy said, and a lecherous smile spread across his face.

As if I was going to do that. I didn't want to risk my mum rekindling her romance with him. I could never understand what she saw in the bloke. He was filthy, and his breath made your eyes water before it knocked you sideways. How could she let him put his hands on her? The thought of it made me shudder. I knew I was a bit of a clean freak, but the bloke needed a good hosing down. He had nothing going for him; his face was covered with permanent stubble, and he had a mouth full of rotten teeth.

'I hate to break up your cosy reunion, but I'm sure I don't need to remind you that I'm paying you to work, not stand around gassing,' Bobby said. 'Get this lot bagged up and get it out on the street, pronto.'

23

Ella

When I'd moved in with Conor, my parents had made it clear they weren't happy I'd started living with somebody I'd only just met. My head understood where they were coming from, but my heart was quick to dismiss my parents' concerns. I didn't listen to them because the heady thrill of my new boyfriend's company was all-consuming. We wanted to spend every waking minute together, so it seemed like the most natural thing in the world. I was falling hard, and when Conor took the lead, I allowed myself to be whisked away by the rapid waters of a whirlwind romance.

Now that I wasn't doing shifts at the Riverside Tavern, and we were both rattling around the house together for long stretches, I realised just how much time Conor spent at home, and it made me question whether he'd been honest with me about what he did for a living. He didn't have a regular nine-to-five job; his work seemed to go from one extreme to another. He was either filling his days pumping iron in the home gym and watching back-to-back series on Netflix or disappearing for days on end.

I probably should have given more thought to the fact that Conor had two phones, but I couldn't blame him for wanting to keep business and pleasure separate; it seemed reasonable to me. The longer we were a couple, the more I realised that he was very secretive when it came to his work. It worried me that everything might not be above board, and I was slightly concerned that there was a side to him I didn't know. But I pushed it to the back of my mind so that I wasn't forced to confront some painful truths I wasn't ready to face. Did you ever really know somebody one hundred per cent?

I couldn't shake the feeling that there was something he wasn't telling me, and kept going over what Mum had said about a fully grown man going out with a teenager. Her words were having a lingering effect on me. I'd initially dismissed her concerns, but the more I thought about it, the more I wondered if there was some truth in what she'd said. I asked myself – if I was almost thirty, would I want to go out with somebody who was technically still at school? The answer was no; end of story. But then I reasoned that I wasn't your typical teenage girl. I wasn't interested in clubbing or the rave scene. Since I'd been with Conor, I was content being a homebody and liked nothing more than a quiet night in. Compared to what my uni friends got up to on any given day of the week, it was pretty unusual behaviour for somebody my age. But I'd never been a sheep and always liked to think for myself.

Cooking wasn't my strong point; Mum used to say I could burn water, but I wanted to surprise my boyfriend, so I spent the day preparing a welcome home meal for him. The trouble was Conor had the skill of a professional chef in the kitchen and had set the bar high. My chicken casserole and dumplings weren't up to his standard by any means, but I was pretty happy with the result all the same. I'd even made the pastry for the apple pie from scratch. Eat your heart out, Jamie Oliver! Mum would have been proud of me, and under normal circumstances, I would have phoned her or sent her some pictures, but things were still strained between us, so I sent the images I'd taken for posterity to Lucy and Amy on WhatsApp instead.

Bet you didn't think I had it in me 😊 😊

Christ on a bike! I never thought I'd live to see the day
😊 Lx

Looks delicious 😊 I'll be right over!! Amy xx

I knew they wouldn't let me down. My girls always had my back, and their texts brought a smile to my face.

'Honey, I'm home,' Conor called as he walked through the front door.

My face broke into a huge beam. 'I'm in the kitchen,' I shouted so my boyfriend could hear me over the playlist that was blaring from my phone.

'Something smells good.'

The casserole had been ready for hours, and it was starting to stick. I'd been trying to carefully scrape it off the base of the pan without damaging it when I heard his voice behind me. I let go of the spatula and fell into his arms.

'Did you miss me?' Conor asked as he lifted me off my feet.

'Whatever gave you that idea?' I replied, planting a kiss on his lips.

'You haven't been cooking, have you?' Conor raised his eyebrows as his beautiful blue eyes stared into mine, then he looked over the top of my head and peered into the pot that was still bubbling on the hob.

'I might have been.'

'Look at the state of my kitchen!' A look of horror spread across Conor's face as he eyeballed the solitary pan containing our dinner.

'Really?' I'd spent ages restoring his kitchen to its former gleaming self and had already cleaned up the pile of dirty pots and wiped down the flour-coated surfaces. He would have blown a gasket if he'd seen it an hour ago. I put my hands on my hips and glared at him. 'I don't want to get into an argument with you over this, but I can't tidy it up until we've eaten.' I could see my boyfriend was stressed out about the so-called mess, but he was making a big deal out of nothing.

'I don't want to argue with you either. I bought you a present.' Conor held a Jimmy Choo carrier bag towards me as he battled to tear his eyes away from the casserole.

'Thank you,' I replied.

I wasn't driven by the compulsion to have material things, but that didn't mean I didn't like them. What girl wouldn't be delighted with a present from Jimmy Choo? Conor had great taste, the bag was exquisite, and the square-toed, block-heeled boots were to die for; I was seriously impressed that he knew my shoe size, but I didn't want to be a trophy girlfriend.

I'd spent the whole day feeling insecure, obsessing about what Conor saw in me, and while I'd been making dinner, I'd been considering asking him outright when he got back. But now that he was standing in front of me, I wasn't sure I'd be able to pluck up the courage.

'Is everything OK? You seem a bit distant.' Conor tilted his handsome face to one side as if trying to read my thoughts.

'This might seem like a bit of a random question, but I can't help wondering why a man like you would want to go out with me?'

'You're kidding, right?' Conor looked bemused and then started reeling off a list of lovely compliments that made me feel embarrassed that I'd felt the need to ask. 'You're beautiful, kind, funny, incredibly smart and an excellent cook. OK, maybe not the last one; the jury's still out on that, I haven't tasted the casserole yet, but everything else is true. I love you, Ella – don't you ever forget that.' Conor pulled me into his arms then planted a kiss on the top of my head.

Conor had put my mind at rest that I wasn't just arm candy. I was annoyed at myself for doubting that his feelings towards me were genuine. Despite what my parents thought, I was glad he was older. He was completely different from guys my age. He was responsible, respected my opinion and was looking for more than just sex. I could never imagine getting a weird text from him and wondering how to respond to it. Conor didn't play games with my emotions. How did that make me feel? On top of the world.

24

Conor

Unemployment was a widespread problem on the Arnold Estate, especially for a person with no qualifications. Without the prospect of a stable job or a good career, I was forced by circumstances to claw my way out of poverty and find an alternative source of income. Roy set me on the criminal path at an early age, but then I set my sights on bigger and better things.

When a well-paid but potentially dangerous job opportunity had arisen, I'd decided to take the risk. I couldn't say no. The money drew me in, and I was desperate to branch out on my own and become a free agent. I knew what I was planning to do was wrong, and although I felt conflicted about it, the earning potential was too good for somebody living hand to mouth to ignore. I'd stumbled upon the chance to break into the drug supply chain, so I grabbed it with both hands and ran with it. That day seemed like a distant dream to me now.

Bobby Parker was back in the game thanks to the quality

of the Gómez cartel's cocaine. He'd made so much money in the last few weeks he now had pound signs rolling around his eyes. The demand for coke was insatiable, and that matched Bobby's greed.

'Get your arse out to Spain and bring back some more of that gear, pronto,' Bobby demanded.

'I'm beginning to think you've got another woman on the go,' Ella said when I was packing my case for my latest trip.

'Don't be daft; I've only got eyes for you.' I was already planning to ask her to marry me when the time was right. I pulled Ella towards me and wrapped my arms around her curves. My body ached for her. Ella reached up and kissed me; when her lips parted, we explored each other's mouths. Holding her close was making me hard, but I didn't have time to make love to her now, so I reluctantly pulled away. 'It's a pity I've got a plane to catch. You're going to be in serious trouble when I get back.' I laughed.

Diego seemed keen to show me how the Gómez operation ran. Juan, his interpreter and right-hand man, explained that because the cartel began working for a Colombian firm as low-level employees – so that they could learn the ropes from the inside – their business, wholesaling the drugs themselves, had become a huge success. The Spanish authorities were cracking down on companies that imported goods from Latin America. Most of which were specifically created to be a front for cocaine distribution. So the Gómez cartel came up with a different tactic. They established contacts in Guinea-Bissau and used that as an alternative route. Having set up legal fruit and fish businesses, they imported the drugs via commercial channels. Both sides of the businesses, legal and illegal, were flourishing.

'To be successful, you have to be one step ahead of the competition,' Diego said as he sipped his espresso from a small glass cup.

Wasn't that the truth?

'Guinea-Bissau is a tiny state in West Africa where poverty is rife, and so is corruption. By placing money in the right hands, our shipments are able to leave the country undetected.' Diego grinned.

'Everything has a price, darling,' Valentina added, rolling her r as she stroked her chihuahua's head.

I listened as Diego spoke to Juan in Spanish, and then the interpreter turned to face me.

'Once the shipments arrive, the cartel use migrant workers, many of whom are illegal immigrants, to distribute the drugs. They live under the radar with no passports or legal documents to prove their identities,' Juan explained.

'I see,' I replied.

'The migrants are essentially ghosts, living under an alias. With the absence of a paper trail, if the authorities arrest the cartel's workers, they are impossible to trace and can disappear into thin air without taking the kingpins with them.' Juan gestured to Diego, Pedro and Valentina.

The principle was the same the world over, I thought.

'So your customer was happy with our product,' Diego said, giving me a knowing smile.

'Yes, he was very impressed.' I nodded.

'Now they can't get enough of it.' Valentina laughed, and her dog's bulbous eyes sprang open. It had been dozing in her arms, and the sudden noise had startled it. 'Sorry, my little one,' she said as she covered its tiny head with kisses, leaving behind red lip prints on the dog's cream-coloured coat.

'How did you guess?' I replied.

'If you are serious about working with us on a regular basis, we have one condition,' Diego said, flicking his long grey hair over his shoulders and fixing his eyes on mine.

'OK. What's the condition?' I asked, intrigued to hear what he had to say.

'The cartel has set up a secret phone network for their members and underworld contacts using encrypted SIM cards in adapted BlackBerry handsets,' Juan said. He'd been given the task of explaining the details to me.

'That sounds interesting,' I replied, not having encountered anything like this before.

'Diego controls the entire system, which cannot be penetrated by law enforcement agencies. If you want to continue to do business with the Gómez family, you will need to join the network,' Juan continued.

That sounded like a reasonable request. 'I don't have a problem with that.'

'Good. These measures are essential for the cartel's security. If one of the phones ever ends up being seized by the police, Diego can send a text to the handset that destroys any information stored on it.'

'You're a genius! What a brilliant idea!' I said, hoping my comments would butter him up.

'Thank you.' Diego beamed with pride.

My confidence in my business partners was growing by the day, and our meeting couldn't have gone any better.

Diego must be an incredibly intelligent man if he could set up a network capable of erasing incriminating evidence if it fell into the wrong hands.

'What do you think, Conor? Do we have a deal?' Diego asked.

'Yes.' I smiled. 'I'm very excited to be working with you.'

25

Ella

November

'Thank God you're back.' I flew into Conor's arms the minute he walked through the front door.

Conor peeled himself out of my grip so he could look at me. 'What's the matter? You look exhausted.' Conor stroked my hair and planted a kiss on the top of my head as I buried my face in his chest.

'I barely slept a wink last night. There was a prowler in the garden,' I said before I pulled away from his embrace.

'It was probably just a fox or something. We get loads of wildlife around here because we're so close to Hampstead Heath. Haven't I told you about the resident muntjac? It's a pain in the arse. I don't know how it gets in, but it eats all the heads off of the flowers.' Conor laughed, glossing over the situation.

I wasn't about to let Conor dismiss my concerns. 'I know you don't believe me, but I definitely saw a man's outline. It might have been dark, but I can tell the difference between a human and a small, hump-backed deer.' My words were laced with sarcasm.

'You're a regular David Attenborough, aren't you?' Conor joked.

'It's not funny. I was absolutely terrified.' I could feel tears stabbing at my eyes as I recounted my ordeal. Why was Conor being such an insensitive prick?

'Oh shit, I'm sorry, Ella. Don't cry,' Conor said when he realised he'd upset me. 'I just thought maybe it was an animal. We get a lot of foxes around here.'

'Well, if it was a fox, it was man-sized and wearing a hoodie!'

'Were the lights triggered?' Conor asked.

'Yes.'

'That's good. There's no point spending a fortune on high-tech security if the bloody thing doesn't work.' Conor took hold of my hand and walked over to the full-length windows that overlooked the garden. 'Where did you see him?'

I pointed outside the window. 'He was right there, and then he disappeared into the shadows. I was scared he was going to try and break in, so I ran around like a lunatic, switching on all the lights. Your house was lit up like a Christmas tree by the time I'd finished.'

'Oh, Ella, I'm so sorry this happened while you were here on your own. No wonder you were scared.' Conor wrapped his arms around me and held me tightly.

'I was terrified, I didn't know what to do, so I hid at the front of the house until I heard the man climb over the gate. If I was on good terms with my parents, I would have got in a taxi and gone straight round to the flat even though it was four o'clock in the morning.' But that hadn't been an option. I could feel myself begin to tremble as I relived the experience.

'Don't be scared. You're safe now, Ella. I won't let you come to any harm; I'll protect you. I promise I'll always look after you; don't ever doubt that.'

When Conor looked into my eyes, my worries melted away. He had an emotional maturity and stable temperament my previous boyfriends hadn't possessed, which made me feel safe and secure. Now that Conor was home, he'd sent my anxiety about the situation packing. I believed his promise; I'd thought no harm would come to me while we were together. But that couldn't have been further from the truth.

26

Conor

Diego was insisting that I fly in to oversee our shipment's distribution personally. The news went down like a lead balloon when I broke it to Ella.

'After what happened while you were away on your last trip, I'm not staying here on my own,' Ella said.

'I'm not expecting you to.'

I couldn't really blame her for being jumpy. She had every right to be terrified of the late-night prowler. If he'd managed to force his way into my house, there was no telling what he might have done. I couldn't put her at risk by leaving her home alone, so there was only one thing for it. As Ella broke up from uni in a couple of days for the Christmas holidays, there was no reason she couldn't join me.

'I want you to come with me.'

Ella's heart-shaped face lit up at my proposal. 'Oh my God, I'd love to.'

'But I'm going to have to work, so you'll have to entertain yourself while I'm out on business.'

'I think I can manage that.' Ella beamed. 'Are we going to Spain?'

'Yes, but before you get too excited, we're going to the north-west. It's a popular destination for Spanish holidaymakers, but it's a relatively unknown region for foreign tourists.'

'That sounds like my idea of heaven.'

I didn't want Ella to cross paths with the cartel, so I chose some accommodation a short drive from Diego's headquarters in Vigo. I'd booked us into a hotel in Baiona. It was located on the headland, surrounded by the Atlantic and flanked by pine woods. The exterior was like a castle, with a semi-circular stone staircase leading up to a solid wood arch-shaped door with forged iron hardware. Several suits of armour were positioned just inside the lobby and looked like they were standing guard over the main entrance.

Ella's big brown eyes were wide like a child's on their first visit to Hamleys as she followed me inside. I looked over my shoulder and smiled at her, but she didn't notice. She was too busy drinking in her surroundings as she pulled her trolley case across the black-and-white chequerboard tiles to the reception desk.

'This just gets better and better,' Ella said as she began exploring our room. 'This place is huge; it's bigger than my parents' flat!'

I wanted to make sure my girlfriend was well catered for, as she'd be spending some of the trip alone, so I'd booked a junior suite. By the look on her face, splashing out on the accommodation had been a good move. I was confident Ella would be safe here as the hotel had round-the-clock security patrolling the manicured grounds.

'It's not too shabby, is it? So do you think you'll be able to entertain yourself while I'm out?' I smiled.

'I can try,' Ella replied, grinning back at me.

'Our coastline, although beautiful, is made up of jagged inlets, coves and bays, so we use speedboats to deliver the drugs, not container ships,' Diego explained as we sat side by side in the back of his black Audi RS3 while the rolling green scenery whipped past the window.

The region of Galicia in the north-western corner of Spain was surrounded on two sides by the wild Atlantic Ocean, which had carved its rugged coastline, so it wasn't that surprising that most of the imported drugs entered the region via that method.

'Our supplier sends a fishing boat or a freight ship with the cargo, and then we cross the ocean in small vessels to meet them at a designated point. We bring the packages back to the shore where men are standing by to collect the cargo from the beach.' Diego smiled with pride as he explained the procedure.

'That sounds dangerous,' I pointed out.

We couldn't see the waves below us, but I could hear them crashing against the rocks through the open window as the Audi passed a forest of pine and eucalyptus trees on the opposite side of the road.

'It is; our smugglers go to extraordinary lengths to get the drugs across the water. They sometimes travel at one hundred miles per hour in extreme weather conditions, often in the middle of the night to reduce the chance of getting caught.'

'One hundred miles per hour! It sounds more like a rocket than a speedboat! That must be a thrilling ride.' I laughed.

'The boats my crew use are superior vessels. They are twenty metres long and have seven, three-hundred-horsepower motors. The craft can take them all the way to Cape Verde, off the west coast of Africa, if need be.'

'I have to say, I'm impressed by your set-up.'

'Thank you, but wait until you see my men in action.' Diego smiled, and the puffy bags under his eyes bulged in response.

I was beginning to understand why Diego wanted me to oversee our shipment's distribution. He was very proud of his operation and wanted me to know how well everything ran.

'Come with me,' Diego said after his driver parked up on a clifftop. 'This area is called Costa de Morte – that means the coast of death. Lots of people have drowned here.' Diego laughed.

What was funny about that? As we stood on the rocky outcrop that jutted out into the wild ocean below, I could see how people might lose their lives in the inky water. Even though we were on land, I felt like we were still in a precarious position as we tried to stay upright while being battered by the wind.

'The Romans thought this place was the end of the world and the gateway to the afterlife.' Diego grinned before taking a set of binoculars out of his coat pocket.

I had to stifle a laugh when I smiled back at him. The breeze had whipped his long grey hair up, and it danced freely above him. If Diego had been carrying a trident, he would have been a dead ringer for Neptune and looked more like a ghostly mythological figure than the leader of a Spanish cartel.

Diego lifted his binoculars to his eyes and scanned the choppy water for signs of life. From our vantage point high above the deserted beach, we could see for miles. I found it hard to believe a speedboat could stay afloat in such conditions as I stood looking out at the fierce Atlantic waves roaring towards us.

'The waters are dangerous along this stretch of coast; many shipwrecks line the bottom of the sea.' Diego gestured in front of him with one hand as the other held the binoculars in place. 'That's why we use local fishermen to land our cargo. They are brave men and know how to navigate the treacherous currents and rocky shoreline. The owners of the speedboats work on commission. It's a good way for them to supplement their income.'

I had a newfound respect for the smugglers who risked their lives for the sake of a few thousand euros.

'Here they come,' Diego said, waving out to sea with his free hand.

The light was starting to fade, so I squinted into the distance, but I couldn't see anything at first. Then I caught sight of a boat travelling through the waves towards the shore. As they neared, the driver of a white van reversed onto the slipway. Diego and I watched from the cliffs above as the men, dressed in dark clothing, unloaded the drugs with military precision into the back of the transit before it headed off to a safehouse.

*

Ella was gazing out of the floor-to-ceiling windows when I walked into our suite. She turned around to face me, and as she did, her dark brown hair swung over her shoulder and fell in ripples down her body.

'You're missing a spectacular sunset,' Ella said, tearing her eyes away from mine.

I walked over to my girlfriend, stood behind her and wrapped my arms around her. When she leaned back against my chest, we watched the sky change from coral to crimson as the golden sun sank below the horizon.

'Look at the colour of the water; it's turned dark pink,' Ella said, tilting her face towards mine.

'I hope you weren't bored while I was out; I got back as soon as I could. What have you been up to?'

'I went for a long walk around the grounds. You know I love taking photos and never miss a chance to post things on Instagram. There are amazing views on every side of the fortress walls, so I wasn't disappointed; deep blue sea, rugged cliffs, soaring seagulls...'

Ella scrolled through the photos she'd taken on her phone to show me what I'd been missing. I was glad she'd come with me. It put my mind at rest to know she was safe while I was at work. I'd felt bad leaving her at the hotel on her own, but she didn't appear to be bothered by my absence; she seemed to be having a great time. I'd resisted being in a relationship for the longest time. I thought I'd always be chronically single, but now that I'd met the right person, it had changed my mindset, and I was loving being part of a couple.

Unlike Bobby's previous supplier, the Gómez cartel wanted me to take an active role in our business arrangement. The location of this hotel was stunning, and it was only a short drive from Vigo, which was an added bonus. But my visits to Spain were about to become regular, so I'd decided it would be better to have my own place here. A while ago, I'd registered with a UK-based estate agency that had an office in Galicia and had instructed them to find me a property. If I bought somewhere, then I could come and go as I pleased. It beat living out of a suitcase any day.

I couldn't imagine Ella would put up any resistance to that idea. By the look on her beautiful face, she was in her element here, embracing the country and all the culture had to offer. Ella would be moving to Spain in September to work during her gap year; I was sure she could find some employment in the local area. If I bought a house close by, I could base myself here too so that she wouldn't have to move on her own. It made no real difference whether I lived in the UK or Spain, and it would solve the issue of having to embark on a long-distance relationship. Something I definitely wasn't looking forward to.

Aside from that, I didn't want the fact that I'd started making visits to the area to look suspicious. I needed to stay under the radar so the authorities didn't start sniffing around. The more I thought about it, the more the holiday home option seemed like the best solution; the timing couldn't have been more perfect.

When Diego and I arrived at his safehouse later that day, two of his men were busy stuffing packages into secret compartments in the car's walls and roof, which would transport the cocaine. Diego had employed a Spanish couple to act as the drug mules. Along with their young child and an elderly relative, they would pose as a family going to the

UK on holiday and drive the specially adapted car from the Galician coast to Santander before taking the twenty-four-hour crossing to Portsmouth. I'd hired a holiday rental for the family to stay in on the south coast, where the exchange would take place. Once I received the shipment, I'd cut the cocaine and deliver it to Bobby. Then his network of local dealers would distribute it. The plan looked good on paper, but only time would tell if the group would be able to make it through customs with the shipment of cocaine undetected.

Diego assured me that the first leg of the journey was the riskiest. The inlets and coves had long been a smugglers' paradise, so it was an area of interest to the local police. The further away from the coast the cocaine made it, the greater the chance the shipment would reach its final destination.

I was travelling along the motorway in Juan's car, which was the third vehicle in the convoy, when I spotted a police presence in the distance. 'There's something going on up there,' I said, feeling my heartbeat quicken.

'Don't worry, the cops always try to catch us out this way, but we have a very effective system in place,' Juan replied.

Because the police routinely set traps for the couriers, the cartel had developed sophisticated evasion techniques to protect their assets. The first car in our convoy sped towards the partial roadblock. Instead of stopping when the officer flagged the car down, Diego's driver put his foot down and shot past the official. Several officers jumped in their car and gave chase.

Juan turned to me and smiled. 'Relax, Conor, everything's under control.'

The second vehicle in our convoy was the car laden with cocaine driven by the unthreatening-looking family. They came to a stop at the checkpoint, and the male driver had a brief conversation with a police officer before being waved through.

'Thank God for that; I thought they might search the car,' I said, letting out a slow breath.

'If the police had tried to go down that route, the family would have driven off, and you would have been in for the ride of your life,' Juan replied. 'If a pursuit had begun, it would have been our job to help them escape by crashing into the police.'

I sat in the back of Juan's car, peering over the headrest. I could feel beads of sweat break out on my upper lip as our car prepared to stop.

'Let me do the talking,' Juan said as he lowered his window.

Juan explained in Spanish that he was a taxi driver and was taking me to the airport so I could catch a flight back to the UK. The officer didn't question us any further and, much to my relief, allowed us to continue on our way.

27

Ella

The landscape surrounding the medieval fortress where we were staying was idyllic, but rattling around the spacious suite or strolling through the manicured gardens on my own was losing its appeal. Conor had been out on business pretty much constantly since we'd arrived, which was to be expected, as he'd come to the area for work and not for pleasure. I hadn't told Conor I was feeling lonely because I didn't want him to regret bringing me, and didn't want to make him feel guilty for leaving me alone.

I enjoyed walking as much as the next person, but the blisters on my feet were telling a different story. I'd covered some serious mileage in the last couple of days to try and pass the time, but the hours were dragging by. On a positive note, my vitamin D levels had received a huge boost by doing laps, several times a day, of the circular coastal walk. The fresh air and breath-taking scenery were good for the soul, but I'd never been a solitary creature. I loved to socialise and thrived on spending time with other people; it boosted my happiness and gave me a sense of belonging.

I'd done a lot of thinking over the last couple of days and had come to the conclusion that if it hadn't been for my social media apps, I would never have survived the trip. Thank God for modern technology! Having Lucy and Amy on a WhatsApp group made me feel connected to them and stopped me from becoming completely isolated, but it didn't really make up for face-to-face interaction. I decided to FaceTime them to give them a virtual tour of our suite and our balcony's incredible views.

'This is the bathroom,' I said, turning my phone around so that they could see the marble-clad space.

'Ooh, look at all those lovely toiletries!' Lucy said as she eyed the miniature cobalt-blue bottles lined up on the glass shelf above the double sinks. 'If you've got any left at the end of your trip, will you bring them back for us?'

'Of course,' I replied as I walked across the vast bedroom towards the balcony.

'That is the biggest bed I've ever seen,' Amy pointed out when I passed the massive four-poster in the centre of the room.

'And this is the view,' I said, stepping out onto the flagstoned terrace.

'Wow! How the other half live,' Lucy said. 'We're not a bit jealous, are we, Amy?'

'Not at all. Your hotel is only slightly more upmarket than the mobile home I stayed in when I went to Skegness last month.' Amy laughed.

'You won't want to come home,' Lucy added. 'I've never seen anything so luxurious before apart from in a magazine.'

I hadn't been trying to make my friends envious of where Conor and I were staying, but I was desperately missing them and craved their company.

'Well, if it's any consolation, girls, I wish you were here.'

'So do we!' Amy replied.

While we'd been chatting, I'd found myself playing down how I was feeling. I was so lucky to stay somewhere as incredible as this and was aware that I would come across as being ungrateful if I started whinging. Not many people got the opportunity to wake up in a castle. How could I be bored? I reasoned that life was better when you shared experiences with your friends and family, wasn't it?

I couldn't help craving the company of others; I wasn't a lone wolf and had always fared better with a network of people around me. But I was determined not to waste this once-in-a-lifetime experience. It was pretty obvious that the secret to getting through the solitude and staving off the boredom was to keep myself busy. Then I could avoid being alone with my thoughts, which I wanted to do at all costs. It was time to embrace the opportunity so that I would get the most out of the trip.

'What have you been up to?' Conor asked when he came out onto the balcony.

'I walked into the town and practised my Spanish on the unsuspecting locals.' I laughed. 'How was your day?'

'It was fine,' Conor replied. Then he dangled a set of keys in front of me. 'Guess what?'

'I have no idea.'

'I've bought a villa along the coast from here,' Conor said as though he'd popped into Tesco for a loaf of bread.

'Really?' I stared at Conor, open-mouthed. I'd had no

idea he was thinking of buying a second home. 'You kept that quiet. So that's what you've been up to on your secretive trips away, is it?'

'I wanted it to be a surprise. I thought I'd take you over to see it once we've checked out in the morning,' Conor said.

'I'd love that,' I replied, and I felt my lips stretch into a broad beam.

'What made you decide to buy a place here?' I asked as Conor drove our hire car towards his new house. Not that I wasn't delighted by the prospect of spending more time in this little piece of paradise with sandy beaches, crystal-clear water, warm sunshine and excellent food.

'I'm going to be spending a fair amount of time here for work. As I'll be a frequent visitor, I thought it made sense to have a base here.' Conor flashed me a bright smile. 'I take it you won't mind accompanying me on my business trips. And anyway, come September, you'll need a place to live...'

I'd been dreading organising my placement for next year, but now that Conor had bought a house, I wouldn't have to leave him behind, so I suddenly felt excited by the prospect. I hadn't realised Conor was planning all of this in the background; he was one step ahead of me.

This was a beautiful part of the world, and I'd loved walking through the craggy arches sculpted by the bracing wind and wild, frothing sea. The deserted beaches, backed by sheer cliffs, were to die for. North-west Spain was very different from the other parts of the country that I'd visited on various holidays with my parents over the years. It was a million miles away from the crowded Spanish Costas, with epic Atlantic scenery, rolling hills covered with pine and eucalyptus trees, green valleys and rugged mountains. Because there were no direct flights from the UK, Galicia wasn't overrun with British tourists demanding full English breakfasts and live-streamed *Coronation Street*. Those types of Spanish resorts, England with the sun, were my idea of hell. I liked to see the real country.

We'd been travelling along the main coast road, a traffic-less highway with spectacular sea views, when Conor turned off and drove down a newly tarmacked driveway. As we came to the end of it, Conor pressed a fob on the keyring, and an automatic gate opened, exposing landscaped grounds and the rugged coastline beyond. When he drove the car inside, I got my first glimpse of the three-storey ultra-modern villa with far-reaching views of the Rias Baixas and the Atlantic Ocean.

'Wow,' was all I could say at first. 'It's like a bright, white version of your Highgate home. You clearly have a type,' I joked.

The six-bedroomed villa was located just outside the beautiful historic town of Baiona, Pontevedra, and had everything money could buy. As we got out of the car, my eyes scanned over the wrap-around gardens peppered with palm trees until they settled on the pool.

'Let me show you around.' Conor tugged me by the hand and led me around the interior, which was tastefully furnished and had English oak parquet flooring throughout.

'Why on earth have you got a wine cellar?' My eyes lit up at the sight of the fully stocked floor-to-ceiling racking.

'Why not?' Conor replied, and a smile spread over his handsome face.

'I have to say, I think that's the height of excess as you never touch the stuff! But it would be a shame to waste it, so I'll be more than happy to start working my way through the collection.' I laughed.

'I thought as much. So do you like the villa?' Conor asked when he'd finished giving me a guided tour. We stood holding hands on the terrace next to the jacuzzi, gazing at the distant view of the Cíes Islands.

'Do you really have to ask?' I replied.

'I value your opinion,' Conor said, pulling me towards him, holding me in his arms while he waited for me to reply.

'The place is incredible.'

'I'm glad you approve.' Conor beamed. 'We'll stay here tonight, but then I need to go back to London tomorrow for a business meeting. Why don't you arrange to see the girls? My meeting's likely to drag on.'

'OK. I'll see if Lucy and Amy fancy going for a coffee.'

'I think we can go one better than that.' Conor opened his wallet, took out a bundle of notes and handed them to me. 'Treat the girls to lunch. I'm sure you've got lots of catching up to do.'

'I can't take that,' I replied.

'Yes, you can,' Conor insisted, forcing the money into my palm and closing my fingers around it.

28

Ella

'How are you going to pay for that?' Lucy asked when I said I'd treat her and Amy to lunch. 'Have you just robbed a bank?'

'Of course not. Conor's given me some money, and he suggested we go out for a catch-up. I know how much you two love Mexican food, so I thought I'd push the boat out and take you to this great restaurant in Trafalgar Square. I wasn't expecting to have to twist your arms,' I replied.

We tucked into our chilli-glazed rib-eye steaks, chips and spicy rice as we put the world to rights. I'd really missed my best friends' company, but when the conversation came around to mine and Conor's relationship, I couldn't help detecting an undercurrent of disapproval from them.

'Don't get me wrong, it's very generous of Conor to pay for our lunch, but don't you ever feel like he's buying your loyalty and affection?' Lucy said as she speared a chip with her fork and plunged it into a pot of mayonnaise.

'No, I don't,' I replied, and my cheeks flushed. I didn't

appreciate being portrayed as a gold digger; I thought she knew me better than that. I felt Lucy was being a bit hypocritical as she was more than happy to take the free lunch. 'Maybe some women are attracted to their partner's lifestyle, but the money and the cars don't impress me. I want more than just the material package.' I wasn't sure why I felt I owed them an explanation.

'You don't need to be so defensive,' Amy said, sweeping her beautiful long red hair over her shoulder before she reached across the table and squeezed my hand. 'It's not that we don't like Conor...'

I had to stop myself from rolling my eyes. Even before Amy continued to speak, I knew there was a *but* coming.

'He seems nice enough, but Lucy and I don't think he's right for you. I hate to say it, but you've changed since you've been going out with him.'

When Amy offered me a lacklustre smile, I was tempted to wipe it off her face. My so-called friends were patronising me, showering me with their superior knowledge. Lucy and Amy had only met Conor once, but they'd formed a strong opinion of him and thought that qualified them to dissect our relationship layer by layer. They'd obviously been discussing my love life behind my back, and I had to admit the idea of that was pissing me off. They'd been bitching about me, and here I was, trying to do something nice for them. Who did they think they were?

'No offence, Ella, but don't you think he's a bit old for you?' Lucy piped up before she polished off the rest of her steak.

I was aware our relationship might be viewed with suspicion and disapproval, provoking snide remarks like that from people I didn't know, but I hadn't expected my friends to go in on my boyfriend. I felt like screaming and slamming my fists down on the table, but instead, I let out an audible breath; I'd heard it all now! Lucy had a very selective memory. Only a short while ago, she'd asked me if Conor had got any brothers, and when I'd said he had two, she'd replied, 'Oh, fantastic! We can have one each, Amy'. So they were either winding me up or as jealous as hell.

What had got into everyone? First, my parents had voiced their disapproval and now my two best girls. I was tempted to say if that's how you both feel you can pay for your own lunch, but I didn't want to fall out with Lucy and Amy over this, so instead, I made a joke out of it.

'The way you're going on, anyone would think I'm dating an old age pensioner.' I laughed.

Lucy and Amy exchanged a look, but neither of them replied.

Conor looked younger than he was, and I'd always been told I looked older, so unless we publicised the fact, nobody would realise the age gap between us spanned a decade. For the life of me, I couldn't work out what all the fuss was about; everyone always remarked that I was very mature for a nineteen-year-old. Ever since I'd been a young girl, I couldn't wait to be an adult. Mum was always trying to put the brakes on to stop me from growing up too fast.

I was midway through my white chocolate and raspberry cheesecake while my friends scoffed rich, indulgent chocolate cake smothered in vanilla ice cream when my mobile rang. I craned my neck to see the name on the screen. It was Conor, so I swiped to answer the call.

'Hello.'

'Hi, Ella. I've finished my meeting. Do you want me to come and pick you up?' Conor asked.

'That would be great,' I replied, ending the call. Since we'd had words earlier, an awkward atmosphere was hovering over the three of us, and I had to admit, I couldn't wait for our lunch to be over.

Lucy and Amy didn't say anything when I told them that Conor was on his way to collect me. After our earlier conversation, I was half expecting them to make a sly comment, but I was pleasantly surprised when they didn't.

I took the bundle of notes out of my purse to settle the bill. As I glanced over at the waitress to get her attention, I couldn't help noticing Lucy's cornflower-blue eyes were like saucers.

Conor was leaning against the passenger door of his BMW dressed in dark blue jeans and a black leather jacket when we walked out of the restaurant. He looked absolutely gorgeous, and I noticed he'd caught the eye of more than one female passer-by. The fact that other women found my boyfriend attractive made me feel proud, not jealous, as he gave me no reason to feel insecure.

'How was the food?' Conor asked as he slid his arm around my waist and planted a kiss on my lips.

'It was delicious. We've had a great time. Thanks for treating us,' I said.

Lucy and Amy both echoed their thanks. I was glad they hadn't forgotten their manners. But even though they were polite to my boyfriend's face, I could sense they didn't like him.

'Any time,' Conor replied.

I kissed Lucy and Amy on both cheeks, then I got into

the car. We'd promised to meet up soon, but I had a feeling that wasn't going to happen. There seemed to be a distance between us, which was a shame – although we hadn't been friends that long, we had quickly become inseparable at uni.

'I'm glad you had a good time, but I get the distinct impression that your friends don't like me,' Conor said as he pulled his car out into the rush-hour traffic.

'What gave you that idea?' I asked, trying to be diplomatic. But my boyfriend was obviously a good judge of character. His ears must have been burning after the conversation we'd had around the table.

'Just a hunch. But for the record, I can't say I'm overly keen on the girls either.' Conor laughed.

His comment took me by surprise. Conor had been his usual charming self both times he'd met my besties.

'I had no idea you hadn't taken to my friends.'

Conor shrugged but didn't elaborate.

I was curious to know why. I hated confrontation and hostile situations and wanted to keep the peace between everyone important to me. My boyfriend and my two closest friends had only met on two occasions, but they seemed to have taken an instant dislike to one another. There had to be a way around this problem, but if I didn't know what was behind the issue, I'd never be able to sort it out.

'So come on then, spill the beans; why don't you like Lucy and Amy?'

'I'm not sure, really; I just don't feel comfortable around them.' Conor paused for a moment. He was deep in thought. 'Maybe it's because I've got nothing in common with them, and they come across as being immature.'

'That's interesting. Would it surprise you to know Lucy

and Amy are both older than me?' I laughed, and my mum's words rang in my ears: old head on young shoulders. That pretty much summed me up, I suppose.

I should have been on cloud nine after the slap-up lunch Conor had treated us to, but Lucy's comment about my boyfriend buying my loyalty and affection was bothering me. Perhaps she was right? I was living in Conor's house, with no money of my own to speak of, so the balance of power between us was on a perilously unhealthy tilt. I knew if I voiced my concerns about how our life looked to other people, Conor would just brush them aside.

Not for the first time, I felt torn between continuing with my education and getting a job. I'd promised myself I wouldn't be financially dependent on anyone, but I'd struggled to juggle everything, and when the pressure was mounting, I'd buckled. I knew I worried too much about what people thought of me, but I couldn't help it. After Lucy's barbed remark, I was regretting resigning from my job.

When Amy had told me that I'd changed since I'd been going out with Conor, and I knew she didn't mean in a good way, it hurt my feelings. I might have stopped going to parties with the girls, and I guess I spent most of my free time with Conor now, but I wasn't trying to neglect them; it was to be expected. I wasn't single anymore. I was sure they would have done the same thing if they were in relationships.

My parents had been keeping their distance since Conor and I came back from Mexico, which was a pity because I missed my mum and dad so much. The last thing I wanted to do was become isolated from Lucy and Amy too. If that happened, I'd be completely dependent on Conor for everything. It felt like everyone close to me was gradually withdrawing from me, and I wasn't sure what to do about it; I didn't want to have to choose between allegiance to my parents and friends or my boyfriend.

29

Conor

Ella had a purity and innocence about her, so if she believed I'd been house-hunting while I'd been away in Spain organising shipments of cocaine, that was fine by me. She was wrong, but I didn't want both of my worlds to collide. The deception was necessary to keep Ella safe and as far away as possible from the shady side of my life. Anyway, a little white lie never hurt anyone, did it?

I'd given the detailed criteria of the property I was looking for to the UK-based agency and let them do the donkey work. The white-washed villa close to Baiona Marina and all the amenities hit the spot perfectly. I'd only viewed it once before I signed on the dotted line.

'I have good news for you. The family breezed through customs without a hitch, and they've just arrived at the holiday rental. Being a former police officer has its perks. I have many useful contacts,' Diego said. I could tell by the tone of his voice that he was smiling.

'That's excellent! I'll let my client know.'

Now that he had plenty of stock, Bobby was keen to re-establish his position and reclaim his turf, but his greed had got the better of him, and he'd started flooding the area with cut-price cocaine, something that hadn't gone down well with the other local dealers.

Leo Carr had been bending my ear about the issue all afternoon, but there was nothing I could do about it. Bobby was his own man – he didn't take orders from me, or anyone else for that matter.

'You might want to tone things down a bit. You're pissing off the other pushers,' I said, trying to deliver the warning with tact and diplomacy, but I should have realised the meathead would ignore my words of advice.

'If I wanted your fucking opinion, I'd ask for it,' Bobby replied.

I'd needed to buy myself enough time to drive to the coast, cut the cocaine and deliver it to Bobby, so I'd suggested Ella take her friends out to lunch. My girlfriend liked the simple things in life, even though we were surrounded by the trappings of luxury. I loved that about her; it helped to keep me grounded.

When I'd phoned Bobby to arrange the handover, he'd declined to mention his men had received fresh threats from the competition the previous night. I didn't find that out until much later on.

Bobby's driver pulled the black Range Rover up outside what should have been a secret location, a terraced house in Stepney Green that he used as a storage facility. Before we had a chance to get out of the car, I heard the roar of a motorbike then the screeching of brakes.

'Get down, boss,' the driver shouted before a man

wearing a black balaclava under his crash helmet jumped off the back and shot him at point-blank range through the front windscreen. When the bullet hit him between the eyes, Bobby's driver slumped back in his chair, having died instantly.

'What the fuck's going on?' Bobby drew his weapon, but he didn't have time to use it.

The shooter flung open the back door and blasted him in the chest with a shotgun. Then the gunman turned his attention to me, and Bobby rolled out of the car onto the pavement.

'Help me,' Bobby screamed, but nobody was going to be brave enough to come to his aid.

Bobby managed to drag himself a short distance, but the effort was too much for a dying man. There was nothing I could do for him; I'd been pulled out of the other back passenger seat by the marksman, and he was holding a gun to my head.

'Put your hands up, you fucker, or I'll blow your brains out.'

'Listen, mate, I don't want any trouble,' I said as my life flashed before my eyes.

He wouldn't need to ask me twice. I slowly held my palms out in front of me. Whatever had just gone down was Bobby's beef; it had nothing to do with me. I was just unlucky enough to have found myself in the wrong place, at the wrong time, so I didn't want to end up taking a bullet for him.

I stood by and watched Bobby bleed out in the residential street in broad daylight. The man lying motionless on the ground just feet from me was dead; there was no doubt about that, and it scared the shit out of me. I kept picturing the sight of Ella's beautiful face and wondered if I'd ever get to see her again.

'Let's get out of here,' the motorbike driver said.

I couldn't see his face; it was concealed behind a dark visor. I stood in a trance in the middle of the road, watching the high-powered bike roar off into the distance. Bobby and his driver's lives had been snuffed out in an instant, victims of a gangland execution. I could have easily been in the same position. I hadn't thought they'd let me live to tell the tale. I had been sure the shooter was going to put a bullet in my head.

Bobby Parker had a lot of enemies. Whoever had done this might change their mind and come after me. I wasn't sure why the gunman had let me go. Surely it would have made more sense to finish all of us off. Leaving a person alive who could retell the sequence of events seemed madness from where I was standing. Not that I wasn't incredibly grateful. I was elated that I was able to walk away completely unscathed, but the shooter's actions were unfathomable to me. If I'd been a snitch, it could have ended up costing him his freedom.

As far as I knew, I was the only witness to the men's murders, so my first instinct was to go to ground. If I laid low, I could see how things would unfold in the coming days. But I wouldn't be able to do that without making Ella suspicious and potentially putting her at risk. I wasn't prepared to do that, so I'd have to spin another web of lies. But if I did, that would prick my conscience, and the layers of guilt were building up. I'd been walking an impossible tightrope between feeling secure enough to open the lock, give Ella the key to my heart and let her into my life by being honest about who I was, and carrying on with the deception for fear of losing her. I didn't want to have to keep Ella in the dark about my work, so maybe it was time to start drip-feeding her information about what I did for a living. It was bound to come out sooner or later, and if our relationship was going to work, I needed to be able to trust her.

Today's events had shaken me to the core, but I didn't want Ella to pick up on my unease, so I'd put on a front to cover up how I was feeling. She would quite rightly be terrified if I told her what I'd witnessed. I tried to put the execution of Bobby and his driver out of my thoughts and carry on as if nothing had happened, but it wasn't easy. My nerves were on edge.

Whoever ordered the hit could still come after me. Never leave behind any loose ends that might come back to haunt you – an unspoken underworld rule. My evidence could put the murderer behind bars, so I was still potentially at risk from the gunman.

For the life of me, I didn't know why I'd been spared, but I was sure the reason would become clear at some stage. The way I saw it, I had two choices. I could leave the area or stay and face the consequences. It was a tough decision to make.

First and foremost, I needed to protect Ella. I didn't want her to get caught up in the backlash, so maybe I should give some more thought to going into hiding. But, for some reason, being in the public eye seemed like a safer option than shying away from the people who might, or might not, be a threat to me. I felt like I was damned if I did, damned if I didn't.

Ella and I should be safe enough behind the walls of my house in Highgate. I liked living in a suburban cul-de-sac because nobody could casually drive past and blast you to pieces. Apart from that, it was kitted out with all the latest high-tech security gadgets. It had to be. Since I'd started my role as a middle man, I had cash and coke stashed in secret compartments all over my home. I was the person who received the shipments from the supplier, so I needed a secure place to run the illegal operation. My house might appear to be a statement of grandeur to an outsider looking in, but it was an essential investment.

Losing Bobby so suddenly was a stark reminder that a person could be here one minute and gone the next. I didn't want Ella caught up in this business; it was too risky. The people involved in the drugs trade were lawless. I wish I could have considered taking up a less dangerous profession for my girlfriend's sake, but the money was too good to walk away from; no other job came close to paying the same hourly rate, and I had bills to pay. That was how I justified being involved in this game when I wasn't a user myself, and I despised the weakness of those who took drugs. But without them, I'd be unemployed.

What else would I do? I didn't have any qualifications or skills to do anything else. I hadn't put a lot of focus on my education; I had been too busy playing the surrogate parent to my brothers and sisters, so I'd resigned myself to the fact a long time ago that once I ventured into this line of work, I'd be stuck in it. But this was my world; this was where I felt comfortable; this was what was familiar. And I knew I was good at my job.

30

Ella

Conor and I lay entwined in each other's arms, still breathless from making love, when I thought I heard a noise outside.

'What's up?' Conor asked as I lifted my head off the feather pillow and stared into the darkness.

'I think somebody's in the garden,' I replied before I tightened my grip on my boyfriend.

Conor had his back to the door, but he rolled over, picked up his boxer shorts that lay discarded by the side of the bed and pulled them on.

'Stay here, and I'll go and check.'

Conor opened the drawer of his bedside cabinet and took out a black patterned tubular object. At first, I thought it was a torch, but the more I stared at it, the more I was certain it was something more threatening than a simple light source.

'What's that?' I asked, pulling the quilt tightly around my chest.

'It's an extendable steel baton,' Conor replied, and with a flick of his wrist, it tripled in size.

It reminded me of a magician's wand, but I was sure it was far more deadly. 'Be careful,' I whispered as he disappeared out of the door.

The thought of Conor having to fight off an intruder was terrifying, but at least he had an effective weapon to defend himself with. I just hoped it was a false alarm, and he wasn't going to have to use it.

Once Conor had left the room, I quickly threw my pyjamas on and tiptoed out of the bedroom, being careful to stay in the shadows. With my heartbeat pounding, my eyes fixed on Conor's broad shoulders as he crossed the open-plan living area and walked towards the full-length windows. He had the steel baton gripped tightly in his right hand. I watched from a safe distance, with my arms wrapped around myself. Conor stared out into the garden; the first thing that struck me was how dark it was – it should have been floodlit.

'I can't see anything suspicious, and the lights haven't triggered, so it must have just been a cat or something,' Conor said, then he turned on his heel and began walking back towards the bedroom. 'It's OK, Ella, there's nobody outside.'

As soon as the words left his mouth, I heard the perimeter gate rattle and the sound of feet landing hard on the pavement. Conor charged towards the back door without a moment's hesitation and slid open the patio doors. He ran out onto the terrace, and down the steps, in hot pursuit of the intruder. With my pulse beating wildly in my neck, I took tentative steps towards the wide-open space. I stood shivering in the doorway before it occurred to me to slide the glass panel back into place before the cold December night robbed the house of all its warmth.

Conor bounded up the steps two at a time, and as soon as he was close enough, I fell into his arms.

'Let's go back inside; whoever was out there is long gone.' Conor took hold of my hand and led me back inside the house.

'Why didn't the security lights come on?'

'I'm not sure, but there's nothing I can do now; we'll worry about it in the morning.'

'You must be freezing,' I said as my eyes scanned over his semi-naked frame.

'I'm OK,' Conor replied.

I put my arm around his waist and snuggled into him. Conor's skin was like ice, but he was too pumped full of adrenaline to notice he was stone cold.

There was no denying this was a beautiful house, I thought as I climbed back into bed, but it was the second time I'd been scared by an intruder in the space of a month. It didn't matter how nice the surroundings were, if you were too scared to open your eyes and appreciate them, they were completely worthless.

'I know you're scared, but try not to worry.' Conor kissed my lips, then lay on his back and looked up at the ceiling.

'What do you think's going on?' I asked. After what had just happened, my mind was too active to try and sleep.

Conor rolled onto his side and propped himself up on his elbow before he rested his head in the palm of his hand.

'My guess is it's just some lowlife crackhead looking for

their next hit. Whoever was in the garden knows there's going to be valuable stuff in a house like this. If they manage to break in and steal something, they'll sell it to buy their next fix. That's how scum like that operate.'

31

Conor

We either had a very persistent thief doing the rounds, or Bobby Palmer's murderer had come back to finish the job. When Ella said she'd heard something outside, I'd thought the gunman was coming to get me. But logic told me if he had been, he wouldn't have disappeared into the night, would he?

It seemed to take her an eternity to drop off, but when she finally did, I left Ella sleeping while I went outside to survey the damage. Even though they hadn't triggered, just like before, the lights hadn't been disabled, which made me think the same person was responsible. Strange as it might seem, that thought brought me a lot of comfort. The first incident had happened before I'd witnessed the senseless murder of two men, so I was pretty sure my other theory was correct. Out of the two options, a burglar, who had set my house in his sights was the better one, especially as whoever that was wasn't a very proficient one.

*

My girlfriend wore her heart on her sleeve. When I'd told her I had to pop out, I could read her expressions like a book. Although she was trying to put on a brave face, her dark eyes were wide with fear. I knew she didn't want me to leave her alone, but Leo Carr had summoned me to a meeting. My first instinct was to blow him out, but then I decided to use the opportunity to lay down some ground rules. I wanted to look him in the eye and make sure he understood he was no longer the puppet master. I worked for myself these days; battling against people who kept trying to control me was a massive ball-ache that I didn't need right now. I had no intention of wasting precious time on him, so before I'd left, I'd assured Ella I'd be back before she knew it.

Leo's rented space was hardly a des res, situated in the shadow of the Bow Flyover in a not very salubrious part of town. When I parked my car outside the grey, lifeless building positioned on a site that was little more than waste ground, I thought twice about leaving it unattended. This was the sort of place you could turn your back for ten minutes and find either your motor had been nicked or, if it was still there, it was propped up on bricks, having been stripped of anything valuable.

'Come on in,' Leo said when I pushed open the flimsy metal door.

He was sitting behind a large desk at the far end of the space, dressed in a pinstriped suit and cufflinks, trying to look the part. But he was failing miserably. Appearances counted for everything. Instead of making a good first impression by operating out of a luxury office space, Leo was conducting his business from a run-down Portakabin with a fan heater positioned opposite him to keep the cold weather at bay.

'Take a seat,' Leo said, gesturing to the stained typist's chair wedged in under the desk.

'Nah, I'm good, thanks,' I replied when I saw the state of the filthy fabric. I didn't want to come into contact with it, so it was safer to stand.

I didn't intend to be here long. I'd just come to the grimy office space to make sure Leo got the message once and for all. My days as an underworld enforcer were well and truly behind me, so he'd need to find somebody else to do his dirty work. I was about to deliver the speech I'd prepared earlier when he stopped me in my tracks.

'I ordered the hit on Parker. The shooter who executed Bobby and his driver at point-blank range was one of my men,' Leo boasted, running his hand over his swept-back, thinning hair.

I was lost for words. Even though I'd heard the news from the horse's mouth, it shocked me to the core. The man had grown a pair in recent weeks. When Leo had entered the turf war, he was the underdog. I wouldn't have thought he was capable of bringing Bobby Parker down, but he had.

'You look a bit surprised.' Leo laughed, having given me time to digest his confession.

'It's a cut-throat business; survival of the fittest,' I replied, not really knowing how to respond.

Bobby and Leo were born streets apart in Mile End, before it became a trendy, vibrant East London neighbourhood. They were your typical Cockney geezers who had graduated from the same school of hard knocks, but Bobby had clearly underestimated his old nemesis. We all had. Leo's actions reminded me that life was fragile. None of us were indestructible.

'I know you witnessed my guy's handiwork,' Leo said. His eyes bulged as he studied my reaction.

For a moment, I considered denying it, but what good would that do? Leo obviously knew I was with Bobby at the time he was slain.

Leo pushed his chair back and stood in front of his desk, gripping onto the sides of it. 'I'm sure I don't need to tell you how important it is for you to keep quiet about the murders. If you blab, I'll have to pay a visit to your family. It would be a terrible shame if something unfortunate happened to your mother and siblings, wouldn't it?'

I wouldn't let my family come to any harm, even though Mum and I were at odds and, thanks to her, I hadn't had the best home life.

'You've got nothing to worry about; I'm not going to say a word,' I reassured him.

Leo didn't need to threaten me. There was no way I was going to go running to the cops. If I went down that route, it would amount to a death wish.

Leo walked over to the side of the cabin, where a small rust-speckled fridge hummed in the corner. He opened the door and took out a bottle of Bollinger from the milk rack, then picked up two mugs that sat on a tray next to the kettle on the top of the fridge.

'I suppose you're wondering why your arse was spared.' Leo grinned.

The way Leo put it, anyone would think I was mildly

curious when in reality, I'd been racking my brains since I'd watched Bobby, covered in claret, take his last breath. Unless they were completely incompetent, shooters never left behind any loose ends. They usually worked on the premise that dead men couldn't talk. I knew it hadn't been a case of Lady Luck smiling down on me that day while removing me from the hit list; the person who had ordered the bloodbath had something in mind for me.

I nodded, then folded my arms across my chest. 'The thought had crossed my mind.' I had to play the game; I couldn't afford to let Leo think I was rattled in the slightest by the threat he posed to me, or the balance of power between the two of us would shift.

As Leo stood in the middle of the room, holding the mugs and champagne, his bulging brown eyes were out on stalks. He tilted his head to one side before he walked over to his desk, placed the mugs down and began easing the cork out of the bottle. I could feel beads of sweat settle on my upper lip. I hoped he wasn't expecting me to drink something that had come out of a fridge that should be declared unfit for use, but thankfully, he stopped short at removing it completely.

'So you didn't lose any sleep over it, then?' Leo laughed.

'I can't say I did,' I lied.

'That says a lot about your character, Conor. Your balls must be made of steel! Now let's get down to business; I have a proposition for you,' Leo said.

I took a deep breath and exhaled it slowly as I braced myself for the moment I'd been dreading.

'Now that Bobby's out of the picture, I want you to

supply me with coke instead. I've built up a client base in recent weeks, and I'm not about to walk away from it.'

I could see why Leo thought this was a logical step, but the guy had caused me nothing but aggro over the years, and I was desperate to keep my distance from him. If it had been anyone else, I wouldn't have had a problem with the new arrangement; business was business. I didn't owe Bobby my loyalty. But Leo Carr was a different kettle of fish.

As the silence stretched on, I noticed Leo eyeballing me, and I felt pressured to make the right decision. I was relieved that his proposal didn't involve the use of pliers or power tools, but if it had, my decision would have been simple, I would have turned him down flat. This needed careful consideration. I was obsessed with making money, and I stood to make a lot out of him if I agreed to become his supplier. Let's face it, since I'd branched out on my own, I'd sometimes had to partner with people I didn't like. But I detested Leo, so I wasn't sure we'd be able to make this work.

As I ran the offer through my head, I was beginning to see Leo in a new light. He was more than just a violent individual; he was a shrewd businessman. By playing the part of a nonentity, he'd slipped under the radar and placed himself in a position where he was able to seize opportunities as they arose. He might have lacked a formal education, but he was streetwise and that more than made up for anything he could have learned at school. I reasoned that it would be better to keep him on side than make an enemy out of him, but any arrangement we made would have to come with strict guidelines.

'I'll agree to supply you, but I have some conditions,' I said.

'Fire away,' Leo replied.

'I want to make it clear to you that I don't work for you; I'm my own boss. I call the shots and name the terms of any deals we make.'

I was finally making a name for myself, carving a path in a successful business, and I wasn't about to go back to being an errand boy. As long as Leo didn't try to overstep the boundaries, I was prepared to give things a go.

'That sounds reasonable.' Leo nodded, then popped open the cork and poured the expensive champagne into the mugs. 'I'm looking forward to doing business with you,' he said, handing me a drink. 'Cheers.'

I peered into the top of the tea-stained mug and steeled myself, but I couldn't bring myself to take a sip. This stuff might cost the earth, but it was vile, so even if the mug hadn't been filthy, I wouldn't have wanted the bubbles to touch my lips. Would Leo see my refusal to drink as a snub? I didn't waste time on the thought; I didn't give a shit if I offended him.

'It's a funny old world we live in, isn't it? Who would have thought, poor old Bobby would be here one minute and gone the next,' Leo said, slapping me on the top of my shoulder before he tried to refill my mug. He didn't seem to notice I hadn't touched a drop.

'Not for me, thanks; I've got to drive,' I replied.

I placed the mug on the side of his desk and walked across the balding blue carpet tiles to the window. After reluctantly clearing the condensation away with my fingertips, I peered out to check whether my BMW was still in one piece.

'Take it from me, Conor, even though you're a young man, you should live every day as if it's your last. Stay in the fast lane and maximise the benefits easy money brings. You never know when everything might be taken away from you.'

I wasn't sure whether Leo had just issued me with another threat or some friendly words of advice. But one thing was certain: from here on in, I would never underestimate him again.

32

Ella

I'd always been told I was mature for my years, probably because I'd identified as a good girl from an early age, going through life making the safe decisions, the appropriate ones. I wanted my parents to be proud of me, so I always tried to do the right thing, and in doing so, I'd found myself pigeonholed.

When Conor had appeared on the scene, he'd opened my eyes to a different way of living, and I'd suddenly realised I was missing out on all the excitement and felt I wasn't in charge of my own life. As usual, I was doing what was expected of me. The fact of the matter was, I was fed up of only expressing the conservative side of my nature. There was another side of this equation. I wanted to kick back and do something unexpected for a change. I wasn't a natural risk-taker by any means, but confining myself to the play-it-safe role was restricting my life experiences to a fraction of what they could be. I was pretty certain that if I was brave enough to scratch beneath the surface, both ends of the spectrum existed within me.

We'd become inseparable almost overnight, so I didn't resist when Conor plucked me from my surroundings and transported me to a different world where wealth and sophistication reigned. My parents and friends were concerned that it was too much too soon. But for once, I didn't listen to the people who knew me best; I jumped in feet first, which came as a shock to everyone around me.

The time I spent with my new boyfriend was exciting, and I yearned for his attention. I couldn't get enough of him. Conor had such an easy way about him; he drew people towards him. Anyone who experienced his campaign of flattery first-hand would find him difficult to resist.

Although it was no secret I hadn't been planned – my parents being teenagers when I was born – I never doubted I was loved. My mum and dad always made me feel as though I was their top priority, no matter what else was going on in their lives. But recently, there'd been an unfamiliar distance between us. It was unsettling, and something told me that the gap might become too difficult for us to fill if I wasn't careful.

The hands of time moved slowly while I waited for Conor to come home, and the events of last night played heavily on my mind. I felt isolated and alone and was more convinced than ever that I needed to reach out to my parents before it was too late. We'd barely spoken since Conor and I had come back from Mexico.

The problem was, I felt awkward contacting them; lately, they seemed to disapprove of my actions and the choices I'd made. Their behaviour was alien to me, and I didn't know how to deal with it. I'd always been obsessed with the way people viewed me; I knew it wasn't a good way to be. It played havoc with my positivity. But these people weren't random strangers; they were my parents, so I should be able to turn to them without fear of being judged. Instead of distancing myself from the people I loved, I should be building bridges.

'Hi, Mum. How are you?' I tried to make my voice sound breezy, but I wasn't sure I'd managed to pull it off.

'I'm fine, thank you. It's lovely to hear from you, Ella. I've been meaning to call you.'

Mum would never know how pleased I was to hear her say that. Realising it wasn't too late to put our hostility behind us brought a smile to my face. As we caught up on each other's lives, the conversation between us flowed easily. I let out a sigh of relief; I was so glad I'd taken the plunge and made contact now.

'Would you and Conor like to come over for dinner tomorrow night?' Mum asked as we were about to end the call.

'That would be lovely,' I replied, accepting the invitation without bothering to check with my boyfriend first. I couldn't help myself. Mum had offered me an olive branch, so I couldn't afford not to take it.

When Dad opened the front door the next evening, my face broke into a smile. He was dressed in a pale grey shirt and smart black trousers. That was very out of character for him. But this was the first time Conor had been to my parents' flat, and Dad clearly wanted to make a good impression. I couldn't help wondering if it was my mum's idea, though, knowing that my dad wasn't easily parted from his jogging bottoms and oversized T-shirts.

'You scrub up well,' I said, kissing Dad on the cheek.

'You don't look so bad yourself, stranger,' Dad replied, giving me a sheepish grin. 'Come on in; your mum's in the kitchen.' Dad shook Conor's free hand and ushered him into the front room.

'Nice to see you again, Scott. I've brought some supplies,' Conor said, handing Dad the crate of Stella Artois he had tucked under his arm.

'We'd best get that open then, hadn't we?' Dad chuckled.

Mum was crouched down, peering into the oven when I walked into the room. The mouth-watering smell of chicken wafted up my nostrils. Mum stood up and then untied her apron before lifting it over her head. She was wearing a bright red jersey dress, which flattered her slim figure and looked stunning against her dark brown shoulder-length hair.

'Something smells good.' Unlike me, who couldn't boil an egg, Mum was an excellent cook, so whatever we were having was going to be delicious.

'I thought I'd keep it simple and do chicken with all the trimmings.'

My eyes widened. That might seem simple to Mum, but I wouldn't know where to start!

'You can't go wrong with a roast, can you? It's nearly ready now, so I hope you're hungry.'

'I'm starving!'

'That's what I like to hear.' Mum smiled.

Conor and I had stopped off at the florist to pick up a large mixed bouquet. 'This is for you,' I said, holding it towards her.

Mum's hands flew up to her chest, and her mouth dropped open before she took the flowers from me. 'They're absolutely beautiful, but you shouldn't have,' Mum said as her eyes scanned over the hot pink and orange flower arrangement.

'You look lovely,' I said as I went to kiss her.

Mum threw her arms around me and held me close. 'So do you, darling,' she replied, placing a kiss on the side of my head. Mum loosened her grip on me but held on to my hands so that she could look at me at arm's length. 'I'm so glad you're here. I've missed you so much, Ella.'

I noticed tears glistening in Mum's eyes before she turned away and a pang of guilt stabbed at my heart.

'I pushed the boat out and got us a lovely bottle of plonk from Sainsbury's, as it's a special occasion. Can we have a drum roll, please?' Mum grinned, then she opened the fridge and took out the cut-glass bottle of Freixenet Italian Rosé. 'I don't know what it tastes like, but the bottle's gorgeous, isn't it? It's almost too nice to open.'

'Thank you for the lovely meal, Joanne. You're an excellent cook,' Conor said as he polished off the remains of his homemade sticky toffee pudding.

'You're welcome.' Mum smiled as she started clearing the plates away.

'I'll give you a hand,' I said.

'It's been lovely spending time with the two of you,' Mum said, squirting Fairy Liquid into the sink as it was filling with water. 'Dad and I had a long chat about the situation, and we've realised we're smothering you, and if we don't loosen the apron strings and give you some space, we're going to end up losing you.' Mum's eyes glazed over before she continued to speak. 'There's no way either of us is prepared for that to happen. It's hard to let go, but we have to let you find your independence and try different experiences.' Mum smiled as she handed me a plate to dry.

'I'm so glad you said that. And I'm not trying to hurt you by doing things you don't agree with, but I need the freedom to choose my own direction in life, even if I end up regretting it at a later stage. I know the decisions I make today could affect the events that happen further down the line.'

'We understand that. We're sorry we had words about you going on holiday. It was none of our business, and we should have been more supportive. Dad and I know only too well what it feels like when people interfere.' Mum offered me a guilty smile and handed me another plate, then took her hands out of the sink and dried them on a towel.

'I'm sorry too. I didn't want it to cause a rift between us. I hate being on bad terms. Not being able to pop over or pick up the phone to you is torture.' I smiled and locked eyes with my mum.

'I feel the same way. I've been desperate to call you too, but I was scared I might push you away.' Tears suddenly tumbled down Mum's cheeks, and she wiped them away with the back of her hand. 'Anyway, life's too short to hold grudges, so let's learn from this and put it behind us,' Mum replied.

So I'd misjudged the situation; my parents hadn't turned their backs on me – they were just giving me space to grow. Which was what I'd wanted, wasn't it? Listening to my mum explain their side of the story made me realise how difficult things had been for them. My parents had struggled to adjust to letting go, which had made them come across as interfering, making me more determined to push against them and the path they wanted me to follow.

The last few months had been a learning curve for all of us. As a family, we'd never experienced such a turbulent time before, but we were all at fault; none of us had gone about things very well, and we had almost damaged our relationship beyond repair. Our breakdown in communications could have had serious implications if we hadn't cleared the air. I wished I'd reached out to them sooner now, instead of bottling up my concerns. No good came of keeping things to yourself. After our chat, I felt a weight had been lifted. Mum and Dad had been frightened to contact me too, so I was glad I'd made the first move and achieved what I'd set out to do.

33

Conor

Leo had taken advantage of the lack of leadership after Bobby Parker's death, and now that his old rival was out of the picture, Leo had begun running Bobby's turf. He was gobbling up all of the local competition, and his firm had rapidly risen up the ranks. Leo's interest in me hadn't waned, and he wanted me to join his ever-expanding empire. This time as his right-hand man, but I'd had enough of taking orders years ago, so I wasn't about to go back to it for any amount of money. I needed to keep him on side, though, for my own safety. Now that I knew what the man was capable of, I'd rather have him as a friend than an enemy.

The shooter responsible for Bobby and his driver's murders disappeared the day after he'd blasted holes into them at point-blank range. The guy was last seen getting into a van and appeared to vanish into thin air. The word on the street was that the gunman was dead, a fact that Leo was only too happy to confirm. His newfound status seemed to have gone to his head. He was knocking people off like an actor on the set of an old spaghetti western.

'The fucker was a liability, so I had to do away with him,' Leo said. He fingered the large mole on his left cheek while he waited for me to respond.

'That's fair enough,' I replied with a shrug of my shoulders.

'The bloke was a heroin addict and a bit of a loose cannon. That's not a good combination.' Leo laughed.

'Sounds like a lethal one,' I agreed.

'I couldn't trust the bloke not to start shooting his mouth off, so he had to go,' Leo explained as if to justify his actions.

That was the way things worked. It was a simple case of trimming the dead wood; now that the man had carried out the gangland slaying, he was no longer useful and needed to be eliminated from the equation before he could do any damage.

I wasn't surprised Leo was worried the junkie might implicate him in the murder. Scum like that would do anything for their next fix. It was widely believed that, like many an underworld victim before him, Leo's marksman was now buried under some building works, never to be seen or heard from again.

'Did you have him laid to rest in some foundations?' I asked, curiosity getting the better of me.

Leo grinned. 'How did you guess?'

All the talk of disposing of human remains prompted me to have a sudden flashback to a time before I got involved in this game. Roy and I were on our way to pick up some dodgy gear that he was going to flog on his market stall when we witnessed two men running away from the scene of a burnt-out car.

I'd been eating dinner in front of the TV that night when the incident came on the news. Firefighters had pulled two bodies from the wreckage of a vehicle abandoned on a deserted industrial estate on the Thames Estuary. Both victims had been shot dead before their car was set alight. The police were appealing for the public's help – but I knew, without even having to be told, that Roy and I wouldn't be volunteering any information. People like us put as much distance as possible between ourselves and the cops.

After listening to the grisly report, I lost my appetite for my Iceland ready meal, not that it was that palatable in the first place. As an impressionable young man, the memory of that day stayed with me for the longest time, but it taught me a valuable lesson: silence was golden.

'I have to go to Spain in a couple of days, on business. Do you want to come with me?' I asked Ella when we sat down to eat the chicken madras and basmati rice I'd rustled up.

'Is that even a question you need to ask?' Ella replied. She looked up from her plate and flashed me her beautiful smile.

'Now that you're back on good terms with your mum and dad, I thought you might want to stay behind.'

Ella's eyes grew wide. 'Well, you thought wrong, Mr Baxter.'

Apart from the obvious risks involved, selling drugs was an easy way to make a living. I was raking in so much money I had to hide the stash all over my house. I didn't want to draw attention to the extent of my operation by spending too much at any one time.

I was lounging on the L-shaped sofa with a beer in hand while Ella was soaking the day away in a bathful of scented bubbles when something caught my attention. I was pretty sure there was a prowler in the garden again. I'd done some research on the internet and knew there'd been a spate of robberies in recent weeks. No doubt the uninvited guest suspected I kept cash in my house. What they probably didn't realise was that I also had a large supply of coke hidden on the premises. It was time to teach this fucker a lesson they wouldn't forget in a hurry.

Armed with my steel cosh, I crept out of the house and took up position in my driveway on the other side of my gate. Thanks to my smart-home technology, I was able to switch the lights on all over the house remotely. As soon as the rooms lit up, I heard the sound of scurrying feet.

When the burglar landed with a thud next to me, I grabbed him by the back of his hoodie, pulled him upright and spun him around to face me. He hadn't even noticed I was there until we stood toe to toe. He dropped the crowbar he was gripping, and held his hand up in front of his face.

'You don't give up, do you?' I shouted as I squared up to the scruffy-looking bloke who was wearing a balaclava. He was dressed all in black with the hood on his jacket worn up. 'This is the third time you've tried to break into my house, but get this through your thick skull, it's going to be the last.' I was about to belt seven bells of shit out of the bastard with my cosh when the hooded man spoke.

'Wait, Conor, it's me,' he slurred as he tried to extract

himself from his face covering. His gloved hands scrabbled at the fabric, but he kept losing his grip.

Even though the man's features were still concealed, I'd recognise that voice anywhere. 'What the fuck do you think you're doing, Roy? You deserve a good hiding for trying to break into my house, you lowlife scrote.'

When he finally managed to free himself, Roy rocked on his feet and looked at me with a glazed expression on his face. He was either stoned or pissed; knowing him, he was probably both.

'I'm sorry, mate. I've been a bit down on my luck recently. Since Bobby went to meet his maker, I've lost some of my regular income, and I'm desperate for money.'

'So you thought you'd steal from me.' I shook my head as I looked at the waste of space standing in front of me. That excuse didn't wash with me. Bobby wasn't in the ground when the first attempt was made on my house.

'I left your house until last,' Roy replied, as though that was some kind of compensation.

'That was good of you.' I felt like telling him he'd scared my girlfriend half to death with his pathetic attempt at breaking and entering, but I didn't want to give him the satisfaction. It was better to keep Ella out of the conversation, in case I put ideas in his head. He was the type of man who would do anything for money. I put my hand in my pocket and tossed him a twenty-pound note. 'Now get out of my sight and don't come back here again. If you ever try and pull a stunt like this again, I won't be as generous.' I swung the steel baton backwards and forwards, catching it in the palm of my hand to drive the point home, so my mum's ex was in no doubt that if he darkened my doorstep again, he wouldn't be walking away without being physically harmed.

'I promise I won't. You have my word, Conor,' Roy said as he bent down and scrambled to pick up the note blowing around at his feet.

Roy's word was as good as nothing, but I was certain he'd take my threat seriously. Now that I'd caught him out, Roy knew better than to try and cross me again. I wasn't a brawler by any means, but if somebody I cared about was put at risk, it brought out my protective side. It wasn't in my nature to back down; I'd earned a fearsome reputation from my days as an enforcer. I'd just given Roy a little reminder of what was in store for him if he went back on our agreement.

Ella's dark, glossy hair was piled on top of her head when she reappeared from the bathroom. She walked across the floor with a towel wrapped around her, hiding her killer curves. I didn't tell her that while she was soaking in the tub, we'd had another visit from our nocturnal visitor – it would have scared her unnecessarily, and that was the last thing I wanted to do.

34

Ella

Conor's work was erratic. It was all or nothing. I sometimes wondered how he managed to maintain his extravagant lifestyle when he only worked for a matter of days out of an average month. On the plus side, we got to spend loads of time together, now that I'd broken up from uni for the Christmas break.

It was mid-December, but the sky was as blue as in mid-July when we arrived at Conor's six-bedroomed three-storey villa. It was only the second time we'd been here, but everything seemed so familiar. I opened the door of the rental car and stepped out onto the driveway. It might have looked like a summer's day, but the fresh breeze coming off the Atlantic Ocean hit me full force, whipping my hair around my head.

We'd been chilling after the journey when Conor's phone rang; he got up from the sofa, walked over to the bi-fold doors, slid back the glass panel and stepped out into the garden. Although he had every right to have a private conversation, the fact that he took himself off every time his mobile rang made me feel like he didn't trust me. Was that a reasonable doubt?

I watched Conor as he walked backwards and forwards in front of the pool with a serious look pasted on his handsome face, engrossed in the conversation. His body language was telling me it was something important. Why wouldn't he take calls in front of me? What was he trying to hide? Was I blowing things out of proportion, or should I confront him about it? Jumping to the conclusion that he was hiding something from me probably spoke more about my level of trust than anything.

I didn't want to turn into one of those whiney girlfriends who complained every two minutes about something when I really had nothing to grumble about. Most people never got to experience the kind of lifestyle I was living, so I should be grateful that Conor had given me this opportunity; he treated me so well. I had a lot to be thankful for, so why did I have this nagging doubt that everything wasn't as rosy as it seemed?

I tried to stop myself from overthinking the situation while I waited for Conor to return. It was a beautiful, bright, sunny day, but the wind was blowing a gale, so unlike the last time we visited, strolling hand in hand along the nearby picture-postcard beaches wasn't going to be an option. What else could we do to fill in the rest of the afternoon? Conor slid open the patio doors, and the sound broke my train of thought.

'Sorry about that,' Conor said, waving his mobile at me.

There was my opportunity to confront him, but instead of speaking up, I replied, 'No problem.' What the hell was the matter with me? Why was I so scared to question him? Was I frightened I wouldn't like what he was hiding?

'I've got to slip out and meet a business associate in a little while. I won't be long.'

That made me see red; we'd only just arrived, and he was doing a disappearing act without giving me any details. The words were out of my mouth before I could stop them. 'Something's bothering me, and I need to get it off my chest. Why do you always leave the room when your phone rings?'

'I don't,' Conor lied. He seemed genuinely confused that I found his actions concerning.

'Yes, you do. What's the matter? Don't you trust me?' I fixed my eyes on Conor, and although he was trying to play it cool, if I wasn't mistaken, he was squirming ever so slightly.

'Of course I trust you.'

'So what's with all the secrecy? What are you hiding from me?' I wasn't trying to poke my nose into his personal life, but his behaviour was making me feel edgy and insecure, and now I was acting like I was a paranoid crazy person.

'I'm not hiding anything from you. Trust me, Ella, you're overreacting. I was just taking a work call and stepped outside so that I could give it my full attention. I feel bad that I've got to go out, but I shouldn't be too long. And when I get back, I'll make it up to you.'

Conor placed his hands on the back of the sofa, either side of my head, and fixed me with his blue diamonds. He'd offered me a logical explanation, so who was I to doubt it?

'Will you be all right on your own?'

Conor knew I didn't like being alone at his Highgate house, but that was because we'd had an intruder in the garden, so it wasn't that surprising. Nothing bad had happened here though. The villa was tucked away from prying eyes near a sleepy little village, and I felt safe here; I had no reason to be nervous.

'I'll be fine.' I smiled. 'I'll no doubt find something to entertain myself with.' Watching Spanish TV would be a good way to hone my language skills and pass the time. 'I might even brave the pool!'

Conor raised his eyebrows. 'That will be lovely! I didn't know you were into cold water conditioning. I hear it's a great way to boost your energy levels and improve mental concentration, but it sounds like pure torture to me.'

'That's because you're a wimp.' I laughed.

'Oh, I am, am I?' Conor had a glint in his eye as he tickled me.

'Stop... stop...' I protested between bouts of laughter. I couldn't take any more.

'So, Isabella, do you still think I'm a wimp?' Conor said as he lifted me off the sofa and carried me off to the bedroom.

35

Conor

Ella had taken me by surprise when she'd grilled me about the phone calls I took in private. She didn't have any solid evidence to base her suspicions on, so I hoped I'd managed to bluff my way out of the sticky situation. Since we'd been a couple, I'd become an expert at skirting the subject of exactly how I made a living, but I'd have to be careful now that she'd voiced her concerns. I didn't even want to consider what the consequences might be if Ella found out my secret, but I was scared that if she knew the truth, I might lose her.

Diego wanted me to experience the thrill of the handover first-hand. So, he suggested I joined the crew on the speedboat when they went out to meet the fishing boat carrying our latest shipment.

'It will be a great experience for you,' Diego said as we watched the men preparing the boat.

It would be interesting to see how the operation worked, but I felt a little uneasy going out on the water in this weather, which surprised me as I didn't have myself down as a fair-weather sailor.

'Don't the guys wear lifejackets?' I questioned as his men got into position and beckoned me towards them.

'Lifejackets are for pussies.' Diego laughed. A sudden gust of wind lifted his long grey hair, and it swirled around him.

'You're joking, right?' I was beginning to realise Diego had a strange sense of humour.

'Don't look so worried; you'll be in safe hands. My men will look after you. They are expert navigators.'

I usually loved the sea, so I never thought I would be nervous going out on the open water in a small vessel, but I hadn't experienced the might of the Atlantic Ocean in such close proximity before. As we headed away from the beach, the grey roiling sea unleashed its fury, tossing our powerful craft around like a leaf in a hurricane.

I glanced over my shoulder as Diego slowly began to fade into the distance. Considering the speedboat could outrun any pursuers, it was struggling to make progress through the choppy ocean. As the inky-black water lashed at the side of the boat and the icy-cold spray stung the skin on my face, I wished I'd bottled the endurance test I'd unwittingly been entered in. It wasn't as though the weather had caught us out; we'd knowingly gone out in the gale-force winds capable of rolling a boat over.

When Diego had told me his crew went out in extreme conditions to reduce the chance of getting caught, I hadn't given it too much thought. But then his words swam around in my head. He'd found it amusing that this area was called the coast of death and that many people had drowned here. As I gripped onto the fibreglass edge while our boat bounced off the water, for the life of me, I couldn't see what was funny about that.

The fishing boat was in sight. Thankfully we hadn't had to travel all the way to Cape Verde; the handover of the drugs was taking place in local fishing waters to avoid detection. Our skipper shut down several of the engines to allow us to drop speed before he drew the craft alongside the trawler and did his best to hold the speedboat steady as the crew lowered black holdalls over the side of the vessel. One of Diego's men untied the rope, and it was pulled back on board. I was sure the process would have been simple enough if the elements hadn't been battering us.

Once the last bag was on board, the skipper opened up the throttle, and we headed back to shore while the waves crashed down around us. The light was beginning to fade by the time we made it to safety. I couldn't have been happier to get back onto dry land and away from the storm-tossed sea. I'd somehow managed not to get seasick even though I'd felt green around the gills for the entire journey. The contents of my stomach had been spinning around like clothes in a washing machine.

'Did you enjoy the ride?' Diego asked as I walked towards him on jelly legs.

'I wouldn't go as far as saying I enjoyed it, but it was character building.'

Diego laughed, then slapped me on the back. The motion was too much for my fragile insides to cope with after the terrifying experience, and before I could stop myself, I threw up all over the sand. I wiped my mouth on the back of my saltwater-encrusted hand, wishing I had something to take away the sour aftertaste of vomit.

I couldn't wait to get back to the villa and hold Ella in my arms. I'd had a horrible feeling I was never going to see her again. As we'd been tossed around the unruly sea, I'd kept picturing her beautiful face. I'd wondered if I'd ever get the chance to kiss her lips again, scared that our lives together would be over before they'd really begun. I couldn't bear the thought of that. Ella meant the world to me; she'd taught me how to love.

Every agonising second I was on the speedboat, I'd thought the ocean was going to claim it, and myself and the crew would perish. How did Diego's men willingly put themselves through an experience like that just to earn a living? I couldn't get my head around it. My part of the deal was dangerous but in an entirely different way.

36

Ella

'Thank God you're back; I was starting to get worried,' I said when Conor finally walked through the front door.

'I'm sorry I've been gone a while; the meeting took longer than expected,' Conor replied.

'Is it raining?' I asked.

'No, it's just blowing a gale,' Conor replied.

'Why are you soaking wet?'

Conor looked like a drowned rat. His black bomber jacket and jeans were dripping wet.

'It's a long story,' he replied.

This was another example of my boyfriend refusing to elaborate when I asked him a question he didn't want to answer, but after our earlier conversation, my patience was wearing thin. I was more certain than ever that he was hiding something from me.

'Luckily for you, I've got plenty of time to hear it.'

I wasn't about to be fobbed off, so I followed my boyfriend into the bedroom.

'I'll tell you what happened after I get out of these wet clothes,' Conor said.

I sat on the edge of the bed, studying my boyfriend's well-defined muscles while he stripped off his jeans and long-sleeved shirt that was clinging on to him for dear life. Conor walked into the en-suite and peeled off his Calvin Kleins. As they dropped to the floor, I stole a glimpse of his naked torso before he dried himself on an extra-large bath sheet. After he put on some boxers, trackies and a sweatshirt, he took hold of my hand and led me into the living area.

'My client thought it would be a good idea to take me along the coast in a speedboat for a spot of sightseeing.' Conor laughed.

'That would've been a lovely idea on a nice day, but in this weather?'

Conor didn't reply, and that signalled the end of our conversation. I didn't want to get into an argument with him, so I decided not to probe any further, even though his excuse sounded fishy to me. I tried not to dwell on it, but I couldn't help feeling upset that he'd robbed me of a decent explanation. I so desperately wanted him to be able to open up and trust me.

Conor and I walked hand in hand into a beautiful beachfront hotel. He'd made a reservation for us to have dinner to apologise for leaving me home alone for hours. As we were being shown to our table on the covered terrace, a man with long grey hair and weather-beaten skin beckoned us towards him. He was sitting towards the back of the restaurant with a glamorous-looking older woman and a dark-haired man with the bushiest sideburns I'd ever seen.

'You're looking a lot better than you did a couple of hours ago,' the grey-haired man said.

I quickly put two and two together and realised this must have been the client Conor had gone to see.

'I hope it's nothing serious,' the lady with the dark red lipstick said. She had a strong Spanish accent, and I couldn't help feeling her behaviour was slightly inappropriate as her dark brown eyes took in every inch of my boyfriend. 'I didn't realise you'd been unwell, darling.'

That was news to me too, so I glanced up at Conor with a questioning look on my face. He shifted from foot to foot, appearing awkward in the people's company, but he didn't offer me an explanation.

'I sent Conor out with the crew on the speedboat this afternoon so that he could witness the handover, but the sea was a little bit lively,' the grey-haired man said in Spanish when my boyfriend failed to reply.

The black-haired man with the thick moustache and bushy sideburns nodded. 'No wonder he was ill.' He laughed.

I was glad somebody had provided clarity, as I was still completely in the dark. Conor told me he'd gone sightseeing. At the time, I'd thought that was odd, but when I'd questioned him about it, he'd fobbed me off. He hadn't mentioned witnessing a handover. A handover of what? I had no idea what they were talking about, but the one thing I did know was that my boyfriend was lying to me, which was painful to accept. What I hadn't worked out at this stage was why.

'I trust you were impressed by our operation?' The lady leaned back in her chair and crossed her arms over her chest. Her manicured fingers drummed against the tops of her arms as she fixed Conor with her heavily made-up eyes.

Conor had suddenly become mute. I watched with interest while he did the smile-and-nod routine, scared to say anything in case he made the situation worse. But it was as plain as the nose on his face that he was hiding something from me and was desperate to put an end to this chance encounter before he dropped himself in it.

'I'm Diego Gómez. This is my cousin, Pedro and his wife, Valentina.' The grey-haired man smiled as he pointed towards the other people sat around the table. 'You haven't introduced us to your charming companion, Conor.'

'My name's Isabella, but everyone calls me Ella,' I piped up as Conor seemed lost for words.

'It's been a pleasure to meet you, Ella,' Diego said as Conor led me away from the table.

'Likewise,' I replied over my shoulder.

Conor picked up his menu and pretended to be engrossed in it, but I could tell he was just scanning through it to avoid an awkward conversation.

'What was all that about?' I asked, but Conor kept his eyes glued on the pages. 'Diego said you went out with the crew to witness the handover.'

Conor's beautiful blue eyes found mine. 'I don't want to discuss this now. Let's enjoy our meal, and we can talk about it later.'

I got the distinct impression my boyfriend was trying to buy himself some time. If everything had been innocent, he wouldn't have needed to do that, would he? At the back of my mind, I had an inkling that Conor made his living from something illegal; he was always too private, too guarded when it came to discussing his work. Unlike most young self-made men, bragging would never prove to be Conor's downfall. He preferred to keep me out of the business side of his life. The only part he exposed me to were the incredible benefits of his luxury lifestyle.

We'd had a lovely three-course meal, but after our encounter with Diego, Pedro and Valentina, a tense atmosphere had settled around Conor and myself. The only way it was going to lift was by talking things through. I wasn't sure that would happen; my boyfriend had always been cagey about his business dealings. But if his work was legitimate, what did he have to hide?

He seemed on edge about something. I'd considered questioning him about it once we were in the car on our way back to the villa, but that would more than likely make him clam up. I knew Conor well enough by now to realise he wasn't going to open up and talk to me until he was good and ready. It looked as though things weren't as clear-cut and rosy as they'd once appeared.

Conor and I were sitting at opposite ends of the sofa like bookends, with a nightcap in hand. He edged along the black leather towards me and took hold of my hand.

'I haven't been completely honest with you,' he began, fixing me with his mesmerising blue eyes.

I'd managed to work that much out for myself, but I said nothing. I didn't want to interrupt Conor in case the conversation went off on a tangent before he'd had a chance to elaborate.

'I am involved in distribution…' Conor paused as if he was trying to find the right words.

I sensed there was a *but* coming, so I squeezed his hand to offer him some encouragement.

'But I don't handle IT equipment.'

There it was, the dreaded *but*. Although Conor had confirmed he hadn't made his fortune in technology, he'd omitted to mention what line of work he was in. I'd hoped the alcohol might have loosened his tongue, but getting my boyfriend to open up to me was like pulling teeth.

'So what exactly do you distribute?' Up until now, I hadn't asked questions about how Conor earned a crust. But that was about to change. For my own sanity, I needed to know what was going on. I knew he was hiding stuff from me, and I was fed up of being kept in the dark.

Conor exhaled loudly, and I wondered if it was for my benefit. He no doubt wanted me to know he wasn't finding this easy. 'I distribute cocaine,' my boyfriend said after a long pause.

My heart pounded in my chest. Conor locked eyes with me and watched my reaction. As his words began to sink in, I struggled to accept what I'd just heard. I didn't want to believe that someone I cared about so deeply had been lying to me since the beginning of our relationship. I'd placed my trust in him, and he'd just blown that to pieces. His revelation changed everything. It suddenly dawned on me that Conor wasn't the man I thought he was. He was a dishonest, shady character hiding behind the veneer of a well-groomed businessman, and the thought of that horrified me.

'I wasn't intentionally cutting you out of the picture, but

the reason I kept quiet was I thought you'd run a mile if you knew the truth. I'm sure you understand why I was hoping to keep my profession a secret,' Conor said, and his voice brought me back to reality. 'I shouldn't have lied, but I was trying to protect you; I didn't want you to get involved.'

'Well, it's too late for that! You should have been honest with me from the beginning. I knew you were hiding something from me. I could sense it. But I had no idea it was something as serious as this.'

'So where does that leave us? Do you still want to be my girlfriend now that you know the truth?'

'I don't know, Conor. I need some time to digest this.'

A million things were whirring around in my head. Conor's question had blindsided me because I didn't have the faintest idea what the consequences of being a drug distributor's girlfriend might be. What would my parents think if they knew the truth? I guessed they would be as shocked as I was; Conor had duped all of us. He was easy on the eye and had a charming way about him; I would never have thought he was a drug distributor. He didn't fit the profile of the guys who hung around our estate pushing spliffs and bags of pills.

I'd grown up protected from the darker side of the estate I lived on. Half of it was dominated by hooded teenagers who openly took drugs and left discarded needles everywhere. And the other half was made up of people, like my parents, who were law-abiding citizens who worked hard for a living. I'd seen what addiction could do to a person, and from an early age, I'd known which side of the fence to stay on to avoid getting into trouble. That was until Conor Baxter waltzed into my life, and I'd allowed myself to be seduced not just by him but also by his lifestyle. This was a wake-up call; it wasn't the perfect fantasy I'd imagined, and the realisation of that made me feel stupid and naïve. I wasn't sure I was as mature as everyone thought. Now that I was left to my own devices, I didn't want to make hard adult decisions.

Conor dropped to his knees in front of me and took hold of my hands. 'Don't shut me out, Ella. Tell me how you're feeling and what's going through your head.'

'That's rich coming from you,' I shouted, pulling my hands out of his grip. 'If you hadn't clammed up every time I tried to question you, we wouldn't be in this mess now. You've been lying to me for months, Conor. How do you think that makes me feel?' Tears of frustration and rage sprang from my eyes, and I swiped them away.

'I'm so sorry. I wish I'd told you sooner. Believe me, I wanted to, but I was scared you wouldn't want to be with me if you knew the truth. I love you, Ella. I can't bear the thought of losing you.' Conor looked into my eyes as a tear slid down his cheek.

'How can we possibly stay together? Our whole relationship has been built on secrets and lies. You've ruined everything.'

I stomped out of the room and up the stairs. I couldn't bear to look at Conor and needed to put some distance between us. I had a lot of thinking to do. Why did life have to be so complicated? I'd thought Conor was my perfect match; our romance had blossomed quickly, and we'd been on a crazy adventure. I'd loved being swept away by the tidal wave. But now the truth had come out, the undertow of insecurity and doubt was pulling me down. The sense of betrayal was all-consuming, and I couldn't see a way out for us, which was devastating.

Conor was my whole world, and I loved him more than I could say. I didn't want to face the future without him, but if we stayed together, I'd have to go against everything I believed in. I was a self-confessed rule-follower and good girl, so accepting that my boyfriend made his living from coke distribution wasn't going to be easy. Even if I turned a blind eye and didn't get my hands dirty, I'd be guilty by association.

I spent a restless night mulling things over. If we hadn't bumped into Diego earlier, I very much doubted Conor would have come clean, and that wasn't easy to come to terms with. Nobody liked being lied to, did they? If we didn't have trust, we had nothing.

I felt like I'd suddenly been catapulted into a grown-up world that I'd previously been entirely sheltered from, and I wasn't sure I felt equipped to deal with it. I'd always taken the safe bet; I didn't take risks. I was a people-pleaser, but that didn't mean I was going to let Conor seduce me from my straight path into the underworld. I genuinely didn't know what to do. Should I follow my head or my heart?

'I'm so sorry, Ella. I should have been honest with you from the start. Please forgive me,' Conor said when I walked into the kitchen in the morning.

His beautiful eyes were red-rimmed, and he looked like a broken man. There was a vulnerability about him that I'd never seen before; it was something he would usually hide at all costs. In my eyes, that went some way to redeem the mistakes he'd made. It showed me that he was letting his guard down and finally letting me inside. Maybe we would be able to rebuild the trust if we tried hard enough. I felt compelled to give him one more chance; the pull towards Conor was too strong for me to resist.

'This probably sounds like a pathetic excuse, but the longer I kept what I did for a living secret, the harder it was to come clean about it.' Conor cast his eyes to the floor.

I understood that logic, but it didn't make it right. Now that I knew what Conor had been hiding, it explained a lot of things. He was extremely suspicious of people he didn't know and could be incredibly paranoid. He only ever answered phone calls to numbers he could positively identify and hated having anyone in his home. In hindsight, ignorance was bliss. Now everything was out in the open; there was no going back. Part of me wished I was still clueless as to what was going on.

'I love you so much. Please don't leave me, Ella.' Conor stepped towards me and wrapped his arms around me.

I was too emotionally invested in him to walk away now. I was genuinely infatuated by him. 'If I stay, you need to be one hundred per cent straight with me from now on; no more secrets and no more lies.'

'You have my word,' Conor replied.

I had a feeling I was about to kiss my carefree existence goodbye, but instead of being frightened by the danger Conor's way of life would inevitably bring, I was starting to feel intrigued by it.

37

Conor

Being with Ella made me feel like a better man; she brought out a side of me that I liked. But I'd almost lost the woman of my dreams because of my own stupidity. I should have been honest with Ella from the start, but my issues were deep-rooted. My mum had a lot to answer for; so many of my problems stemmed from my unstable childhood. The inability to trust became woven into the fabric of who you were from an early age, and in my experience, it emerged at different points depending on the situation. I was too scared to let my guard down, especially to those closest to me; that would make me vulnerable and susceptible to being hurt. But if I didn't learn to open up to Ella, our relationship was doomed. She'd agreed to give me another chance, so I couldn't afford to fuck it up.

A high-ranking military official had accompanied the latest shipment from Guinea-Bissau, which added fuel to the rumour that the country's ruling party was directly involved in drug smuggling.

'Conor, this is Rodrigo Almada,' Diego said. 'Unfortunately, he doesn't speak English.'

I recognised him instantly. Rodrigo was directing the crew onboard the fishing boat when they offloaded the cocaine yesterday. I smiled as I shook his hand, but the man, dressed in full uniform, seemed uninterested to meet me.

Diego explained that the cocaine they imported from Guinea-Bissau was grown in South America. Rodrigo, moonlighting from his day job, had volunteered to oversee the coke's smooth transfer and guarantee its safe passage following a tip-off that armed pirates were patrolling the waters looking for cargo to loot or a vessel to hijack.

When he wasn't protecting his country, Rodrigo controlled the shores situated in an ideal location for drug smuggling; lying close to where the Geba River met the Atlantic Ocean. Because of the threat posed by the pirates, he was keen to discuss alternative delivery arrangements with the cartel. I wanted to be part of the talks, as the outcome directly affected my part in the supply chain.

More often than not, I was out of my depth when I was in the cartel's company. The language barrier was proving to be a real issue. Today's meeting had been particularly stressful. The conversation between the Spanish speakers had carried on without my input because I couldn't understand a word they were talking about.

While I was meeting my business partners, Ella would either chill out at the villa or sometimes she'd jump on a bus and go shopping in one of the towns dotted along the coast. I knew she got bored when she was on her own killing time, and I felt guilty about that. As I was driving back to my villa, an idea suddenly came to me. Once I got home,

I'd speak to Ella and see what her thoughts were on the matter.

'How did the meeting go?' Ella asked when I walked into the kitchen and kissed her on the cheek.

I let out a loud sigh. 'Not good,' I replied, shrugging off my jacket and hanging it over the back of a chair.

'Why? What happened?'

'There was some high-ranking official there who couldn't speak English, so the cartel kept talking in Spanish; I've no idea what they discussed. Not being able to speak the language is a major disadvantage for me.'

'I could teach you,' Ella suggested.

That was a good idea, but it was a long-term goal. It wouldn't help me out of my current predicament. When we'd first met, Diego had tried to lead me to believe that the Gómez family had a poor grasp of the English language. I was well aware that they were a lot more proficient than he wanted me to realise. Although their accents were strong, Diego, Pedro and Valentina spoke English perfectly well, which left me with an unanswered question. Why had the cartel spent the entirety of the recent meeting speaking in their mother tongue? I'd felt excluded from the conversation, and that raised my suspicions.

During our previous dealings, I'd had to rely on Juan to translate certain aspects of the conversation. I was never one hundred per cent sure his interpretation was word-for-word accurate. But I'd had no option other than to go with it. Now that Ella knew what I did for a living, it had potentially opened up a different possibility.

'There's no problem if you don't want to, but I know you've always wanted to be an interpreter. How would you feel about coming with me to the next meeting to act as my translator?'

Ella initially looked taken aback by my suggestion, and her reply was filled with hesitation. 'Oh, I don't know about that. I'm not sure I want to get involved.'

'No problem. I wasn't trying to put you on the spot, but I feel out of my depth not being able to speak Spanish,' I replied, trying to keep the disappointment out of my voice.

'I'm not surprised.' Ella opened the fridge door and handed me a cold bottle of beer. 'You look stressed.'

'I am. The situation's frustrating me, but there's nothing I can do about it. Juan is meant to be translating for me when the cartel discusses things between themselves, but I don't know if he's telling me everything or holding back some of the information. I have a feeling he's giving me a watered-down version of the conversation.'

'You might be right. I feel bad for you. If I went with you, do you think I'd be out of my depth?'

I wasn't trying to force Ella to do anything she wasn't comfortable with, but I was glad that she was at least considering my suggestion.

'I wouldn't have asked you if I'd thought you wouldn't be able to handle it.' Ella's safety was first and foremost in my mind. I wouldn't put her in a situation where I thought she'd be in danger. 'You've already met Diego, Pedro and Valentina, so you won't be walking into a room full of strangers, and I'll be right by your side.' I hoped that would reassure my girlfriend.

'OK, I'll give it a go.'

'Do you want to think about it and let me know tomorrow?'

'No. I might talk myself out of it. I feel a bit uneasy about becoming involved in the drugs trade, but you do so much for me, and I know you're struggling with the language barrier, so it's the least I can do.'

'Are you sure you don't mind?' My eyes scanned over my girlfriend's beautiful face, but her earlier hesitation seemed to have lifted.

'I'm not thrilled about committing a crime, but since I gave up my job, you've been paying for everything. I want to show you how much I appreciate you supporting me by going to the next meeting and acting as your translator,' Ella replied.

38

Ella

At first, Conor's idea had met with some resistance; all the dangers of getting involved with a drug cartel were foremost in my mind. My parents had tried to shield me from the dark side of the estate I grew up on; because it was denied to me, it had always fascinated me.

Conor's world represented danger, risk and intrigue. I'd spent my whole life playing goody two shoes; it was time I allowed my halo to slip. I felt safe with Conor; he made me feel invincible. So instead of being scared, I was excited by the prospect of my new role. I was a little fazed by the thought of being in the company of drug dealers, but Diego, Pedro and Valentina had seemed pleasant enough when I'd met them the other evening, so I was sure my concerns would come to nothing.

'Diego likes to conduct his business as a cloak-and-dagger affair, with the minimum amount of people in the room, so he could be offended if I ask to bring my own interpreter to the meetings. He might think I don't trust him. We'll need to play this smart and come up with a good strategy,' Conor said.

Because of the sensitive nature of the cartel's work, I understood why Diego would be reluctant to allow anyone but a select few around the negotiating table. Even though my presence would have been a perfect solution to Conor's problems, the Gómez family were going to take some convincing before they'd let me into their inner circle.

'I just called Diego and suggested he join us for breakfast tomorrow, and he's agreed.' Conor smiled, hoping the casual introduction might allow me to get a foot in the door.

'How are you enjoying your time in Spain?' Diego asked as he shielded his eyes from the bright winter sun.

'I love it. I'm studying languages at uni, so it's a fantastic opportunity for me to try out my Spanish,' I replied in his native tongue before taking a sip of my frothy coffee.

Thanks to the mild December weather, we'd opted to sit outside on the café's large terrace, which overlooked the sheltered, yacht-lined harbour and Baiona Marina. Diego explained to the waitress that we were tourists and asked her to bring us some of the café's specialities. Moments later, she appeared carrying a tray groaning with food. She placed plates packed full of assorted pastries, waffles and croissants with oozy cheese spilling from the sides onto the table.

As we engaged in general chit-chat, Diego seemed to be warming to me, unlike Valentina, who eyed me suspiciously. I wasn't sure why she had such a problem – unless she was worried I was going to uncover something they weren't sharing with Conor when I translated their conversations. Whatever it was, she had her barriers firmly in place as she sat on the opposite side of the table with her chihuahua tucked under her arm. Pedro only had eyes for the food. He rubbed his well-rounded belly before he helped himself to a portion of everything on the sharing platters. He then devoured a savoury croissant while his wife sat glaring at me as she stroked the top of her dog's tiny head with her red-tipped fingers.

Our breakfast introduction had gone well, and by the end of it, Diego had brushed aside Valentina's objections and agreed to allow me to sit in on the cartel's next meeting. I could see by the look on Valentina's face that he'd reached his decision on behalf of the Gómez family without consulting the other members. He hadn't tried to bring the rest of the cartel around to his way of thinking; he'd overruled them. There was no doubt about it, if it had been up to Valentina, I would have been left out in the cold and deprived of the eye-opening experience.

'I want to introduce a different delivery process while the threat of piracy is present,' Rodrigo said in Portuguese.

My pulse pounded in my temples; then my heart thumped as a wave of adrenaline washed over me. The situation was surreal; I was sitting around a table with a drug cartel while they discussed business.

'What I'm proposing is that we drop the cocaine off by private plane at a small airport on the outskirts of Marrakesh. My contact will then organise drug mules to transfer the shipment by land to northern Tunisia. Local smugglers could take the coke on its final leg to Europe by cargo ship,' Rodrigo continued.

'I'm not completely sold on the idea. There are too many links in the chain for my liking,' Diego replied in Spanish before rounding up the meeting.

I was able to translate several languages in the same conversation, so my skills were invaluable to Conor. I was pulling my weight for once instead of being a financial burden, and that gave me a real buzz.

'I can see why you felt out of your depth. Diego was speaking Spanish, and Rodrigo was answering him in Portuguese,' I said once we were in the car.

'I would never have realised that; the only thing I knew was that I couldn't understand a word they were saying.' Conor laughed. 'I thought you only spoke French and Spanish.' Conor looked at me with a puzzled expression on his face.

'I do, but Portuguese and Spanish are similar, so I was able to work out what he was saying,' I replied before filling Conor in on the details of the meeting.

'I'm not surprised Diego was hesitant. Except for some trusted outsiders, family members are responsible for all areas of the business. Instead of simplifying the process, Rodrigo Almada's complicating it,' Conor said.

'Rodrigo said he'd only agreed to accompany the latest consignment so that he could discuss the issue with the cartel. He told Diego that he was a high-ranking military official, so he couldn't just disappear from his post every time a ship set sail. But if he didn't oversee the coke's transfer, he couldn't guarantee its safe passage across the high-risk waters. Armed pirates regularly patrol the area looking for cargo to loot,' I said, brimming over with confidence that I'd been able to hold my own in Conor's complex world.

'Whether Diego likes it or not, importing the cocaine from Marrakesh might be the only viable option he has,' Conor said as he parked the car on the driveway of his villa. 'By the way, you were brilliant. Thanks for acting as my translator.'

'My pleasure.' I beamed, still hyped up and wired from the experience.

'If you hadn't come to the meeting, I wouldn't have had a clue what was going on.'

'I've never done anything so illicit before, and I was nervous at first, but once I got into the swing of things, it was thrilling.'

I was on a real high. I hadn't expected to feel a rush like this, and I suddenly questioned what lay beneath the excitement. Was I sweeping my doubts and fears under the carpet because I felt so fantastic at this precise moment?

'It would be a shame to waste all that pent-up energy,' Conor said, pulling me into his arms and kissing the side of my neck.

I closed my eyes and pictured the two of us falling into bed together. 'My thoughts exactly, Mr Baxter.'

39

Conor

Since Bobby had bled out on the pavement in front of me, it wasn't the first time it had crossed my mind that he might have had a spy in the camp. Somebody must have tipped Leo off to the whereabouts of his rival's safehouse, as the address of the terraced house in Stepney Green was a closely guarded secret.

Leo's desire to conquer the market hadn't waned while I'd been away. If anything, it had reached new heights. Now that he'd experienced the huge profits to be made selling coke, Leo had seized the opportunity to make his fortune and run with it. I saw a tendency to self-destruct in everyone I knew to one degree or another, and Leo's greed would be his downfall if he wasn't careful.

Both Leo and Bobby had been on the law enforcement radar since their early teens. Working their way up the criminal ladder, they progressed from petty crime to more lucrative enterprises. Now that he was the only one on the scene, Leo was keen to expand his clientele. The United

Kingdom was the third-largest consumer of cocaine in the world, and Leo had every intention of being one of the main distributors. The problem was Diego knew the best way to remain undetected by the authorities was to keep his operation as small as possible.

When I'd walked into Leo's grotty Portakabin, I'd done a double take. Stumpy was propping up the Formica sideboard next to the yellowing plastic kettle.

'Fancy seeing you here,' I said.

'A few things have changed around here since you've been away sunning yourself in the Costa del Sol,' Leo replied.

The fact that Galicia was in north-western Spain and nowhere near where Leo thought I'd been would be lost on him, so I didn't bother to correct his mistake. The man was an ignorant piece of shit. Leo wore the hallmarks of a misspent youth; he'd bunked off of school for most of his childhood, so it didn't particularly surprise me that his knowledge of Spain's geography was poor.

'Stumpy works for me now; isn't that right, mate?'

Leo grinned at the shaved-headed giant of a man with the bushy ginger beard.

'Aye,' Stumpy replied.

Leo's new employee was a man of few words, which was just as well as he sounded like he was speaking an entirely different language on the rare occasions he did strike up a conversation. He preferred to get his point across using his fists. If you so much as looked at him the wrong way, he'd rip your head off. No questions asked.

'Stumpy and I have made a gentleman's agreement. Now

that Bobby no longer requires his services, he's done the sensible thing and jumped ship.' Leo grinned and smoothed back his balding hair even further off his forehead, drawing attention to his widow's peak.

Bobby Parker would be turning in his grave if he knew that his main confidant was working for the enemy. The story could have ended very differently the day Bobby and his driver were slain in broad daylight in the middle of a residential street. If Stumpy hadn't been diverted to deal with an emergency, he would have been in the car alongside his former boss, and the chances were, he wouldn't have lived to tell the tale.

'So when's my latest shipment due to arrive?' Leo asked. He couldn't get his hands on enough product at the moment. He was ignoring the obvious risks involved; expansion was the only thing on his mind.

'Any day now,' I replied.

Diego's English-speaking migrant contacts, acting as couriers for the cartel, were due to arrive in Folkestone tonight. That was as long as the cocaine-loaded people carrier they were driving made it through the Channel Tunnel. I didn't want Leo to get wind of that. Otherwise, he'd be breathing down my neck, so I kept the information under wraps to buy myself some time.

'Why is your supplier so slow?' Leo's brown eyes bulged.

'I don't think he's slow, but he's thorough.'

Diego Gómez was a former police officer, and he did everything by the book. He paid out a small fortune so that his ex-colleagues looked the other way.

'By the time the gear gets here, I'll have run out of stock.

Get him to double the amount he sends us next time. On second thoughts, triple it.'

That was going to be a tall order. Diego deliberately kept his shipments small for good reason.

'I'll see what I can do, but don't hold me to it.'

'Listen, Conor, your supplier should be ripping your hand off for an order this size. If he's not up to the job, look for another one or I'll cut you out of the deal and buy my coke elsewhere.'

Leo had overstepped the mark, and his attitude was seriously testing my patience. He seemed to have conveniently forgotten the terms of our agreement. 'I name the terms of any deals we make, not you. But if you want to go elsewhere, that suits me fine.'

I couldn't wait to get out of this place; it made my skin crawl. I turned on my heel to go, but before I reached the door, I could hear Leo's footsteps behind me.

'Wait, Conor, I didn't mean it. I'm sorry I lost my rag, but your guy is seriously winding me up. Sort him out, will you, mate?'

It was at moments like this I felt I'd never escape the hooks that tied me to my past.

40

Ella

'I've got to drive down to Folkestone tonight to pick up the latest shipment,' Conor said.

'Can I go with you?'

'I don't think that's a good idea. If I get stopped by the cops, you'd be implicated by just being in the car with me.'

Conor was right, of course. What the hell was I thinking? It was a case of my mind telling me one thing and my heart telling me something else.

'I'm not staying down there, so traffic permitting, I'll be there and back in about four hours.'

Conor arrived back just before midnight. 'I'm shattered,' he said as he walked through the front door carrying two large black holdalls.

'Is the cocaine in there?'

'Yes. I've got to cut it before I can give it to the local dealer, but I'm too tired to do it now. Let's go up to bed.'

Conor walked into the larger of the two spare bedrooms at the front of the house, and I stood in the doorway watching him. I felt my eyes widen when he pushed what I'd thought was a fixed shelving unit, and it folded in half to reveal a hidden room. Since I'd seen the film *The Lion, the Witch and the Wardrobe*, I'd been fascinated by the idea of secret doors.

'That's so cool,' I said, crossing the room so that I could get a closer look. Now that my boyfriend's career was no longer under wraps, the trust had grown between us.

'It's great, isn't it? I've got compartments like this hidden all over the house.' Conor laughed. 'It's not as though I can put my money in the bank, is it?'

I supposed that was true; I hadn't given it much thought up until now. 'You've got more cash than the Bank of England.' There were piles of crisp fifty-pound notes stacked on top of each other in the corner of the room. I'd never seen so much money before.

Conor laughed again. 'Making money's the easy part; finding legitimate ways to spend it is more difficult.'

Conor placed the bags down and then slid the black bi-folding shelves back into place. They had been expertly made; the hinges and sliders were completely concealed to the untrained eye. If you hadn't known they were there, you wouldn't have noticed them in a million years.

'It's such a brilliant idea; you would never expect there to be a hidden compartment behind that unit.'

Now that I knew there were more of them, I was obsessed with finding the others. Not for any reason other than curiosity, so when Conor went out the next day, the first thing I did was go through all the rooms in the house looking for them. I would never have made a detective as I didn't manage to find any. It was time to get back to the job in hand – Conor and I were flying to Spain this afternoon, and I was meant to be packing. I opened the wardrobe door, took out my hard-shell Ted Baker cabin case and put it on the edge of the bed.

As I placed a few outfits onto the pale pink lining, it suddenly occurred to me why Conor didn't like inviting people over. I'd seen the huge piles of money he had stacked in secret compartments; it looked like he'd robbed a bank. Not that my friends or family would ever steal from him, but if you had cash and coke hidden all over your house, you were bound to be wary of others.

My parents might be hard up, but they had better morals than anyone I knew. They'd both worked hard all their lives in minimum-wage jobs but would give their last fiver away to help somebody out. I knew Conor respected my parents, but I felt a bit offended that he didn't trust them enough to have them in his house. He was a naturally suspicious person and thought people had a hidden agenda, but there was a time and a place for suspicion. For our relationship to flourish, he'd need to let go of the demons that haunted him; they were holding him back.

I'd decided to dress to impress and had put on an ivory lace top, a high-waisted pair of black trousers and black high-heeled Christian Louboutin court shoes with the iconic red sole. I wanted to make a good impression at the meeting so that all of the cartel members would take me seriously. The last time we'd come face to face, Valentina had barely tolerated my presence, so I was keen to try and win her over.

'You are looking radiant, my dear,' Diego said as he greeted me with a kiss on either cheek.

'Thank you,' I replied as I took my seat at the table next to Conor.

'Business is booming in London, so my client is keen to increase the size of his orders,' Conor said.

'I don't know how much you know about cocaine production. But the raw ingredient is coca leaf. The world's supply is grown in relatively few places.'

'What's with the history lesson?' Valentina piped up in Spanish.

'I want Conor to understand the background of the supply chain,' Diego replied in his mother tongue.

'Why do you have to keep interrupting? Let the man finish, Valentina,' Pedro added as they chatted away to each other like they were the only people in the room.

No wonder Conor got frustrated in the meetings. The family weren't displaying much professionalism by talking among themselves at the conference table when they knew he wouldn't be able to understand. It was the height of bad manners, especially as all of them were able to speak English.

Conor turned to face me, and I discreetly rolled my eyes. I'd fill him in on the details of the conversation later.

'The farmers we source the coca plants from in Bolivia are distant relatives of ours. The family bond ensures I get the best price and complete exclusivity of the crop. We currently take everything they produce. If you need a larger amount, we would have to try and source the coke from multiple farms scattered around the Andes so that I can keep the transactions small enough not to ruffle any of my rivals' feathers,' Diego explained.

'We have contacts in Colombia and Peru we could use,' Valentina said.

'But we haven't bought from them before. I like to check my suppliers out thoroughly before I do business with them.' Diego glared at his cousin's wife, and I sensed an undercurrent of trouble pass between them.

'My client is threatening to take his business away from me if I can't increase the amount I supply,' Conor said.

'I understand,' Diego replied. 'But sourcing the coke from many small farms instead of one will be a logistical nightmare.'

'Stop creating obstacles that don't exist. You know full well we can do that; we have enough contacts to make it possible,' Valentina said in Spanish.

'And you know as well as I do, the more links there are in the chain, the more chance there is that something goes wrong,' Diego replied through gritted teeth.

41

Conor

The fact that Ella spoke fluent Spanish was proving to be a major advantage for me. Since she'd been acting as my translator, I was beginning to build up a bigger picture of the people I was doing business with. Before, I hadn't realised so much bickering was going on. There was an undeniable tension between the cousins and, from what I could see, Valentina was at the root of it.

Valentina was a natural-born troublemaker. In the beginning, she'd put up some bitter resistance to Ella being present at the meetings. I wasn't sure why she had such a problem with my girlfriend now that I knew the conversations the cartel were having in Spanish were primarily family disputes and not discussions about swindling me. So, I put it down to a simple case of jealousy. Ella was a beautiful young woman, whereas Valentina looked like an ageing dollybird with a cosmetic surgeon's mobile phone number on speed dial. Her permanently raised eyebrows and expressionless face were a testament to the whole host of injectables she used. I couldn't help thinking that she was fighting a losing battle in her quest to remain ever-youthful. Although some highly paid professional had tried to work their magic on her, instead of wiping away the years, her jet-black hair and frozen features had the opposite effect.

'Against my better judgement, I will agree to supply you with a larger volume of coke,' Diego said.

'Thank you,' I replied before shaking his hand. 'My client is struggling to keep up with demand. Londoners can't get enough of your product.'

We'd spent countless hours sat around the negotiating table, trying to hammer out a new deal. After much persuasion, Diego had finally agreed to import a large quantity of their product from multiple sources so that they could fulfil Leo's order. I could tell Diego wasn't happy about it, but he'd bowed to pressure from the other cartel members.

Thanks to Diego's background, the Gómez family had extensive ties to the Spanish federal police and military. Hopefully, their presence would ensure the smooth running of the operation.

Leo's greed could end up costing us all dearly. I had more than enough cash hidden away to live comfortably for the rest of my life, and I briefly considered walking away from this deal. I couldn't put my finger on it; I had a bad feeling about it. But I was ambitious, and I'd worked hard to get to where I was today. My desire to be successful and a big player outweighed any concerns that I had.

'As the shipments are coming from different sources, we're going to import the drugs using a variety of methods. The Port of Vigo is the largest fishing port in the world. It receives millions of containers a year. The authorities try to check them all, but in reality, it's not possible,' Diego continued.

It was common knowledge that the big ports were black holes. With the correct handling, cargo could disappear without a trace. That was reassuring to know.

'We chose the Port of Vigo for a couple of reasons. Firstly, it is on our doorstep, and secondly, the headquarters of a multinational fishing company is based there. We'll use that as a cover for the import and export of the shipments. Some of the cocaine will arrive by trawler concealed within the vessel's catch. We'll wait until it all arrives, then the bricks will be packed into boxes of seafood and exported to the UK.'

I'd expected Diego to ship the consignment in dribs and drabs as and when he received it. 'Will that cause much of a delay?' I asked, knowing how Leo would feel about that. He wanted the product yesterday, so he wouldn't be impressed if the lead time increased.

My question was left unanswered when Valentina suddenly leaned forward in her chair and flashed me her crepey cleavage. She put her elbows on the table and rested her chin on her knuckles for a few moments before she spoke.

'Our new contacts are going to use submarines to smuggle the drugs into Spain.' Valentina smiled, delighted that she'd been able to be the one to share this nugget of information with me.

'I was just getting around to telling Conor that.'

Diego spat his words across the table towards Valentina, clearly miffed that she'd disclosed the news. But she batted away his remark with a waft of her long, bony fingers. She'd made sure she'd stolen Diego's thunder before he'd had a chance to tell me about the exciting information himself. The woman couldn't help herself; she loved to be the centre of attention.

'This is a new method for us, but it is a tried-and-tested one when the shipment of cocaine is large enough to warrant the cost involved. The purpose-built narco submarine will cross under Atlantic waters following marked coordinates. Once the crew arrive at the designated handover, they will move the cocaine onto one of our speedboats. The rest of the operation will be the same as before. You remember how that worked, Conor?'

'Yes,' I replied. I'd never forget the experience as long as I lived. 'What happens to the submarine?'

'The crew transfer onto another vessel, then they sink it.'

'Really?' That seemed like an incredible waste of money. A purpose-built narco submarine must be worth a small fortune.

Diego nodded, then smiled. 'Don't look so surprised. My contact tells me the bottom of the ocean around here is littered with sunken vessels.'

This might have been a tried-and-tested method for some suppliers, but not for the Gómez cartel. Any concerns I'd had that something wasn't right hadn't been put to rest. But Diego seemed confident that everything was OK, and he'd always been very thorough, so I'd have to trust his judgement and go with the flow.

42

Ella

'Are you OK? You seem really on edge.' Conor looked like he had the weight of the world on his shoulders.

'I have to say, I'll feel a lot better when the cocaine arrives in the UK. If Leo's orders are going to cause me this much stress in the future, I might have to consider jacking this all in.' Conor laughed.

'Why don't you?'

Conor considered my question for a few moments. 'What would I do with myself all day? Being successful makes me feel good about myself, fulfilled. I thrive on the buzz the risk gives me.'

I knew what he meant about the excitement; I hadn't understood what the rush felt like until I'd got caught up in Conor's world and become seduced by it. Conor had made me realise I'd been suppressing a fear of missing out. But breaking the rules made me nervous. My parents had taught me right from wrong from a young age, so following an honest path had always been easy for me. Getting involved in such a dangerous business was filling me with self-doubt.

What we were doing was wrong; I was nervous about being caught, but I went along with it anyway. That was very out of character for me. But Conor had asked me to do something to help him. He treated me like a princess, and in return, I'd do anything to please him. When you were young and in love, you didn't always see things the way they really were. I was guilty of that; I had the capacity to block out the parts that I didn't like. Since I'd met Conor, I'd been swept away on a wave and had a distorted view of reality. At the moment, I was so content it was as though a warm fuzzy glow was surrounding me; life with my boyfriend was euphoric, and that was all that mattered to me.

Conor was a closed book and lived a very private life. He rarely opened up about anything, but I could see something was troubling him, so I wanted to get to the bottom of it.

'You never did tell me how you got into this line of work.' I looked up into Conor's eyes. They were deep blue and framed by thick, dark lashes. The kind of eyes you could get lost in.

'I just drifted into it; I'd been involved in shady stuff since I was a boy. Looking back, it was inevitable I'd end up getting involved in bigger things.'

'What makes you say that?'

'My mum was a single parent and had a history of gravitating towards unsuitable men; all of us have different dads. Most of them were class acts and shot through before we were born,' Conor said without a hint of emotion in his voice.

It made me sad to think my boyfriend had grown up like that when I'd had such a happy childhood.

'I learned from an early age, I had to take care of myself; nobody was going to do it for me. Not only that – because I was the oldest, I got lumbered with looking after my four brothers and sisters all the time.'

'Eat your heart out, Daddy Day Care.' I laughed to try and lighten the mood, but Conor looked back at me with a stony expression on his face.

'You're not far off the mark. My home life was a mess. If my mum had devoted more time to her kids and focused less on her latest squeeze, my life might have taken a different direction.'

I was beginning to understand why Conor distanced himself from his family now, and didn't blame him one bit.

'Mum never really gave a shit about what we were doing and who we were mixing with; as a parent, you have to put boundaries in place if you don't want your kids to go off the rails,' Conor said.

What Conor had said made a lot of sense. Even though we'd grown up streets apart on the same council estate, I'd never been involved in anything illegal... until I started going out with him, that was. But unlike Conor's mum, my parents invested all their time and energy into my upbringing. Despite this, I'd still ended up walking down the criminal path – just like my boyfriend. They would be devastated if they knew what I'd got myself involved in after they'd done everything they could to steer me away from trouble. A pang of guilt stabbed at my heart.

'When I was a kid, my mum was always skint. There was never any spare money, and we survived on benefits. Mum struggled to make it through every month with five kids to feed,' Conor admitted.

In some ways, our childhoods had similarities. My parents were also hard up. Although they eventually married when I was five, they never added to our family as they couldn't afford to. They could barely make ends meet as it was. We might not have been cash-rich, but I never went without. Every penny Mum and Dad had they spent on me. We might not have had holidays at Disney World; we went camping in Europe instead. But I didn't feel like I was missing out on anything; I loved every minute of it. My parents taught me to appreciate simple pleasures, and that was a valuable lesson.

'When you've lived hand to mouth, it's easy to become obsessed with money.' Conor cast his eyes over the expensive interior of his immaculate house.

I'd also been raised on the breadline, and I'd thought I had a different outlook. Material things didn't really impress me. I could take them or leave them. But on reflection, I knew that couldn't be right. Otherwise, I wouldn't have been seduced by the glamour and luxury of Conor's lifestyle.

43

Conor

To fulfil the size of Leo's order, Diego had to source the cocaine from multiple suppliers. Instead of shipping the batches as they arrived, he'd decided to compile them into one large consignment. Valentina and Pedro had been the driving force behind that idea. They'd insisted that it would cut down on the cost, red tape and workforce needed if they only had one shipment to deliver. I understood that, but there was a huge amount at stake. If it was seized, we'd lose everything. It was doubtful that all of the shipments would fail to make it through if Diego sent them separately.

I'd brought Ella with me to finalise the details of the agreement. On a deal of this size, there was no room for error. My girlfriend shared my concerns, so she'd tried to help me convince Diego to send the cocaine in smaller quantities, but unfortunately for us, he'd made his decision, and he was sticking to it.

I didn't want to have to keep travelling backwards and forwards to Spain every time we needed another consignment.

But until we cemented some trust between us, that was the only option. At least I had a base in Baiona where I could conduct my side of the business from now. That made things a lot easier all around.

I sat behind the driver's wheel of the transit van on a frosty morning at the end of February, waiting for the ship to dock at Felixstowe. I couldn't have asked for better conditions. The port was shrouded in fog, and the visibility was incredibly poor. I closed my fingers around the paper cup and sipped at the bitter-tasting coffee I'd bought from the mobile food truck parked in a nearby lay-by. As expected, it was foul, but it was warm and wet and nowhere else was open at this unearthly hour of the morning, so I had to grin and bear it. I placed the cup into the holder in front of my dashboard, then stuck my hand inside the paper bag I'd left on the passenger seat and pulled out a white, flour-dusted bap. As I lifted the lid and stared at a thick ring of white fat surrounding the undercooked bacon, which had barely been shown the pan, I suddenly lost my appetite.

A short while later, the Spanish plated van pulled into the bay next to mine. It was instantly recognisable as it had been kitted out with some self-adhesive graphics of a fish wholesaler's logo down either side to make it look legitimate. I got out of the transit and opened up the back doors as the driver jumped out of the cab. I could see the man's breath swirling in the misty air in front of him as he walked towards me.

'Is it cold enough for you?' I said, rubbing my hands together.

'You think it's cold out here? Wait until you feel the temperature in there,' the dark-haired man replied before he swung open the doors. He climbed into the back of the refrigerated Nissan and began handing me the boxes that contained our shipment.

Now that Ella knew the nature of my work, I could head straight back to London with the consignment and cut it in the privacy of my own home. I wouldn't have to waste time taking it to a safehouse first. The sooner I could hand Leo the gear, the better. Once he'd received the coke in his hot little hands, he'd pay the balance he owed Diego. We'd agreed to different terms on this deal because of the size of the order – half the money upfront and half on delivery.

Back at home, Ella sat on the other side of the kitchen counter, watching me with wide-eyed fascination while I placed the polythene-wrapped bales in a row on the black granite next to a box of testing kits. I carefully unwrapped the first bundle, then snapped the lid off of an ampoule containing a chemical identification reagent. Picking up a small amount of the powder on a metal spatula, I dropped it into the test tube and gently shook it so that it dissolved into the liquid.

'What are you doing?' Ella asked.

'It's just routine, but I have to test the product. The darker the colour, the purer the batch.' I smiled.

Ella's dark brown eyes fixed on the tiny bottle while we waited for the result to appear.

The smile soon slid from my face. 'Something's wrong. Whatever's in that bale isn't cocaine.'

'Are you sure?' Ella questioned.

'Yes, there's no doubt about that.'

'How can you be certain?'

'The liquid in the vial should have turned blue, and it hasn't changed colour at all. For fuck's sake,' I shouted, slamming my fist down on the counter. Guilt washed over me when I saw Ella jump out of her skin. 'I'm sorry; I didn't mean to scare you.'

'It's OK. Maybe the test was faulty. Why don't you try another one?' Ella suggested.

I shook my head. 'They're normally incredibly accurate, but I suppose it could have been a dud one. I'll need to check all of the bales.'

'I'll help you,' Ella said.

We went through the packets one by one until we'd tested them all.

'It looks like somebody's switched the product,' I said now that I'd had the opportunity to analyse the whole batch.

'Who would have done that?'

'I have no idea.' Working alongside gangsters always carried an element of risk, but something had felt different about this job right from the off.

I couldn't believe this was happening. I could hear the blood whooshing in my ears. My head felt like it was about to explode. My worst fears had been confirmed; Leo had just paid a small fortune for this latest shipment. He was expecting to receive one hundred kilos of cocaine, with a street value of four million pounds, but instead, he'd been sent a batch of self-raising flour or a similar useless substance. He was going to lose his shit when I broke the news to him. I'd had a bad feeling about this deal right from the start. I wished I'd trusted my gut now and pulled out while I'd had the chance to.

'What are you going to do?' Ella looked at me with concern written all over her beautiful heart-shaped face.

I blew out a loud breath. 'I'll have to get on to Diego and let him know what's happened.'

'Don't you think he might have had something to do with it?'

'I doubt he'd be stupid enough to pull a stunt like this. He'd be out of business in no time if he did that to his customers.'

'What do you think happened?'

'It's more likely the coke was switched at some stage along the supply chain. Members of the criminal underworld aren't known for their honesty.'

'Do you really think Diego's innocent?' Ella tilted her face to one side as she looked up at me.

'Yes, I do.'

I'd heard a rumour that the Gómez family tortured and murdered couriers who lost their product or failed to deliver on time, but I didn't want to share that information with Ella.

'Well, you know him better than I do,' Ella said.

'But the cartel use migrant workers, many of whom are illegal immigrants, to distribute their drugs. They're badly paid, so if you put temptation in people's way, sometimes they can't help themselves.'

'That's true,' Ella agreed.

'Juan is a fine example; he's Diego's main man, but he's little more than a glorified drug mule. He has all the danger for hardly any reward, but that doesn't seem to concern him. He's just happy to be a part of the cartel's operation.'

'But not everyone's that obliging or trustworthy, and

there were a lot more people involved this time,' Ella pointed out.

'I know, which makes it much harder to keep track of things and leaves a lot more room for error.'

'I'm scared, Conor. I've got a horrible feeling that this isn't going to end well,' Ella said.

I threw my arms around my girlfriend's neck. 'Don't be scared; I'll sort it out.'

'But, how?' Ella asked with worry etched on her face.

'I'm going to fly out to Spain and speak to Diego in person. I can't discuss this over the phone.'

'Can I go with you?' Ella asked.

'What about uni?'

'This is more important. I'll catch up on the lectures I miss when we get back.'

'As long as you're sure.'

'I am.'

While Ella went to pack a bag, I gave Leo a call. 'There's been a problem with the shipment.'

'What the fuck's the matter now?' Leo's dulcet tones boomed down the phone at me.

'Diego didn't say, but I'm going to fly out to Spain and sort it out.' I'd decided not to give Leo too much information and keep the details sketchy for the time being.

'We've had one fiasco after another. Tell your supplier if he doesn't get his act together sharp-ish, this will be the last time I'll give him my business.'

I held the phone away from my ear as Leo ranted and I pictured his eyes bulging in his head; it wasn't a pretty sight.

44

Ella

I gazed out of the plane window as wispy pink clouds resembling spun candyfloss floated past us. Out of the corner of my eye, I could see Conor check his watch for the hundredth time since we'd taken off twenty minutes ago. We couldn't arrive soon enough for his liking, but as he'd said himself, the corner of north-west Spain we were heading to wasn't easy to reach from England. That was why he'd had to go to the expense of chartering a private four-seater plane.

When my boyfriend decided he needed to pay the cartel an urgent visit, we'd flown out from Biggin Hill airport in south-east London at a moment's notice. The fact that Conor could arrange to do that at the drop of a hat spoke volumes about his connections. I put that thought to the back of my mind; I had more than enough to worry about at the moment without adding to the list.

'It'll be late by the time we arrive, so I'm going to arrange to see Diego first thing in the morning,' Conor said.

'I'll come with you to give you some moral support.' I faced my boyfriend and smiled as we sat side by side, behind the pilot.

'I appreciate the offer, but there's no need.'

I was surprised that he'd turned me down, given the cartel's track record of talking among themselves. 'Won't you need me to translate?'

'Not this time.'

I would have thought it would be essential to have an interpreter present at this meeting, more so than any other I'd attended. 'You know what the family are like; if they're hiding something, they'll end up speaking Spanish, and you won't have a clue what's being discussed.'

Conor considered my reply for a moment. 'I'll be OK.'

'Are you sure? I'm happy to go with you.' I didn't want Conor to know that wasn't the case; I was scared witless, but I wanted to be there for him if he needed my support.

'No, honestly, I want you to stay at the villa; it'll be safer. The conversation's likely to get pretty heated, so I don't want to involve you in it.'

'I'm tougher than I look, you know; I can handle a lively discussion.' I smiled, but I was putting on a front.

The danger and intrigue I'd found exciting in the beginning had suddenly lost its appeal. Conor and I weren't part of a glamorous world; the people who shaped it were dangerous criminals, and when I thought about what we were mixed up in, it sent a shiver down my spine.

After a fretful night's sleep, Conor and I sat opposite each other at the kitchen table, discussing our next move.

'I wish you'd let me come with you so that I can translate.'

'There's no telling how the cartel members are going to

react when I tell them about the shipment. I know you want to help, but I need you to stay here; I don't want to put you in danger.' Conor leaned towards me and planted a kiss on my lips. 'I'd better make tracks.'

My boyfriend placed his coffee cup down on the table and pushed back his chair. He stood up and began walking towards the front door, leaving his breakfast untouched.

'Be careful,' I said when I caught up with him. Standing on tiptoes, I draped my arms over Conor's shoulders and kissed him.

'Don't look so worried; I'll be back before you know it.' Conor smiled and then disappeared out of the door.

But his words offered me little comfort. I couldn't help feeling concerned. There was a huge amount of money at stake, and I had a horrible feeling that things weren't going to end well.

45

Conor

Much as I was going to miss Ella's translation skills, it was likely things would turn messy at the meeting, so I wanted her to stay as far away from the drama as possible.

'What's so important that you needed to call an emergency meeting with us?' Valentina asked when I arrived at the cartel's office in the heart of Vigo.

'There's a problem with the shipment,' I replied, getting straight to the point.

'Don't tell me the cargo's gone astray on the last leg of its journey,' Valentina added, and a faint smile played on her lips.

'The driver made the handover, but when I tested the product he gave me, I discovered whatever's in the packages isn't cocaine.'

'That's impossible,' Diego said.

I was pretty sure he was going to say that, so I'd come prepared.

'This is one of the bales the driver delivered,' I said,

opening up my rucksack and placing the wrapped package on the table in front of the family. Then I got out the testing kit to back up what I'd been saying.

Diego's eyes flashed between Pedro and Valentina when the result showed the sample didn't contain cocaine. I could see panic begin to set in as Diego realised the coke was missing.

'Do you really expect us to believe you didn't receive the shipment we sent?' Valentina said. 'More likely, your client is having trouble coming up with the cash he owes us.'

'I've shown you what I received.' I was doing my best to be tactful, but I couldn't keep the irritation out of my voice.

'Conor, darling, how do we know you're not saying this to try and swindle us?' Valentina fixed me with her heavily made-up peepers. She looked like Alice Cooper's sister with thick black liner caked all around her eyes.

'I'm the one who's been swindled. I wanted to give you an opportunity to put things right before I tell my client what's happened.'

'We only used reputable suppliers, so the mistake can't have been at our end,' Diego attempted to reassure me.

'I don't know when the cocaine was switched, but if your suppliers are one hundred per cent genuine, it must have happened at some point after the handover at sea.'

As Ella predicted, a conversation in Spanish began, and after several minutes of raised voices and animated hand gestures, it stopped. I didn't know what they'd said, but if I'd had to read between the lines, I reckoned they were trying to pin the blame on each other. Although he was keeping quiet about it now, I hadn't forgotten Diego had been reluctant to source the cocaine from the Peruvian and

Colombian contacts, preferring to stick with his relatives in Bolivia. None of us had been working together long, and we were still trying to build up trust between us. A fuck-up on a grand scale like this would do nothing to strengthen our partnership.

'I don't appreciate the accusations you're making,' Diego said, wagging a gnarled finger at me before fixing me with a glare.

I held my palms up in front of me to reinforce my words as I tried to pacify him. 'I haven't come here looking for trouble; I need your help to get to the bottom of this.'

'Despite what you're insinuating, my employees wouldn't dare double-cross the Gómez cartel. They know we wouldn't hesitate to sacrifice their families if they did,' Diego continued with a scowl plastered onto his weather-beaten face.

As the head honcho of the growing empire, Diego essentially held his employees at gunpoint to ensure their loyalty. He retained control over his migrant workforce through fear and intimidation.

'I hear what you're saying loud and clear, but I also know what I received. The shipment I collected from Felixstowe didn't contain an ounce of cocaine. I didn't tamper with the consignment, so the only other explanation is that somebody on your side did.'

Diego pushed his chair back, stood up and gripped on to the side of the table. I watched his nostrils flaring as he stared at me.

'I have already explained to you that none of my staff would be brave or stupid enough to try to get away with switching the product.'

Diego and I were getting nowhere; we were going around in circles. Whether he wanted to believe it or not, the error had come from his side. Everyone had a price, so it stood to reason that one of the poorly paid drug mules was responsible. But we weren't going to be able to resolve the issue until he was prepared to open his eyes and see the bigger picture.

I was fully aware that time was ticking. If we didn't track down Leo's cocaine soon, I'd be forced to tell him what had happened. Then Diego would have a lot more to worry about than loyalty within the ranks.

46

Ella

Conor and I were sitting in silence, eating breakfast. As I spooned cereal into my mouth and lazily chewed it, I looked out at the fog being burned off by the rising sun.

'Once this clears, I think it's going to be a lovely day. We could go for a walk on the beach when I get back if you like,' Conor said before he finished the last of his coffee. He put down his mug and checked the time on his watch. 'I'd better get going. I shouldn't be too long.'

Conor was right; once the fog had lifted, it left behind a beautiful sunny day. It was pretty warm, considering the time of year. We never got weather like this in England in February. Conor was meeting Diego, Pedro and Valentina to discuss the ongoing saga of the missing cocaine. So, instead of rattling around in the sprawling mansion trying to kill time, I'd decided to relax out in the garden. There was nothing more therapeutic than feeling the sun on your skin, was there? And after a long British winter, my vitamin D levels were in serious need of a top-up.

The sun was still low when I went outside and stretched out on the pale grey wicker day-bed that took centre stage on the raised patio of Conor's luxury home. The biggest decision I had to make this morning was whether or not to brave taking a dip in the pool or stay where I was and continue reading the book I was engrossed in. While I mulled over what to do, I glanced up and admired the view of the deep blue Atlantic in the distance. Life could be tough sometimes.

Lounging around was hard work, and I suddenly felt restless. I sat up, swung my legs over the side of the day-bed and slipped on my rhinestone-encrusted flip-flops before I walked the short distance to the pool, overhung by palm trees. Instead of turquoise tiles, dark shimmery mosaics lined it, creating the illusion that you were swimming in a mysterious natural water source and not a man-made structure. I crouched down and trailed my hand through the cool water as I decided whether or not to take a dip.

The next thing I knew, a set of nicotine-scented fingers covered my mouth. I could feel something digging into the small of my back and instantly knew it was a weapon of some sort. I was yanked backwards and onto my feet as I struggled like a fish caught on a line. I tried to sink my teeth into the man's palm. When that failed, I clawed at his hands with my long nails then tried to prise his fingers off, but just as I managed to pull one of them away, and I reach for the next, the first would clamp down over my lips again.

'Settle down, Isabella,' the man said in Spanish. His voice had a gravelly quality to it.

I was alarmed that he knew my name.

'If you don't want me to hurt you, you need to stay calm...'

I'd been trying to, but my heart was pounding wildly in my chest as the desperate urge to survive kicked in. Whatever this man had got in store for me, I wasn't going to give in easily. I was determined to fight back, but no matter how much I tried, there was nothing I could do to free myself from my attacker's grip. I bucked and kicked like an untamed horse, but I couldn't break his hold. He was too strong for me to overpower.

Then a second man appeared, holding a gun out in front of him. Our eyes met, and my pulse went into overdrive. His face was inches from mine. 'Don't make a sound,' he threatened in Spanish before covering my mouth with tape.

Even though he'd warned me to stay quiet, the desperate urge to alert somebody took over me. When the other man removed his fingers from my lips, I attempted to scream, but he quickly muffled the sound.

'If you do that again, it will be the last sound you ever make. Do you understand?' His dark eyes peered out from the balaclava and bored into mine.

As I couldn't reply, I nodded my head.

The men were speaking to me in what I assumed was their native tongue. Both of them had dark eyes, tanned skin and a generous covering of dark hair on their exposed forearms. I would have been surprised if they weren't local.

Before binding my wrists and ankles with thick cable-tie restraints, the second man placed a black hood over my head, which plunged me into darkness. My pulse raced in response. I felt myself being lifted off my feet before being carried a short distance and placed headfirst into a small space. I lay on my side, concentrating on the sounds around me. My bare arms were resting against a scratchy fabric, possibly carpet. Terror coursed through my veins as I heard something above me latch shut, entombing me within it. Even though I couldn't see anything, I knew I was in the boot of a car.

I battled to focus, but it was impossible to think straight. Ever since I was a little girl, I'd been afraid of the dark. I'd struggle to get to sleep at night because I thought a monster was hiding under my bed. Fear programmed at such a young age tended to linger; this was the stuff of nightmares.

How could this be happening? The villa was tucked away from prying eyes near a sleepy little village, and it was broad daylight. I kept hoping that Conor would arrive home in the nick of time and come to my rescue. When I heard the car's engine start, I knew that wasn't going to happen. That was when I lost control of my emotions.

Since I'd been bundled into the boot, I'd tried to focus all my energy into making it through the journey uninjured, but that was easier said than done as I didn't have the use of my arms or legs. It was virtually impossible to stop myself from rolling around and bashing into the sides as the car sped along the road.

The heat inside the boot was unbearable; it was intense. As I struggled to breathe, I was sure I was going to die. I could feel my nostrils flaring every time I tried to inhale. My chest ached with the effort of trying to get air into my lungs. I knew the worst thing I could do was panic, but it was almost impossible to keep calm. My breathing had become rapid and shallow, so I focused on it until I was able to take slower, deeper breaths.

Being locked in a cramped, dark space was playing havoc with my emotions. Fear was threatening to overcome my rational thinking. I knew I should try to take in any details that might be useful later on, but the panic that was spreading through my brain was suppressing any logical thoughts I might have had. I was being driven to an undisclosed destination. I realised I might never see Conor or my friends and family again. As the hopelessness of the situation dawned on me, tears rolled down my cheeks. I'd held them in as long as I could, but my bravery had deserted me.

The car lurched forward, and I hit my head against the hard wall of the speeding vehicle. Since the terrifying ordeal had begun, the coarse fibres of the carpet were scraping at my bare arms, making my skin itch. The air was heavy, and the heat was oppressive in the enclosed space, and my chest heaved with the effort to breathe.

I felt like I was slowly sinking into a pit of quicksand on the agonising journey. I'd lost all concept of time, so I didn't know how long ago I'd been kidnapped. Suddenly, the car slowed, and the road surface deteriorated, which heightened my sense of fear; we were obviously heading somewhere remote. Every time the wheel hit a pothole, I smashed my head against the metal side as it lolled around uncontrollably. The restraints were digging into my limbs, making my skin sting. I tried to stay strong, but I wasn't sure how much more I could take.

I tried not to think about where the men were taking me and what they were going to do. Instead, I focused on memorising details, no matter how small and insignificant they seemed at the moment. I knew they might be useful later on and help the police catch whoever was responsible if I survived the experience. My life flashed before me;

I was only nineteen. That was way too young to die. As the hopelessness dawned on me, tears rolled down my cheeks again. I tried to hold them in, but I was fighting a losing battle. If I somehow made it through this experience, I knew it would haunt me for the rest of my life.

When the car eventually came to a stop, a feeling of relief washed over me, but the moment quickly passed as reality hit home. I didn't know who had taken me, or more importantly, why? But I was fully aware that whoever it was wouldn't waste time making idle threats. I should never have got involved in the first place. Why had I been so stupid and naïve? These people were ruthless. If they didn't get what they wanted, they wouldn't hesitate; they'd kill me. The thought of that sent me into another spiral of despair.

When I heard two doors open and then slam shut, I focused on what was happening outside the car to stop myself from going into a total meltdown. I trained my ears on the sound of the two pairs of feet walking across the hard ground. The footsteps and inaudible muffled voices grew closer. Then the boot finally opened and fresh air flooded into the confined space; I knew this wasn't the end of my ordeal. It was the beginning of my worst nightmare.

47

As soon as I opened the front door, I realised something was wrong. I could sense it.

'Ella.' I called out a couple of times, but there was no reply.

My heart hammered in my chest as I ran through the house, checking all the rooms, but there was no sign of my girlfriend anywhere. I pulled open the patio doors and stepped outside. My eyes scanned around the garden; the book Ella had been reading was lying discarded on the day-bed, so I knew she'd been out here.

A sinking feeling suddenly hit me, and fearing the worst, I rushed over to the pool and checked it for signs of life. I wasn't sure why; Ella was a good swimmer, but sometimes freak accidents happened, and people got into trouble in the water and drowned, didn't they? As I couldn't offer myself another explanation for my girlfriend's whereabouts, it seemed like a reasonable assumption to make. She couldn't have just vanished into thin air.

I tried to steady my breathing; I needed to calm down and think logically so panic wouldn't set in. It was a beautiful day; Ella might have gone for a walk. Who could blame her? The weather was lovely, exceptionally mild for the time of year, and she loved the countryside surrounding the villa.

Not knowing what to do for the best, I considered my options. There were so many unanswered questions whirring around in my head. None of this made any sense. Why would Ella have gone out without me? She knew I wasn't going to be long. Maybe I should take the car out and drive around the local area and see if I could spot her.

I'd been so alarmed to find the house empty, I'd forgotten to do the most obvious thing. I should pick up the phone and call her. Because of the nature of my work, sometimes I was guilty of being paranoid, creating situations that didn't exist. As I dialled her number, I heard her phone ring, then I noticed her mobile sitting on the glass table next to a full tumbler of fruit juice. I was suspicious of anything and everything and made a habit of jumping to conclusions, but this time being on my guard was justified. My hunch was correct. Something was definitely wrong. Ella wouldn't have gone out and left her phone behind. My girlfriend loved taking photos and never missed an opportunity to post stuff on Instagram, and on top of that, the patio doors were unlocked. Ella knew how cautious I was about security, so she wouldn't have ventured out without locking the villa up first.

If something bad had happened to Ella, I'd never forgive myself. I shouldn't have let her come to Spain with me this time; it would have been safer if she'd stayed with her mum and dad while I'd sorted out the mess. In my line of work, a person made a lot of enemies; that went without saying. I had a horrible feeling that Diego and the other members of the cartel were behind my girlfriend's sudden disappearance. Now that I'd got that thought planted firmly in my head, I couldn't seem to shake it, and they always say you should trust your intuition, don't they?

My imagination was beginning to run away with itself, but this wasn't the right time to lose my head. I forced myself to focus on the facts; nothing seemed out of place, so maybe there was a different explanation. As I started to walk back towards the house, my eyes were drawn to something dumped over by the side gate. On closer inspection, several heavy-duty cable ties and two sets of black gloves had been discarded in the flowerbed. When I looked up from them, I noticed that although the gate was pulled across the driveway, the lock had been forced. Now I was in no doubt that somebody had come onto my property and taken my girlfriend. I felt the contents of my stomach rise as the realisation hit me; Ella had been kidnapped, and at that moment, my world began to fall apart.

What the hell was I going to do? It wasn't as though I could go running to the police. I'd have to interrogate the most obvious culprit; Diego must know something about this.

48

Ella

The temperature instantly dropped several degrees when the hot, stagnant air escaped from the enclosed space I was confined in. As I lay in the darkness, wondering what was going to happen next, a pair of hands slid under my body and lifted me out of the boot. I couldn't see a thing, but I knew it was still daylight because I could feel the warmth of the sun on my arms. The silence that surrounded me told me in no uncertain terms that I'd been taken to the middle of nowhere. My hopes were dashed; there wouldn't be any way for me to alert a passer-by from this remote location.

It felt like I'd been bumping around in the boot for an eternity; I'd lost all concept of time and had no idea how long I'd been held captive. The car's trunk wasn't airtight, but I'd still been finding it difficult to breathe with a hood over my head and tape over my mouth. Morbid as it may seem, I'd begun to wonder how long a person could live for if they were left tied up and gagged with no food or water.

The passage of time was going to be a crucial element to my survival. I wished I wasn't having such trouble estimating it.

As the two men moved away from the car, one of them carried me in *An Officer And A Gentleman* style, scooping me up with one of his arms under my thighs while the other was across my back. But it wasn't a sweeping romantic gesture or a fairy-tale sugar-sweet scene at the end of a movie. It was purely the most practical way to move a blindfolded and bound hostage from one place to another. I listened intently while they walked, looking for clues as to where I might be, but apart from the sound of their shoes making contact with the ground, there was silence. The men paused then I heard a key turning in a lock before a door creaked open.

To stop myself from losing hope, I focused on the fact that I hadn't been brought here for no reason; I was a valuable asset. So it was in my kidnappers' best interests to look after me. I was going to get out of this; I just had to try and stay positive. It was a case of mind over matter. If I repeated that over and over, I might start to believe it.

The sound of the men's footsteps changed as they stepped over the threshold; they were now walking on bare floorboards or some other kind of wooden flooring. I had no idea where I was, but if I had to guess, I'd say I was being held in a derelict building or possibly on a disused farm miles away from civilisation.

The man carrying me came to a stop, then lowered me onto my feet. He lifted the hood off of my head, and I squinted until I became accustomed to the light. I cast my eyes around the space where I'd be staying for the foreseeable future. It was grim, for want of a better description. As the men turned to leave, a wave of panic washed over me and threatened to crush me. But I wouldn't allow myself to crumble. If I wanted to get out of this situation, I'd have to stay strong.

'We hope you enjoy your stay,' one of the men said in Spanish, and they both laughed. The sound echoed around the sparsely furnished space.

I felt tears stab my eyes, but I wouldn't give my captors the satisfaction of breaking down.

After closing the door behind them, the balaclava-clad men turned a key in the lock and then slid two bolts across, one at the top and one at the bottom, to further secure the room. I looked around the makeshift prison and focused my eyes on a tiny pinpoint of light coming from outside the place I was locked in. The sun was forcing its way through a small hole in the corrugated steel used to board up the windows like rustic shutters. I thought about shuffling towards it, but my limbs were aching from being bound tightly, so I decided against it. I should conserve my energy.

It was clear from the room's poor condition that wherever I was had been empty for a long time. Plaster had crumbled from the walls, and what was left was covered in damp patches emitting an overpowering smell of mould. Cobwebs covered the inside of the windows, Mother Nature's net curtains, and when I glanced up, a broken light fitting was hanging by bare wires above me. There was a disused fireplace in the centre of the wall opposite a makeshift bed, consisting of a filthy, half-inflated air mattress covered with an olive green threadbare blanket that looked like it had come from an army surplus store. I knew even without touching it that it would feel unbearably itchy.

The sound of footsteps nearing distracted me from my surroundings. I could only hear one pair of feet approaching this time. The man unlocked the door, which was as secure as Fort Knox, then closed it behind him. He walked across the room, avoiding the gaping holes in the floorboards that let in a tremendous draught, and dragged a spindle-backed chair that had seen better days towards me.

'Sit,' he said, pushing down on my shoulder after he placed the rickety wooden chair behind me.

When he ripped the tape off my face, I winced. The skin around my mouth and lips throbbed, but my hands were still bound, so I couldn't press down on the rawness to stop the stinging. The man held a plastic bottle to my lips to give me a sip of water. I almost refused it, thinking it might be drugged, but I'd seen him break the seal, so I started to gulp it down. My throat was so dry, it hurt to swallow the cold liquid. The man pulled the bottle away from my lips and placed it on the ground. Then he slid off the roll of duct tape he was wearing as a bracelet, and before I could protest, he sealed my mouth shut again.

49

Conor

I needed to confront Diego about Ella's disappearance, but I couldn't afford to burst into his offices with both barrels loaded, no matter how tempting that thought was, just in case my suspicions were incorrect. I wasn't sure how to play this; I'd have to come up with a plan en route. I didn't have time to waste. The sooner I jumped into my car and began driving to Vigo, the sooner I could confront the Gómez family. I wouldn't bother phoning ahead. The last thing I wanted to do was tip them off. The chances were they were going to deny any involvement in my girlfriend's disappearance, so I'd turn up unannounced and see if I could catch them off-guard.

As I drove along, Leo's number flashed up again. I almost lobbed my phone out of the window in frustration. I'd lost count of the number of times he'd called me since I'd left England. I'd told him I'd be in touch as soon as I had some news, but he seemed to find it impossible to get that information through his thick skull. I let his call connect to my voicemail while I tried to regain composure. I had more important things to deal with at the moment than pacifying an East End villain who was getting too big for his boots.

'What a surprise to see you again, darling. We are honoured that you've come back twice in one day.' Valentina smiled as she ran her witch-like scarlet nails over the top of her tiny dog's head. 'Is it business or pleasure this time?'

'I think you all know why I'm here,' I replied before looking daggers at her. I wasn't interested in massaging her enormous ego by engaging in idle chit-chat. I dragged my eyes away from Valentina's startled face and turned my attention to Diego. 'Where's Ella?'

Valentina's cackle broke the silence. She was lucky she was a woman, or I would have launched myself at her and wiped the smile off her face.

'Where's the cocaine?' Diego replied without answering my question. As he spoke, he wore a hostile expression on his face.

'I've already told you. I didn't receive it.' I clenched my jaw as I faced the old grey-haired man and tried to keep my cool.

'I know what you said, but I don't believe you.'

'What can I do to convince you?'

'Nothing. I smelled a rat right from the beginning when you tripled the size of your order.' Diego narrowed his eyes and glared at me.

'You know that was to try and keep up with demand. The appetite for cocaine is insatiable in London.'

'It seems like a bit of a coincidence that a deal of this size would disappear into thin air, doesn't it? After all the times I've supplied you without any problems.'

I stood looking at Diego, dumbfounded. Even though I knew I had nothing to do with the product switch, I could see why he might think I had tried to double-cross him. The situation was grave. I had no way of proving that I wasn't involved, and with such a huge amount of money at stake, none of us wanted to be the ones out of pocket.

'Look at me, Conor. I'm an old man, I wasn't born yesterday. I knew you were up to something when we started negotiating this deal. Until this shipment, we've always sourced our coke from Bolivia, and it's always arrived safely under Rodrigo's protection. You knew I was reluctant to change anything, but you forced me into it.'

'As you just said, everything went smoothly when you sourced the cocaine from Bolivia. You have my word that I didn't do anything underhand. Just consider the possibility for a minute that the blame lies with your Peruvian and Colombian contacts. The bulk of the order came from them, after all. Are you sure you can trust them? You hadn't bought from them before, and you said you liked to check your suppliers out thoroughly before you did business with them.'

A flash of anger spread over Diego's face when I called him out. But instead of responding, his eyes flicked sideways as he considered what I'd said. Then he wagged a gnarly finger at me. 'If that had been the case, there would only be a problem with the Peruvian and Colombian part of the order; the coke coming from Bolivia should have arrived intact. Don't bother to try and focus the attention away from yourself. I know you received the shipment.'

Diego had a point, so that blew my theory out of the

water. But whatever had happened, something had gone seriously wrong.

'How many times do I have to tell you, your courier delivered one hundred kilos of flour to me, and as I don't work for Hovis, it's not a lot of use.' I shook my head; I could feel my blood pressure rising as my temper bubbled under the surface. Any minute now, I would explode with rage.

'Let me make something clear. If you want your beautiful girlfriend back in one piece, I suggest you ask your client to pay the two million euros that he still owes – right away,' Diego said. 'Otherwise, my men will be forced to dismember Isabella bit by bit.'

I felt bile start to rise in the pit of my stomach at the thought of somebody hurting the woman I loved, but my fury suppressed it. I slammed my fist down, then leaned forward and gripped on to the side of the desk so that I could get right up in Diego's craggy face. I could feel my nostrils flaring; I was as mad as hell and about to lose my shit.

'Don't fuck with me.' I jabbed my finger in Diego's face and saw one of his eyes twitch. 'There will be serious consequences for kidnapping Ella. If you harm one hair on my girlfriend's head, I will destroy you, one by one.' My glare lingered on Diego, Valentina and Pedro in turn.

I needed to get out of the room before I lost control and took my anger out on the old man. Taking Ella in retaliation was a low blow; she'd had nothing to do with the cocaine's disappearance, but I was determined to figure out what had happened to the missing coke so that I could get Ella back safe and sound.

50

Ella

By now, the light was fading fast. The tiny pinhole in the corrugated steel, which was my only connection to the outside world, had almost disappeared. As I watched it seeping away, fresh panic rose up within me. I was alone and afraid, and I would be in total darkness soon. Then my imagination would take on a life of its own, and if I wasn't careful, it would get the better of me. My lips quivered as I fought back tears. Before I lost the last trace of daylight, I scanned the room but wished I hadn't when my eyes started to play tricks on me, and shadows appeared to move as if they were alive.

All of my senses were heightened, and I looked over my shoulder into the darkness when I suddenly heard distant footsteps growing louder. One of the men was approaching. When he stopped outside the room and unlocked the door, the sound echoed around the sparsely furnished space, which made my pulse rate spike. Was he going to free me, or was something more sinister about to happen? The door creaked open, but I couldn't see a thing. It was pitch-black. The man crossed the room, and even though I couldn't make out his silhouette, I sensed he was near me. I could hear him breathing. Waiting, but he said nothing. He just stood inches away from me for what seemed like the longest time. Not knowing what was going to come next was terrifying. My heart was hammering in my chest.

The man switched on a super bright torch and shone it in my face; as he tore the tape from my mouth, a scream escaped from my lips.

'Please don't hurt me,' I begged. My eyes blinked and watered as they tried to adjust to the light.

'There's no point in crying out, Isabella; nobody can hear you,' the man said in Spanish before he placed a plate in my lap.

I'd guessed that would be the case, but I hadn't wanted him to confirm the fact. I looked down at the chipped edges of the crockery so that he wouldn't see the tears in my eyes.

'I brought you some food,' the man continued.

I glanced up into his balaclava-covered face. My hands were tied behind my back, so I wouldn't have been able to pick up the baguette even if I'd wanted to, not that I had any appetite. I was a bundle of nerves. Food was the last thing on my mind. How could I eat at a time like this? The man stared at me for several seconds; then, he pulled something out of his pocket. My heartbeat sped up when I saw the metal glinting in the torchlight. I was terrified he was about to hurt me, so I backed myself into the chair as he moved closer to me.

'If you want me to cut the restraint off, you'll have to sit forward.'

I did as instructed, and once my limbs were freed, I shook out my numb hands then took it in turns to clasp my fingers around my throbbing wrists. The double-looped cable ties had left a red ring behind on my skin. By cutting the restraints off, the man had placed his trust in me. I wondered if I should take the opportunity to promise not to try and escape or tell anyone what had happened if he let me go or whether I should wait until I'd built up a better rapport with him. But I hesitated too long and lost my nerve.

The man took several paces backwards and stood watching me. 'Eat up,' he said, then he folded his arms across his chest.

'I'm not hungry.' That was true, but I wouldn't have eaten it anyway; the food might be drugged. 'I need to go to the toilet.'

I'd thought the man would cut off the restraints binding my ankles and lead me out of the room so that I could get some insight into where I was being held. But instead, he gestured to a dirty bucket by the side of the air mattress. At that moment, my heart sank, and my hopes were dashed.

The man left, and I found myself alone again with only my thoughts for company. With my hands out in front of me to guide me, I shuffled over to the mattress and sat down on it. My surroundings were eerily quiet, but the occasional noises I heard seem to be amplified in the darkness. I'd always been scared of the dark, which was something considered normal when young children experienced it, but I'd never grown out of it.

My mind kept travelling to scary places where women found themselves raped and murdered in situations like this. I tried to distract myself from the unwanted, intrusive images that were bombarding my brain, but as fast as I banished one to the back of my mind, another quickly replaced it.

Thoughts of my parents drifted into my head. I wished I was at home with them now, surrounded by their love, tucked up in the safety of my childhood bed. But no matter how much I longed to be with them, I knew escape was not an option. A failed attempt would more than likely result in my death. Even if I was brave enough to try and make a run for it, I had no idea where my kidnappers were holding me, so the chances of making it to safety were slim.

It was cold in my unheated room, so I lay down on the mattress and pulled the itchy blanket over me. It felt disgusting and smelled musty, but I tucked it around me to stop myself from shivering. As the scent of mould wafted up my nostrils, I tried not to think about fungi spores that were potentially growing and multiplying in the fibres. Yet another nightmare-inducing thought to add to the ever-growing list. It was going to be a long night.

I couldn't believe this had happened to me. One minute I was dipping my hand in Conor's amazing pool, minding my own business, and the next, I was grabbed from behind and bundled into the boot of a car. As I replayed the events, everything seemed to happen in slow motion. I lay trembling under the blanket, wondering if I could have done something differently to have prevented this. Then the realisation hit me like a thunderbolt. I'd behaved like a complete idiot. If I hadn't become involved with the cartel, I wouldn't have ended up in this position. I'd been stupid and naïve to think I could court danger and indulge in risky behaviour and get away with it. It was time to take a long hard look at myself.

Tears rolled down my cheeks as reality hit home; my stupidity could end up costing me my life. I lay in the darkness, rocking backwards and forwards, wishing I could turn back time. The fog clouding my judgement had lifted, and now that I viewed the situation with wide-open eyes, I didn't like what I saw. Actions sometimes carried consequences, which made me realise how stupid I'd been to be so trusting in the first place. I promised myself that if I got out of this alive, I would become a different person who lived differently and made different choices. Safe choices. The conservative side of my nature had never looked more attractive than it did right now.

I must have dropped off at some stage during the night because I woke with a start, and for a brief moment, I'd forgotten where I was. It was pitch-black, so I couldn't see a thing, but I could sense I wasn't alone in the room. I focused on the silence, and then, just when I'd thought things couldn't possibly get any worse, I heard the unmistakable sound of rodents' feet scurrying by the side of my bed, triggering a fresh wave of anxiety that threatened to engulf me.

51

Conor

Since I'd told the cartel the cocaine destined for the streets of London had disappeared without a trace, a major feud had erupted between me and the Gómez family. They were convinced I was lying about the shipment's whereabouts, and they'd kidnapped Ella and threatened to hurt her unless Leo handed over what he owed. As agreed, Leo had paid half the money upfront and was due to pay the balance when the coke was delivered. But he wasn't going to pay for drugs he hadn't received, was he? There wasn't even a remote possibility that was going to happen. So there was no point in asking him.

I'd spent a restless night at my villa trying to come up with a solution. I had enough money stashed in my house in the UK to pay Diego, but it didn't seem right to leave Spain without Ella, and anyway, that didn't solve the other problem. Leo's shipment was still unaccounted for, and he wouldn't be fobbed off about that.

Ella's safety was at the forefront of my mind. Torturing,

maiming and disfiguring people was a regular occurrence for some of the drug barons, and the cartel was known for their brutality; they'd learned from the best. I just hoped Diego wouldn't go quite as far as his Colombian ex-employers, who didn't draw the line at decapitating their victims. In some of the lawless states, many a rival had received the severed head of their loved one in a box.

The cartel's reputation had never bothered me until now. But suddenly, the knowledge that the family kept a network of kidnappers and assassins on their payroll wasn't sitting well with me. Bad things didn't just happen to bad people. I had to get Ella back before it was too late. But finding the location of the missing coke was going to be virtually impossible.

Then a thought sprang into my mind. Diego always embedded his shipments with GPS tracking devices. He used the measure for added security, so this had to be a set-up. He would have known instantly that the drugs had gone off track if somebody had switched them.

'I need to speak to you in private. Can you meet me somewhere?'

'What time is it?' Diego replied and then cleared his throat.

I'd been up all night, so I hadn't thought to check the time before I'd made the call. The Spaniard's voice was husky and groggy. It sounded like I'd woken him up; I didn't give a shit about that. I was desperate to confront him and put an end to the situation, but it was clear Diego hadn't lost any sleep over the matter.

'Six-thirty,' I said. I wasn't about to apologise for the daybreak call. We had important issues to discuss, but they were too sensitive to speak about over the phone, so the sooner we could meet face to face, the better.

'Have you got the money?' Diego asked.

'Not yet, but I have some information regarding the missing shipment.'

'You have until tomorrow morning to deliver the money. When your client pays me what he owes, we can talk. But until that happens, I have nothing to say to you, Conor.'

Diego ended the call before I could say another word. Leo had left me another voicemail to say he wouldn't tolerate any more fucking about; his patience had worn out. He was threatening to send Stumpy to Spain to obliterate the cartel members for failing to deliver his gear on time. If they hadn't been holding Ella captive at a secret location, I'd have been only too pleased to take him up on his offer.

52

Ella

I'd somehow managed to make it through the night, and
when I saw the light start to stream in through the hole
in the shutter, it filled me with hope. I was sure Conor
would be doing everything he could to find me or negotiate
my release.

I lay on the air mattress listening to the sound of my
stomach rumble, thinking about how different my life had
become in the blink of an eye. Now that I looked back
on things, I realised I'd gradually become alienated from
everyone I knew. It wasn't an issue, to begin with; when
you were in a new relationship, you couldn't get enough of
each other and wanted to spend every moment with your
partner. But as time wore on, the isolation increased.

Working with Conor hadn't happened overnight. I was
introduced to his business dealings gradually. I wished I'd
kept my distance now. They say you can never have too
much of a good thing, but that wasn't true. At first, Conor's
lifestyle seemed so glamorous and exciting, but the novelty

had worn off. Once I'd scratched beneath the surface, I'd revealed a different story, a terrifying one.

A tear rolled down my cheek as I glanced down at the restraints around my ankles. And to think, when Conor plucked me from suburbia and deposited me into a life of luxury, I'd thought I was the luckiest girl in the world. I'd imagined my life was about to become the stuff of dreams. But that couldn't have been further from the truth; in reality, I'd just stepped into a nest of vipers.

The sound of voices growing closer grabbed my attention. As the locks opened on the door to the room, the two men walked in, one behind the other. I swung my legs over the side of the mattress as they approached.

'You're coming with us, Isabella,' one of the men said, then pulled me onto my feet and placed a hood over my head.

I was so frightened; my legs turned to jelly. My heart hammered in my chest; something was about to happen, and I was genuinely scared for my life. The man cupped my elbow with one of his hands and led me out of the room.

As I shuffled along beside him, fearing the worst, I allowed myself to consider the possibility that good things were coming, maybe my ordeal was finally over, and the men were going to let me go. The man stopped walking, put his hand on the top of my shoulder and forced me onto a chair. He pulled off my hood, and my eyes darted around the room, which was the filthiest kitchen I'd ever seen. The tiles covering the floor were obscured by dirt. Empty spaces lay where gleaming appliances should be standing, and the grimy cupboard doors were hanging off their hinges.

The moment I took in the stomach-turning sight, I knew

I was right not to eat the food my captors had brought me. I was ravenous now, so it was difficult for me to refuse, but the fear that it might be drugged overrode everything else. Now that I'd seen the unhygienic place it was prepared, the chances were I would have gone down with a bad case of food poisoning if I'd consumed anything made here. It was just as well I'd decided to play it safe and stick to the sealed bottles of water the men gave me instead.

I'd been so distracted by the condition of my surroundings, at first, I hadn't noticed the shiny new blowtorch and power tools, which seemed out of place in the decrepit room, lined up on a rickety table in front of me. As I cast my eyes over them, I didn't need to be told they were torture instruments.

I kept hoping that Conor would burst through the door and rescue me, but this wasn't a scene from a Mills and Boon novel, so that wasn't going to happen. Nobody was coming to help me; I needed to accept that fact. I knew I had to stay strong and build a rapport with the men before they subjected me to horrific physical and mental abuse, but fear controlled my actions, and I was in danger of falling to pieces.

'Please don't hurt me,' I said in Spanish.

Then one of the men suddenly picked up a roll of duct tape and wrapped it around my thighs and chest, pinning me onto the chair.

'Your boyfriend missed the deadline. He hasn't paid up,' one of the men replied.

'Where is the coke?' the other man shouted at me.

Tears sprung to my eyes as my interrogation began, and I willed them not to spill down my cheeks, but I was fighting a losing battle. I couldn't stop my tears from starting to flow.

'I don't know,' I sobbed.

'That's not the answer I was looking for, so I'll ask you again: where is Diego's cocaine?'

'I promise you, if I knew, I'd tell you.' My pulse was racing, and panic coated my words.

'Perhaps this might help you remember.'

I hadn't noticed the bucket full of water on the floor by the leg of the wooden table until the man picked it up and tipped it over my head.

'Jesus!' I yelled before gasping for breath.

The ice-cold liquid had drenched me, instantly chilling me to the bone. It had never occurred to me before that being warm and dry was a simple luxury that I took for granted. Who would have thought an unpretentious act like that would result in something so unpleasant?

'I swear to you, I don't know anything about the cocaine.' My teeth were chattering, and my breathing was so rapid I could hardly get my words out.

The other man tore off the tape that was binding my body to the chair before he placed the hood back over my head. Then he led me out of the kitchen and back to my room. I was visibly shaking from being soaked to the skin and the terrifying experience I'd just endured.

After the man left, I sat on the edge of the mattress, violently shaking. Warming myself up was paramount, or it was a dead cert I'd be miserable for hours. My clothes were stuck to my skin, so I needed to take them off quickly. But I didn't have any spare things to change into, and I had no way of drying off unless I wrapped myself in the scratchy blanket. If I did that, I'd make that wet too, and the temperature dropped rapidly at night at this time of year. My survival instincts suddenly kicked in; I stripped off my top, but I couldn't remove my jeans because my ankles were bound. All I could do was peel them down so that the fabric wasn't in contact with the majority of my legs.

A bitter sob escaped from my lips as I burrowed beneath the musty blanket. Wrapping my arms around myself, I curled into a tight ball. Fear was playing havoc with my mental state, and with only my thoughts for company, I imagined what other twisted things my kidnappers had in store for me. I couldn't get the vision of the power tools out of my head.

I'd never been religious, but I suddenly found myself praying to a God I wasn't sure I believed in, hoping for some divine intervention. I wished something would interrupt the disturbing thoughts that were running riot in my head before I lost it completely. I'd always been a good person to have around in a crisis. Out of all of my friends, I was the dependable one, the one with the level head. But my calm, rational nature seemed to have deserted me in my hour of need, and I was falling apart.

My childhood had been a happy one; I owed my parents so much more than gratitude for keeping me on the straight and narrow. And look how I'd repaid them for everything they'd done for me. A deep sense of shame settled over me. What would they say if they knew I'd thrown the morals they'd instilled in me back in their faces?

I scrunched my eyes tightly to try and block out the images popping into my head, but it didn't work. I kept seeing flashbacks to moments I'd shared with the people closest to me and wondered if I'd ever get to see them again. During the long periods of isolation, I thought about my parents. I thought about Lucy and Amy. I thought about Conor, who I loved with all my heart. But most of all, I thought about how stupid I'd been and how I'd got myself into this mess when I should have known better.

I was furious with myself for making the decision that changed the course of my life, and angry tears purged themselves from my eyes. I couldn't seem to stop them. They were my body's release valve for my pent-up emotions, and with no end in sight, I was overcome with feelings of despair, anxiety, frustration and regret.

As I lay under the blanket shivering, I knew there was a very real possibility that I wasn't going to get out of this hell-hole. I could lose my life due to my own carelessness and reckless behaviour. That thought struck me with paralysing fear. Which left behind a question: if I ended up dying, what would my last thought be?

53

Conor

Diego was either a good liar, or he was as much in the dark about the whereabouts of the missing cocaine as I was. When we'd first starting discussing a new deal, he'd been reluctant to change the terms of our agreement, preferring to keep the volume of the orders small. Why change what wasn't broken? He had a highly sophisticated set-up with excellent transport links, direct access to the motorways and ocean-side distribution.

Diego had been happy to sell us the drugs, but he'd kept us at arm's length. While the cartel had acted as a wholesaler, and Rodrigo's involvement ensured the cargo's safe arrival, we'd never had any issues with the supply chain. That was until Leo had become greedy and forced Diego to outsource the importation of the cocaine to other groups. Once the Peruvian and Colombian contacts had joined forces, it heralded the arrival of trouble. That seemed like quite a coincidence if you asked me.

I'd known Diego wasn't happy with the new arrangement,

but he'd eventually come around to it. By engaging in a bit of good old bribery and corruption, he'd managed to keep the officials on his side. The police in these countries were underpaid, giving them little incentive to bring a kingpin to justice, which was good news for all of us. But they weren't the only threat to the operation. Hispanic gangs and the Spanish mafia dominated the scene, so Diego liked to stay under the other cartels' radar by keeping his shipments small.

At this stage, it was too early to rule out the big players' involvement; it was better to try and keep an open mind. But whichever way I looked at it, something had gone catastrophically wrong with this deal. I racked my brain to work out what could have happened, and I kept coming back to the same thought. The only thing we'd done differently this time was to use unknown Peruvian and Colombian suppliers that Valentina had been keen to vouch for. That had to be where the problem lay, but how could I get Diego to acknowledge the issue if he wasn't prepared to discuss it?

54

Ella

'**I**'ve brought you some breakfast,' I heard one of the men say as he walked through the doorway.

I tried to lift my head from the mattress, but it felt like lead.

'Isabella, wake up.'

I could feel a pair of hands on my shoulders shaking me, but I couldn't respond. I felt delirious.

'Something's wrong with her,' the man shouted, and I heard footsteps running towards the room.

'She's burning up,' one of the men said after he put his hand on my forehead.

He then pulled the blanket off me. I tried to wrap my arms around myself to stop myself from shaking; I felt so cold.

'You better phone Diego,' the other man said as the conversation carried on around me.

The next thing I knew, my ankle restraints were cut off, and my jeans were pulled over my feet. I was vaguely aware that I was only wearing my underwear, and I wondered if the men were going to take it in turns to rape me. I was terrified, but I was too weak to try and fight them.

'These wounds are infected, which is why she has a fever,' an official-sounding voice said.

That was when I realised somebody else was in the room. 'Please, help me,' I managed to say.

'You cannot keep this young woman here; the conditions are appalling, and she needs antibiotics.'

Strong fingers tapping a vein in the crook of my arm and a sharp scratch from a needle were the last things I remembered before darkness engulfed me.

55

Conor

'At ten o'clock, I want you to come to the marina opposite my offices – where my yacht, *La Vida Loca*, is moored. We have things to discuss,' Diego said.

That was a turn-up for the books. I hadn't paid the two million euros yet, so something must have happened to prompt his call. Although I was glad to hear from Diego, I couldn't help wondering why we couldn't conduct our meeting on dry land. I had a horrible feeling that if things didn't go well, I might find myself disposed of at sea.

I'd be lying if I said I wasn't apprehensive at having been summoned to Diego's yacht, but if it opened up lines of communication between us, I'd have to go through with it. I owed it to Ella to do everything in my power to secure her release. Diego had always got on well with my girlfriend, so I had to believe hurting her would be a last resort. Maybe I could use this opportunity to appeal to his better nature and convince him to let her go.

While I walked along the jetty towards *La Vida Loca*, I

could feel the T-shirt under my jacket sticking to my skin as I tried to second-guess what was about to unfold. The closer I got, the more uneasy I felt. And after my last experience on the water, when I was a passenger on the speedboat collecting the drop from Diego's supplier, I couldn't say I was looking forward to venturing out of the harbour any time soon.

When I arrived, Diego was waiting for me on the deck. The cruising yacht stood out from the other all-white modern vessels it was nestled between because of its navy blue hull and portholes, which gave it an old-world charm. Diego reached his gnarly fingers towards me and shook my hand as I boarded the yacht. A sudden gust of wind lifted his long, grey hair off his shoulders and made it dance in the breeze behind him.

'Thank you for coming,' he said.

So far, so good, I thought. His initial welcome was friendly, so I hoped things didn't go downhill from here.

'The others are downstairs,' Diego said. He turned his back on me and began walking towards the stairwell.

My heart was pounding as I followed him below deck. As I descended the stairs, I wondered what I was walking into; anything could be waiting for me once I was hidden away from public view.

My eyes scanned around the traditional teak interior of the main saloon. I spotted Pedro and Valentina sitting at a polished wood table on blue velvet chairs, sipping espresso from tiny white cups. Ella's absence in the room was notable, and I felt my pulse rate begin to soar. I'd hoped Diego had come to his senses and had brought me here to call an end to this situation. But it looked like I was mistaken;

nothing indicated that he was about to hand over my girlfriend.

'Take a seat,' Diego said.

As I pulled out the chair opposite Valentina, I could see her toy-sized dog making itself at home on the sofa at the other end of the open-plan saloon.

'How lovely to see you, darling,' Valentina said.

While she waited for me to reply, she clasped her long, bony fingers together in front of her face as if she was in prayer.

I offered the ageing dollybird a weak smile, but I couldn't bring myself to answer her. The woman was vile. As usual, she was wearing a face full of slap and an inappropriately low-cut top. She held herself in such high esteem – as though she was a Galician goddess that men found irresistible.

Pedro was the only cartel member who didn't speak to me, which didn't particularly surprise me at first. He was a man of few words and totally overshadowed by his domineering wife. As we sat at the table, Pedro started behaving strangely, like he felt uncomfortable in my presence. I fixed my eyes on him, but he averted his gaze. Beads of sweat appeared on his forehead as he sat fidgeting next to Valentina. If you asked me, he looked like a man with something to hide.

'Where's Ella?'

As I asked the question, I noticed the scenery change. The harbour view began to glide past the windows, and a knot formed in my stomach when I realised we were heading out to sea.

'I can assure you, she's being well looked after,' Diego replied.

'I'd like to see her.' I needed some kind of reassurance that the cartel hadn't hurt her.

'I'm sure you would.' Diego smiled. 'But first, we have things to discuss; business before pleasure.'

'I don't think you're in any position to be making all these demands, darling.' Valentina wagged her bony finger at me, then she smiled before letting her full red lips settle back into her trademark pout.

'Would you like some coffee?' Diego asked.

'Yes, please,' I replied, but if truth be known, I'd much rather have had a stiff drink to steady my nerves.

'It's a beautiful day. Why don't we sit out there? You'll have a much better view of the coastline.' Diego gestured with a nod of his head towards a decked area.

Carrying a drink in either hand, Diego led the way across the shiny teak floorboards towards the social space. I took a seat with my back against the chrome railings, facing the open-plan living area. That way, nobody was going to be able to sneak up behind me without me noticing.

'I'm sure you're wondering why we invited you here,' Diego said as he placed an espresso cup and saucer down in front of me.

'Yes, I am.' I fixed the head honcho with my eyes as I tore the end off a sachet of sugar.

'Can you explain to us why your client missed the deadline? He still hasn't paid the outstanding balance.' Diego kept his eyes trained on mine as he leaned back in his chair and took a small sip of his coffee.

'I would have thought that would was obvious?'

'Well, it isn't. Perhaps you would care to explain.' Diego's reply was curt as he placed his cup back on the saucer.

I'd hoped a new development in the situation had prompted Diego's invitation today, but that had been wishful thinking on my part. Nothing appeared to have changed, and we were still going around in circles.

'As I've already told you, my client is refusing to pay for cocaine he didn't receive,' I said.

Leo still didn't know his shipment had been switched, but I wasn't about to share that nugget of information with the cartel.

'Well, then we have a big problem.' Diego shook his head slowly from side to side and exhaled loudly.

Now that Diego had brought up the shipment, he'd opened the door for a discussion. 'I want to ask you a question.'

'Go ahead,' Diego said.

'Do you always use GPS devices on your shipments?'

I was certain I knew the answer, but I just needed confirmation before I made my next point. The demand for black-market goods was insatiable – I should know, I'd spent many teenage years working for Roy peddling knocked-off gear in the local market. So if container loads of handbags and trainers went astray, it made sense that the same thing would happen to valuable shipments of drugs. Suppliers would be negligible if they didn't protect their cargo.

Diego nodded.

'In that case, the GPS would have recorded every inch of the journey the cocaine made.' I smiled, feeling slightly smug. At long last, it seemed like I was beginning to make progress.

'That's true, but I don't understand where you're going with this,' Diego said, scratching his head.

'My client wants to see the recording.'

'For what reason?' Valentina narrowed her dark eyes and drummed her blood-red talons on the table in front of her.

'It will prove to you that we didn't receive the shipment, and then we can put this unpleasant episode to bed,' I replied.

'Your client is very demanding,' Valentina continued. 'What if we refuse to retrieve the records?'

A conversation in Spanish broke out around the table. I should have expected as much.

'If you are that desperate for proof, Pedro can arrange this. He is the administrator,' Diego said.

I felt like I was finally getting somewhere.

'But it will take time to get the information. Pedro will need to access his email to gather the data collected from the journey,' Valentina added.

That sounded like a stalling tactic if ever I'd heard one. Retrieving the information I'd requested didn't seem like a big deal, and it made me wonder why Pedro didn't just pull up the recordings on his phone now instead of glaring at me with his hands on his hips. Sensing this was going to be the end of the conversation, I stood up to take in the view.

'My client would appreciate it if you could make this your top priority,' I said, looking Diego's cousin in the eye.

Pedro didn't bother to reply, but a flash of anger spread across his face before he pulled a gun from the back of his trousers' waistband. Everything happened so fast; I didn't have time to react before the bullet hit me in the chest.

56

Ella

I tried to let out a scream with everything I had in my lungs as the shot rang out, but my cries were muffled by the tape covering my mouth, so nobody heard me. I watched in horror as Conor was thrown backwards by the force of the bullet. He toppled over the side of the yacht, and I pressed my face against the porthole's glass so that I could see what was happening. Conor landed with a splash and floated face down in the freezing water. As soon as he hit the Atlantic Ocean, his blood seeped into the blue water and turned it red.

I had a bird's eye view from my elevated position, but I wasn't sure I wanted to watch. I felt like the bullet had hit me as well, as a searing pain ripped through my body. I desperately wanted to help my boyfriend, but there was nothing I could do but stand here and watch the drama unfolding; each second dragged agonisingly by.

'What the hell have you done?' Diego shouted at Pedro

in Spanish before he turned to his crew and ordered them to help Conor.

Two men immediately jumped overboard and swam over to Conor. One of the men flipped him onto his back and towed him to the side of the yacht. As he was hauled on board, I was sure my boyfriend was dead. Blood was running down the side of his head, and his blue eyes were closed.

'Check if he's breathing,' Diego said.

I held my breath and waited as one of the crew checked my boyfriend's vital signs. The colour had drained from Conor's face; he was deathly pale and unresponsive. Time seemed to stand still.

'He is, sir,' the crew member replied.

I felt my shoulders drop when I heard his response, and tears sprang to my eyes. Conor was still alive, so at least that gave him a fighting chance.

'Take him inside,' Diego instructed.

I stood on tiptoes and craned my neck to get one last look at Conor. One man lifted his ankles while another slid his hands under Conor's shoulder blades. They scooped him off the deck before they carried him into the saloon. I dropped down on the floor, hooked my bound wrists over my knees and hugged them into me as I sobbed my heart out. My thoughts were interrupted when I heard Diego shouting orders at the crew.

'Lie him down over there and get the doctor here immediately.'

My tears dried instantly; I had to pull myself together. I wouldn't be able to hear what was going on if I kept sobbing. Although they were directly below me, it wasn't easy to make out what they were saying. Why didn't they just turn the yacht around and head back to shore? Surely that would be quicker than summoning medical help to come to us.

The more I thought about it, the more I realised from the cartel's point of view, treating a gunshot wound victim in the middle of the Atlantic Ocean was a better option than in the centre of a bustling harbour. In a situation like this, discretion was everything, so they were bound to go down that route. I just hoped the delay wouldn't end up costing Conor his life.

When I'd first heard the sound of my boyfriend's voice, I'd wanted to shout his name out, but my mouth was taped shut. I'd tried to bang and stamp on the floor, but the thick carpet dulled out the sound I was making. Diego had locked me in a room above the saloon. I hadn't been able to see Conor until he'd stepped out onto the lower deck and took a seat at the back of the yacht. I'd tried to get his attention by knocking on the glass, but it was virtually impossible to aim my fists, joined together at the wrist, into the recessed porthole. He didn't even glance in my direction, so I knew he couldn't hear me.

Even before Pedro fired the gun, I knew something dodgy was going on when the cartel members began speaking in Spanish. Conor didn't know that Diego had told Pedro to go along with what he was saying to humour my boyfriend. He had no intention of retracing the cocaine's journey. Diego was convinced Leo was having a cashflow crisis, so Conor had come up with the idea of saying they hadn't received the coke to delay the transfer of the funds. Diego thought Conor was asking to see the data collected from the GPS as a stalling tactic to buy his client some time before he had to hand over the money. It didn't seem to matter what Conor said; he couldn't convince the kingpin he was telling the truth. It was so frustrating. I knew my boyfriend wasn't lying; I'd been with him when he'd tested the shipment.

I didn't understand why Pedro had pulled his gun on my boyfriend. Maybe he'd sensed the net was closing in on him, and he'd panicked, shooting Conor in an attempt to silence him. But he'd behaved recklessly, and now he'd made it look like he had something to hide.

After what seemed like an eternity, I heard the sound of a speedboat approaching, bouncing over the waves as it raced through the icy water. The revs dropped, and it pulled up alongside *La Vida Loca*. I listened as somebody climbed on board, and then they ran across the deck and down the steps.

'Bring me some water, blankets and clean towels,' a man's voice said. I presumed it must belong to the doctor.

'We think Conor must have hit his head against the side of the boat and knocked himself out when he fell. He was unconscious when we pulled him from the water,' Diego explained.

'OK, I'll check him out, but first, can one of you help me take off his clothes?' the doctor said.

I had a sudden flashback to my time in captivity. Why had they left Conor in soaking wet clothes? I knew only too well how miserable it felt. And aside from that, his body temperature was in danger of dropping rapidly. Cold, wet clothing drew the heat from a person's body like a magnet.

By leaving Conor fully clothed, Diego had put him at risk of developing hypothermia.

When I heard Conor yell out in pain, it brought me back to reality. Even though it was hard to listen to my boyfriend crying out in agony, I knew it was a good sign. I'd watched enough episodes of *Casualty* to understand that generally speaking, the more noise a patient made, the less seriously injured they were.

'Hold still. I need to examine you,' the doctor said.

Everyone was speaking Spanish; it must be so confusing for my boyfriend. I would have given anything to be by Conor's side right now, holding his hand and helping him through the ordeal, instead of having to picture the scene in my mind.

'Aargh.' Conor cried out in pain.

The sudden sound made me jump; my nerves were in tatters.

'The bullet is lodged beneath his skin next to his sternum,' the doctor said.

'It's still inside him?' Diego questioned.

'Yes. It's embedded itself in the wall of his pectoral muscle.'

'Is that a good thing?' Diego asked.

'It would have been worse if the bullet had hit his lungs, heart or a major blood vessel,' the doctor replied.

From the loud moans coming from my boyfriend, I could tell he was in excruciating pain.

'Can I see the gun?' the doctor asked.

There was a pause, and I presumed he was checking over the weapon that had injured my boyfriend.

'Luckily for you, the bullet hasn't entered the chest cavity.'

When the doctor finally began speaking in English, I couldn't help thinking, it was about time he included Conor in the conversation instead of talking about him as though he wasn't in the room.

'You will require a minor surgical procedure to remove the cartridge and clean up the wound,' the doctor continued.

'Are you going to do it now?' Conor asked.

My heart skipped a beat at the sound of his voice.

'No, I'll perform the procedure at my medical facility. The bullet came from a small-calibre weapon, and it doesn't look like it's punctured anything important. But you'll need an x-ray to confirm that.'

'Juan, get the speedboat ready and take the doctor and Conor to shore,' I heard Diego say.

In a roundabout way, Pedro had done Conor a favour when he'd shot him. His reckless action wasn't the behaviour of a man with nothing to hide, so it might make Diego come to his senses.

'What the hell were you playing at?' I heard Diego shout as the sound of the speedboat faded into the distance. 'You could have killed him.'

'Well, I didn't, did I?' Pedro responded without trying to hide the irritation in his voice.

'Why did you shoot Conor?' Diego asked.

His question was met with silence.

'Your actions make no sense – unless perhaps Conor has been telling the truth all along, and you wanted to stop me finding out,' Diego continued.

As I listened to Diego putting the pieces of the puzzle together, I was suddenly overcome with emotion. Pedro had inadvertently planted the seed of doubt in his cousin's mind, so it felt like we had won a small victory.

'How could you do this to me?' Diego was enraged and pounded the table so hard, the sound resonated around the room. Even though I wasn't a ring-side spectator, I could tell the tension between the cartel members was palpable.

'I don't know what you're talking about,' Pedro replied.

'I trusted you, and this is how you repay me,' Diego bellowed.

'I haven't done anything,' Pedro shouted back, having lost his cool.

'I don't believe you. I might be old, but I'm nobody's fool.'

Diego continued screaming; I pictured his face contorting and turning red before I heard a scuffle break out.

'Get your hands off him. You're choking him,' Valentina screeched. I could only presume Diego had discharged his anger on his cousin.

'You are family, and I have zero tolerance for betrayal. If I find out you've blindsided me in such a twisted way and double-crossed me...'

'Let him go! Conor is a liar. He is the one who double-crossed you,' Valentina wailed, trying to lay the blame away from Pedro's door.

'The woman you married is pure evil; she's poison.' Venom coated Diego's words. I could hear Pedro coughing and spluttering and presumed Diego had finally loosened his grip. 'Tie them up and take them out of my sight,' Diego said to his crew.

'Yes, sir,' was their response.

'You two are going nowhere until I have an opportunity to check the GPS records for myself,' Diego spat.

My lips strained against the tape as they attempted to stretch into a smile at the thought of Pedro and Valentina being placed in confinement. Even though it had been the day from hell, I felt we were making progress. Pedro's reckless behaviour could have cost Conor his life, but thankfully it hadn't come to that. Instead, it had been the catalyst that raised Diego's suspicions.

57

Conor

The fact that I was young and healthy meant the doctor discharged me a matter of hours after he'd removed the bullet from my chest so that I could recuperate at home. He recommended bed rest for two to three days and a course of antibiotics. I was happy enough to take the tablets, but I couldn't justify lounging around the house while Diego was still holding Ella. I needed to strike while the iron was hot.

'Have you had a chance to check the data?' I asked.

'Yes. Can you come to my offices? I want to show you the results in person,' Diego replied.

As yet, I didn't have concrete proof, but I was ninety-nine per cent certain that Pedro and Valentina had masterminded the cocaine scam and had stolen the missing cargo. My money had been on the two of them from the moment the shipment vanished. However, convincing Diego of that had turned out to be nigh on impossible because whoever was responsible had done their best to frame me for the coke's disappearance.

Even though the cartel had a volatile relationship, Diego was adamant that a member of his family wouldn't double-cross him. He'd refused to believe that I was telling the truth about the missing shipment, but with any luck, the kingpin was about to make a massive U-turn. I could feel my skin prickle the closer I got to Diego's offices as the suspense heightened.

'How are you feeling?' Diego asked when I walked into the conference room.

'I've been better,' I replied, shaking his outstretched hand.

'Take a seat,' Diego said, gesturing to the chair next to his.

'I've checked the data from the tracker, and it would appear you were correct. The GPS signal should have been coming from London, not from locations all over Spain,' Diego said, pulling up a document on his laptop.

I wanted to let out a sigh but decided not to tempt fate; it looked like this nightmare was finally going to come to an end.

'Pedro and the driver would have been in two-way communication in case there were any issues along the way. He was the only person who would have known the shipment had been switched.' Diego paused for a moment and considered what he'd just said. 'Scrap that idea. Valentina's the driving force in their relationship, so I'm sure she would have been the instigator.'

I had to agree. There was no doubt that Valentina wore the trousers.

'Why do you think they decided to steal the cargo?'

'Since this came to light, I've made contact with the Peruvian and Colombian suppliers we used, and they confirmed that this wasn't the first time they'd done business with Pedro and Valentina. I've had the locations of the GPS signals checked, and it appears my cousin and his wife have been using them as safehouses. They've been hiding secret shipments of drugs and money there for a while now.'

'Why would they do that?' I asked.

'They must have been planning to split from me for some time,' Diego said.

He seemed surprised by his discovery, but the news that the leaders' turbulent relationship caused its eventual demise didn't shock me. The Spanish camp's internal politics had always been dicey; our meetings were often conducted on shaky ground.

'So now that you know my client didn't receive the drop, will you let Ella go?'

'Of course. Juan, can you go and get Isabella?'

'How long will it take you to organise the shipment?' Leo was breathing down my neck, and I wouldn't be able to stall him much longer.

'I'm just finalising arrangements; the cocaine will leave shortly,' Diego replied.

'My client will be pleased to hear that.'

I stood up when Juan walked back into the room. Ella came into view a moment later. She charged across the room and threw herself into my arms. I felt myself wince with pain as her head made contact with my chest.

'I'm sorry; I didn't mean to hurt you,' Ella said, running the tips of her fingers over the front of my T-shirt, which concealed the dressing covering my wound.

'There's no need to apologise,' I replied, wrapping my arms tightly around my girlfriend.

Ella turned her beautiful face towards mine, and tears streamed down her face. 'I wasn't sure this day would ever come.'

'I've been so worried about you.' I fixed Ella with my eyes. 'Are you OK?'

'Yes,' Ella replied, wiping away the wet patches on her cheeks with the back of her hand.

I knew she was putting on a brave face for my benefit. There was no denying, Ella was a natural beauty, but she looked like a shell of her former self. After the ordeal she'd been through, she looked pale and drawn. My heart lurched when I looked down at her. I'd let the love of my life down in the worst possible way. I should have protected her; I knew what these men were capable of when I got her involved in my business. They'd kidnapped Ella to teach me a lesson because they thought I'd double-crossed them.

Ella had gone to hell and back for me. Diego hadn't even apologised for putting my girlfriend through her terrifying ordeal or for doubting my version of events. If he'd been willing to listen to me in the first place, all of this could have been prevented. But I should have expected as much. The Spanish cartel never felt remorse for their crimes. Their mantra was, if people got in their way, they'd have to suffer the consequences.

As Diego stood watching our emotional reunion, I could feel the anger rising within me. I was delighted to be holding Ella in my arms again and didn't want to spoil the moment. So I turned my attention away from him and back to my girlfriend. I cupped her face in my hands and planted a kiss on her soft lips.

I wanted to get Ella as far away from Diego as possible in

case he had a sudden change of heart. The man had proved to me that he couldn't be trusted, and although I'd have to go through with the deal to keep Leo off my back, it was the last time I was going to do business with the Gómez cartel. I wasn't prepared to work with people who threatened my nearest and dearest if things didn't go their way. It was time to take stock of my life and reconsider my options; almost losing Ella had forced me to rethink the future. I was never going to risk her safety again; she was far too important to me.

58

Ella

Conor and I stayed up long into the night, reliving the ordeal we'd both been through.

'I can't explain why, but as soon as I opened the front door that day, I knew something was wrong. I could sense it. I didn't know you'd been snatched at that stage, but as I started searching for you, I had a strange feeling in the pit of my stomach.' Conor held my hand as he spoke.

'I didn't realise the men were there at first. I was trying to decide whether to go for a swim or not when I was grabbed from behind. The next thing I knew, two men were binding my wrists and ankles with thick cable-tie restraints. I tried to fight them off, but I wasn't strong enough.'

Conor squeezed my hand, then looked deeply into my eyes. 'You must have been terrified.'

'I've never been so scared in my life. When the men taped my mouth shut and put a hood over my head before they bundled me into the boot of a car, I genuinely thought they were going to kill me.' I was trying to hold it together, but my voice cracked with emotion as I retold the story.

Conor pulled me towards him and placed a kiss on the top of my head.

'When I realised you were gone, I was petrified they were going to hurt you. So I didn't lose hope, I made myself cling to the fact that you'd always got on well with Diego. I reasoned he'd only become physical with you as a last resort. You don't have to answer this, but did the men torture you?'

I felt tears spring to my eyes as the memories came flooding back. 'The men strapped me to a chair and questioned me about the missing shipment. I told them I didn't know anything about it, so they poured a bucket of freezing cold water over me. It might not sound like much, but it was horrific. I had no way of getting warm and dry, and I was soaked to the skin and chilled to the bone.'

Conor wrapped his arms around me and rocked me backwards and forwards as I cried. 'You've been so brave. It must have been awful for you.'

I pulled away from my boyfriend's embrace and looked him straight in the eye. 'Do you know what the most terrifying part was?'

'I have no idea,' Conor replied.

'I hated being alone in the dark.'

I had an age-inappropriate fear of darkness. It was, at best, embarrassing and at worst debilitating. It stopped me from doing everyday things that other people took for granted. I'd avoid certain circumstances like the plague, and just the anticipation of being somewhere without light could bring on a full-blown panic attack.

'I've always prided myself on being a tough cookie. If I could have seen what I was up against, I'm pretty sure my stress levels would have instantly reduced. But the darkness intensified my fear tenfold. Well, that and the sound of rodents running around under my bed…'

Conor's mouth dropped open, and his eyes widened until his irises resembled the yolks in sunny-side-up eggs. He would have freaked out if he'd seen how dirty the place was.

'Do you have any idea where they were holding you?'

'No, but it must have been in the middle of nowhere. There was no sound of passing traffic. It was eerily quiet. I think the building might have been a farmhouse once upon a time, but it was in a dilapidated state. The windows were boarded up with corrugated steel, and it had the filthiest kitchen I'd ever seen.'

Conor stared at me with a look of horror on his face. I knew that would get to him. My boyfriend was a clean freak. He might be strong and tough on the outside, but he'd go into meltdown at the thought of a food-splattered cooker hob and dirty pots and pans. But that's what made him the person he was. We all had our own Achilles heel, and soiled items, especially in the kitchen, were Conor's. He put the quest for cleanliness above everything else. Although that seemed alien to me – life was too short to lose sleep over going to bed without doing the washing up – it was the sort of thing that gave my boyfriend nightmares. I liked to think my phobia was more rational. But I'd never got to the bottom of whether my fear was the darkness itself or the unknown dangers that lurked in it.

I pulled my legs up onto the sofa, and as I went to tuck my feet under my body, my skinny jeans rode up a little.

'What happened to you?' Conor asked when he noticed the bandages covering the healing skin around my ankles.

'The ties the men were restraining me with were so tight they were digging into my flesh. The wounds ended up becoming infected, which was a blessing in disguise.'

'That's a funny thing to say,' Conor said, raising an eyebrow.

'Maybe it is, but it kick-started the chain of events that led to my freedom. If I hadn't needed to see a doctor, I might still be stuck in that grim place. Every cloud...'

Conor was looking at me with a puzzled expression on his face.

'The doctor insisted I was moved as the conditions were appalling.'

'Where did they take you?'

'I was out of it at the time, so I don't really remember what happened, but when I woke up the next morning in a four-poster bed, I discovered I'd been taken to Diego's house. What a contrast that was; his home was like a palace.'

'That doesn't surprise me.'

'You didn't know I was onboard *La Vida Loca* when you came to meet the cartel, did you?'

'No.' Conor shook his head.

'I was locked in a room above the saloon. I couldn't see you at first, but I heard everything that was going on.'

'I was hoping Diego had summoned me because he was going to release you. I wasn't expecting to get shot in the chest for my trouble.' Conor smiled.

'This probably doesn't seem much like a silver lining, but

if Pedro hadn't shot you, things might have turned out very differently. Diego had no intention of retracing the cocaine's journey.'

Conor crossed his arms while he mulled over what I'd just told him. 'Really? He told me he was going to retrieve the data they'd collected from the GPS.'

'I know he did, but he was just humouring you. Diego was convinced you had come up with the idea of saying you hadn't received the coke because Leo was having a cashflow crisis, and you were trying to delay the transfer of the funds. He only became suspicious that something wasn't right when his cousin fired the gun. If Pedro had kept his cool, the outcome could have been very different.'

'I suppose, in that case, taking a bullet was a small price to pay.'

'I wouldn't go as far as saying that.'

'It's an occupational hazard in my line of work. It's not the first time I've stared down the barrel of a gun, and I'm not convinced it'll be the last. But, luckily for me, it's hard to kill a bad thing.' Conor laughed.

How could my boyfriend find the idea of being gunned down even remotely amusing? 'I didn't know you'd been shot before.'

Conor pulled up his T-shirt and pointed to the faint line running down the centre of his stomach. I remembered asking him where he'd got the mark from, and he'd told me it was an appendix scar. At the time, I'd thought it was in an odd place, but I'd brushed that idea away; why would Conor need to lie about something like that? Now I knew what he'd been hiding.

'I was unlucky enough to be in the wrong place at the

STEPHANIE HARTE

wrong time and got caught up in the violent tit-for-tat feud between Bobby Parker and Leo Carr.'

'Oh my God. What happened?'

'I was standing on the pavement minding my own business when a guy inside a car opened fire. I still don't know who ordered the hit. But either way, whether the bullet was meant for Leo or Bobby, it managed to miss both of them, and it hit me in the stomach.' Conor shook his head, and a smile played on his lips.

My boyfriend's words tripped off his tongue. He was so casual about the whole thing, but I was shocked that he'd been the victim of a drive-by shooting. It was scary to think that violence like that was part of his everyday life. The murky world he did business in was a dangerous place. To think that before my ordeal, I'd been too starry-eyed to see it.

59

Conor

Once I delivered Leo's coke, I'd break the news to him that he'd need to find a new go-between. We'd had a close call, so I needed to take heed of the warning and retire from the action before things got really out of hand. I'd always wanted to be the main player, and I'd had a good run, but being powerful came at a price. It was time to get out of the game. The bigger the name you made for yourself, the more enemies you acquired along the way.

'It still doesn't seem real. The last time I was in this villa, two men abducted me at gunpoint,' Ella said, derailing my train of thought. 'Even though I love this place, I don't feel safe here after what happened.'

'Trust me, Ella, I'll protect you; I won't let anyone hurt you again. First thing tomorrow, we'll fly back to England. OK?'

'OK,' Ella replied, giving me a half-smile.

I felt a shiver run down the length of my spine. The outcome of the situation could have been so different. Seeing the red marks around my girlfriend's ankles was a stark reminder that innocent people got tortured and sometimes murdered when they got caught up in a drug cartel's business. It was one thing Diego wanting to punish me, but taking Ella in retaliation for the cocaine's disappearance was a low blow.

'You've been through so much because of me. You look exhausted.' I cupped the back of Ella's head with my hand, leaned towards her and placed a kiss on her lips.

'I'm shattered. Maybe we should go to bed, but do you mind if we leave a light on?' Ella said, stifling a yawn.

As Ella and I were packing up our belongings the following day, a call came through on my mobile from Leo.

'Unless you want Stumpy to rearrange your features, I suggest you stop fannying about and get your arse back to Mile End with my long-overdue order. I don't trust Diego's crew, so I want you to personally accompany my gear. It's the least you can do to make up for the delay.' Leo's voice boomed down the phone, so I held it away from my ear and rolled my eyes.

He wasn't the only one who had reservations. After what had happened last time, I wasn't sure we could trust the Spanish couriers to deliver the shipment in one piece either. But if I travelled with the cargo, to make certain nothing went wrong, where would that leave Ella? It was too dangerous for her to hitch a ride in the van. I didn't want her to be implicated in the deal, and if the drugs were seized, she would be. I knew she wouldn't be happy, but I couldn't risk there being any more issue with Leo's order, so Ella would have to fly back to the UK on her own.

'You're not serious, are you?' Ella's eyes flashed with fury, and they bored into mine when I broke the news.

My girlfriend's usual mild manner seemed to have deserted her, but I supposed after what she'd just been through, her personality was bound to have been affected. I'd never seen Ella take such a stand before; she wasn't holding back. She obviously felt strongly about the situation and wanted me to know she wasn't happy with the arrangement.

'Your selfishness astounds me sometimes, Conor. Correct me if I'm wrong, but didn't you tell me last night that we were going to fly back to England first thing in the morning? Both of us?'

'I know I said that, but I hadn't spoken to Leo at that stage.' I felt bad going back on my word, but I was only doing it to protect her.

'I can't believe after what I've been through, you're going to put me on a plane and leave me to travel alone.'

Tears sprang into my girlfriend's big brown eyes, and I felt a pang of guilt as I watched her wiping them away. I could see where she was coming from, but it wasn't as though I'd bought her a ticket on a packed scheduled flight. She was going back to the UK on the private plane I'd chartered. I was in the doghouse, so I reached across the table and took hold of her hand. But instead of winning her over, she wrenched the two fingers I'd caught hold of out of my grip.

'I don't want to go on my own.' Ella's tone was petulant. 'Why can't I go in the van with you?' Ella crossed her arms over her chest and fixed me with a glare.

'It's too risky.'

'And flying alone isn't?'

'It's not as if you're flying economy class on Ryanair. I've booked the four-seater to take you home, and I'll have a car waiting at Biggin Hill airport for you. It might be best if you stay with your mum and dad until I get back, though. Just to be on the safe side.' I offered Ella a smile, but she didn't reciprocate the gesture.

60

Ella

I turned my face away as Conor went to kiss me goodbye when he dropped me off at the airport. I knew it was a childish thing to do, but I was still furious with him. It was about time he realised he couldn't always charm his way out of situations.

'Don't be like that, Ella. I'll phone you when I get to Portsmouth,' Conor said, flashing me a bright smile.

Without saying a word, I took my bags out of his hands and marched off towards the private jet.

'Thanks for letting me stay,' I said before I put my luggage down in the front room of my parents' flat.

'Don't be silly. You know you're always welcome. You might not live here anymore, but this is still your home, Ella,' Mum said, smiling at me.

I couldn't tell them the real reason I was taking refuge within their walls. Mum and Dad would be worried sick if they'd known what I'd just been through, so I decided it was best to keep them in the dark.

'I hate rattling around in that big house on my own while Conor's away on business. You know what I'm like; I'm a sociable creature and crave people's company.' Being around my parents would help me to feel less isolated and take my mind off my recent ordeal.

'Well, we're delighted to have you here. Aren't we, Scott?'

'Absolutely, we don't see nearly enough of you these days. Loverboy hogs all of your attention,' Dad said, throwing his arm around my shoulder before he placed a kiss on the side of my head. 'Stay as long as you like.'

I suddenly felt bad for neglecting them. I was lucky to have such a good connection with my parents, but it was part of growing up to spread your wings and leave home. Dad had a point, though. Since I'd been with Conor, I had started seeing less and less of them.

'You and Conor seem to be going from strength to strength,' Mum said as we sat side by side on the sofa immersed in the simple pleasure of dunking shortbread fingers into mugs of tea.

I didn't want to admit that our relationship had hit rocky ground because I knew Mum would ask why, and I wouldn't be able to tell her what was behind it. Mum would be horrified if she knew Conor's business partners had kidnapped me over a disagreement.

'When you two were newly an item, I have to say Dad and I were worried you weren't right for each other. I'm glad you proved us wrong.' Mum smiled at me before she took a bite of her biscuit.

I smiled back, remembering how Conor had kept

chipping away at them until he'd had them eating out of the palm of his hand.

'We'd been concerned about the age difference,' Mum explained.

'I get that.'

Pretty much everyone I knew had had the same reaction when I'd told them my boyfriend was twenty-nine.

'Maybe if you weren't nineteen, the gap wouldn't have seemed so extreme.'

I couldn't see what all the fuss was about; Conor was ten years older than me – big deal. But I understood what Mum meant; the gap somehow seemed larger because I was still a teenager. If I'd been thirty when we'd met, I doubted people would have the same issue.

'You make a lovely couple, Ella. Dad and I are delighted for you. I'm going to sound like I'm a hundred years old now, but you fell so hard for him; we were worried about his intentions.' Mum threw her head back and laughed.

'What can I say? I'd never met anyone like Conor before; he swept me off my feet, so it was hard to keep them on the ground…'

'The two of you are like love's young dream. Conor takes such good care of you, and he's been incredibly generous to us. He's definitely a keeper. You've bagged yourself a thoroughly nice guy,' Mum concluded, grinning like she was a star-struck fan.

'I'm glad you approve,' I replied with a smile on my face. But if Mum only knew the half of it, I thought.

Conor's persistence had paid off. By persevering and smothering them with lashings of Baxter charm, he'd managed to push through my parents' resistance to our relationship, and now they adored him.

I looked down at the square floral face of my Gucci watch and realised that the ship should have docked by now. Conor hadn't called me yet. I spent a tense hour sitting on the sofa next to Mum, pretending to be engrossed in the TV while discreetly glancing down at my wrist at regular intervals. Time seemed to be dragging. My anger was dissipating by the minute, and worry was rapidly replacing it.

61

Conor

Although I'd earned my living from questionable means, and I'd got into a few scrapes in my time, I'd never been in trouble with the police before. Somehow, I'd always managed to keep my nose clean, which was more than could be said for a lot of people I did business with.

It wasn't just myself and Leo who were edgy; Diego didn't want to take any chances with the shipment this time either, so Juan was going to drive the van to Santander, and I'd take over once we reached British soil. The fact he was entrusting the job to his main man hadn't gone unnoticed; he'd taken a small step towards repairing the trust between us.

Everything had gone smoothly on the Spanish side. We were almost home and dry; there was just one more hurdle to cross. Juan sat in the passenger seat with his dark eyes fixed on the windscreen, staring straight ahead. As the car in front began to move, I put the van into gear and joined the procession as the convoy crawled down the ramp.

I felt my heartbeat speed up a little as we approached customs officers wearing hi-vis jackets, but it went into overdrive when one of the officers waved me into a bay. I had to resist the urge to glance sideways at Juan.

'Don't panic; this happens all the time. Because we're carrying freight, they probably just want to check our booking details,' Juan said.

Diego had warned me that the ferry operators did spot checks at the port to catch commercial vehicles travelling on passenger tickets.

As I stopped the van, I had to loosen my grip on the steering wheel before I discreetly wiped the palms of my hands down the front of my jeans. Juan sat next to me, displaying the sort of calm exterior I could only dream about; I wasn't normally the nervous type, but a lot was riding on this. Nobody had to tell me that I would give the game away if I didn't get a grip. Two officers walked around the outside of the van like sharks circling potential prey. I lowered the window and waited for them to approach.

'Good evening, sir. Can I see your passports and tickets, please?' the officer asked.

Juan handed me his, and I passed both booklets through the open window along with a copy of our booking.

'Thank you,' the man said before he checked them over. 'What is the purpose of your visit?'

My lines were well-rehearsed, but I hoped my voice wouldn't give away my nerves. 'My friend and I are starting up a small business selling handcrafted leather goods, and we're bringing over some stock.'

'Can you both step out of the vehicle, please?'

'Is there a problem?' I asked as the man's words swam

around in my head. He didn't answer, so Juan and I both did as instructed.

'Please take a seat over there,' the other officer said. 'My colleague and I need to carry out a search of your van.'

They were the words I'd been dreading since we left Vigo more than thirty hours ago. Juan and I sat side by side in silence on two plastic chairs, watching the other passengers drive down the ramp and out of the port without being stopped. Why had they chosen us? My gut feeling was that it had to be a tip-off, and if it was, Pedro and Valentina's names were written all over it.

Two immigration officers examined the outside of the van while other members of staff armed with carbon dioxide, heartbeat and passive infrared detectors got to work testing for the presence of clandestine illegal immigrants. Even though I knew we didn't have any stowaways on board, my pulse raced. I had to stop myself from sighing with relief when they gave the all-clear.

But my joy was short-lived, and my heart sank when I saw a floppy-eared black-and-white springer spaniel come bounding into view, its tail turning like a propeller. The dog's lead strained as it dragged the handler, armed with a tennis ball, behind it. It was so keen to get in on the action, the spaniel could barely contain its excitement as two of the officers unloaded the cargo and laid it out on the ground for the dog to sniff. The handler unclipped the dog's lead from its harness, and it took off like a contestant on *Supermarket Sweep*. I watched it weaving in and out of the boxes with its pink tongue sticking out of its mouth as it ran around looking for signs of drugs.

When it didn't indicate it had found anything, the handler

caught hold of the dog's collar and led it to the back of the van. My heart hammered in my chest. I knew we were in real trouble. The handler made the dog sit in front of the van's open back doors so that it could refocus, which must have been difficult because anyone could see the springer had a high drive for search and retrieve.

'Ready…' The handler pointed his gloved finger in front of the dog's face for several seconds. 'Go, Zorro,' he said, signalling for the dog to jump up into the empty space.

Even though my stomach was twisting in knots, I couldn't help smiling. What a great name for a dog with black patches around his eyes, I thought. Zorro's markings made him look like he was wearing a mask. But it was time to face reality. The customs officials might have the most sophisticated state-of-the-art technology known to mankind, but there was nothing better for finding a consignment of concealed drugs than a well-trained dog's nose.

Zorro's handler stood in front of the van's doors as the dog scampered around the interior. After several nail-biting moments, the spaniel's black-and-white face reappeared in the opening.

'All clear. Good work, Zorro,' the handler said, throwing the dog's tennis ball in the air as a reward. Then he turned to his colleagues and smiled. 'Proud Dad moment; this was his first job.'

I could have run over and given the dog a hug when Zorro leaped out of the van with the ball in his mouth. He waited obediently with his tail wagging while the handler clipped his lead onto his harness. Then he dropped to his knees and fussed over the dog.

'Good boy,' the handler said, praising the spaniel, giving Zorro one last pat on the back before leading him away.

Good boy indeed, I thought as the original two men began loading the boxes back into the van. As the newly recruited springer spaniel hadn't indicated the presence of anything illegal, they'd called off the search. Although the hidden compartments were difficult to spot, the customs officers may well have noticed them if they'd paid close attention to the panels. And thankfully, as we'd hoped, the pungent smell of the leather had masked the odour of the drugs, so Zorro hadn't picked up the scent.

As I drove along by the quay, I glanced over at Juan. Now that we were heading to safety, his calm exterior had deserted him; he looked like he'd aged ten years since the officers had carried out their search.

'Stop the van,' Juan shouted. He flung open the door, jumped out of the passenger seat and threw up all over the grass verge.

62

Ella

When my mobile rang in my hand, and Conor's name flashed up, I swiped at the screen to answer the call. 'I'll be back in a minute,' I said to Mum as I walked into my bedroom and closed the door behind me. 'Why are you so late?' I whispered into the handset. I wasn't sure why I did that; it wasn't as though Mum would be able to hear our conversation over the sound of the TV.

'The boat was late docking, and we were the last ones off,' Conor replied.

'That's a relief! Thank God you got here safely. I was starting to get worried. I thought something had gone wrong, and you'd been arrested.'

'No, nothing like that.' Conor laughed. 'Everything went smoothly. I can't wait to see you. Shall I come and pick you up when I get back to London?'

'No, leave it until tomorrow. It'll be late by the time you get here, and I don't want to disturb Mum and Dad; they get up early. I'll stay at the flat tonight.'

'OK, fair enough,' Conor said, his words laced with disappointment.

It was true; I didn't want to disrupt my parents' evening, but there was another reason I was stalling going back to Conor's. I wanted to make sure my boyfriend had cut and delivered the coke to Leo before I stepped foot in his house again.

I didn't want to discuss the sensitive matter over the phone, but I was never going to be comfortable living at Conor's place if he continued to hide cash and cocaine there. I thought back to when that intruder had plagued us. Conor had told me it was probably some lowlife crackhead looking to steal something so they could fund their next hit. After everything that had happened, it made me question his theory. If you asked me, it seemed too much of a coincidence that his house was targeted twice by a random burglar.

'What time do you want me to pick you up?' Conor asked.

The sound of my boyfriend's voice broke my train of thought and brought me back to the present. 'About ten o'clock,' I replied.

'You've got yourself a date.'

Conor's voice was cheerful, and I knew without even seeing his handsome face, a big smile was pasted across it. He was carrying on as if nothing had happened, but the harrowing ordeal of being kidnapped would poison my life if I let it.

I was naturally a very trusting person; some people would say I was naïve. But being young and inexperienced wasn't a crime. Recently I'd become quite cynical. I didn't like feeling this way. But I was almost certain being in this state of mind wasn't a conscious decision, and I hoped it was a temporary phase I was going through. I'd always been a positive person, a glass-half-full kind of girl. I couldn't think of anything worse than having a negative outlook on life.

I hadn't told my parents or friends about what happened. How could I? They'd quite rightly be horrified, but now I was stuck in a rut. I wished I had somebody I could confide in – keeping stuff bottled up wasn't a healthy thing to do; it took a lot of energy to suppress strong emotions. I attempted to channel everything into putting the terrifying experience behind me, but the more I tried to shut out the memories, the more they resurfaced. I kept waking in the night in a cold sweat, imagining I could hear the sound of scurrying feet, and I couldn't seem to get the smell of mildew out of my nostrils.

I was trying to put on a brave face, but it wasn't easy; my nerves were torn to ribbons, and I jumped at the slightest thing. I felt like I was trapped beneath a heavy weight that was slowly suffocating me, squeezing the life out of me little by little.

63

Conor

I could hear the concern in my girlfriend's voice when she'd asked why we'd arrived so late. I didn't like lying to her, but I reasoned on this occasion, it was better to shield her from the truth. It would only distress her to know how close I'd come to getting caught with a van-load of Class-A drugs. Spinning her the line that the ship docked late and we were the last ones off accounted for a lot of the lost time; it was just as well we'd arrived when expected and were one of the first to disembark.

If Ella had known the customs officers went through the van with a fine-tooth comb, it would have scared her to death. Even after carrying out a sensitive search, with the help of Zorro, the bottom line was they hadn't managed to locate the cocaine. I was grateful that we'd used a different smuggling method this time. Instead of concealing the blocks inside the cargo, Diego's men had stashed the coke in the wall panels and behind the false ceiling. It's just as well they did. Otherwise, Zorro would have detected the scent, and the officers would have found it.

Although Ella seemed to buy my excuse, I did feel guilty that I'd lied to her again, but it was in her own best interests not to know how close Juan and I had come to getting caught. After what she'd been through because of me, I wasn't sure she'd be prepared to wait for me if I got sent down for a long stretch. And who could blame her? She was a beautiful young woman with her whole life in front of her.

'Well, well, look who it isn't. About fucking time too,' Leo said when I walked into the run-down Portakabin next to the Bow Flyover he used as an office space.

He was sitting behind the desk dressed in his trademark pinstriped suit and cufflink combination, twiddling a Bic biro in his hand.

'I see you haven't channelled any of your profits into upgrading your premises,' I remarked as my eyes scanned the shabby interior.

Leo's short, stocky frame shot out of his seat, and he gripped on to the desk in front of him as he fixed me with his bulging eyes. 'Less of the fucking attitude, Baxter. Where's the coke?' Spittle flew from Leo's mouth when he spoke.

I lifted up the large black holdall I was carrying and dropped it on the table.

'Is that it?'

'The rest's in the car.'

I hadn't wanted to draw attention to myself by bringing the whole shipment in at once.

'Go and get it. I need to check it's all there,' Leo said to Roy and Stumpy.

I rolled my eyes and handed the Scotsman my keys. 'Do you think I'm trying to short-change you?'

'You can never be too careful.' Leo gave me a sideways glance before he unbuttoned his suit jacket, slipped it off and hung it over the back of his chair.

I checked the time on my watch. This had better not take long, or I wouldn't make it to Ella's by ten.

'Am I holding you up?' Leo asked.

'I've got another appointment soon.'

'Is that so? Well, too fucking bad; you'll have to wait until I carry out a bit of quality control.'

Leo turned his attention away from me. He opened the holdall and took out a baggie, then tipped a small amount of the cocaine onto his desk. Dipping his finger into it, he rubbed it onto his gums.

'Where do you want us to put it, boss?' Roy asked.

'Bring it over here. I need to check it.'

I let out a loud sigh so Leo would know how I felt about him scrutinising the delivery.

'Don't get your fucking knickers in a twist, son. You've got a nerve huffing and puffing after the shit you put me through. I have every right to examine what I've just purchased, so settle down until I've finished. And if I hear another peep out of you, I'm going to put a bullet in your head,' Leo said.

I knew that was no idle threat, but the clock was ticking, and I could tell Leo was dragging his heels, not to be thorough, but for the sake of it. He was trying to flex his newly acquired muscles and exert his power over me. I was in danger of losing my shit any minute. The whole reason I'd branched out into becoming a middleman in the first place was to get out from under the thumb of men like Leo. But I didn't want to prolong the meeting, so I held my tongue.

'I'm out of here,' I said. Now that the handover was complete, I was going to collect Ella.

'Give my regards to Trisha next time you see her,' Roy piped up as I was walking out of the door.

I turned around and looked him in the eye. I should have just ignored him, but I decided to offer him a bit of advice instead. 'Do yourself a favour and stay away from my mum. She doesn't need an old scrote like you back in her life.'

'The way you're talking, anyone would think Trisha was something special. Let's face it, Conor, your mother's a tramp. Everyone knows she's the local bike. We've all had a ride on her, haven't we, lads?' Leo threw his head back and laughed.

When Roy and Stumpy joined in, the sound bounced off the flimsy walls and echoed around the room. Leo's comment made me see red, and the atmosphere changed in an instant. I didn't have a close relationship with my mum, but that didn't mean I was going to stand by and let the fucker disrespect her.

'You shouldn't have said that.' I glared at the jumped-up little wanker while he ran his thumbs down the inside of his braces.

Leo glared back at me while he contemplated his next move, then he very wisely decided to back off. He held the palms of his hands out in front of him as he walked towards me.

'Settle down, son. I was only joking. You know what I'm like; I'm a straight talker. I call a spade a spade.'

I could see Stumpy eyeballing me, waiting for me to make a move. The man was a mad bastard with an evil temper, and it didn't take much to rattle him. He'd rip a person's head off if he didn't like the way they were looking at him. But I'd reached the end of the line with Leo. This latest deal had been a disaster from start to finish, and I'd promised myself as soon as it became viable, I'd get out of the game. Now seemed like as good a time as any to break the news to him.

'You're going to need to find yourself another mug to do your dirty work. I'm sure I don't need to remind you that I'm a free agent, and as of now, I've officially retired.' The words felt good as they left my mouth.

'Did you hear that, boys? If he thinks he can just walk away, he's more stupid than I gave him credit for.' Leo laughed. 'Do you want to end up in the foundations with the marksman? I have no loyalty to you. You seem to have forgotten, I only kept you alive because you were useful to me, but if that's no longer the case...'

That was a death threat if ever I'd heard one. I knew witnessing the bloodbath would come back to haunt me. I'd have to think long and hard about my decision now that Leo was holding his trump card over me.

'Conor, you've got shit for brains, and I have to say that didn't come from my side, so you must have inherited your intelligence from your mother.'

'What the fuck are you going on about now, you stupid bastard?'

'You're the only bastard around here. My folks were legally hitched when I was conceived. I might have knocked Trisha up, but I wasn't prepared to put a ring on her finger.

If I'd ever ventured down the route of saddling myself with a ball and chain, my intended would have had a bit of class. Let's face it, son, nobody could accuse your mother of ticking that box.'

I stood open-mouthed, staring at the balding man in front of me as his words bounced around the inside of my head. It was too much for me to take in. He had to be lying to wind me up. There was no other feasible explanation. I'd like to think we didn't bear even a passing resemblance to each other. It was a hideous enough thought that Leo's DNA ran through one of my siblings' veins, but I didn't want to consider the fact that he was my father. Trying to get my head around that was proving to be impossible.

Leo's words were the touchpaper that threatened to set our whole relationship alight. He couldn't have picked a worse time to drop his bombshell; the last thing I wanted was to be in a bad mood when I picked Ella up. But his words kept replaying in my mind. They were stuck on a continuous loop. I had to put some distance between us, so I stormed out of the Portakabin and jumped behind the wheel of my car. Then I pulled out onto the dual carriageway and floored the accelerator.

When I pulled into the Arnold Estate, I thought about texting my girlfriend to say that I'd wait in the car for her, but I knew how that was going to look; it would come across as being rude, and I didn't want to offend Joanne and Scott. I blew out a slow breath as I rang the doorbell, trying to block all thoughts of Leo from my mind.

'Hello, mate. Long time no see. Come on in,' Scott said when he opened the front door.

Ella and Joanne were in the kitchen drinking mugs of tea, chattering away for all it was worth when I walked in.

'Hello, Conor,' Joanne said. 'I'll put the kettle on. Would you like a cuppa?'

'Not for me, thanks.' I walked over to where Ella was standing with her back against the countertop, slid my arm around her waist, then stooped to kiss her. 'So what are you two gossiping about?'

'Wouldn't you like to know?' Ella replied.

'I bet my ears are burning.' I laughed.

Ella put her mug in the sink and went to wash it.

'Leave that, love; I'll do it when you've gone,' Joanne said.

Ella walked out of the kitchen and reappeared several minutes later, dragging her Ted Baker luggage behind her.

'Thanks for having me,' Ella said before kissing her mum and dad on the cheek.

64

Ella

Conor didn't seem himself on the drive back to his house. He was quiet and distracted, considering we hadn't seen each other for days. You didn't need to be a genius to work out that something was bothering him. I'd been having some doubts about our relationship, but seeing Conor like this tugged at my heartstrings and made me want to reach out to him.

'Are you OK?' I asked, touching Conor's arm as we sat in silence, waiting for the traffic lights to turn green. The only sound in the BMW Z4 was the engine idling.

Conor turned towards me and gave me a half-hearted smile. 'I'm fine.'

I knew that wasn't true. But being a man who kept his cards close to his chest, he wasn't about to confide in me, no matter how much I would have liked him to. If I wanted to know what was wrong, I'd have to try and coax the source of his problem out of him. That would be an uphill battle. Conor's reluctance to open up would test the skill of the most experienced therapist. How was somebody like me, who was completely untrained in the art of delving into the inner sanctum of another person's thoughts, meant to do that? Especially as my boyfriend was an expert at being guarded.

Conor's mobile was in the hands-free unit attached to the windscreen when it rang. I saw Leo Carr's name flash onto the screen before my boyfriend declined the call.

'Why didn't you pick up?' I wasn't trying to be nosy, but curiosity had got the better of me.

'That wanker has nothing to say that I want to hear.' Conor's response was sharp.

'Fair enough, but you don't need to bite my head off. I just asked you a simple question, so I'd appreciate it if you didn't take your bad mood out on me.'

'I'm sorry I snapped at you, Ella. I shouldn't have spoken to you like that, but I've had as much as I can take from Leo for one day.' The words had barely left my boyfriend's mouth when Leo's name came up on his phone again. This time Conor swiped at the screen to answer it. 'I have nothing to say to you. If you phone me again, I'll block your number,' Conor said before he disconnected the call.

Conor's car sped into the drive like Usain Bolt coming out of the starting blocks. He leaped out of the driver's seat and slammed the door behind him, bounded up the front steps, then stomped into the house. I trailed along behind him, wondering what could have happened between the two of them to make Conor react this way.

'I take it your meeting didn't go well.'

Conor opened the fridge and took out a bottle of San Miguel. He flipped the cap off of it before downing half the contents in one swallow. I thought about commenting as it wasn't even eleven o'clock in the morning, but I decided against it. If Conor felt the need to have a drink at this time, something bad must have happened.

'Do you want to talk about what's bothering you? I'm not trying to pry, but I always feel better when I get things off my chest.'

Conor took a seat at the table and wrapped his hands around the bottle of beer.

'It hurts my feelings that you never let me in,' I said, taking a seat opposite him. 'I only want to help you. I wish you wouldn't shut me out.'

Conor looked at me with his amazing blue eyes. 'I'm sorry, Ella, I'm so used to dealing with things on my own, I didn't even realise I was doing that.'

'It's OK.'

I understood why Conor pushed people away. He'd had a tough childhood. His mum had let him down so many times that now he found it difficult to trust anyone.

'I've had the morning from hell. This latest shipment's turned out to be the biggest ball-ache; there's been one disaster after another. Then Leo started mouthing off about my mum. You know how I feel about her, but I couldn't stand by and let him slag her off either.'

'Of course not.'

'So I thought fuck it, enough's enough. I've had it up to here with that bastard.' Conor held his hand over his head to emphasise his words. 'I told Leo I was a free agent and wasn't working for him anymore.'

'Really?' After what happened in Spain, I desperately

wanted Conor to consider a career change, but I never thought he actually would.

'And do you know what he said?'

I shook my head. I was fairly certain the news hadn't gone down well. 'I imagine he was pissed off.'

'That's an understatement, and as I was about to leave, Leo only went and dropped the biggest bombshell,' Conor replied.

'What happened?' I was glad Conor was finally opening up to me.

'He told me something that's been a closely guarded secret for almost thirty years.' Conor knocked back the rest of his San Miguel, then placed the empty bottle on the table in front of him and wiped his lips on the back of his hand.

'What did he say?' I asked when Conor clammed up.

'He reckons he's my dad.'

I could hardly believe what I'd just heard. 'I wouldn't be too worried; I'm sure he just said that to rattle you.'

'But why would he say something like that if it wasn't true?'

'I don't know. He probably wanted to get back at you and knew that would mess with your head. But if you think about it logically, he can't be your dad; the two of you are polar opposites in the looks department.' My boyfriend was tall and handsome, whereas Leo was short and balding. Conor had the most beautiful eyes I'd ever seen, and he certainly didn't get those from the bug-eyed man claiming to share the same gene pool as him.

'Much as I don't want to accept it, Leo's story does add up.' Conor stared into space. He looked like a man whose

STEPHANIE HARTE

numbers had come up on the lottery, but he'd lost the winning ticket.

'I suppose it's possible he's telling the truth, but it's also just as likely he said it to piss you off.' And if that was what Leo Carr had set out to do, he'd well and truly achieved his goal.

Conor locked eyes with me. 'Leo was enjoying every minute of rubbing my nose in it. I came this close to smashing the bastard's face in,' he said, and he held his thumb and forefinger an inch apart to illustrate his point.

'I'm not surprised.'

'One of the main reasons I think Leo's claim might hold water is because he was so smug when he told me. It was as though he'd been waiting a lifetime for the opportunity. And I suppose he had. The guy's a complete scumbag, and that's another reason my mum would have been drawn to him like a fly on shit. Her taste in men is legendary.'

Conor looked so sad. I wanted to take his pain away, so I reached across the table and took hold of his hands.

'Leo, Roy and Stumpy were having a great laugh about Mum being the local bike. Leo reckoned they'd all had a ride on her.'

Conor shook his head and cast his eyes to the floor. I could see he was tormented by the idea, but I didn't know what I could say to make things better, so I decided to keep quiet. I might not be able to offer him any words of wisdom, but I could be a good listener and let him get it off his chest instead.

Conor looked up, and his eyes met mine. 'Nobody wants to think that their mum's a slag, but I know Leo was being honest when he'd said she'd done the rounds. I've witnessed enough of my mum's relationship fails to last me a lifetime. Her appetite for cock is insatiable.'

I drew a sharp intake of breath. That was a terrible thing to say. I knew Trisha and Conor had a difficult relationship, but I was shocked to hear him lash out at his mum after he'd fallen out with Leo defending her. I slumped back in my chair while I waited for my boyfriend to continue.

'Mum's world revolved around enticing as many men as she could into our flea pit of a home. If she'd channelled as much energy into bringing up her kids as she did opening her legs, mine and Leo's paths might never have crossed.'

Conor's words were laced with bitterness. 'What makes you say that?'

'I know we had very different childhoods, but you'd have to agree that an absent father's a recurrent theme on our estate.'

I nodded my head; Conor was right. I was in the minority, coming from a two-parent household.

'It doesn't take a genius to work out the connection between wayward teenage boys and the lack of a decent role model. The absence of boundaries has a lot to answer for, if you ask me.'

I didn't agree with Conor. Not all children raised in one-parent homes went off the rails. Far from it – women and men did a great job of raising their offspring alone. It was tough to be both a mum and a dad to a child. But judging from my boyfriend's current mood, I decided to keep my opinion to myself.

'The streets I grew up on were a breeding ground for all sorts of criminal activities, which is the root of the problem. It's easy to get led astray when your mother doesn't give a shit about what you're getting up to or who you're hanging around with.'

Trisha's ears must be burning, I thought. I heard what Conor was saying; I didn't deny he'd had a tough childhood, but he was forgetting one crucial fact. I grew up on the same estate, and I didn't experience any of the same problems he had. I wasn't saying petty crime wasn't an issue, but he was painting a very grim picture indeed.

'Poor people in society are vulnerable. They're easy targets for criminals to groom because they have nothing, so they have nothing to lose.' Conor put his elbows on the table and interlocked his fingers.

My boyfriend's rant was endless, which was understandable. He was angry at the world and had spent years bottling up his emotions. At least he was opening up about his frustrations for once.

'I agree that our estate houses low-income families, but not all the residents are involved with drugs or are part of a gang.' I knew Conor wasn't going to like what I'd just said, but I was entitled to have my own opinion.

'Open your eyes, Ella; criminality is rife among local residents.'

'I think we'll have to agree to disagree on this. My parents raised me to have a strong work ethic. Their mantra was if you want something in life, you have to go out and get it yourself. Nobody's going to hand it to you on a plate.'

As soon as the words left my mouth, I realised how hypocritical they sounded. I'd followed my heart and got in way over my head. I'd given up my job and lost my independence before I'd allowed myself to be coerced down the criminal path. Conor talked about being led astray, but he'd done the same thing to me, grooming me into his perfect accomplice. I was embarrassed to think toeing the line came so easily to me. But then again, I'd never been the rebellious type.

'You grew up in a loving household, so you have no idea what it was like for me. It's inevitable that children like me, who are left to our own devices, end up on the wrong side of the law.'

I couldn't argue with that, so I changed the subject. 'Why did you say your path might never have crossed with Leo's?'

'Leo has literally lived around the corner all my life, but he's never bothered with me, apart from in a business capacity, since the day I was born.'

I couldn't imagine for one minute not having a relationship with my dad.

'If my mum had been stricter and cared about how I'd got on at school, I might have left with some qualifications and been able to get an honest job. Then I would never have encountered the lowlife who reckons he's my dad.'

'Don't lose sight of the fact that it might not be true,' I replied.

'I'm fed up with playing the guessing game; it's time Mum and I had this out. Not knowing who to believe will end up driving an even bigger wedge between us than there is at the moment.' Conor leaned back in his chair and let out a long sigh.

'Try not to fall out with her. I know the two of you aren't close, but she's still your mum.'

Conor was lashing out because he was hurt, and he didn't want to admit it. He was putting on this tough exterior and making out he didn't care, but my boyfriend wouldn't be reacting like this if he wasn't bothered.

'What are you going to do?'

'When I've calmed down, I'm going to confront the only person who knows whether Leo's telling me the truth or not.'

'I'll go with you.'

I'd offered to go with Conor to give him some moral support, but I had to admit as he reversed out of the driveway, a bundle of nerves formed in the pit of my stomach. The peacekeeper's role wasn't an easy one to play at the best of times, and Conor was so furious about the situation, I was sure he was going to burst through the door with both barrels loaded.

Having never personally met the enigma that was Mr Leo Carr, I didn't know what to make of his revelation. I'd only observed him on a couple of occasions when he'd been talking to Conor. Time was about to tell if he was a man of his word or not.

65

Conor

As I drove towards the Arnold Estate, fresh anger rose inside me. How could Mum have so little respect for herself that she'd sleep with a man like Leo Carr? Admittedly, I hadn't known him back then, but men like Leo never changed; once a dickhead, always a dickhead.

The smell of tobacco hit me as soon as Mum opened the front door, instantly reminding me that the prospect of inhaling her second-hand smoke was one of the many reasons I didn't often bother to visit.

Mum looked a little startled to see me. I wasn't sure who she was expecting. Only a brave person or somebody well oiled would venture over her grubby threshold. 'What are you doing here?' she said.

I wasn't surprised by the coldness of her greeting, but it would have been nice if she'd at least pretended to be happy to see me.

'I need to talk to you. Can I come in?'

Mum turned on her heel and began walking along the

hallway, lined with tobacco-infused yellowing wallpaper. Over the years, the smoke had seeped its way into every fibre of the flat's interior. If it hadn't already got there, it must be reaching complete saturation by now.

As I looked around the grotty front room, I couldn't help thinking it was amazing that my siblings and I had managed to stay healthy while being in daily contact with the toxins Mum exhaled into our air, but she didn't give a flying fuck about our developing lungs. If she had, she wouldn't have exposed all of us to danger while we were still in the womb. She was a selfish piece of shit.

'This is my girlfriend, Ella, by the way.'

'Pleased to meet you,' Ella said, offering Mum a wide smile.

Mum was too busy to answer immediately; she was preoccupied with trying to light the cigarette dangling from her mouth with a plastic lighter whose spark had seen better days. We waited as she dragged the pad of her thumb repeatedly over the metal wheel until it eventually produced a small flame. She lit the tip, inhaled deeply, then turned her attention to Ella.

'Pleased to meet you too.' Smoke wafted out as the words spilled out of Mum's mouth. 'Let me make you a cup of tea.'

'Not for me, thanks.' I didn't want to stay here any longer than I had to, so I followed Mum into the kitchen. The place was a state as usual, and I felt my blood pressure spike. I was glad I'd remembered to block off my nostrils before I walked into the stinking space. As she filled the kettle with water, I decided to get straight to the point. 'Leo Carr told me he's my dad.'

I locked eyes with my mum to gauge her reaction. She'd

just taken a long drag of her cigarette and coughed and spluttered as it went down the wrong way. When she regained herself, she looked at me, kettle in one hand, fag in the other, with a horrified expression on her face. She must have thought the purpose of my unexpected visit was to introduce Ella to the family. And although she'd battled to keep her expression indifferent, I noticed her face drop at the mention of Leo's name.

'What on earth did he say that for?' Mum said, doing her best to look perplexed, but she'd never been a very good actress.

'I have no idea, Mum. You tell me.'

With her cigarette clamped between her lips, Mum swirled the teabag around for at least two seconds before she fished it out of the chipped mug and dropped it onto the grimy work surface. Without bothering to check how my girlfriend liked her tea, she filled the half-empty mug up to the brim with full-fat milk. My stomach flipped at the sight of it.

'Does your girlfriend take sugar?' Mum asked, tilting her head in the direction of the front room.

'No,' I replied, without taking my eyes off Mum's fag as it bobbed up and down in her mouth when she spoke.

I was mesmerised by the inch-long ash that was doing a balancing act on the end of the cigarette, and hoped it didn't drop into Ella's tea. On the other hand, it would probably improve the taste, I thought as Mum walked out of the kitchen and handed the mug that had seen better days to my girlfriend.

Mum plonked herself down on a stained, lumpy armchair that looked like it had come out of a skip. 'Leo must have been trying to rile you up. Have you done something to upset him?'

I had, but that was beside the point. I knew what Mum was doing; she was trying to skirt around answering the question. 'Why would he drop a bombshell like that if it wasn't true?' I cautiously lowered myself onto the sofa next to Ella, making sure I sat right on the edge so that I had as little contact with the dirty fabric as possible.

'Your guess is as good as mine.' Mum was trying to speak in a breezy manner, but she wasn't quite managing to pull it off.

I could see she was hiding something, so I was going to continue to press her on it.

'Well, if Leo's not my dad, who is?' I'd asked that question a hundred times before, and Mum had never felt the need to answer it honestly. My dad's identity had always been one of my mum's closely guarded secrets.

Mum shook her head before tapping the ash-end of her cigarette into the overflowing ashtray with more aggression than was necessary, then she turned her face towards me and looked me in the eye. 'I've told you before, Conor, I'm not sure.' Mum didn't take her eyes off me as she lit another cigarette.

'Do you have any idea how that makes you sound? What kind of mother doesn't know the identity of the man who fathered her child?' I knew that was a low blow, but I was fed up of skirting around something as important as this.

At least Mum had the decency to look sheepish when she cast her eyes to the floor. I'd come to terms with the fact years ago that I would never have a father figure in my life. It was something that bothered me as a young child, but

I was in good company on the estate, so I soon got used to it being the norm. These days I had more important things to worry about than some lowlife serial shagger who shot his load into anyone and everyone without thinking of the consequences.

'I don't want a relationship with my dad, I just want to know where the other half of my DNA comes from. Surely that's not too much to ask?' I pressed on, hoping my mum would buckle under the pressure, but her lips were tightly sealed, and I was running out of patience. 'If it isn't true, why did Leo say he's my dad?' I couldn't help raising my voice; anger was bubbling just under the surface of my skin, and I was stressed out from being back in the shithole I grew up in.

'I've already told you, I don't know why he said it, but he's lying. If I don't know who your father is. How the hell would he?'

Mum trained her blue eyes on mine as she spoke in a steady voice, but she was all fingers and thumbs as she fumbled with her cigarette pack. When she finally got one out, she lit it from the butt of the one in her mouth. If she was feeling as calm and collected as she wanted me to believe, why was she chain-smoking? One of them was lying, but I had a sinking feeling that it wasn't Leo.

I cast my eyes towards Ella; she was also sitting on the edge of the sofa, mimicking my body language. Her slender fingers were wrapped around an almost-full mug of my mum's dishwater tea. I wasn't surprised she hadn't drunk it; it looked repulsive. But if you bought the bags made from the dust collected from machines at a Sri Lankan tea plantation, rather than decent quality PG Tips, you couldn't really expect to get a proper brew. I should have warned Ella not to accept anything before we arrived, but I'd had other, more important things on my mind.

It brought some momentary light-hearted relief to the situation to watch my girlfriend, who was too well mannered not to try and drink it. The corners of my mouth lifted into a smile as Ella went into battle with the foul-tasting liquid. She was moving the mug around, trying to find a piece of the edge that wasn't chipped so that she could take a sip. But every time she lowered her face towards the mug, she backed off before her lips made contact with the surface. Ella had suffered enough horrors recently to last her a lifetime, without this experience being added to the list. I felt obliged to rescue Ella from the tea-flavoured nightmare she was currently stuck in.

'So if Leo Carr isn't my dad, who is?' I thought I'd have one last stab at extracting the truth from my mum before I admitted defeat.

'I don't know. I was seeing a few guys at the time that would have been in the frame.'

Mum didn't even try to sugar-coat the truth, and her reply made my skin bristle. I didn't want to think about the existence of her sex life, let alone with multiple partners. I looked daggers at her, wishing my glare could bore holes through her skull and read her mind.

'Don't look at me like that.' Mum laughed. 'Anyone would think I was the only woman since time began who didn't know who the father of my baby was. It happens all the time, probably more than you realise.'

'So it's a case of eeny, meeny, miney, mo, is it?'

Mum threw her head back and laughed. 'Did anyone ever tell you, you're hilarious, Conor?'

That was my cue to get out of the hell-hole she called home. It was clear we weren't going to get anywhere with this conversation; I felt like I was going to explode with rage. I picked up my car keys, turned to my girlfriend and stood up.

'Let's go, Ella.'

The best thing I could do was take myself away and give my mum time to digest what had happened and hope her conscience might get the better of her. From the way she was acting, it was clear she knew more than she was letting on.

66

Ella

My heart bled for Conor. I'd thought he was being over the top when he'd described his tense relationship with his mum, but now that I'd seen it for myself, it was every bit as bad as he'd painted it, if not worse.

Trisha was an overweight peroxide blonde, carrying most of her poundage around her stomach, which was hardly surprising as she'd given birth to five children. Her frizzy shoulder-length hair had three inches of dark brown regrowth streaked with silver and echoed the crimped style women rocked in the Eighties. My boyfriend's mum spoke with a cigarette hanging out the corner of her mouth and wouldn't have looked out of place in the cast of *Shameless*. In fact, if I hadn't known better, I'd have thought I'd just stepped onto the set mid-shoot.

I couldn't deny I was messy; my old bedroom used to be chaotic, to say the least. My mum was forever complaining about it, but Trisha's flat wasn't just untidy; it was filthy. This was the first time I'd stepped foot into her home, so when she'd gone to make me a cup of tea, my eyes followed her into the room. I was shocked to see piles of dirty crockery and pots and pans covering all the surfaces of the galley kitchen and spilling out of the sink. It looked like she hadn't washed up for weeks. No wonder Conor was a clean freak. Now I understood why he was so particular about everything he owned. My boyfriend wasn't exaggerating when he'd described the place he'd grown up in as a flea pit. I'd be tempted to go one step further and call it a hovel.

As I'd sat on the sofa listening to Conor and his mum's cringe-worthy conversation about her past conquests, I could feel my cheeks flush with embarrassment. I had a great relationship with my mum, but I couldn't imagine discussing the nitty-gritty details of her love life. Some things between a parent and child are better left shrouded in mystery. But Trisha seemed happy enough to chat away to her son about who might have sired him. She was completely unfazed by the situation.

I know you shouldn't judge a person if you haven't personally experienced what they've been through, but if I'd been in her position, I'd be mortified that I couldn't narrow the odds of who my child's father was down to two men. Trisha was almost proud of the fact that there was a list of possibilities. I couldn't see his face because he had his back to me, but Conor's posture stiffened when his mum shared that piece of information with him.

Conor never talked much about his family, but I wondered if he was the only one of the siblings in this position. My guess would be probably not. From the little he'd said, they'd grown up without any male intervention. This told me that if Trisha knew the identities of her children's fathers, none of the men stayed around to help her raise their offspring.

Trisha had put Conor and his brothers and sisters in a horrible position. I was beginning to understand why my boyfriend was so paranoid. He'd probably spent his whole life being whispered about behind his back; the butt of people's jokes and the victim of gossips. The human race could be so cruel sometimes for no apparent reason. It pained me to think that the world was full of people who said nasty things about others just for the sake of it, but it was a fact of life.

'Are you OK?' I turned to face Conor, but he kept his eyes fixed on the windscreen.

'I can't believe my mum didn't even have the decency to look embarrassed when I questioned her about my dad. She said there were a few men in the frame, but I'm not convinced she even knows the names of the men she slept with. Knowing how carefully Mum selects her partners, she probably picked them up at the end of the evening when she was drunk out of her mind.' Conor shook his head.

I was about to offer him some words of comfort, but before I could, he began talking again.

'I'd hoped by putting Mum on the spot, there might be a different outcome to the mystery this time. I haven't asked her about my dad since I was a kid, and I wouldn't be bringing it up now if Leo hadn't put ideas in my head.'

It wasn't fair of Trisha to keep her son in the dark over something as important as this. She was robbing Conor of his true identity.

'And to think, I jumped to her defence when Leo called my mum the local bike. Everything he said about her was true. She openly admitted she'd had sex with multiple men and couldn't be sure which one of them got her pregnant. She's a real piece of shit, isn't she?' Conor glanced across at me before turning his eyes back to the road.

I didn't reply. Whatever I thought about Trisha, she was still his mum, so it wasn't my place to slag her off. But he had every right to be furious with her. She'd been irresponsible and reckless. There was a way for Conor to find out the truth, but I wasn't sure he was likely to go down the route of having a DNA test carried out; he just wanted his mum to be honest with him. This wasn't a game show where contestants lined all the possible suspects up against the wall and weighed up the probability of which one of them was the father. This was Conor's life.

'Why can't she just tell me the truth?' Conor said, turning to me as he parked his car on his driveway.

'Maybe she is; your mum might not be lying when she says she doesn't know which one of the men fathered you.'

I cringed at the thought. Poor Conor. What a horrible situation to be put in. I could see why only having half of the picture made him feel like he was in limbo.

I couldn't begin to imagine what it must be like going through life without both of your parents being able to fill in the gaps in your childhood and recount facts about your heritage. I was forever hearing stories about our extended family and the things I did in my early years that I was too young to remember for myself.

When I thought about how Conor and his siblings had been brought up, it was a miracle that none of them had ended up in care. From what Conor had told me, it was clear that they'd all suffered from neglect, both physically and mentally. I was the unplanned product of a teenage romance, but my childhood couldn't have been more different than my boyfriend's.

'The worst thing about all of this is my mum thinks it's all a big joke.' Conor's dark brown hair flopped forward as he bowed his head.

I reached over and squeezed his hand, realising that he was finding this difficult to deal with. I didn't know Trisha, but my gut feeling was she was putting on a front so that she didn't lose face. She might have thought she was displaying a confident façade, but if you asked me, it was false bravado. Her body language gave away how uncomfortable she felt by the confrontation on more than one occasion. But that didn't change the fact that my boyfriend was no better off now than before he went to see his mum. In some ways, he was worse off. Trisha had cheerfully admitted she was sleeping with multiple men when she fell pregnant, as if it was something to be proud of, and up until this point, Conor had been spared that painful fact.

'It might not seem like much of a silver lining, but the one thing your mum didn't confirm was that Leo Carr was even in the running to be your dad,' I said, offering him a glimmer of hope.

In the days that followed our visit to Trisha's, the mood in Conor's house was sombre. We both had a lot on our minds. I hadn't been back to uni since I'd been kidnapped; the ordeal was too fresh, and I couldn't concentrate on studying. But with time on my hands, I found myself reliving the terrible experience. I'd been terrified, but now I wasn't in danger and was in a place of safety, anger replaced my fear. Conor was doing his best to put everything right, but I couldn't help being pissed off with him. Being cooped up together wasn't healthy for our relationship. We were bickering about small things instead of focusing on the wider picture.

'What are we like? The two of us have been moping about for days; maybe I should book us a nice holiday. We could do with a change of scenery. Name me one person who could resist the offer of some winter sun.' Conor smiled.

I let out a loud sigh before I could stop myself.

'What's the matter?' Conor's smile had disappeared, and a frown replaced it. 'I thought you liked being whisked off to exotic places.'

He was right. What person wouldn't like flying first class to locations they'd always dreamed of visiting? But this was a situation that Conor couldn't buy his way out of; even if we went on holiday, the issues that were troubling us would come along for the ride. We couldn't just leave them behind and deal with them when we got back.

'We could go back to the Banyan Tree. You loved it last time we went there,' Conor continued, undeterred by my silence.

That was an understatement. Love wasn't a strong enough word to describe how I'd felt about the place. I'd never stayed anywhere like the luxury beach resort before and probably never would. 'I know I did, but running away isn't the answer. If we don't face our problems head-on, we'll never be able to move on from them.'

'I don't know what more I can do. I know you're struggling to put what happened in Spain behind you, which is understandable. It must have been horrific for you, but going away might help to take your mind off things.'

I let Conor voice his opinion on how I must be feeling, but as far as I was concerned, he wasn't qualified to comment as he hadn't been in the situation himself. He would never understand what I'd gone through. I was extremely fortunate to get out alive; other people in a similar situation weren't so lucky. I'd be eternally grateful that I escaped serious harm, but the experience would stay with me for the rest of my life. It was going to take time for me to put this behind me and get back to normal. I couldn't just brush it under the carpet and pretend it hadn't happened.

Being held against my will had forced me to find out what I was made of. I'd discovered that no matter how scared I was, I could manage to be resilient. I'd like to say there were no lingering after-effects from my time in captivity, but I'd be lying. I was a changed woman. My trusting nature would never be the same again; it had taken a severe battering during the ordeal.

'It's an incredibly generous offer, but I really don't feel up to going away. I'd much rather stay at home. I feel safer behind familiar walls.' I couldn't believe I'd just said that. I sounded like a spoilt brat, turning my nose up at an all-expenses-paid holiday in a five-star resort. But I couldn't help the way I felt.

Conor respected my decision, and we spent the next few weeks confined to the house with only each other for company. But be careful what you wish for; after a couple of days, cabin fever well and truly set in, and I felt stifled. Since I'd said I felt safer behind familiar walls, my boyfriend had taken it literally. In his quest to protect me, he became so security conscious that he insisted we withdrew from everyone around us. We became virtual prisoners stuck inside Conor's house. Despite the beautiful surroundings, I was miserable and fed up with being in isolation. I'd always had a lot of friends. But recently, the members of my social circle had dwindled in number to the point of extinction.

'I'm going to meet Lucy and Amy for a coffee later,' I casually dropped in while Conor and I were eating breakfast.

The look of horror on my boyfriend's face let me know what he thought about that idea without him needing to comment. This set-up might have suited Conor down to the ground; he didn't have any close friends and rarely saw his family. Because of the nature of his work and his upbringing, he found it hard to trust anyone. He'd always been a bit of a loner. In the past, we'd either go out on our own, or Conor would socialise for work. But recently, we weren't even doing that. Conor had become completely paranoid about my safety, and his fear had taken over my life. It was time to make a stand.

I knew Conor didn't approve. He'd made it clear that he didn't want me going out alone; he pictured enemies lurking around every corner, but I was coming to terms with what had happened and felt the time apart would do us good. We were seeing too much of each other and getting on each other's nerves. It wasn't healthy to closet yourself away from the rest of civilisation. I was going stir-crazy and desperately needed some contact with my friends.

Conor walked into the bedroom while I was getting ready; I could see him eyeing the pile of clothes I'd discarded at the end of the bed.

'Look at the state of this place,' Conor said, shaking his head from side to side.

I rolled my eyes when I saw the look of horror on his face. It was clear; we had very different tolerance levels for mess.

'Are you intentionally trying to wind me up? It makes my blood boil when you disrespect my home like this. You're so inconsiderate.' Conor stared at me with his hands on his hips.

Did a few pieces of clothing bother him that much, or was he picking a fight to stop me from going out?

'Stop making a huge deal about nothing.'

'Your untidiness is a huge deal to me. I'm constantly picking up all of your shit, and it does my head in.' Conor's eyes were blazing.

I was so fed up with his nit-picking behaviour. 'Nobody asked you to,' I replied through gritted teeth while shoving my unfolded tops back in the drawer in an act of defiance, knowing that would infuriate him. 'Happy now?' I glared at Conor before I walked out and left him to stew.

'Hello, stranger. You're looking really well. Are you feeling better now?' Amy said as I pulled out a chair opposite her in Costa.

I nodded. 'I must have caught a bug while we were away,' I lied and promptly changed the subject. 'You're looking well too.' The bright spring sunshine picked out flecks of copper and bronze in Amy's beautiful red hair as she swept it over one shoulder.

'So don't keep us in suspense; tell us all about your latest trip. Which exotic location have you been to this time?' Lucy's platinum blonde bob bounced on her collarbones as she pulled her chair closer to the table and adjusted herself in her seat.

'The north-west corner of Spain. It's wild and rugged, but I'm not sure I'd call it exotic – even though it's breathtakingly beautiful. The locals say it's the costa the crowds forgot.'

'How lovely; tell us more...' Lucy said, beaming at me.

'The scenery's incredible, but Galicia's on the Atlantic coast, so it can be wet and windy and the water's freezing.'

'It sounds exactly like England.' Amy laughed.

'The weather's not that dissimilar. It rains more in that region than anywhere else in Spain!' I was aware I was painting a gloomy picture, but I knew in my heart I'd never go back there.

'I could live with a bit of rain if it meant going on holiday; it's not as though it's something we're not used to,' Lucy continued.

'Sod the weather. You're lucky to get the chance to travel. Even if it is to somewhere battered by the wind and rain,' Amy added.

'Absolutely, anywhere would seem incredible if you hadn't been away in years like me,' Lucy agreed without an ounce of bitterness in her voice.

A pang of guilt hit me; I hadn't meant to be so insensitive. 'I've missed you two so much,' I said, changing the course of the conversation. Seeing my besties in the flesh suddenly made me realise how much I'd been craving the company of people my own age.

'We've missed you too, Ella,' Amy replied.

'It seems like ages since we've seen you,' Lucy said.

Conor didn't like me going out without him these days, so I hadn't seen my friends for weeks. He'd insisted he wanted to protect me, but was it that, or did he want to control me? Could he sense I was slipping away from him?

'So how is the sex god these days?' Lucy giggled.

When she laughed, Amy did too, but instead of joining in with them, my eyes glistened with tears. My friends gave each other a sideways glance before they turned their attention back to me.

'What's the matter, Ella? Lucy was only joking.' Amy reached over the table and covered my hands with hers.

That was all it took. One gesture of kindness and a few words of concern, and I dissolved into floods of tears. I reached under the table and grabbed hold of the handle of my designer handbag. Pulling the black Michael Kors tote onto my lap, I unzipped the top and delved my hand inside. I retrieved a pack of Kleenex, took one of the tissues out and dried my tears on it. After composing myself for a moment, I looked across the table at my friends, and two pairs of worried blue eyes looked back at me.

'We keep bickering like an old married couple. Before I came out, we had words over a couple of tops I'd left on the bed because I couldn't decide what to wear! He's so fussy and has such high standards, which are impossible to maintain. I'm finding it hard to live up to his expectations.'

'Poor you, neat freaks are the worst. He'd have a fit if he saw our place.' Lucy laughed.

'It's not just that, since I've been going out with Conor, I feel like I've lost my identity and become quite isolated, which is making me miserable.' My current situation was only compounding my feelings.

'I wasn't going to say anything, but now that you've brought it up, you have been behaving differently. You were always so sociable, and now you're a virtual recluse,' Lucy said, laying it on the line.

'Your presence from our little group has been sorely missed,' Amy added, giving me a half-smile.

I valued my friends' honesty. I hadn't realised everyone around me had noticed I was behaving differently, but why wouldn't they? It wasn't as though it was a subtle change; my personality had undergone a huge transformation.

'I'm going to tell you something, but you have to promise to keep it to yourselves.' I suddenly felt the need to confide in my friends.

'We will,' Lucy and Amy replied.

'I'm having doubts about my relationship with Conor,' I blurted out. I could see the look of shock on my friends' faces, but now I'd voiced my concerns, I couldn't take them back. It was too late to regret it. I'd said it, so I had to own it.

'I thought he was the man of your dreams?' Amy's eyebrows knitted into a frown.

'So did I, but I'm beginning to wonder if I've made a terrible mistake.'

The more I thought about it, the more I realised the dynamics of our relationship were all wrong, and I was starting to resent the compromises I had to make to live in his space. Everything was so perfect at the start, but it was too perfect. I should have known our relationship was doomed to failure.

'What are you going to do?' Lucy asked.

'I'm not sure. It's complicated. I love Conor so much, but because we're constantly around each other with hardly any interaction from anyone else, he's getting on my nerves.'

'It sounds like you just need a bit of space. Now that you're feeling better, you'll be able to come back to uni. Then you'll have a reason to get out of the house and have some fun,' Amy said.

'And the three of us could start doing this regularly,' Lucy suggested.

'That's a great idea. Same time next week?' I smiled.

I'd always craved interaction with others, whereas Conor was a loner and comfortable being on his own. For me, the novelty of being together twenty-four-seven had lost its appeal. I felt stifled living in each other's pockets. Our living styles were very incompatible and a source of friction. I was messy; he was tidy. There was no right or wrong. They were both legitimate ways of living, but I found it impossible to maintain Conor's standards, which added to my stress.

I was beginning to wonder if I'd mistaken Conor's protective behaviour for romance; was he in love with me, or was he trying to control me? The unhealthy pattern we'd slipped into had crept up on me, but it was slowly beginning to dawn on me that Conor's manipulation would know no boundary if I didn't challenge it. He was using an arsenal of tools to isolate me from my friends and family while hiding behind the role of being my knight in shining armour.

67

Conor

As soon as I'd heard Ella close the front door, I had run down the stairs and armed myself with a bottle of multipurpose antibacterial spray and a microfibre cloth. When I felt like I was losing control, I cleaned to calm myself down. I'd started rage-buffing all the surfaces in the house while ranting to myself about how Ella was completely content to live like a filthy, disgusting slob. I was fed up of coming into conflict with her because she was naturally messy. I liked order and just wanted her to respect the way I did things. Was that really too much to ask?

Much as I hadn't wanted my girlfriend to go out yesterday, it seemed to have done her a world of good, and she came back with a smile on her face. Our argument was a thing of the past; neither of us mentioned it.

I propped myself up on one elbow as I lay on my side, watching Ella sleep. She looked so peaceful; her long dark eyelashes began to flutter as she woke up.

'Good morning,' she said as she opened her big brown eyes and smiled at me.

'Good morning,' I replied, planting a kiss on the end of her nose. 'I've got a surprise for you downstairs.'

Ella yawned and stretched out her limbs while rubbing sleep from her eyes.

'Last one in the kitchen cooks for the rest of the week,' I said, knowing that would get her moving. I couldn't think of anything worse than allowing Ella to have free rein over my domain. It played havoc with my mental state when my environment was disordered.

'Hell no! Eat my dust,' Ella said, then her smile spread into a grin. She flung back the quilt, leaped out of bed and scampered down the stairs like a child on Christmas morning when they'd realised Santa had been.

I followed two paces behind her. Considering she'd just woken up, Ella moved with a spring in her step. She rushed into the kitchen and looked around the bare surfaces.

'So where's my surprise then? I thought you'd made breakfast,' Ella said, looking up into my face.

'Seeing as I lost the race, I will make breakfast, but first, I want to show you the surprise.'

'Have you bought me a puppy?' Ella asked.

'Close your eyes.' I took hold of Ella's hand and led her towards the front door.

'Where are we going?' She giggled.

'You can open your eyes now,' I said once we were standing in the driveway. 'This is for you.' I handed Ella a car key then watched the smile slide from her beautiful face as her eyes scanned over the shiny red paintwork of the convertible Fiat 500. 'What's wrong? Don't you like it?'

My girlfriend didn't need to reply; her expression had given the game away. I was surprised by her reaction; every time we passed a car like the one I'd just bought her, she always remarked on how great they were. I was convinced she would love the present, but it was clear that I'd missed the mark.

'It's not that I don't like it; it's amazing, Conor, but I don't know how to drive!' Ella said, ever the diplomat.

'That's easily remedied. I'll book you some lessons.'

Ella seemed underwhelmed by my gesture; I thought she'd be over the moon. I knew I made a habit of flashing my money around. It stemmed from me being insecure. Ever since I could remember, I'd tried to buy friends; I wanted everyone to like me. You'd think I'd have learned my lesson by now; the tactic didn't work. But I had a blinkered view where money was concerned, I firmly believed that if you spent enough of it, you could get a foot in the door of the person you were trying to impress. I might need to rethink my technique; it seemed to be failing miserably at winning over my girlfriend.

I was trying my best to ignore it, but there'd been a definite change in Ella's behaviour since Diego's men had abducted her. She seemed distant with me and was a nervous wreck, scared of her own shadow. I hated seeing her like that and felt responsible for what she was going through. Guilt had been gnawing away at me, and I was determined to make it up to her.

68

Ella

Love was a complex thing. Relationships often struggled because a couple didn't spend enough time together. Conor and I had the opposite problem. In the early days, my obsession with my boyfriend had fanned the flames of passion, but the infatuation had burnt out. The honeymoon period was over. I was bored with our daily lives and needed some normality to ground me.

At first, the sheer excess of Conor's lifestyle took my breath away. I never thought you could have too much of a good thing, but I was wrong. My boyfriend was charismatic and incredibly generous, but he was also paranoid and insecure. I'd worked hard to build up the trust between us and didn't make the mistake of expecting too much too soon from Conor in that department. I knew it would take time before he felt comfortable enough to open up to me. I was fine with that; I'd thought we had all the time in the world.

I hadn't foreseen that along the way, Conor would begin

moulding me into his perfect partner. But as a teenage girl, I was easy to manipulate. The large age difference between us created an imbalance in power. We almost had a parent and child relationship. My lack of life experience left the door wide open for Conor to start to dominate me. His house rules were becoming unbearable. I was doing my best to keep everything neat and tidy, but we kept coming to blows over my untidiness. I didn't want to be trained in the correct way to mop a floor. Life was too short to worry about things like that.

There was a very fine line between being caring and controlling, which made it hard for me to distinguish between the two sometimes. It would appear that stereotypes didn't apply when it came to abusive partners. My boyfriend certainly didn't fit the profile; Conor wasn't a bully who belittled me and everyone he encountered. He didn't tell me how to dress or style my hair, and he definitely wasn't physically abusive. Conor was much more subtle than that, but the end result was the same. By withdrawing me from my family and friends, he'd curbed my freedom and stripped me of my support network.

'You look nice,' Conor said when I walked into the kitchen.

'Thank you,' I replied, looking down at the pale pink floral shirt I'd tucked into my skinny jeans. Conor had bought me so many beautiful clothes, but I never had the opportunity to wear them because we rarely left the house. 'I thought I'd make an effort for the girls.'

'Are you going out again?' Conor asked, his expression changed when he asked the question.

'I'm just going for coffee with Lucy and Amy,' I said, putting my iPhone into the zip compartment of my bag.

'But you saw them last week,' Conor protested in the tone of a five-year-old child being told to turn off the TV because it was bedtime.

'I know I did.' I wasn't about to change my plans or apologise for wanting to meet up with my friends.

Conor bowed his head. 'I thought you might have checked with me first.'

'I didn't realise I needed to ask your permission.' The last thing I wanted was to get into an argument with Conor over this, but I had to stand my ground.

Conor fixed his eyes back on mine. 'Don't get narky with me, Ella, but we might have had something on...'

I had to stop myself from rolling my eyes. Our diary was hardly overflowing with social engagements, so I didn't think me popping out for a catch-up with my besties would be this much of an issue. If this was the way things were going to be every time I wanted to step foot outside the house, I'd have to resort to Conor's level and start lying about where I was going and who I was seeing. For some reason, he seemed to have a major problem with Lucy and Amy; maybe I should have told him I was going over to Mum and Dad's instead.

'Please don't make a big deal out of this. I'm only going out for a couple of hours.'

'Let me give you a lift,' Conor said.

'There's no need.'

'You're never going to guess what Conor's gone and bought me this time,' I said, taking a seat opposite my two friends.

'A Coach shoulder bag by the looks of it.' Amy smiled, then held her hands out towards me.

Amy's observation was correct. The bag was a recent present from my boyfriend, but it wasn't the one I was talking about.

'Ooh, it's lovely. Isn't it a beautiful colour!' Amy said.

'It's called Dusty Rose,' I replied.

'Of course it is.' Amy's greeny-blue eyes sparkled as they scanned over the candy-floss-coloured exterior while she twisted it around in her hands.

'Let's have a look. Wow, it's gorgeous,' Lucy concluded after Amy passed the bag to her, and she ran her fingers over the smooth surface of the chunky chain handles. 'When did Conor buy you that?'

I tilted my head to one side as I considered the answer to her question. 'A couple of weeks ago.' I almost added *I think* but decided against it.

I couldn't be one hundred per cent certain when Conor gave me the bag; he bought me so many presents – it was hard to keep track of them all. I decided not to elaborate as I could imagine how that would come across. I didn't want my friends to think I was being ungrateful, but it made me feel uncomfortable when he flashed his money around. Although I was sure his intentions were good, sometimes it came across as an insult and made me feel as if he was trying to buy my loyalty and affection, a thought that Lucy had previously put in my head.

'If you ever get fed up with it, you can pass it my way,' Lucy said as she handed the bag back to me.

'I know it's amazing, but I wasn't talking about the bag.'

'Well, don't keep us in suspense,' Lucy said.

'Conor handed me the key to a convertible Fiat 500 this morning.'

'You're kidding?' Amy looked at me with wide eyes.

'No, it's parked on his driveway as we speak.'

'The man must have money to burn,' Lucy said.

'So it's not just me who thinks it's ridiculous? I mean, who buys their girlfriend a car before she's even had her first driving lesson?'

Lucy and Amy sat across the table from me, completely dumbstruck. It didn't happen often, but my best buddies were lost for words.

'I'm speechless,' Lucy eventually said, shaking her head.

'I wouldn't mind finding a man who lavished me with expensive presents every day of the week.' Amy laughed.

But it wasn't funny. Instead of making me feel special, I felt as though Conor was treating me like a commodity, but he didn't own me. I was starting to resent the financial control he had over me. I should never have given up my job to focus on my uni course. By doing so, I'd lost my independence. Conor had gained his lifestyle through illegal means, and the longer I was exposed to it, the more it played on my conscience. I didn't want to be worrying where he was, who he was with and what was happening to him if he didn't come home at night. Living with Conor came at a price, and I wasn't sure I was willing to pay it anymore.

69

Conor

I couldn't work women out sometimes. I thought I'd done a really nice thing buying Ella a brand-new car, but you'd think I'd suggested she should eat a plate of live locusts for breakfast the way she recoiled in horror when she saw the shiny red car sitting in pride of place in the middle of the driveway.

Ella had been so excited when she'd run down the stairs before breakfast; her reaction had completely blindsided me. I'd wanted to talk to her about what was bothering her, but she'd suddenly decided she wasn't hungry after all and went off to have a shower. The next time I saw her, she was on her way out. My girlfriend had decided that giving me a wide berth was the best way to deal with the situation, but I felt like I was in limbo while I waited for her to come back. If the car was causing her this much distress, I'd happily take it back to the dealer's, but something told me Ella's issues ran deeper than that.

'How were the girls?' I asked when Ella walked into

the kitchen. I didn't give a shit about the two of them, to be perfectly honest, but I thought I'd better ask just to be polite.

'They were great. I'm enjoying seeing Lucy and Amy socially again,' Ella said as she placed her bag down on the kitchen tiles.

'That's good,' I replied, but I didn't mean it.

I didn't want Ella meeting up with her friends so often. They were both single, and I was worried my girlfriend might question whether she was too young to be tied down to one man. I wouldn't put it past them to try and put ideas in her head so that they could come between us. I hated to admit it, but I was jealous of the close relationship they shared. Ella seemed to prefer their company to mine these days.

'Can we talk?' I reached over the black granite work surface and took hold of her hand.

Ella nodded her head, and her dark brown curls bounced up and down.

Even though I didn't think I'd done anything wrong, I'd unintentionally upset my girlfriend, so I decided to open up the lines of communication with an apology.

'I'm sorry you didn't like the car. I can take it back if you don't want it.'

I smiled at Ella, but she cast her eyes to the floor while she thought about how to respond. I could see she was trying to choose her words carefully, but as the silence dragged on, the atmosphere between us became awkward. Since she'd come home, she'd seemed incredibly distant with me.

I was desperate to make amends; Ella's happiness was the most important thing to me. I let go of my girlfriend's hand and opened my laptop that was sitting on the counter next to me. I pasted a smile back on my face, then swivelled it around so that she was able to see the screen.

'You seemed excited this morning when you thought I'd bought you a puppy, and that got me thinking. How about I take back the car and get you a dog instead?' I took hold of Ella's hand and squeezed it.

Ella's dark brown eyes scanned over the page I'd left open, showing the ten best-recommended breeds for first-time owners. Instead of jumping with joy as I'd expected, she pulled her hand out of my grip. A moment later, she closed the lid before she looked up into my face.

Ella shook her head. 'You just don't get it, do you?'

I could pretend I understood exactly why my girlfriend was behaving the way she was, but I would be kidding myself. I was a man, so the complex inner logic of a woman's psyche was, and always would be, alien to me. I considered sharing that information with Ella, but I doubted that was the answer she was looking for, so I decided to take a different approach.

'You haven't been yourself lately, so I wanted to cheer you up,' I replied, then I let out a long sigh for Ella's benefit.

'I don't want you to keep buying me things. I know you're trying to be nice, but it makes me feel cheap.'

Ella's words hit me like a slap around the face. 'That's the last thing I'm trying to do; I just want to make you happy.'

Ella bent down and picked up her bag, then turned around and walked back out of the front door before I had a chance to speak. I couldn't seem to do anything right at the moment. I was damned if I did and damned if I didn't.

Ella felt I was trying to buy her affection, but I didn't

see it like that; I loved her and wanted to treat her to nice things. I could feel her slipping away from me, so I was trying everything I could to hold on to her, but unlike a lot of other girls, Ella wasn't a gold digger, so showering her with expensive presents wasn't winning her over. Deep down, I knew her well enough to realise that wouldn't work, but I was desperate to hold on to her, and desperate times called for desperate measures.

70

Ella

I swiped my tears away as I stomped along the pavement towards the station.

'Hi, Ella, I wasn't expecting to hear from you so soon,' Lucy said when she answered the phone.

'I need to speak to you and Amy. Is it OK if I come over?'

'Of course, is everything all right?'

'I'll explain when I get there.'

Lucy and Amy lived in a shared terraced house in Islington, close to the Barbican underground station, with three other students.

'Come in,' Lucy said, throwing open the half-glazed front door. 'Excuse the mess.'

That was music to my ears. I smiled as I followed her along the narrow hallway littered with coats, shoes and other personal effects. It made a pleasant change to see a proper lived-in house. Everything at Conor's place had to be tidied away, which was hard to maintain for a messy person like myself. Clutter of any sort was off-limits in his show home; he had a zero-tolerance policy to it. Lucy led the way into the first room on the right. It was a small lounge, packed with an abundance of mismatched worn-out furniture, that looked out onto the street.

'We've pushed the boat out for you and made Nescafé Gold Cappuccinos and opened a pack of chocolate digestives.' Amy beamed when I came into view.

They were laid out on one end of the coffee table; a large pile of books and magazines were perched up the other end, precariously balanced like a literary edition of Jenga – one false move and the lot would come tumbling down.

'By the look of you, you might need something stronger. Have you been crying?' Amy asked when I took a seat in the squishy fabric armchair closest to the door.

'Is it that obvious?' I thought I'd done a good job at camouflaging my red eyes and tear-streaked makeup, but nothing got past my observant friend.

'What's the matter? Have you and Conor had a fight?'

'Not exactly; it's difficult to explain. I feel suffocated by him, and the more he tries to be nice to me, the worse he seems to make me feel.'

I couldn't tell the girls that I was also still traumatised from the events in Spain. I probably needed some professional counselling to help me come to terms with the ordeal, but if I went to see a therapist, it would raise questions that I wouldn't be able to answer without putting myself and Conor in danger. I was stuck in a rut and didn't know what to do for the best.

Since I'd been kidnapped, I'd changed so much I wasn't sure I recognised myself anymore, and if I was brutally honest about it, I didn't like the person I'd become. A jumpy, nerve-jangled wreck wasn't a good look for a young woman. The ordeal I'd been through had damaged my emotional constitution, and that had taken its toll on my relationship with Conor, which had begun to unravel at an alarming rate. My boyfriend had become very overprotective, and it was making me feel irritable and claustrophobic. Your partner should bring out the best in you, not the worst, shouldn't they?

'When you moved into Conor's house, Amy and I were worried it might be too much too soon,' Lucy said as she plonked herself down on the arm of my chair.

'What can I say? When we first started going out, I was living for the moment. I didn't really focus on the future.'

'That's fair enough,' Lucy replied.

'I'm thinking of leaving Conor,' I suddenly blurted out. The look on my friends' faces told me that they were surprised by my news.

'Oh, my God! I'm sorry to hear that,' Amy said before covering her mouth with her hands.

'I didn't realise things were that bad between you. Has something happened? He hasn't cheated on you, has he?' Lucy quizzed.

'No.' If only it were that simple, I thought.

'You don't have to tell us if you don't want to. We're not trying to pry. We're just concerned about you,' Amy added.

Much as I wanted to open up and confide in somebody, I couldn't tell my friends what had been going on, so I replied, 'It's complicated.'

I saw my friends exchange a sideways glance and realised I owed them a better explanation as to what was behind my change of heart. They thought Conor was a successful businessman and made his money legitimately. They would be beyond shocked to learn the truth.

'I think it's a classic case of a whirlwind romance fizzling out.'

'I see. Once the fog of sexual desire cleared, you discovered you didn't have much to talk about when your mouths weren't clamped together snogging.' Lucy laughed.

'Yeah, something like that.'

'Conor's a great guy, but I never really thought the two of you would end up together permanently. Relationships should be fun, but not necessarily for life,' Lucy said before sweeping a strand of my hair over my shoulder.

I knew exactly what Lucy meant; she'd hit the nail on the head. I'd intended to enjoy our time together and have fun while it lasted. Love was a drug, and the effects were wearing off. Why was I so distressed to think we might have reached the end of the road?

I was guilty of having a rose-tinted view of romance. My parents portrayed a beautiful vision of everlasting commitment, but not many people were lucky enough to ever find that, especially at my age. My first flush of love had been everything I'd ever hoped it would be; Prince Charming came into my life and swept me off my feet. But now, instead of wooing me, Conor was suffocating me.

Before I could stop myself, I was pouring my heart out. If I explained my dilemma to my closest friends, the people who knew me best, perhaps it would help me to reach a decision.

'The longer Conor and I are a couple, the more cracks seem to be appearing, and now I don't know what to do.'

I bowed my head because I didn't want my friends to see the tears that were threatening to spill from my eyes.

'Maybe you should move back to your parents' and see if things settle down between you,' Amy suggested.

That was good advice. Conor had become very possessive recently, and it was making an already stressful situation even more difficult to deal with; his overprotectiveness was making me feel stifled.

'Moving in with your partner is a big commitment at any age, but you're only nineteen, Ella,' Lucy added. 'Putting some distance between you might be all you two need.'

'I wish you wouldn't keep running off every time things get a bit tough,' Conor said when I walked through the front door. He was standing at the kitchen counter, getting ready to prep the dinner.

Talk about being cut down to size by one sentence. He'd made me feel like an immature child hauled up in front of the headmistress.

'So what did the girls have to say for themselves this time? No doubt, their input into our relationship was invaluable to you.' Conor's voice was laced with sarcasm.

I had to stop myself from jumping to their defence. Conor took so little interest in my best friends; I wasn't even sure he knew their names. Truth be told, instead of meddling in our affairs, Lucy and Amy were trying to help me solve the problem.

'Why are you being so nasty?' I glared at Conor, then suddenly burst into tears. I was annoyed with myself for losing control. So much for the pep talk I'd given myself on the tube. I'd shed more than enough tears this afternoon and was determined to be cool, calm and collected when I came face to face with my boyfriend. But I justified my actions because it was easy to let your emotions get the better of you in stressful situations.

Conor put the knife down on the chopping board. 'I'm sorry, Ella, I didn't mean to make you cry.' My boyfriend went to take a step towards me, but then he decided against it. 'I just want to make you happy, but I seem to keep fucking up.'

It wasn't all Conor's fault. He was literally standing on his head while jumping through hoops to please me, but every time he did something nice, it seemed to irritate me beyond words. It wasn't fair on either of us to carry on like this; we were making each other miserable.

'Things have changed so much between us recently. I think we need to talk.' I looked Conor straight in the eye when I spoke.

'I'm scared I'm going to lose you. Just tell me what I need to do to put things right between us.'

As Conor's blue eyes searched mine, I realised he'd given me the perfect opportunity to voice my opinion, so I would be stupid not to use it.

'I've tried to put what happened in Spain behind me, but I'm finding it hard,' I said, hoping my emotions didn't get the better of me.

'You don't need to tell me that,' Conor replied with guilt written all over his face.

'I won't risk something like that happening to me again. There's no place in my life for violence, so if you want to be part of my life, I want you to give up your job.'

Being kidnapped had been a huge turning point that opened my eyes and made me realise how stupid I was for being so trusting. Now that I had experienced the danger first-hand, I hated the world Conor was mixed up in. I'd been worried about having this conversation. But I felt a huge sense of relief now that the words were out of my mouth.

'If that's what it takes to make you happy, then consider it done.'

I felt my lips stretch into a smile. 'Really?' I was sceptical that Conor would walk away from his business dealings as easily as that. 'Do you mean it? You'd give up your work just like that?'

'Yes, I mean it.' Conor smiled.

Perhaps our relationship wasn't doomed after all. Don't get me wrong, we still had areas of tension to work on, but they seemed minor in comparison. Conor's compulsion to clean and tidy everything was a major headache for me. Before I began living with him, I had never met a person who got so much joy out of buffing surfaces to a reflective shine. I felt like I was walking on eggshells because I knew I couldn't maintain his high standards – standards which, incidentally, I thought were ridiculous. He could be anal about hygiene; I sometimes felt he was happier spending time with his steam cleaner than with me. But if we were going to live in harmony together, he would need to relax his regime, and I would do my best to stop being a slob. Wasn't compromise a wonderful thing?

'I wasn't sure you wanted to be with me anymore; I thought you were going to finish with me,' Conor said and broke my train of thought. His eyes glazed over as he spoke and it tugged at my heartstrings. 'I can't bear the thought of losing you. I love you so much.' Conor wrapped his arms around my waist and lifted me off my feet.

'I love you too,' I replied before Conor's lips met mine.

'Time to keep the spark alive, I think.' Conor winked as he led me up the stairs, and I smiled. He was one of those rare individuals who could manage to pull off a manoeuvre like that without a trace of creepiness.

71

Conor

Although I'd promised Ella I'd jack it all in, Leo's threat was hanging over me. He'd only kept me alive because I was useful to him, so it would be impossible for me to cut ties with him and go into retirement without seeing this latest deal through, at least. I needed time to plan my exit from the game. I wished I could have just explained that I was mid-way through a deal and couldn't walk away until it was finished, but Ella had made it clear I had to choose between her or my work, and I couldn't risk losing her. I knew I'd made my girlfriend a promise I couldn't keep, so I'd have to keep her in the dark one last time. But once the shipment landed, I'd come good and walk away from it all.

My heart pounded when a text came through from Diego; I opened it with guilty fingers on the encrypted handset while Ella slept soundly beside me.

You need to make arrangements to come over.

There was no way I was going to be able to fly out to Vigo without rousing my girlfriend's suspicions. I looked at Ella's beautiful face nestled into the pillow. She looked so peaceful, curled into a ball in the foetal position. I didn't want to disturb her, so I quietly slipped out of bed and made my way downstairs.

I had a sinking feeling I was making a mistake. Was it too late to come clean? Maybe I should be honest with Ella and tell her it was too late for me to back out of this latest shipment. She was scarred by what had happened to her and quite rightly wanted to distance herself from the shady characters who inhabited the underworld. She would be horrified if she knew I was still working with Diego after what he'd done to her. But finding a new supplier took time, and that was something I didn't have. I was caught between a rock and a hard place, so I decided to pull my usual stunt and gloss over the truth; it was justified in this case. What Ella didn't know wouldn't harm her.

'It's good to hear from you, Conor,' Diego said when he answered the phone. 'When are you coming over?'

'I can't fly out to Spain at the moment; I have another commitment that I can't get out of.'

That wasn't true, but I couldn't tell him the real reason I was reluctant to accompany the delivery this time. It wouldn't do my street cred any good for my supplier to know my teenage girlfriend had told me to quit my job and I was worried about how she would react if she found out I hadn't done what she'd asked.

'That's not good news,' Diego replied.

'I know, but there's nothing I can do about it.' I was determined to stand my ground on this. I couldn't please everyone, and Ella's happiness was far more important to me than Diego's. 'Can't Juan bring the gear over like last time?'

Diego and I both knew he was more than capable of delivering the shipment and his loyalty to his boss was unquestionable.

'No, I don't like to use the same people too often; it's not good for security.' Diego's tone was dismissive.

'If that's the case, why do you want me to travel with the shipment?' I replied, calling him out.

Was he trying to set me up? The Spaniard could be a slippery bastard, so that wouldn't surprise me. A long silence stretched out between us while he considered how to respond.

'Leave it with me,' Diego finally said. 'I'll try and find a courier to deliver the order. Apart from having a suitable mule, everything's ticking along fine at my end; I'm expecting the consignment any day now.'

That was exactly what I wanted to hear; it wouldn't be too long before my involvement with Diego would come to a natural end. Then, to grant my girlfriend's wish, I'd cut ties with Leo and hope he didn't carry out his threat. Only time would tell if he was all mouth and no trousers. In the meantime, I'd have to keep the deal a secret from Ella for the next week or so until things were sorted. Surely that wouldn't be too difficult.

72

Ella

After making love last night, Conor and I fell asleep tangled in each other's arms with our limbs entwined. When I woke and opened my eyes, it was still dark outside, so I knew it must be early. I ran my hand over the cotton sheet and was surprised to find Conor's side of the bed was empty. At first, I thought he'd got up to use the toilet. I checked the time on my phone while I waited for him to come back. I let out an involuntary groan when I realised it was just before six. I lay staring up at the ceiling with the quilt tucked under my chin and a faint smile playing on my lips.

I rolled onto my side and checked the time on my phone again. What was taking him so long? A couple of minutes later, when he still hadn't returned, I decided to investigate. The light in the en-suite was off, so I knew Conor wasn't in there, but I pushed the door anyway just to be certain.

I opened the bedroom door, and my eyes scanned the corridor. Everything was in darkness, so I wasn't sure where Conor had gone. I wanted to stay in the safety of the bedroom, but I dug deep and forced myself to look around the house. I had a sudden sinking feeling my boyfriend was up to something, so I tiptoed down the stairs without switching on any of the lights. If Conor was hiding something from me, I didn't want to alert him to my presence, but my heart was pounding so loudly he would probably hear me coming. The house seemed bigger than usual as I swiftly padded across the floors trying to track Conor down. The longer it was taking to find him, the more convinced I was that all was not as it should be. As I approached his man-cave, I heard the sound of my boyfriend's voice, and it stopped me in my tracks.

'Let me know when the shipment's ready to leave Spain,' Conor said.

I didn't hang around to hear the rest of the conversation. I hot-footed it back up the stairs with my racing pulse pounding in my ears. My fear had been replaced by anger. I was absolutely livid. Conor had crossed the line; he'd promised me last night that he was going to get out of the game, but he'd lied to me again. I thought I'd made it clear there was no place for violence in my life. Conor had told me he'd leave his criminal past behind him; just yesterday, he'd said he'd give up drug smuggling if it would make me happy. I should have known he had no intention of keeping his words; he'd agreed to my request too readily. How could Conor lie to me about something so important?

As I made my way back to the bedroom, I rampaged through Conor's house, pulling things out of the kitchen cupboards and making a mess. I knew that would drive him insane. I raced into the bedroom like a human whirlwind and threw clothes around, tipping out drawers into the middle of the floor before hurling the pillows and quilt off the bed. All the while, thoughts of Conor's betrayal swam around in my head.

It wasn't as though Conor needed the money; he wasn't short of cash. But he knew the business like the back of his hand, so what else could he do for a living? Conor was a big spender, and no other job could match the hourly rate he earned. Convincing my boyfriend to go straight was a lost cause, but I couldn't be part of this world anymore. I'd given him an ultimatum, but keeping Diego and Leo sweet was more important to him than I was. He'd made his decision, so now I'd made mine. It was time for me to go. I had to walk away from all of it. That was… if Conor let me. I wasn't at all sure he was going to let me leave that easily.

I had no idea how Conor was going to react. I knew all his secrets. I was the only person in his trusted inner circle, but now that I'd made my mind up, I had to follow it through and trust my gut. The instinct to end our relationship was overriding everything else, and if something felt that right, how could it be wrong? The longer I stayed, the harder it would be to leave. I knew what I had to do, so now wasn't the time to lose my nerve. As sad as it was, Conor and I had reached the end of the road. So why did I feel like I was about to fall to pieces?

I took my case out of the cupboard and began flinging my belongings into it with more force than necessary to relieve some of my pent-up anger.

'What's going on?' Conor said when he walked back into the bedroom with a shocked expression written all over his face.

'You lied to me, again...' I panted, breathless from the exertion of messing up his house.

I stood glaring at my soon-to-be-ex-boyfriend with steam coming out of my ears. He was trying to pull off being perplexed, but who was he trying to kid? He knew what was coming. I could sense it; watching him trying to act all innocent made my anger step up another notch.

'I overheard you on the phone arranging another shipment after you told me you'd give it all up to make me happy.' I fired my words into his startled face and wondered if he was going to be stupid enough to try and deny it.

Conor pushed my suitcase backwards, then he took a seat on the edge of the bed and took hold of my hand, which was going to make the conversation we were about to have so much harder.

'Ella, please stop for a minute. You're overreacting.'

I pulled my fingers out of his grasp. 'Don't you dare say that to me! Lies trip off your tongue so easily, half the time I don't think you even realise you're doing it.' I shook my head, then pulled my case towards me and carried on packing the clothes and possessions that I'd arrived with into it.

'I promise you, this is the last shipment.' Conor flashed me one of his winning smiles, but I wasn't going to allow myself to be hoodwinked by him this time.

Previously, I was so besotted with Conor that I would have overlooked anything, and I'm embarrassed to say I did. But now that I'd come to my senses, he was about to enter uncharted territory.

'I don't believe you.' My words were cold.

'What do I have to do to convince you?' Conor threw out the palms of his hands and fixed his blue eyes on me.

It was easy to bring someone round to your way of thinking when they wanted to believe you. But I wasn't going to allow myself to be swayed that easily. Trust had to be earned and Conor had just proved to me that he didn't deserve to have mine.

'This isn't working. I'm going to move back to my mum and dad's.'

'Please don't do that; I love you, Ella.'

I still had feelings for him, too; I couldn't switch them off just like that, but I wasn't about to share that with him. It would only complicate matters and give him false hope. Sometimes you had to be cruel to be kind. The last thing I wanted to do was hurt Conor, but I also had to do what was right for me.

'I know you've been through a terrible time, and that was down to me, but I promise you we can put all of this behind us and start again.' Conor caught hold of my hands and tried to pull me down onto his lap; when I resisted, he let go of me.

Part of me wanted to believe my boyfriend; his beautiful eyes looked so sad, and knowing I was causing him to feel that way, made guilt stab my conscience, but I had to be strong. Otherwise, I'd never be able to go through with it. I needed to put a stop to this conversation before he talked me out of leaving. Conor was doing his best to convince me to stay, and he could be very persuasive, but I had to trust my instincts and take a leap of faith. I couldn't let him cloud my judgement.

'At least give me a chance to explain, and if you're still determined to leave, I won't try and stop you.'

The art of winning a person over was a coveted skill. It came more naturally to some than others. I couldn't deny Conor was blessed with a silver tongue, but no amount of arm-twisting was going to make me buckle.

I'd given Conor an ultimatum last night in an attempt to save our relationship, but he'd chosen to go back on his word. He was so used to calling the shots; he didn't seem to take anything I said seriously, which highlighted the fact that we weren't equal partners. Up until now, he'd led, and I followed. But that was about to change.

'I'm sorry, Conor, I have to go. It's for the best.' I zipped up my case with a heavy heart, completely disillusioned with what initially seemed like a dream.

'You're the only person in this world who I trust, Ella.'

Tears sprang into Conor's blue eyes as the words left his mouth. My first reaction was to comfort him, but if I did that, I'd be sending him mixed signals, and he might think he could sweet-talk me into staying. I knew what he'd just said was true, and I felt bad about that, but I couldn't let guilt influence my decision. As I lifted the case off of the bed, Conor went to take hold of my hand, but I pulled my fingers out of his grip.

'Ella, please don't go.'

There was no point in me stalling; it was prolonging the agony for both of us. I needed to get out of the room and put some distance between us. Even though I was the one leaving, it was the hardest thing I'd ever had to do.

Conor sat on the edge of the bed looking shell-shocked

as I took off the jewellery that he'd bought me and placed it on the bedside cabinet.

'What are you doing? I bought those things for you; I want you to keep them.'

Despite what I'm sure some people thought, I'd never been interested in the material package that accompanied Conor. It was time to get out of here and leave the trappings of wealth in the past where they belonged.

'So that's it – you're going back to your old life, are you? I have to say, I'm shocked that you're prepared to give up the lifestyle you have with me to become a penniless student again.' Conor shook his head.

But instead of placing doubt in my mind, his words confirmed I was doing the right thing. Having money can make a person's life easier and provide opportunities, but it couldn't buy love or happiness, and those two things were more important to me than anything.

'Well, if that's what you want, you know where the door is.'

Conor's words were cold. He sat on the bed with his head in his hands as I walked out of the bedroom, pulling the case behind me. My pulse was pounding as I paced along the hallway. The huge house was suddenly claustrophobic. I felt like I had no air to breathe. When I opened the front door and stepped out into freedom, I let out a sigh of relief.

'I can't believe you're just going to walk out the door without giving me a chance to explain,' Conor shouted after me; he must have been calling my bluff.

The minicab I'd ordered was waiting outside Conor's house, and as it pulled away from the kerb, I forced myself to keep my eyes fixed on the front windscreen. I knew if I turned around in my seat, Conor would be standing in the doorway sandwiched between the blue hydrangeas and windmill palms. I didn't need to look; I could sense his blue diamonds boring into the back of my head. I heard my mobile beep inside my bag and knew the message would be from my now ex-boyfriend.

Please don't go. Come home, Ella. I love you xx

I decided not to reply to the message. The hardest part of leaving was taking the first step, and now that I'd done that, I couldn't allow myself to go back. That would be too easy. I needed time to adjust. Believe me, I wished things had turned out differently, but after everything that had happened, I didn't have another option.

I knew there was only one place I could go at this unearthly hour of the morning. Tears were streaming down my face when Mum opened the front door.

'What's the matter, Ella?' Mum said, ushering me inside.

'Conor and I have split up, and I've never felt so guilty about anything in my whole life.'

Mum held me in her arms and stroked my hair the way she used to when I was a little girl. I cried like a baby while Dad hovered in the periphery, not knowing what he could do to help. I was inconsolable. Even though I'd been the one to walk away, it hadn't been an easy decision. I knew I was the only person that Conor trusted; the weight of that responsibility was suffocating. He'd have nobody to turn to now that I'd left him, so he would have to go through the breakup on his own without anyone to support him.

'Don't worry, love. Conor's a grown man; he'll get over it,' Mum said, rubbing my back to soothe me as I cried in her arms.

73

Conor

I'd never seen Ella react like that before. She was normally such a placid, docile creature. When I'd walked into the kitchen and saw the destruction she'd left in her wake, I realised the game was up. My plan had backfired in spectacular fashion. Ella knew the mess would be a huge deal to me, but I had to try and ignore it; easier said than done for a man with OCD. Not only did I have neat-freak tendencies, but I was also a control freak. The sight of my organised cupboards' contents spilling onto the tiles made my brain fry and took me straight back to my mum's filthy kitchen and the chaos of my childhood. As an adult, I'd reassured myself that everything in my life was under control by keeping a clean home. Even before I faced Ella, I knew that wasn't the case. When I walked into the bedroom and found Ella packing her case, my pulse went into overdrive. She was madder than a hungry grizzly bear with its snout caught in a trap.

Ella had walked out on me, and I had nobody to blame

but myself. I was my own worst enemy. I should have been honest with her, but I knew she'd be scared if she realised Leo had threatened to put me on the hit list if I didn't continue to supply him with cocaine. By keeping it to myself, Ella felt I'd betrayed her, and now she didn't trust me.

After I'd drifted into a life of crime, I'd made a habit out of distorting details and keeping people at arm's length to protect myself from giving too much away, on both a personal and business level. This time, my behaviour had cost me dear. I'd fucked up on a grand scale and lost the only person who was important to me.

When Ella walked down the path and closed the cab door behind her, I'd sat on the bottom step with my head in my hands in a complete daze. I wanted to drop onto my knees and beg her to stay, but I couldn't have done that to her; it wouldn't have been fair to try and make her feel guilty. There was nothing remotely attractive about a clingy partner who had desperation seeping from every pore of their body. I'm glad I managed to stop myself from running after the cab; at least I'd managed to hold on to a small amount of my dignity.

Whether it was intentional or not, Ella couldn't have picked a worse moment to split up with me; talk about kicking a man when he was down. She was the only person I trusted, and now I'd lost her. It felt like somebody had taken a machete and hollowed out my insides. My life was falling apart.

I was trapped in a world of my own making and couldn't see a way out without blood being shed. Ella didn't want to go out with a criminal, and who could blame her? I'd give anything to get out of the game and not be the middleman anymore. But it wasn't going to be easy to stop working with the other parties. I knew too much about their illegal goings-on to simply cut ties. Quitting would be dangerous. When you dealt with career criminals, the best advice was to keep your head down, mind your own business and do what was expected of you.

I knew how Leo felt about the situation, but I hadn't broached the subject with Diego before. I had a pretty good idea how he'd react. Holding the title of the cartel's most wanted man and having a bounty on my head wasn't high up on my wish list. If I didn't stick to my side of the agreement and tried to walk away, it was almost certain Diego would put a bullet in my head. He would never let me leave and live to tell the tale. Maybe that wouldn't be such a bad thing. Now that I didn't have Ella to go home to, I didn't really care what he did to me. I wasn't sure I wanted to wake up in the morning if her beautiful face wasn't on the pillow next to mine when I opened my eyes.

At this stage, I didn't need the money. I had more than enough cash stashed away to last me for the rest of my days. I would happily give it all away if I could convince Ella to come back to me, but it looked like she'd made her decision, and she was sticking to it. The only thing I could do was give her some space and hope she calmed down.

They say you shouldn't have regrets, but the two biggest mistakes I ever made were walking down the criminal path in the first place and lying to my girlfriend. If I could turn back the clock, I'd take a different route.

It suddenly struck me that everything in my house reminded me of Ella. She'd left me because I'd taken away her option to stay. The space felt too big without her.

My eyes teared up as I thought about what I'd just lost. Ella was the sweetest person; she didn't have a bad bone in her body. Pity the same couldn't be said for me.

74

Ella

The decision of whether to leave Conor or not had been yo-yo-ing backwards and forwards in my head for days. Just when I'd thought I'd made my mind up, I changed it again. It had been agonising, and the stress had been starting to wear me down. But when I'd overheard him on the phone to Diego, everything seemed to fall into place. I should have realised Conor wouldn't keep his word to me.

'I know when we met the other day, you were having a wobble, but I didn't see your split coming. I thought it was just a bump in the road,' Amy said. Her greeny-blue eyes were full of sympathy as I held court at our usual table in Costa.

If I was totally honest, neither had I. Even though I'd been considering moving back in with my parents, when push came to shove, I wasn't sure I'd actually go through with it. Conor and I loved each other, but we'd been going through a rough patch. All couples do, but not all of them split up over it; they find a way to work things out, and everything turns out great. After all, love conquers all, right? Wrong.

It was difficult to explain, but when I'd overheard the tail end of Conor's conversation, it was as though somebody had switched on a light and allowed me to see clearly. I'd suddenly realised our relationship's success hinged on deeper and more important values than who left the lid off the toothpaste. The bottom line was, if I couldn't trust Conor, we didn't have a future together. Even though it was early days, I knew I'd made the right decision.

'If it's any consolation, I think you've done the right thing,' Lucy said as if she'd just read my mind.

'I agree,' Amy added.

I could feel the tears welling up in my eyes and willed them not to start falling. I was the one who had instigated the split, but it hadn't stopped me from feeling heartbroken and miserable.

Lucy reached across the table and covered my hand in hers. 'Don't you dare turn on the waterworks, or you'll have us all blubbing. I know you're hurting, and it feels like the end of the world right now, but things will get better; you just need to give it some time.'

'Wise words indeed,' Amy said.

'Not that I have a great deal of experience in matters of the heart. You know me; I like to keep myself young, free and single, but I've heard people say that and I'm sure it's true.' Lucy laughed.

I blew out a breath, then straightened my posture. 'I'm not sure what got into me. Really, I'm fine,' I replied, pasting a `smile on my face, but my words couldn't have been further from the truth.

Apart from the text he'd sent me while I was in the minicab, I hadn't heard from Conor since I'd left his house. I should have been happy that he was respecting my decision and not trying to make things difficult for me, but I had to admit, I was a bit put out by the lack of contact.

What the hell was the matter with me? It had been my idea to call things off between us, so why was I so bothered that Conor had let me walk away without a backwards glance? Surely if he loved me as much as he said he did, he'd fight for me and our relationship. It was more than just my pride that was hurt by Conor's response. I still loved him with all my heart, and that was making this situation so difficult.

I'd intended to power through the breakup phase with sheer determination and a refusal to be weak. That hadn't happened; I was a snivelling, insecure wreck full of mixed emotions. I'd never been in a position like this before, so I didn't know how to deal with my feelings. When Conor had begged me to stay, I hadn't realised how comforting I'd found that until he stopped bothering to try to win me over. I should have been relieved by the lack of communication; I wanted Conor to leave me alone and let me move on, didn't I? So why was I so confused?

Deep down, I knew Conor was doing me a favour. I wouldn't be able to let go of the past, and the healing process wouldn't start if we were still in regular contact. I had to focus my attention elsewhere, and one day things would get better. I just had to have faith, but I couldn't force the process. Everybody had their own schedule; there was no set time frame to mending a broken heart.

Looking back, my friends and family had raised not-so-subtle concerns about Conor and me living together so soon, but I chose to ignore them, and I moved in with him anyway. If I'd listened to the people who knew me best, maybe I wouldn't be in this mess now. Conor and I had declared our love to the world very quickly, but it wasn't destined to last a lifetime. Hard as it was at the moment, ultimately, I knew we weren't right for each other. On the lonely days that would inevitably follow, I'd have to remind myself of that. The best thing I could do to kick-start my recovery was to keep myself busy.

'I can't believe you left all your expensive clothes behind,' Lucy said, breaking my train of thought. 'If we'd have known, we'd have snapped your arm off for them, wouldn't we, Amy?'

'Absolutely, I'd never be too proud to accept somebody's cast-offs, especially the designer kind.' Amy laughed.

'But seriously, why didn't you bring them?' Lucy questioned. Her blue eyes were as wide as saucers. 'All jokes aside, Ella, were you having a moment of madness or was it a calculated decision?'

'I wanted to make a clean break and felt it was the right thing to do.' I didn't tell my friends I couldn't face being surrounded by all the beautiful things Conor had bought me while we were together. It would be too painful.

'You're a better person than I am. I wouldn't have left anything behind. In fact, I'd have probably helped myself to some of his gadgets too. He had so many; he wouldn't have noticed if a few had gone missing.' Lucy smiled.

I smiled back; I could see she was trying to cheer me up. 'I needed to make a fresh start, and possessions hold too many memories. This is going to be difficult enough without constant reminders of the life I've left behind.' I felt tears stab at my eyes, so I tried to blink them away.

'I get where you're coming from,' Amy said, flashing me a half-smile.

'I hear you too, but I'm just saying, if I'd have been in your shoes, I would have taken everything with me, and if being surrounded by memories turned out to be too painful, I'd have put the lot on eBay.'

Amy flashed Lucy a look of horror.

'What?' Lucy threw the palms of her hands out. 'I'm just putting it out there and sharing my innermost thoughts with you.'

When Lucy let out her infectious laugh, there was nothing Amy and I could do but join in.

'I'm not claiming to be an oracle or have the same knowledge as a wise old Buddhist monk, but I've read plenty of magazines that delve into the lives of others, so I think that qualifies me to comment.' Lucy chuckled.

I'd missed my girls so much. If anyone was going to be able to get me through the next few months, it would be Lucy and Amy. From the first day we'd met, we clicked, and they'd had my back ever since.

'Perhaps you should consider training to be a relationship counsellor,' Amy suggested.

'Maybe, I will. But rest assured, Ella, any pearls of wisdom I offer you will be free of charge,' Lucy countered.

'That's very generous of you.' I smiled.

'I'm a great believer in fate. Everything happens for a

reason. Splitting up with Conor was the right thing to do,' Amy said.

I knew my friend was right. Fundamentally Conor and I were just too different; we weren't meant to be together. He was so guarded about his personal life, whereas I was the complete opposite. I'd share my life history with a complete stranger if I thought they would listen. My mum was forever telling me off when I was little because the minute she'd turn her back, I'd start talking to anyone and everyone. I'd been through a bad experience, but it was time to dust myself off and find the sociable, confident person I knew was lurking somewhere inside me.

75

Conor

Why did everything bad seem to happen all at once? I felt like I was being buried alive under a steaming pile of shit at the moment. Although my heart was breaking, deep down, I realised my girlfriend leaving was probably for the best. Ella's safety was the most important thing to me, and I knew from experience that I couldn't always keep her out of harm's way. I would never forgive myself if something happened to her; in my line of work, rivals took their revenge on the other person's nearest and dearest. Even though Diego eventually released Ella, the stress of what she'd been through left its mark on her.

I didn't want Ella to become paranoid about everyone and everything, like me. I wanted her to be happy; she deserved to be. If letting her walk out of my life was the only way she could achieve that, then it would be wrong of me to try to stop her. If she felt our relationship had run its course, I'd have to do the right thing and sacrifice my own happiness for hers. I loved her with all my heart and only wanted the best for her. Whoever ended up with Ella would be a very lucky man; she was incredible. I would never meet another woman like her. If she ever needed anything, she only had to say the word, and I'd be there for her. I would always look out for her.

Leo had left countless messages on my mobile. He was desperate to know when his cocaine was landing. His order had arrived in Spain, but Diego was still trying to pressure me into coming over; he reckoned he couldn't find a trustworthy courier to deliver the shipment. Diego could throw his weight around all he liked; it wasn't going to influence my decision. I had a gut feeling he was up to something, so I was sticking to my guns. After what he'd done to Ella, I could never trust him again.

I had a sudden flash of inspiration. The more I thought about it, the more it made sense. The man would do anything to make a quick buck, so it was time to give him a call. 'It's me, Conor. I've got a proposition for you.'

'That sounds interesting,' was the reply.

'I know you're short of cash, and the job's well paid,' I continued knowing I'd made the guy an offer he couldn't refuse.

I didn't normally use the facilities when I chartered a private plane from Biggin Hill airport. I always chose to fast-track straight to the departure gate, but I wasn't the one flying today; I was meeting my courier so that I could go over the instructions with him. While I waited for him to arrive, I took a seat in the mezzanine level of the two-storey VIP passenger lounge overlooking the impressive ground-floor space. When Roy's dishevelled shape came into view, it brought a smile to my face. I was sure he wasn't the sort of passenger the doormen, in top hats and tails, were used to greeting.

Roy quickly spotted me as his eyes scanned the double-height space, and he made his way to where I was sitting.

'So you know what you have to do?'

Roy nodded. 'After I deliver the cash to Diego, I fly back with Leo's order.'

'That's great.' I was actually quite impressed that the dimwit had remembered the plan. 'You can call me if you have any problems.'

I wasn't overly confident that Roy would be able to pull this off, but I wasn't prepared to take the risk, so I had to send somebody out to Spain in my place. Roy wasn't the sharpest tool in the box; he had decades of alcohol and drug abuse to thank for his diminished IQ level and impaired cognitive function. But my options were limited, so I had to entrust him with the task. I'd like to think he wouldn't try to shaft me, given his connection to my mum. He was the best of a bad bunch of scumbags Mum had hooked up with over the years. But then again, she hadn't exactly set the bar high.

'The pilot's waiting for you. Any questions before you go?'

'The only one that comes to mind is: when am I going to get paid?' Roy flashed me a rotten-toothed grin.

'Once you've delivered the order to Leo.'

I fished my mobile out of the back pocket of my jeans when it rang. I'd been fully expecting to receive a call from Roy, but I was surprised to see Diego's name displayed on the screen.

'Did you really think you were going to get away with this?' Diego shouted down the phone.

I didn't know what had happened at this stage, but he was furious, so I figured it must be something bad, although it could just as likely be an overreaction to something minor. The man could be a drama queen when the mood took him.

'What's wrong?' I replied, then took a deep breath and prepared myself for the verbal onslaught that was sure to follow.

'As if you don't know.' Diego's words had a sarcastic edge to them.

'I don't. Maybe you'd care to enlighten me.' Frustration coated my words; I wanted this to be over and done with.

'It's just as well I'd been expecting trouble; otherwise, you might have got away with it.'

Diego could rant all he liked, but I couldn't try to put things right if he didn't tell me what was wrong.

'Your stupidity astounds me!'

As Diego continued his tirade, I felt myself bristle. He'd better hurry up and get to the point. My patience was starting to wear thin, and anger was bubbling under the surface.

'Ninety per cent of the notes are counterfeit! Did you really think I wouldn't notice something like that?'

I slammed my fist down on the counter. I should have known better than to trust Roy with the cash. The temptation not to syphon off a large chunk of it for himself was too great for him to resist. I'd always known he was a dopey bastard, but he was dimmer than I'd given him credit for. If he hadn't been so greedy and had just switched out the odd note, he'd have possibly got away with it. I'd take great pleasure in tearing the scumbag limb from limb for causing all this aggro when I got hold of him.

'The deal's off. I will never do business with you again.'

I had to stop myself from cheering. Diego refusing to fulfil the order was great news for me but bad news for Leo. He wasn't going to take the collapse of the supply chain well, but at this stage, I didn't give a flying fuck what he thought.

Roy had actually done me a huge favour double-crossing Diego, so I should have been giving the man a pat on the back and a firm handshake. But the wanker had caused me countless problems over the years, so I wasn't about to pass up the chance to give him a good hiding.

Blood and spittle flew out of Roy's rotten-toothed mouth when my fist connected with his jaw. 'You've caused me a whole heap of shit. I should have known you couldn't be trusted where money was concerned.'

'I swear I didn't swap the notes with fakes, Conor.'

'Do you expect me to believe that?' I got up in his face but had to take a step back when the smell of his breath threatened to knock me sideways.

Roy held his hands up in front of him and backed away from me while protesting his innocence. I had to say, he seemed pretty convincing, and when I thought about it more, I was inclined to believe him. Roy wasn't clever enough to pull one over on Leo, but he was wasting his time begging for mercy. An opportunity like this didn't come around every day of the week, so I wasn't about to let it pass me by; I was going to enjoy every single minute of it.

The first jab I made resulted in a nosebleed; a trickle of blood ran out of Roy's nostril towards his upper lip. The cross that followed it left swelling around my reluctant opponent's eye. A free-standing punch bag would have fought back more than Roy; if he didn't start to retaliate, he would end up getting battered. A cut opened up on Roy's right eyebrow as my blows rained down on the side of his face, but he was still only making a half-hearted attempt to defend himself. The fight was too one-sided to be worth continuing, so I decided to abandon it after giving him one last clump on Bobby's behalf. When the uppercut landed right on target, it rocked him on his feet.

'And that, my friend, is for throwing the man who paid your wages to the wolves. I'd had my suspicions that Bobby had a spy in the camp before his life was snuffed out. When Leo admitted he'd ordered the hit that executed Bobby and his driver at point-blank range, your name popped into my head, and everything fell into place.'

'I swear on my mum's life, I didn't set Bobby up.'

That just about summed the lowlife up. His mother had been dead for at least fifteen years, so that didn't add any weight to his statement. In fact, rather than making me believe he was telling the truth, it had the opposite effect.

Despite protesting his innocence on all counts, he was wasting his breath. Roy couldn't tell the truth if his life depended on it. After I'd finished giving him a pasting, I shook out my hands; my knuckles were throbbing, but it was worth the pain. It felt good to get some of my anger and frustration out. It was shaping up to be the best day I'd had in a long while. Seeing Roy's ugly mug beaten to a pulp gave me a huge sense of satisfaction. It was about time he got what was coming to him. I was only twelve when he'd set me on the wrong path. Things might have turned out very differently for me if he hadn't led me astray.

I parked my BMW Z4 outside Leo's shabby Portakabin and sauntered up to the door for the last time. I didn't want this moment to be over too soon. I could have delivered the news to Leo by text, but I decided to pay him a visit instead; telling him in person would be much more rewarding. Nothing would give me greater pleasure than seeing the look of horror on his face when he realised Roy had come back empty-handed. It would be the cherry on top of a perfect day.

'What are you doing here?' Leo's bulbous eyes scanned over me.

'It's great to see you too.' I laughed.

'Have you got my gear?' Leo quizzed.

'Not exactly.' I wanted to keep the bastard in suspense.

'What's that supposed to mean? You either have, or you haven't.'

I could see Leo's temper start to rise, which gave me immense pleasure.

'The deal's off.'

'What the fuck are you talking about?' Leo stood up from his wheelie chair and gripped onto the side of his desk with his pudgy fingers.

'Diego's pulled out because most of the money you sent was fake.'

'Where the hell is Roy?' Leo asked Stumpy.

'I haven't seen him since he left for Spain,' Stumpy replied.

'When I get my hands on that useless fucker, he's a dead man. It will be the first and last time he steals from me,' Leo bellowed. His response made me realise the news had come as a shock to him.

If Leo wasn't the mastermind behind the counterfeit notes, the net was about to close in on the real culprit. I suddenly smelled a rat; it made me realise maybe I'd been wrong about Roy after all. There was another person who could just as easily be in the frame.

'I've already had words with him about it.' I looked down at my grazed, bruised knuckles before I continued to speak. 'And he was adamant he hadn't tampered with the cash. Credit where credit's due, I don't think he's smart enough to rip you off.'

Leo's eyes widened as he considered what I'd said. He looked like he was wearing a pair of comedy glasses with eyeballs on springs when the realisation hit him. Once the penny dropped, he flew into a rage and completely lost his shit. He turned his attention away from me and ran around the desk.

'You were in charge of counting out and bagging the cash,' Leo roared, grabbing hold of Stumpy's T-shirt.

'Get your fucking filthy hands off me,' Stumpy spat.

Even before the mad Scotsman retaliated, I knew Leo had made a huge mistake. I was sure he was guilty of the swindle, too; we'd exhausted all other possible logical explanations. But I'd had the misfortune of seeing Stumpy in action. Whatever happened from here on in wouldn't be a pretty sight.

Leo screamed like a girl when Stumpy unleashed his fury on him. He grabbed his boss in a tight clinch before he sank his teeth into Leo's earlobe. As he ripped a chunk of it off, Leo let out a blood-curdling scream.

'For fuck's sake, Conor, help me,' he wailed, but he was wasting his breath. After what he'd put me through, I wasn't going to lift a finger to assist him.

Stumpy stepped back and spat the flesh onto the floor, then prodded the discarded body part with his shoe. The huge man's eyes darted wildly as blood dripped from his mouth like a crazed lunatic. The gruesome scene was like something out of a flesh-eating zombie movie. Stumpy didn't need to resort to using a weapon; he was more than capable of doing damage with his bare hands. He wiped the blood away from his mouth before he stomped out of the door, slamming it behind him.

Leo dropped to the floor and picked up the missing part of his ear. 'Don't just stand there. Call a fucking ambulance before I bleed to death!'

That couldn't happen to a nicer guy, in my opinion.

'I can't believe that bastard double-crossed me. I should have known he was capable of turning on me like he did Bobby.'

That was news to me; I'd always thought Roy had fed Bobby to the wolves. He was the obvious scapegoat as he'd secretly been on Bobby and Leo's payrolls at the same time. But none of this mattered now. I was getting out of the game once and for all. It felt good to be back in control. As I drove away from the Bow Flyover, I felt like a weight had lifted from my shoulders.

I dialled Ella's number, but it went straight to her voicemail. That didn't surprise me; I would have been more shocked if she'd answered the call. As I couldn't speak to her in person, I pulled the car over and sent her a text instead. I wanted her to know I'd done what she'd asked and jacked in my job; better late than never. Ella brought out the best in me, so I owed it to myself to try and convince her to give our relationship another go. I knew it was a long shot, but I wasn't going to give up easily; she was too important to me.

> I've got some good news; I've cut all ties with Leo and Diego. As of now, I'm officially retired 😊 I need to get away from it all. There's a beautiful palm-fringed beach on Koh Samui that has my name on it. Can I tempt you to join me? I miss you and still love you more than anything. Please can we put everything behind us and start again? x

76

Ella

I looked down at the screen on my phone, and my heart skipped a beat; it was like I'd seen a ghost from the past. I felt my eyes well up as I read Conor's text, and although my heart ached for him, and I missed him more than anything, his message had come too little, too late.

Conor's charisma never usually failed to let him down – he won over everybody he came into contact with; but I'd come this far, so I needed to stay strong and not give in to temptation, no matter how much I wanted to. I had to remind myself that the longer we'd been together, the more emotionally disconnected we'd become. I'd lied to myself about the state of things and initially ignored my gut instinct to walk away because I'd wanted to believe the fantasy was true.

The stress of my abduction had taken its toll on me; returning to the normality and simplicity of my old life had been just what I'd needed to ground me again. My tightly wound nervous system was beginning to unwind. Despite being slapped in the face by all the red flags my friends and family raised while I was dating Conor, the rollercoaster ride was so intoxicating, I'd chosen to ignore their concerns. When we'd first become a couple, I'd been blinded by love, so I got swept up by the whirlwind, but I came down to earth with a thud when the relationship unravelled. Conor had sold me a dream that didn't exist, which in the cold light of day made me feel stupidly naïve.

I was going from strength to strength, and all the hard work would be undone if I went back to Conor. I was putting the pieces of my life back together; nobody said it was going to be easy, but I was proud of myself. I'd come a long way. I'd spent hours analysing our relationship, dissecting the fabric of it and forming conclusions. Something I'd pondered over and over was how I'd mistaken Conor's controlling behaviour for protectiveness. I hadn't realised what was happening because of the subtlety; the change came about gradually. But by the time we'd split up, I'd lost sight of who I was, which taught me an important lesson: don't sacrifice who you are to make your partner happy; never give up living your own life.

I had to push aside the guilt that kept surfacing on an almost daily basis, knowing I'd left Conor while he was battling his demons, but I'd had to do what was right for me. Much as it might have seemed callous, it had broken my heart to walk away from him. I still loved Conor, but sometimes love wasn't enough to make a relationship work.

Lucy and Amy had rallied around me and lifted my spirits when I'd been feeling low; I couldn't have asked for two better friends. I don't think I'd have got through the tough times without them making me smile through the pain.

I'd been stuck in a bottomless pit of despair and cried too many tears during too many sleepless nights; I needed to find myself again. I was confident that would happen; this was just one chapter of my life, and I was determined that I was going to put it behind me and never look back.

After I left Conor, it would have been easy to stay on at my parents' flat, in my old room with everything familiar surrounding me. But once you'd flown the nest, it was difficult to revert to living under somebody else's roof again. I valued my independence too much, so I got my old job back and moved in with Lucy and Amy.

I'd been due to go to Spain in September for a year, but after my ordeal, I wasn't sure I could face it. The end of term was fast approaching, and I was still deciding what to do when Lucy saw an advert for a job opportunity that was too good to resist and suggested we all apply. The money wasn't great, but the experience it offered promised to be priceless.

Almost a year to the day I met Conor, the three of us jetted off to the south of France. To hone our language skills, we were going to work as general dogsbodies on a French campsite. The job description was suitably vague; serving behind the bar, cleaning static mobile homes, and translating tourists' problems were the main tasks, but the manager reserved the right to change our duties as and when he saw fit, which was slightly concerning.

'Welcome to France.' Lucy had laughed when she'd signed on the dotted line and then she'd turned to Amy and me and muttered under her breath, 'No wonder the workforce is always on strike!'

My parents were understandably worried when I broke

the news to them, but after the intense relationship I'd just come out of, I needed to cut loose, have some fun and live for the moment, and that was exactly what I intended to do. I wanted to embrace being young, free and single like my two besties. I didn't regret my relationship with Conor; I'd learned a lot about myself during our time together. Although I agreed to shoulder some of the blame for the bad choices I'd made, Conor seduced me down the wrong path. But I was back on the straight and narrow now, and that was where I intended to stay.

I'd been through a terrifying experience, and my mind was doing its best to block the details out, but sometimes powerful memories were triggered by the slightest thing, and I was reminded of a time I'd rather forget. But I was a survivor, so I wouldn't allow post-traumatic stress to become my new best friend or part of my daily life.

I'd been travelling along a bumpy road, but recently there'd been more good days than bad days; time was a great healer. Fast-forward three months, and I was in a different place, a good place. This was the happiest I'd felt in a long time. It was as though the dark clouds hovering over me had parted, and the sun was shining brightly. I had Lucy and Amy to thank for that. My best friends' company was a tonic, and drinking local wine, poured straight from the barrel, following an after-work dip in the warm Mediterranean was more therapeutic than I cared to mention. This was shaping up to be the best experience of my life, and I didn't want it to end any time soon.

Part of me would always love Conor; being my first love, he would forever hold a special place in my heart, but that ship had sailed, and I didn't want to be tied to the past. His secrets and lies had broken my trust along with my heart. I picked up my mobile and scrolled through until I found Conor's name in my list of contacts. I'd been meaning to do this for some time, but I hadn't managed to pluck up the courage. Tears welled up in my eyes as I pressed my finger onto the screen and deleted his name. Out of sight, out of mind.

Acknowledgements

Thank you to my fabulous editor, Thorne Ryan, for your help and support. It has been a pleasure working with you.

Thanks to Laura Palmer, Vicky Joss, Nikky Ward, Lizz Burrell and all the team at Aria Fiction. Also, Lydia Mason, Josephine Gibbons, Helena Newton and everyone involved in the production of this book.

A special mention should go to the lovely readers, reviewers, book club members and bloggers. Your positivity and words of encouragement brighten my day and spur me on when the going gets tough!

About the Author

STEPHANIE HARTE writes thrilling gangland fiction. She lives in London with her family.

Hello from Aria

We hope you enjoyed this book! If you did, let us know, we'd love to hear from you.

We are Aria, a dynamic fiction imprint from award-winning publishers Head of Zeus. At heart, we're committed to publishing fantastic commercial fiction – from romance to sagas to historical fiction. Visit us online and discover a community of like minded fiction fans

You can find us at:
www.ariafiction.com

🐦 @ariafiction
📘 @Aria_Fiction
📷 @ariafiction